Back to the Bush

ALSO BY JAMES HENDRY

A Year in the Wild: A Riotous Novel (2011)

'There's family conflict, romance, funny anecdotes, poaching and all kinds of intrigue – in other words, something for everyone.'
– KAY-ANN VAN ROOYEN, *GO*

'It's both delicious and deliciously funny. It draws easy-to-imagine pictures of madness and mayhem; hilarity and horror. And it gives the most fascinating insights into what goes on behind the posh scenes of larney lodges.' – TIFFANY MARKMAN, Women24

'I laughed, cried and basically didn't want the book to end.'
– NICI DE WET, *You*

'…a window into a world juxtaposed between the wilds of Africa and the pampered international guests they attract, who are cosseted by a service contingent catering to their every whim. Staff scandal, sibling rivalry, romantic liaisons and spoofs on South African and international stereotypes [make] for a rich entertaining read.'
– STEPHANIE SAVILLE, *The Witness*

'*A Year in the Wild* is a delight to read [and a] hugely entertaining novel. Don't miss it. If there's a sequel, and I hope there is, I will be first in line to read it.'
– BRIAN JOSS, *Bolander*

'Brilliantly written, sharply witty and excruciatingly funny – a must for anyone who knows the private lodge industry and those who enjoy a good laugh!' – HUGH MARSHALL, involved in guiding and lodge operations for over 25 years

'*A Year in the Wild* is more than an amusing and entertaining account of game lodge goings on; it is also a coming-of-age tale of two brothers who explore life, love, lust and loss.'
– CHRIS ROCHE, Wilderness Safaris

Back to the Bush

Another Year in the Wild

James Hendry

MACMILLAN

To Duncan MacLarty

First published in 2013
by Pan Macmillan South Africa
Private Bag X19
Northlands
Johannesburg
2116

www.panmacmillan.co.za

ISBN 978-1-77010-338-2
e-ISBN 978-1-77010-339-9

Editing by Sharon Dell
Proofreading by Wesley Thompson
Design and typesetting by Manoj Sookai
Cover design by K4
Cover photographs by iStockphoto

Dramatis personae

THE MACNAUGHTONS

Angus
Angus is 27. He is a biologist by training and a ranger at the lodge. Angus has dark hair, angry blue eyes and is shorter than average. He is intelligent, incredibly cynical and sarcastic – he easily puts people's noses out of joint. Angus frequently considers hosting the world's wealthy travellers a hindrance to his enjoyment of the wilderness. He is a talented but introverted musician.

Hugh (String Bean or SB to his brother)
Hugh is 23. There has never been any doubt that Hugh would make a career in hospitality. He is tall, blond, extroverted and jovial – in many ways the opposite of his brother. He loves to act and entertain. Hugh is the manager of Tamboti Camp and thoroughly enjoys his job.

Julia
Julia is Angus and Hugh's beloved sister. She is 25, slightly taller than average, has light-brown hair, green eyes and a pretty, engaging face. Julia is independent, clever and has recently qualified as a lawyer.

Born between the two brothers Julia means different things to each of them. To Angus, she has always been a friend and confidante because she understands him. Their closeness in age meant that they moved in the same circles at school (although Julia was considerably more popular than her sarky brother).

To Hugh, Julia is something of a mentor. In the past she has been a valuable source in the unfathomable world of women. Hugh tells her everything and she, in turn, dotes on her little brother.

SASEKILE LODGE STAFF

Heads of department

PJ Woodstock (43) – General Manager. Calm, collected and highly competent. Lodge life has made him soft around the edges.

Carrie Bartlett (31) – Head Ranger and only woman in the field team. Quiet, butch, highly organised and possessed of excellent bush and leadership skills.

Jacob 'Spear of the Lowveld' Mkhonto (42) – Conservation Manager. Mighty Shangane of immense strength. The 'go-to guy' whenever there is trouble (bush fires, elephants in camp, etc.).

Ronald O'Reilly (36) – Executive Chef. Skilled, passionate and volatile. From Tipperary, Ireland. Pasty white complexion.

Hilda Botha (39) – Head of Finance. 120 kg. Unmarried.

Simone Robertson (22) – Child Minder. Girlfriend to Hugh. Pretty, happy, no-nonsense but full of fun.

Camp management

Amber Thompson (23) – Rhino Camp Manager. Blonde, sexy, fair-weather character.

September Mathebula (46) – Main Camp Manager. A Shangane full of life. Fond of a heavy whisky before dinner. Immensely loveable man.

Jenny Sutherland (24) – Main Camp Assistant Manager. Attractive and competent young woman. From Johannesburg, on a two-year stint in the bush.

Melissa Mandelay (26) – Kingfisher Camp Manager. Ditsy. Severe lisp. No social graces. Massive cringe factor.

Rangers

A team of sixteen, the most important being:

Jeff Rhodes (23) – A trainee ranger. A likeable, yet gormless creature.

Alistair 'Jonesy The Legend' Jones (28) – One of the senior rangers. Good-looking, clever, arrogant. A man's man and a woman-slayer.

Matthew 'Matto' Keys (23) – A trainee ranger. Cousin of Jonesy The Legend. Confident. Sense of entitlement.

Sipho (24), **Jamie** (34), **Duncan** (29), **Richard** (25), **Mango** (23), **Jabu** (26), **Brandon** (27) and various others.

Trackers

A team of sixteen, the most important being:

Elvis Sithole (41) – 118 kg. Angus's field partner. Highly experienced, silent Shangane tracker.

Johnson (55) and **One-eyed Joe** (29).

Other lodge staff

Bertie Mathonsi (25) – Conservation team second-in-command. Young, ambitious, intelligent.

Candice Anderson (26) – Receptionist. Answers phones inefficiently. Elastic morals.

Incredible Mathebula (thinks he's 38) – Butler. Not blessed with a frontal lobe.

Kerry (22) and **Jane** (24) – Trainee chefs. Attractive girls from Cape Town, doing a year's practical training at the lodge.

Richard (46), **Gift** (37), **Petrus** (42) and **Samson** (39) – Chefs of widely varying talents (in exponentially descending order).

Redman (50) brilliant, **Nora** (43) very good, **Auto** (28) fair to middling, **Clifford** (23) insane – Butlers.

Allegra Gordon (24) – Massage therapist. Dark, quiet, formal on the surface. Qualified Physiotherapist educated in Scotland.

Outside of the lodge

The Major (86) – Angus, Hugh and Julia's senile maternal grandfather.

Great Aunt Jill (76) – Easily riled great-aunt.

Arthur Grimble (89) – A kindly old Englishman full of wisdom and subtle advice.

Trubshaw (42 dog years) – The MacNaughton family hound – a profoundly stupid Staffordshire bull terrier.

Phoebe or **'AIDS Cat'** to Angus (indeterminate number of cat years) – Adopted Burmese with severe halitosis. Highly aggressive, infected with feline AIDS.

Places

Sasekile Private Game Reserve – 'the lodge'

Sasekile is a five-star establishment situated on a private game reserve in the north-eastern lowveld of South Africa. It adjoins the Kruger National Park and, as such, is a game-viewing paradise. The nearest town is the dubious settlement of Hoedspruit.

The lodge consists of four beautifully appointed camps: Main – 24 beds; Tamboti – 12 beds; Kingfisher – 18 beds; and Rhino – 6 beds. The camps are situated adjacent to each other on the banks of the annual Tsesebe River.

All operations of the lodge are run centrally (finance, maintenance, laundry, rangers, trackers, kitchen, etc.).

The staff are housed in a widely spread staff village and there are just over 150 people employed at the lodge, most of whom are local, rural Shangane people.

Avuxeni Eatery

The staff canteen.

Twin Palms

Staff bar/TV room and general entertainment venue.

The office

A number of rooms where the administration staff of the lodge work (General Manager, finance, switchboard, maintenance, etc.).

The rangers' room

A large room next to the office where the rangers and trackers gather before and after game drives to shoot the breeze, share heroic stories, sort out issues and use the Internet, etc.

Definitions and terms

Boet – Afrikaans word for brother. Used as one might use 'buddy' or 'mate'.

Boma – Acronym for British Officers Mess Area. Place where soldiers used to surround a central fire with their wagons and a thorn fence in order to keep predators and the enemy at bay. In the lodge, the boma is an outside eating area surrounded by a split-pole fence. It has a central fire place, cooking area and bar.

Bru – Slang for brother. Also used as 'buddy' or 'mate'.

Cattie – Homemade catapult made with a forked stick and some tire tubing.

Doos – Afrikaans word for box. Used as an insult.

Impi – Zulu word for army.

Induna – Headman or chief.

Kak – Afrikaans slang for faeces.

Koppie – Rocky outcrop or hill.

Lowveld – North-eastern, low-lying (approximately 400 metres above sea level) part of South Africa. The Kruger National Park and many of the country's other premier game-viewing destinations are in the Lowveld.

Muthi – Zulu word for medicine or herbal concoction.

Pax – A word for guests or passengers used normally by airline and hotel staff and preferably not by personable lodge staff.

Potjie – a slow-cooked stew made in a three-legged iron pot over an open fire.

Shangane – A group of people who settled in the Lowveld at the turn of the 19th century. They are mainly a combination of the Tsonga people of Mozambique and an Nguni clan called the Ndwandwe.

Sheba – Tomato and onion sauce.

Sjambok – A whip made of hippo hide.

Turbo-lettuce – A slang term for the plant *Cannabis sativa*.

Voetsek – Afrikaans slang for 'go away'.

A weekly journal

The pages that follow are taken from the weekly journal of Angus J.D. MacNaughton – a year's worth of rant, reflection and musing.

Prologue

The year that was ...

The wilderness has a way of bludgeoning the truth home. Through beauty, drama, humour and tragedy, this wild place has been my teacher – an instructor without tact, mercy or concern for my feelings, but that's probably what makes it so effective. I have learned more about myself and other members of the bizarre species that is *Homo sapiens* in the last twelve months than in all the years preceding.

I'd sooner have assaulted my pink bits with a hot poker than have willingly chosen to engage with some of the cretins I've been forced to work with at Sasekile Private Game Reserve in the past year. Anton Muller, the jeep jockey responsible for the farce that was my training; Arno van der Vyfer, the maintenance manager, still bitter about his ancestors' loss in the Boer War; Candice Anderson, the receptionist with a level of ineptitude inversely proportional to her liberal sexual appetite; Alistair 'The Legend' Jones – the putrid senior ranger imbued with a confidence born of his size, sporting prowess and a giant trust fund.

Others I could tolerate either because they were inoffensive or because I found it amusing to watch as they bungled around, lost in an alternate reality. The imbecile Jeff Rhodes, my roommate in the Bat Cave for the first four months; Meliss(th)a Mandelay, the camp manager with a lisp more productive than a fire hose; and Incredible Mathebula, the Tamboti Camp butler possessed of less common sense than a lobotomised lemur.

Then, there are the rare few with whom I feel privileged to have worked: Elvis Sithole, senior tracker, with his quiet confidence and astounding talents, taught me more than anyone else about the wild and its creatures; Jacob 'Spear of the Lowveld' Mkhonto, head of the conservation team, whose presence inspires confidence in the direst of situations; Bertie Mathonsi, rising star in the conservation team, with his eager mind; Carrie Bartlett, the highly competent if slightly butch new head ranger, blessed of impressive leadership and ranging skills.

In general, my attitude to the people around me has moved from blanket contempt to a genuine sense of respect for a few, some fondness for a few more and a mild indifference to most of the rest. Of course, there are still those for whom I reserve a scalding disdain.

The time I have spent with the guests assigned to me also contributed to my education. I know with more certainty now that I'm an introvert. I see my guests as a necessary evil to my enjoyment of the bush. That said, I have come to realise that they are not all evil in themselves (although many are). I just find meeting new people and being nice to them a trial. This attitude is reflected in the fact that I am one of the worst tip earners in the history of Sasekile. Thankfully my skills as a naturalist have also increased exponentially so I can get away with not being Prince Charming all the time.

Mostly, of course, my character was booted from its insular, judgemental malaise by the single greatest joy – and then tragedy – of my life to date.

Anna.

There's still so much about this place that reminds me of her. Sometimes the memories catch in my throat and the pain of reminiscence slices through me. As time passes, however, remembrance brings with it a sense of warmth and a smile. Anna opened my eyes and my heart. She loved me and opened me to the beauty of the world before being brutally torn from my life. I can't believe I'll ever meet anyone like her again. Well, I know I won't but I suppose I need to be open to the possibility that there are women out there who will affect me as deeply – if differently.

Of course one of the major benefits of last year was the development of my relationship with Hugh aka String Bean (SB). When I started here the thought of being in such proximity to the brother with whom I struggled to acknowledge a common ancestry disgusted me. While we're unlikely to ever see the world through the same lens, I am happy to say that I now have a certain amount of respect for String Bean and his talents.

There's no doubt that Anna's dying wish of me – that I should try to see the world and its human inhabitants with a modicum of tolerance and affection – helped to change my approach to SB. A few events after that helped to create the bond that we now share – fixing the roof in the rain, the pantomime we performed, and, of course, the fire on the final night of the Young Millionaire's Society visit. I am still impressed that the two of us managed to put our differences aside for long enough to save the obese form of guest Martha van Dyk, her pathetic husband and their equally over-nourished children from the flames in their room.

As for SB, well he's just as over-excited as usual at the prospect of meeting new guests – serving them great food and wine and doing everything in his power to make their stays at Sasekile unique and memorable.

So I look forward to the year with careful optimism: to adventures with the animals and beautiful places that make up the reserve I live on; to time with the people I enjoy; and to more of the inescapable lessons that the wild has to offer.

Week 1

Beginning and bacchanal

The moon was two days waned from full, and the sky almost clear, with just a few clouds drifting through the summer air like lazy ships. I had just stepped out of the Twin Palms, den of drink and lasciviousness, for some fresh air. My shirt was wet from the exertions of dancing in the windowless room, my mind hazy from the punch. The sound of revelling people mixed with the strains of Johnny Clegg's *Great Heart* as it heralded the changing of the year. I sat down on an old jackalberry stump, took my shirt off and savoured the summer breeze on my skin. The scent of lush vegetation filled my lungs. A water thick-knee called from the waterhole next to the Main Camp and a flock of crowned lapwings squawked a mild objection on the flood plain behind the lodge. Insects sang all around me.

Before I moved to Sasekile, I didn't have a sixth sense. Now, however, I can normally feel when I'm being watched. Sitting there in the night, the hair on the back of my neck began to tingle. I was facing the bush, the camp buildings behind me. I looked up and scanned the trees and low shrubs. Something moved in the shadows and my whole body tensed. The shape was about four feet off the ground. Moonlight glinted off a shiny eye. I sat dead still, staring, knowing that the animal was returning my gaze. After a few minutes he emerged into the blue light – a weathered old nyala bull – satisfied that I posed him no threat. A smile spread across my face.

'Happy New Year, old boy,' I said softly. He sniffed the air and then returned to the shadows. I sighed and relaxed – and then my sixth sense

1

failed. Something touched my shoulders from behind. I shot up and spun round and she yelped in fright.

Jenny.

We stared at each other as the adrenalin ebbed and then we started giggling.

'Happy New Year,' she said re-tying her blonde curls in a bunch behind her head.

'And to you too,' I replied.

'What are you doing out here?' She pulled a stick of lip gloss from her shorts pocket and applied it to her small, neat mouth. The stick replaced, she turned her hazel eyes up to me and smiled.

'Getting some air, considering the universe, that sort of thing.' Her face was extra pretty in the moonlight, her lips shimmering. My punch-mellowed mind decided it would be an excellent idea to kiss her so I stepped forward...and tripped over the stump I'd been sitting on, landing at her feet – face-first in the dirt. She burst out laughing, helped me to my feet and then we wished each other a proper Happy New Year through the medium of a long smooch.

The same time last year was spent with a growing sense of dread at the thought of being stuck in the wilderness with String Bean – all in all, a more positive beginning.

Jenny and I were the least publicly affectionate that night. Jeff and Melissa became so excited that PJ was forced to tell them to 'get a room'. Their enthusiasm threatened to knock over the split-pole fence separating the Twin Palms from the kitchen. The General Manager, for the first time since I've been here, let his hair down (well, as much as one can let down a neat, short back and sides). Every time any South African music was played, he flung his podgy six-foot frame about the room displaying a startling number of violent dance moves which cleared the dance floor.

The New Year dawned with the Sasekile staff in various states of disrepair. The camp was full of guests, most of whom were in the bush to escape the necessity of the obligatory New Year's Eve party. My six, deeply aged Swiss guests were in bed before 22h00. I went to sleep about half an hour before meeting them on deck at 05h30 with a large mug of tar-strength coffee. I smelt like a distillery, my visage akin to a skydiver whose parachute had failed to open.

'Good morning,' said Udo. 'Zis morning vee see lions.'

'In South Africa we say Happy New Year,' I muttered and turned to make my way to the Land Rovers.

In the Main Camp car park, the trackers weren't radiating an aura of five-starness. Jackson, who claims that drinking is against his religion, was leaning against his vehicle groaning audibly. Elvis's headache was obvious from the absence of his ubiquitous woolly hat. The worst, by a comfortable lowveld mile, was One-eyed Joe. He was fast asleep across the bonnet of his Land Rover, his unshaven cheek pressed up against the radio aerial. Sipho had to prod him awake with his rifle as the guests arrived.

The game drive, conducted in heat rivalled only by that at the centre of a neutron star, was a trial. The guests spotted most things well before me. The illustrious Elvis claimed to find tracks of lions about ten minutes out of camp. These he said he would follow alone. The fact that I couldn't raise him on the radio for the next hour indicates that he went to sleep under the first guarri bush he found.

Thankfully, however, Carrie, our uber-competent head ranger, discovered some lions languishing in a river bed. Their New Year meal was a kudu bull killed sometime in the night (miserable year end for him). The pride had eaten its fill and was lazing about in satisfied corpulence. Unfortunately they had opened up the kudu's stomach so the stench was unspeakable. This, combined with the vodka/tequila and possibly diesel-based punch that my bowels were failing miserably to digest, made for an uncomfortable hour of fighting my gag reflex.

The most enjoyable part of the sighting came from Carrie's tracker. While the head ranger is more efficient than a Swiss watch factory, her tracker for the day was not. Samson is normally a chef, and not a very good one. His inescapable lack of talent as a cook is exponentially greater than his aptitude for tracking. He found himself on this game drive because Carrie's regular tracker was at home feeling 'sick'. By 08h00, Samson was still misfiring on rum fumes. He slept through most of the sighting in the passenger seat. Carrie hid this from her guests by placing a bird book in his lap which made it look like he was trying to identify a rare vagrant.

About half an hour after we arrived at the sighting, something startled one of the pride males. He stood up with a loud grunt. This, in turn, woke the recumbent Samson. As his eyes opened, he found eight lions filling his field of vision.

'Lions! Lions! Lions!' he shouted pointing excitedly as if his ranger, her six guests and the other two Land Rovers full of people had failed to notice the pride lying in plain view. This profound utterance bewildered his guests somewhat, made mine scowl, and infinitely improved my hangover.

On returning to camp, I found an email waiting for me. It was from Arthur Grimble – Anna's surrogate father. But for a handwritten thank-you note, I hadn't heard from him since he graciously allowed me to share the duty of scattering Anna's ashes at her memorial. He is pushing 90 now and, to his eternal credit, has just learned to use email (although, he still thought it necessary to put his address in the top right-hand corner). It was great to hear from him.

To: Angus MacNaughton
From: Arthur C. Grimble
Subject: Are you receiving me?

Crocus Cottage
West Road
Wragby
Lincolnshire

My dear Angus,

I do hope that you will receive this. I have just purchased, for the first time, a computer machine. A very patient young man in the village has been round a number of times to help me connect with the interworld.

I hope that you are in excellent health. I am fit and in good spirits and would enjoy hearing some news from you. I shall send more of mine when I have mastered this infernal keyboard. This letter has taken an age to type. I am using just one arthritic finger!

I am very much looking forward to hearing from you.

Best wishes,
Arthur Grimble

Receiving this message brought back memories of Anna. It felt almost like I was connecting with her through the old boy. I replied immediately and filled him in on my life and the goings on at Sasekile.

Then SB sent me the following missive from Kenton a few days later. The Sasekile rumour mill works with the efficiency of the MI5 communications department. I suspect SB's source on this occasion was Redman, his right-hand man at Tamboti Camp.

To: Angus
From: Hugh MacNaughton
Subject: Happy New Year and see you soon

Hey Angus,

Happy New Year!

Well done on your New Year's Eve conquest! I told everyone here in Kenton and they all thought it was an excellent achievement although Mum said it was a bit disgusting because you haven't been on a date with her yet. Simone says that Jenny has had a crush on you for ages (don't tell her I told you).

I've had a lot of time to think about last year while lying on the beach or sipping beer upriver on the old boat. I think it was probably the best year of my life and I've definitely found my calling – I can't imagine a job that I'd rather be doing. While I'm tired at the end of each work cycle, I always look forward to getting back to Tamboti Camp, meeting new people, conjuring new food and wine combinations with O'Reilly, organising special drinks stops in the bush etc. Sasekile has given me the opportunity to practise everything I learnt at hotel school and I think I've got pretty good at my job.

Obviously the fact that I now have a relationship with my brother after 23 years means a huge amount to me. As I said to you at the end of last year, despite what you might think, I have a lot of respect for you.

Also, to have found the fair Simone is awesome – we've been through our ups and downs but we do love each other very much. Speaking of which . . .

It's been fun here but not all roses with Simone. The MacNaughtons are not that easy for girlfriends. Dad has the same dry wit as you (without the vicious sarcasm thankfully) so it's difficult for people who don't know him to figure out when he's joking. Julia was a bit offish to start with and so Simone was the same but they seem to be getting on fine now – they went out for a drink together yesterday while I was skiing.

Mum's been friendly but very formal – we were obviously placed in separate bedrooms so there hasn't been much physical contact, which is frustrating after the freedom of Sasekile. Trubshaw was over-friendly and he knocked Simone clean over as she walked through the front door and then licked her face while Dad tried to pull him off. The Major still doesn't know her name although he perks up when she's in her bikini. He hasn't been informed that she has a German grandfather.

On the whole it's been a fun holiday but I'm quite looking forward to getting back to the bush. I miss the hubbub of the camp and I especially miss sleeping next to the fair Simone every night.

Julia had to leave Kenton early because, as you put it, she has sold her soul to the legal profession . . . Trubshaw and Dad are distraught at the thought of their return to Johannesburg. Anyway, I'll be back in a week and will see you then!

All the best for the New Year!

Hugh

P.S. Mum has just adopted a stray cat. It's a feisty Burmese-looking thing and Trubshaw, despite being unafraid of Great Danes, is pretty scared of her. Mum took her to the vet the other day and apparently she has feline Aids which made Mother love her even more. She's called it Phoebe and it really smells bad.

Astoundingly I'm actually quite looking forward to String Bean's return which confirms that I must have changed. It's difficult to imagine that twelve months ago we could barely stand the sight of each other. It's also impossible to see how we'd ever have forged our fledgling sibling bond without the experiences of beauty, danger, emotion and hilarity that this place and its bizarre assortment of inhabitants (animal and human) have thrown at us.

Week 2

Untrained and untrainable

SB returned at the beginning of the week. The evening he arrived I wasn't driving so we headed to the staff shop for a beer and a general report on the Kenton holiday. All the camp managers were up there and an atmosphere of summer frivolity gathered as SB regaled the assembled company with stories of our senile grandfather and the recalcitrant Trubshaw. When he imitated Dad's language on finding his 'best friend' consuming the lamb leg he'd just seasoned for the New Year's meal, there was a general collapse. Everyone here wants to meet Trubshaw.

My brother was ecstatic to be back. He went about greeting everyone with the fondness of someone who has just returned from a prolonged and dangerous mission to a war-ravaged region of the Rwanda/Congo border. He was especially pleased to be living with Simone again. I find it very amusing to think of SB trying to sneak along the Kenton sprung floors past the Major's room. I suppose his sharing of accommodations with Simone would have pushed our grandfather to lengthy diatribes about the decline of moral standards since the war. I wonder what my mother thinks her baby boy gets up to at the lodge without her supervision.

SB's excitement at his return was tempered slightly by the state of play at Tamboti Camp. He felt the camp's standards had dipped somewhat in his absence. Amber looked after Tamboti while he was away and apparently her eye for detail is not quite as accurate as his. The rusks in most of the rooms were stale, as were the nuts. It mortified SB to think of his guests paying R10 000 a night, sitting down with a G&T after a hot bush walk and then biting into a nut tasting as if it was harvested during the last ice age.

I drove out of Tamboti a few times in his absence and without SB's constant supervision, Incredible's butlering skills certainly did seem to have ebbed. Being a man blessed with little more than a rudimentary brain stem, he must be constantly monitored. The other night, a guest of mine ordered a R500 bottle of Rustenberg John X Merriman. Incredible failed to let the man taste his purchase, and then filled his glass to the brim. The Tamboti red wine glasses are enormous so the man's wife received half a glass.

The other disadvantage of driving from the camp in which Amber works is Jonesy The Legend. Because he and Amber are lovers, he often drives where she is hosting. The Legend, in some ways, is like my former classmate Johnny Danville. Johnny was the Eagle's Cross College 1ˢᵗ XV flyhalf and captain, opening bowler for the 1ˢᵗ XI, head boy and straight-A student. The difference is that Johnny Danville was on a scholarship and his widowed mother could barely afford lunch. Johnny's lowly roots gave him a certain humility. The Legend doesn't know the meaning of the word and, given the size of the Jones family farms, worrying about lunch is not something he will ever have to do.

While waiting for our guests one afternoon, The Legend asked me when SB was coming back. As always, before addressing me he made sure to draw himself to his full height and stand over me – almost as if inviting me to challenge him. I gave him the answer to his question and then, in order to be cordial, asked him where his family holidays over the Christmas period. He, turned, gave a little snort and replied, 'We alternate. Plett one year, skiing the next – Vale normally but sometimes St Moritz.' He looked out over the Tsesebe River, sipping on the post-workout protein shake he insists on consuming at 16h00 every day. The specially insulated dispenser looks more expensive than my guitar. He didn't bother to ask where the MacNaughton peasants travel for the holidays so I thought I'd tell him.

'Us? Well since you ask, we normally dive the Barrier Reef, take a houseboat on the Amazon and then, if Mum's up for it, tootle down to the

Antarctic for New Year's Eve coinciding with the *Aurora Australis*.' I bit into my choc-chip biscuit. He looked at me.

'Your brother's such a good oke. What the hell happened to you?' he asked, relaxed as a monitor lizard. The guests arrived on deck just then and my tension dissipated.

On his first night back, SB organised a special wine tasting before dinner. He'd just received a mixed box of new wines from a friend who is starting up a distribution company in Stellenbosch. There were six couples in camp: some Americans, some Germans, some Brits and the rest filthy rich South Africans. They were hugely appreciative of the effort he made despite the fact that some of the wines tasted like rancid vinegar. The evening progressed with an excellent meal by O'Reilly who came to cook at Tamboti in honour of SB's return.

'Muurveluss, te have ye back, Hugh,' he said on SB's return. 'Oi'll cook ye a cracker tunoight!' And that he did.

As I left Tamboti, String Bean was sipping cognac at the fire with the head chef. The guests had all gone to bed. My brother sighed happily.

'I must say, eating a stunningly seared Cape salmon, dripping in white-wine sauce, sipping a bold and buttery chardonnay, chatting to interesting people with the noises of the bush all around, must be the most blissful atmosphere I can imagine,' he said.

The beginning of the year is often a time for training new staff – Sasekile now has a trainee ranger, a new security guard and two new trainee chefs.

The trainee ranger has arrived, partly to fill the vacuum left by Anton's departure (although Anton was more vacuum than matter). Ah, Anton – a flood of unpleasant memories comes back tempered by the remembrance of his departure after the ego smashing he took during his appalling shooting evaluation. The thought of his failing the test in front of the whole team sweetens the painful recollection of his tenure.

Matthew (or Matto to his friends) is the Legend's lizard cousin. He's over-familiar and puffed up with the unjustified air of arrogance that comes with average intelligence and a vast family business empire to fall into. When I introduced myself to him he slapped me on the shoulder and said, 'Ja, Howzit, cool to meet you hey Mac.' While SB loves this moniker, I have always detested it.

'My name is Angus,' I replied. 'The only other thing I'll answer to is Sir.' I left him to ooze about and shake hands with the rest of the field team. Matto attended one of those over-subscribed private farm schools in the Natal Midlands and I overheard him telling his cousin that he believes his training will be no more taxing than 'scoring a high-school chick at a New Year's party'. Well if he doesn't hop off his high horse soon, Carrie will most certainly push him off it.

In SB's case, new staff meant a new security guard to replace Efficient who has been forcibly retired at age 75 (the most reasonable estimate). SB was a bit sorry to lose the ancient Shangane but he was almost blind. The first inkling he'd have of a charging hippo would be its white ivories as they were about to clamp down around his head. He was also almost stone deaf too, so PJ organised him a hearing aid as a retirement gift. This was good and bad in that as soon as the device was fitted, Efficient called a meeting with the union to demand that he be reinstated. Even the militant shop steward of the Millennium Solidarity Union admitted that this was ridiculous.

Jerry (aged 23) is SB's new protector of guests and their belongings. Carrie trained him to deal with animals in camp and during this process she took the opportunity to test all the other security guards and was horrified at what she found. Unsurprisingly, her predecessor prepared the guards so poorly that it's some wonder we haven't lost a guest to a marauding buffalo. While the security team is being retrained, the rangers have been doing security guard duty.

The most bothersome part of this task is making the early morning coffee. While I realise that they are paying the bills that allow me to live in the wilderness, I find most guests a bit of a chore. Making cappuccinos and skinny vanilla lattes at 04h30 does not improve my disposition towards them.

Thankfully, SB has nearly finished training Jerry in the barista's art. This has been no easy task because Jerry's background hasn't extended to space-age coffee machines and he speaks virtually no English. Apparently his first cappuccino resembled Trubshaw vomit but he is improving – at great cost to the beverage budget.

The two new trainee chefs have arrived to replace Natasha and Ashleigh. Kerry and Jane are attractive, Kerry particularly so, but out here all new girls tend to look sexier than they might in more populated surrounds. This is not a target-rich environment as Duncan put it during a sexually explicit conversation in the rangers' room just before their arrival.

There was some territorial jealousy at their first lunch. When Kerry and Jane arrived to eat, all the male staff fell over themselves to be friendly and welcoming. But for Carrie, there were only muted hellos from the girls.

As soon as they'd left, Simone piped up, 'You guys and your cock fighting are so lame sometimes. It's so gross. Anyway, those girls are not even that hot … are they?' She turned to look at SB who just stared at his food, his ears going red. She had posed an unanswerable female enquiry and my brother was stumped. He simply looked at his watch and remarked that he was late for a training session with Jerry.

'To answer your question, Simone,' said Jamie swallowing a mouthful of spaghetti, 'they are absolutely sssmokin!' This caused general hilarity amongst most of the Y-chromosomes present. O'Reilly seems to have developed a huge crush on Kerry already. This of course is the perfect plot for high drama and comedy. The executive chef is now pushing 40 and his midriff is showing the years of fine food he's sampled. While he has a friendly engaging face, his Irish complexion alternates between ghostly pale and beetroot red – the latter occurring after more than five minutes in the sun. The package is topped with thinning strawberry blond hair and infused with emotional instability. If Kerry ends up with anyone else, there will be great entertainment. This is almost inevitable as she is 21, tall, slim and sassy – and the rangers are already circling.

I too received a training assignment – from Carrie. (I continue to be most impressed by her leadership and ranging skills – both of which eluded her predecessor.) Before I describe my slightly astounding project, I must describe a few of the changes Carrie has wrought since her elevation to the lofty position of head ranger.

While Anton was in charge, the rangers' room looked like a grubby armoury. Empty cartridges littered every surface and the battered old chairs looked like they'd been pilfered from a large buffalo family who hadn't treated them very well.

Since his departure, the space has been transformed. It's a rectangular room with its entrance in the corner of the east-facing short side. Left of the door, Carrie has fitted some enormous shelves and filled them with well-labelled artefacts from the field – an elephant jaw, hippo teeth, complete lion, leopard and hyena skulls and four exquisite arthropod collections in glass cases. To the right of the door, there is a sofa pushed into the corner – its spruced companion sits opposite with a small coffee table in the middle. On the wall between them is a ceiling-high bookshelf full of old issues of *National Geographic, Time, Africa Geographic* and *Science and Nature.*

In the middle of the room, there are two desks set in an L shape, one of them backing onto the sofa. Two computers for the rangers occupy the surfaces. Carrie's desk is at the far end under a window. She sits next to another ceiling-high bookshelf full of reference books – including some very valuable first editions (*Roberts Birds of Southern Africa, Trees of the Kruger Park* and *Smithers' Mammals of Southern Africa*). On her left are the rifle safes, the cleaning kits and a small tool cabinet. Carrie keeps the place spotless.

The rangers' room is now a place of learning and research and its comfortable layout means that the rangers and trackers spend time reading and talking about the things they see out in the field.

Back to the reason for my being summoned ...

I thought perhaps I'd done something wrong but this wasn't the case. Instead, Carrie presented me with a bizarre request.

After more than sixteen months of training, the imbecile Jeff still shows no signs of passing an assessment game drive and his days here have finally been numbered. The long-suffering PJ has decided that Jeff is, rather like the Natal Native Contingent was once described, untrained and untrainable. As far as I'm concerned, this was patently obvious from the moment I met him. However, apparently he comes from a difficult background (I'm not privy to the details but they must include being dropped on his head). He will therefore be afforded one final chance to pass his drive. When Jeff was informed of this and asked if he thought there was anything more that could be done to help him, he replied in the affirmative.

Astonishingly, Jeff nominated me as his mentor. I cannot remember saying one pleasant thing to him – ever. In fact, I believe I've slandered him more or less continuously since we were forced into the same living quarters last year. I've told him that his brain is more miniscule than a Higgs boson; I've suggested that he's more suited to employment as the red flag waver at a roadworks; and I remember telling him that the likelihood of us becoming friends was smaller than the chances of life being discovered on Venus. Just last week I found him in the rangers' room looking at a recently captured dung beetle trying to escape from a glass aquarium. He looked up as I came in.

'Angus,' he said, 'I'm so excited to be a ranger – I need to start earning tips so I can take Melissa on a holiday.' The dung beetle banged its head against the corner of the aquarium.

'Jeff,' I replied, 'I would suggest asking a family member for a loan, because it is my firm belief that the dung-rolling coleopteran you are examining would make a more competent ranger than you.'

How, therefore, he has come to the conclusion that I'm the man to guide him through his final chance at a job in ecotourism is quite beyond me. Carrie was more than a little puzzled herself but said, 'Let's face it Angus, the senior rangers have all tried our best with him. You couldn't do any harm ... well, that's not necessarily true but I'd like you to have a go all the same.'

'Carrie,' I replied, 'with due respect, there are eukaryotes at the bottom of the ocean with greater potential than that cretin – harmless though he might be. And I say harmless only because he's not currently allowed out with a V8 full of guests, armed with a high-calibre hunting weapon.' Carrie smiled – she finds me quite amusing.

'Angus, you are being a little melodramatic, I think. I don't expect much from the exercise but I'd appreciate you giving it a go.'

At this point the pathetic form of Jeff slouched into the room. He's a heavily built fellow with a mop of dirty blond hair. His arms are too long for his body – indeed his whole demeanour gives the observer a hint of man's distant evolution. His uniform is always unkempt and dirty and there is a whiff of body odour about him. That said, my experience over the last year has led me to believe that Jeff Rhodes would do anything in his power to help someone in need — no matter who they were. He'd probably kill or seriously maim them in the process but at least he'd make the effort. There simply isn't a nasty bone in his body.

Carrie looked from him to me as he slumped down at the rangers' computer. 'All he wants in the whole world is to be a ranger and part of the team. You've got four weeks,' she said and then, before turning back to her rifle inspection she added, 'of course that means you'll have to skip your leave but I'll make sure there's a little something extra in your pay this month.'

'It had better be a large something ma'am,' I muttered.

I went off to the Avuxeni Eatery for lunch and there I found a few of the other rangers, The Legend among them. Clearly they'd been told of my new assignment.

'How do you feel about your challenge?' asked Jabu as I sat down to eat my wors roll.

'A bit like Captain Henry Pulain on seeing 20 000 very irritated Zulus streaming towards his camp at Isandlwana,' I answered.

'Total waste of time,' said The Legend picking some wors from his teeth. 'That dude should be doing manual labour somewhere. Besides, you've only been here a year so, what are you going to teach him?' This utterance stung my ego.

'Jones, what say we have a little wager,' I snapped. The table went quiet.

'Anything you like,' said The Legend leaning forward towards me, 'absolutely anything. You don't ... have ... a ... fucking ... hope.' Of course his objective here was to rile me into betting something stupid. He succeeded. I pointed my fork at his arrogant face.

'Okay, Jones. If Jeff passes, you pay his and my bar bills for the rest of the year.' While I'm a bit of a lightweight in the booze department, Jeff has an unrivalled ability to hold liquor.

'No problem,' he leant back in his chair, 'And you pay mine if ... no, no sorry ... *when* he goes.' He stuck out a muscled hand. I dropped my fork and took it.

'I'm going to drink every last cent of your measly income,' he said smiling.

Soon after that, I went back to my room and considered the situation. Jeff remains a hopeless challenge and the pressure was far greater given that

I had probably just bankrupted myself with The Legend's challenge. I sat on my bed and hatched a plan which I delivered to Jeff at tea time. The two most crucial points of the strategy are:

- Carry a notebook and pen at all times. Failure to comply with this will result in no supper for three nights (Jeff loves food almost as much as Melissa).
- No more sex with Melissa until the end of the assessment drive. There is nothing like enforced celibacy to spur a man on. Ask the Zulu army *circa* 1830.

Every hour of Jeff's life for the next four weeks is now accounted for in the timetable I've drawn up. I suspect that someone with the IQ of Forest Gump needs complete structure and discipline for success.

That afternoon, confidence levels in my pupil plunged to greater depths.

I took Jeff on a training drive, the idea being to drive into sightings so that he could practise approaching animals and explaining their behaviour. We travelled north out over the river and I asked Jeff to explain a number of things about the trees around us. I quickly gauged that there was a lot of very jumbled information in his mind – much of it irrelevant to the topics at hand (or any topic for that matter).

I decided that giving him the rudiments of some interesting anecdotes about the vegetation was a good first step. Animals don't always behave in the same way and explaining their behaviour sometimes takes conjecture and fast thinking. Conjecture in Jeff's case would amount to wild fantasy and as for fast thinking, well, the three cells in his head can only be expected to do so much. Trees, however, do not move about and behave unpredictably. There are also any number of interesting local beliefs and medicines associated with most of the plants out here.

So it was that we fetched up next to a rocky hillside, inaccessible to the Land Rover. I knew there was a snot-berry bush on the eastern slope. This tree has very rough leaves and is used for various things including treating septic sores.

We hadn't brought a rifle but I wasn't intending to chase down murderous animals so I figured we'd be fine. We walked up the rocky slope, the grass so long in some places that it cleared our heads. The bushy trees were also covered in thick foliage so visibility in some places was extremely limited.

I should have told Jeff to be quiet but I suppose my mind was on other things as we pushed our way up the hill. One should really be as quiet as possible when walking in the wilderness with hardly any visibility.

'I've never had my own professor!' he said loudly before launching into a treatise on Melissa's perceived attributes.

Some ancient volcanic activity had scattered the top of the hill with huge, haphazardly arranged, granite boulders. Underneath them, smaller rocks were scattered, creating innumerable nooks and cracks for creatures to hide in. We stepped up onto an uneven ledge formed by some closely packed rocks. There were thick bushes growing from the crevices on the ledge so visibility wasn't improved. The hair on the back of my neck began to tingle. I stopped and Jeff bashed into me.

'Oh, sorry,' he said, failing to understand my tension and carrying on with his story, 'and then she said she wanted to go to Zanzibar but I don't really know where that is so I said ...'

'Jeff, shut up.'

'Oh, sorry, okay um, what about?'

'Just shut up and listen.'

'Oh, sorry, okay.'

Far in the distance I heard a Wahlberg's eagle calling its mate.

I gingerly stepped forward and, as I did so, Jeff resumed his yakking. I was about to turn around and admonish him when a sound like two Harley-Davidsons burst from the bush – first on the right and then the other on the left. Jeff went silent, his primitive survival instincts kicking in.

Lionesses.

Very cross.

With us.

The dense foliage and rocks made it impossible to see them but I could hear they were maybe twenty metres in front. Then, another sound, pitched much higher than the first, sounded further to the left – cubs. We'd almost blundered straight between the cubs and their mothers. Jeff's next action was to swear ... loudly.

'Oh bugger fuck crap!' he shouted at the top of his lungs. The lions didn't appreciate this and revealed themselves in spectacular fashion. A blur of snarling tawny exploded out of the grass and thicket on either side of us. Thankfully we both froze – more out of shock than courage. The vegetation was so thick that I could only see the one growling face, teeth bared and ears flat back on her head. The other one, a few metres to the right, was revealed only by the black tip of her swishing tail – making the grass covering her sway angrily. The noise emanating from the cats, obviously convinced that we were about to attack their babies, was as loud as it was terrifying. I swallowed my heart.

'Jeff... hold my belt and take one very slow step back.' The whole point of moving like this is that the chap holding the belt is supposed to navigate while the person facing the threat assesses the situation. Sweat streamed down my back and into my eyes as I stared at the razor claws and sabre teeth threatening to end our short lives. Jeff did as he was told and took a timid step back. The lions remained where they were, growling ferociously. Jeff, of course, was fixated on his impending doom and therefore wasn't watching where he moved.

When the lions didn't maul us after the first step, I told him to take another. He complied and then tripped over a loose rock and off the ledge on which we were standing. His grip on my belt tightened as he went, so we both fell. The lions, believing that we were attempting to hide from them, rushed forward to the rim of the ledge. The first one arrived and took a swat at us as we lay on our backs. I felt the wind on my face as her fully extended claws slashed out at my midriff, missing by a whisker. Both seething cats' faces were now in full view.

We'd fallen into a deep crevice, the lip of which was about two feet below the lions, the walls pressing in on us. There was nowhere to move. Jeff was lying directly underneath me, totally silent. I think the only reason the lions didn't follow us in was that they failed to see a way out. This didn't stop them both stretching down and trying to hook us out. Their claws came so close that I could smell the rancid carrion embedded on them.

It became clear after a few minutes of murderous swiping that we were relatively safe – at least for a while – and this allowed me space to think. The sun was already starting to set so there was about an hour of light left.

'You alright Jeff?' I gasped as a fresh slash cut just above my head.

'Ja no okay for alright now,' he replied.

'Are you hurt?'

'Well, I think maybe, my arm is underneath me and it's really sore.'

'Okay, just sit tight, I can't move right now – we're going to have to wait it out.'

After another few minutes, the lionesses lost interest and stopped swatting at us. Soon after that, I heard the cubs emerging from their hiding place and, in the fading light, I could hear them growling as they fought over a teat to suckle on. By this stage, Jeff and I were both seriously uncomfortable, the sharp parts of our hiding place making themselves felt as the adrenaline levels ebbed.

'How long must we wait?' asked Jeff.

'I have no idea but if we leave now, we'll die for sure.'

'Okay no okay,' said Jeff.

There we lay, as the sky above went from blue to gold to red. As the red darkened to purple, I decided to chance a peep over the edge because I didn't fancy spending the night there. I told Jeff to lie still and then very gently levered myself up on the walls of the crevice. I peered over the edge.

There were no lions in sight but then visibility was terrible even in good light conditions so I had no idea whether the lionesses had gone off hunting or if they were simply waiting quietly for their dinner to climb out of the crevice. Our choices at that point were simple. Walking down the rocky hill on a moonless night would be asking for trouble. Either we waited until morning or chanced a move right then in the embers of the dusk. I looked back at Jeff who was pale and decided we had to chance it now. Visions of spending the night in the same proximity to him as Melissa usually would made me nauseous.

'Jeff, I'm going to climb out. If nothing happens, follow me.' My heart was thrashing against my ribcage and my mouth was so dry I could barely swallow as I eased myself over the lip of the crevice and swung my legs out away from the ledge where the lions had been. I froze, expecting 120 kg of pissed-off lioness to smash into me from behind. But there was just the sound of the breeze in the long grass and the smell of the summer evening.

'Come Jeff. Now – and be as quiet as possible.'

As my charge stood, he yelped and we both froze. Still no lions.

'What's the matter?' I asked irritated.

'My wrist,' he said, 'I think it's broken.' I turned to look. There was no need for an advanced degree in anatomy to see that Jeff's wrist was pointing at an angle it was never intended to. There was no time for sympathy so I just helped him out by his good arm and we started down the slope. As we neared the bottom, it was almost dark and I was starting to feel a bit more relaxed. This is normally when things go bad.

Suddenly, an animal erupted from a bush next to us. We both swung to face our killers as the adrenaline surged up again.

But there were no lions. A duiker had scampered out from its hiding place to find another. We made it back to the vehicle without incident after that.

Jeff was carted off to have his wrist set when we arrived back at the lodge. Carrie made a pretence at being angry with me but she knew that it had been a great learning experience for both of us and that the lionesses had forged a bond between me and Jeff.

My first leave of the year begins tomorrow but because of my training task, all I have is four days. Still, I'm looking forward to some down time and the two nights Jenny and I are going to spend away at the beginning.

Week 3

Kerry and cobra

On the morning of my first day of leave, I was forced to face some of my demons. I was sitting with Carrie in the rangers' room going over what Jeff and I had covered during the last week and handing over what needed to be done in my absence when her radio went ballistic on the desk next to her.

'Carrie, Carrie, Carrie dja cuppy?' crackled the panicked voice of O'Reilly.

'Go ahead,' replied the calm head ranger.

'Dere's a fekken snehk in de kitchen stores, fekken huge ting and it's got Kerry pinned on de flour bin!'

I went cold, the blood draining from my face. Memories of the cobra that bit Anna cascaded into my head.

Carrie looked at me.

'Angus, can you go and deal with that please,' she said casually. Duncan was sitting reading on the sofa.

'If it's all the same to you, given my experience with that thing last year, I'd rather not.'

'I'll do it,' said Duncan.

'No, thank you Duncan,' said Carrie firmly, 'I think Angus needs to do it.'

Her thinking was logical – she knew that I had to face the loathing, anger and terror with which I have viewed all serpents since last year's tragedy.

'Alright,' I sighed, standing. I fetched the snake-catching tongs and goggles. Duncan stood, patted my shoulder and I walked out into the sun.

I made my way to the kitchen and then through it to the store entrance at the back. All the chefs and scullery ladies were standing at the door. They were silent but for the Irishman who was hopping up and down, his head peering into the store every so often.

'Oh fehk, Kerry, ya alright in dere? Just don't move, don't look de fehkker in its aivil oiyes!'

Kerry's reply floated out of the doorway. 'Just calm down, dude. Every time you shout it gets agitated.'

The head chef heard me coming and turned, wringing his hands, shaking his head. By this stage, I was sweating heavily and feeling light-headed. I asked Jane for some water and she went to fetch it.

'Kerry,' I called trying to hide the quaver in my voice, 'can you see the snake?'

'Yes – it's sitting on the floor in front of the flour bin. It's just sticking its nasty forked tongue in and out and looking at me.'

'Just sit tight,' I exhaled, 'I'm coming to get it.' I downed the water Jane had brought and moved slowly in. O'Reilly followed close behind.

'What ur ya going te do in dere?' he asked twice in quick succession – tapping me on the shoulder frantically. I turned to him, the tongs in one hand, goggles in the other.

'I'm going to retrieve some flour and sugar for tonight's malva pudding!' I snapped, 'What the hell do you think I'm going to do in there?!' I swung round again.

'No, no I see, I mean, I'm just, I'm just worried aboat Kerry, ya know.' I ignored him and moved forward.

The kitchen store is separated into two sections by a floor-to-ceiling wire mesh. The fresh produce section is in the front. The dry store is accessed through a doorless frame in the mesh. I walked cautiously past the fruit and vegetables towards the gap while trying to stop my heart bashing a hole in my ribcage. 'Breathe evenly,' I told myself. I peeped through the gap and around the spice shelves blocking my view.

In the far corner of the room I saw the flour bin with Kerry perched on the lid. Her eyes were fixed on a loosely packed pile of 6 kg hessian bags labelled, 'Rwandan Coffee Beans'. I stepped into the room, the snake tongs in my right hand.

'Where is it?' I asked not looking at the trainee chef.

'It's just moved under the coffee, I can see it coiled up a crack.' She looked almost as terrified as I felt but, as the ranger, it fell to me to try and lead the situation.

'O gud, dis is aahful!' bleated O'Reilly, grabbing my shoulders and looking over me.

'O'Reilly, for God's sake!' I hissed, 'I can't do this with you hanging all over me!' He backed away. I looked up at Kerry. 'Just stay put, it's not going to climb up there – it's as scared of you as you are of it.'

'Then it must be fucking terrified!' she whispered.

I had to somehow move around to the front of the coffee bags where the snake was hiding.

'Which side of the pile is it on?' I asked.

'The right,' said Kerry.

'I'm going to come around,' I said making for the left of the pile.

'My right! Your left!' she shouted.

'Okay, okay – don't yell, you'll frighten it,' I said as soothingly as possible, moving to the opposite side of the pile which was about three feet high and five feet in diameter at the base. I edged round and peered down towards where Kerry's eyes were focussed. In a gap between two bags I made out the tail. From the width of its back end I could see it wasn't a tiddler and from its colour I identified it as a Mozambique spitting cobra.

'I'm going to try and grab its tail,' I said, pushing the goggles onto my face.

'Shit,' said Kerry.

I reached forward slowly with the snake tongs, figuring I could just reach it. Sweat dripped down my back and the protective goggles misted up almost immediately. They were useless but attempting to grab a spitting cobra with nothing covering the eyes is plain stupid. I looked up at Kerry– she had a pair of sunglasses tucked into the front of her chef's jacket.

'What are you doing?' she hissed.

'Toss me your sunglasses . . . slowly!' I whispered.

'What?' she was becoming a little hysterical. I took a deep breath and wiped the sweat from my brow.

'It's a spitting cobra. If I'm going to catch it I need something over my eyes. These things have misted up. Throw them over here.'

'What about my eyes!'

'You're standing on a bin, three feet in the air, not about to piss the thing off!' She wheezed and then flicked the glasses over to me. I placed the oversized, fake D&Gs on my nose which made Kerry giggle nervously. I then refocussed on the snake's tail.

'Oh fek,' said O'Reilly.

I reached forward with the tongs. When they were an inch from the scaly tail, I made a lunge and, to my great surprise, the tongs closed around the rear end. My satisfaction was extremely brief however. The cobra didn't appreciate having its tail clamped. First it tried to pull away but quickly realised it was trapped. Then it manoeuvred itself from under the coffee bag and turned to face me.

I watched in horror as it rose up and spread its hood in classic cobra style. As with all situations where adrenaline is saturating every cell in the body, time slowed. I watched with calm, grim fascination as the cobra opened its mouth and then flicked its head forward.

'Fek fek fehhk!' yelled O'Reilly.

Jets of liquid hit the lenses of Kerry's glasses, a drop landing on my cheek. I reflexively wiped it away with my hand – in hindsight not very intelligent given that I may well have had some broken skin there. I didn't have a huge amount of time to think about it because the realisation that the snake was a good deal longer than the two-foot tongs holding it hit me. When spitting didn't result in release, the cobra stood up again and lunged at the tongs, biting them about halfway up. In blind panic, I released the handle and pulled my hand away as it made a second lunge that would have punctured my wrist.

Cobras are slower and less abrasive than their mamba cousins. This is lucky because it meant that I managed to move out of the way as the second lunge came down. A high-pitched yelp (very unbecoming of a ranger) escaped my mouth as I leapt backwards, bashed my head on the shelving behind, slipped and then scrambled up onto the sugar bin – just next to Kerry.

'Oh my Gud, dis is fekken aahful, Angus, ya alright? Oh shit, oh my Gud! It's gonna kill us!'

'O'Reilly,' I yelled, 'get out of here now, or I shall tell it to chase you out! Go and find a bucket and do not come back in here until I tell you to!' He looked mortified and reversed out of the door.

Kerry considered me as I felt the bleeding wound on the back of my head. It stung. I took her glasses off, wiping the venom from them.

'And now?' she asked unable to hide the incredulity in her voice.

Her enquiry and manner were both justified. My performance thus far hadn't been the model of snake handling. The tongs were on the floor and the cobra had retreated back under the coffee sacks – once again invisible. As I was considering the situation, Carrie called from outside.

'What's going on in there? Need some help?'

I should have answered in the affirmative but my ego wouldn't allow for that.

'No, all under control,' I replied, 'he's gone under a pile of sacks. I'll have him out in a second.' I looked at Kerry whose already large eyes became even larger as she listened to me lie. 'I will,' I whispered to her. The look on her face was as unconvinced as I felt.

It came time for me to steel myself and be brave. I picked up a broom that was leaning on the wall behind the bins, pushed the glasses back onto my nose and then climbed slowly down. The tongs were on the floor close to where the snake had disappeared. I retrieved them with the aid of the broom.

The next task was to find the hiding cobra. I began gingerly flipping the bags with the broom. Each time I moved one, I jerked back, expecting the snake to rear up and spit. On bag number five, I found my quarry.

As the bag moved, the snake rose off the ground and prepared to attack. But I was ready for it this time. As the hood spread, I grabbed it just below the flattened skin. Venom flew from its mouth, the liquid hitting the glasses again but not in the same volume as before. The cobra was helpless.

'Carrie,' I called, 'bring the bucket . . . I've got him.'

I then pulled the snake out from his hiding place, both hands holding the tongs, my arms extended in front of me. It wasn't a small snake – a good four feet long. The head ranger came in with the bucket and, seeing the snake hanging from the tongs by its neck said, 'Angus, it can't breathe like that. Let go with one hand and grab its tail.'

The thought of doing this appalled me, but despite myself, I let go with my left hand and reached for the tail which was resting on the pile of coffee. As soon as I felt the dry cool skin in my hand, my body relaxed and I carried the now becalmed cobra to where Carrie had a bucket with a lid. I put the snake in tail-first and released the head as the lid slapped shut.

Relief surged over me.

'Well done,' said Carrie mildly and walked out with the bucket. I looked back at Kerry who was still standing on the flour bin.

'You may come down now,' I smiled, feeling impressed with myself.

'We'll keep that little squeal to ourselves, Mister Big Bad Ranger,' she said climbing off the bin. 'My glasses, please.' I handed them to her and she walked out. I sat there on the coffee sacks for another ten minutes allowing my heartbeat to return to normal.

After that, I was ready for a short holiday. String Bean had called in a favour from a friend so Jenny and I spent a very pleasant two nights in Dullstroom at Jefferson's Country Hotel on our way home to Johannesburg. Its superb reputation was vindicated. Jenny went on and on about how incredible the linen, decorations, furniture and amenities were. Apparently the Thai green curry she had for dinner was 'beyond heaven.' When she returned from her massage at the spa, she looked like she'd reached Elysium and passed out beneath the Egyptian cotton sheets.

While she was asleep, I went for a wander on the vast estate. The highveld up there has a different ecology from the lowveld so there were plenty of new trees and unusual birds to discover. When I arrived back in the room, I resembled a bog monster. Jenny, who was lounging on the veranda in a white robe, sipping some peppermint tea, spat out a mouthful on beholding my muddied visage.

My soiled appearance was the fault of a red-chested flufftail. These birds, although relatively common, live in marshy areas and are notoriously difficult to see. I came across a vlei where one of them was calling and quickly became completely focussed on finding it. I removed my shoes and stepped forward … and immediately sank up to my knees in sticky, black mud. The bird prattled away about three metres in front of me, completely invisible in the reeds and thick grass. I waded forwards slowly and on my fourth step I must have hit an air-pocket because a jet of mud squirted up and hit me in the right eye. This made me swear loudly.

The flufftail took exception to my language and I heard him scuttling off through the vegetation – the bird was no more than a foot away when the bog had shot me. I calmed myself and waded on towards the middle of the vlei. The mud became shallower, so the walking became easier, but the irksome bird was still hidden just a few feet in front of me, calling gently in the undergrowth. Just when I thought it was about to flush, I stood on a long, sharp, vicious thorn.

'Fuuuuck!' I yelled, ripping my right foot out of the mud. This made me over-balance and I flew up and then down, face-first into the mud – almost landing right on top of the bloody annoying bird. It exploded from its hiding place squawking loudly. I just managed to catch the flash of its rufus head and chest as it disappeared back into the impenetrable vegetation.

I rolled over and pulled the thorn from my foot, by now covered in black Dullstroom mud. Unfortunately, the only way back to the room was through the reception area. A large excited group was checking in as I traversed the lobby. Silence descended as they saw me, shoes in hand, dripping mud.

'Good afternoon all,' I said. 'May I recommend the mud treatment at the spa.'

After dinner that evening, Jenny and I went for a walk across the moonlit hills. We found a flat rock high on the grassland and sat for half an hour chatting. We don't have an enormous amount in common – she's not particularly interested in the secrets the universe might reveal as to our existence – but, very unusually, she makes me laugh. She's also not much affected by my somewhat surly outlook on life and teases me mercilessly, which is probably quite good for me.

I felt a strong sense of affection for her sitting there under the stars. I was about to lean over and kiss her when there was a horrific screeching sound from a small stand of trees behind us. Jenny jumped up.

'What the hell was that?' she gasped.

'Barn owl,' I replied, the moment broken.

Back in Johannesburg, I met a number of Jenny's peers. Most of them seemed pleasant enough although there are a number of corporate article clerks who subtly looked down their noses at my current profession – especially when they found out I don't have a golf handicap. Dad suggested I might like to look at the impression I gave them before writing them off completely.

I met Mother's cat for the first time and I have re-christened her AIDS Cat. This startlingly aggressive animal smells like bad fish (apparently on account of her expensive scientifically balanced food). She is the only organism in the world Trubshaw is afraid of and he affords her a wide berth.

AIDS Cat is not the only new resident at the MacNaughtons' Johannesburg domicile. Julia is finally earning enough to live on her own and has left home. This is a good move for her but not necessarily for our parents because it's been decided that the Major is too infirm to look after himself. He has moved into Julia's old room – thankfully semi-detached from the main house.

The positive value of the move for Julia is tempered by the actual place she now calls home. Her one-bedroom apartment is in a complex of at least 300 faux Tuscan units. The horrendous obsession with recreating rural Tuscany in Johannesburg – a vile architectural malady that began with the construction of Montecasino – is more mysterious than the Shroud of Turin. Initially it was just the Fourways region that was afflicted with appalling rip-offs of bucolic Italy but the plague has spread to all parts, with very few suburbs escaping the scourge.

I went round to see the place and conveyed my view of the architecture to her.

'Angus,' she said, 'must you always say something negative?'

'Well, I mean, I like what you've done with the interior. You've got great taste,' I replied. 'Oh and the wine is delicious.'

She shook her head and moved out onto the little balcony which affords a view of the other 299 identical pale baby-shit-brown units (I didn't use this description with her). I joined her outside. The noise of the traffic mingled with the sound of squabbling Indian mynahs in the palm tree growing in the tropically themed pool area.

'The place is brand new and very close to work,' she said.

'Fair enough,' I replied. 'And I really do think you've put some great pictures on the walls and the furniture is beautifully matched.'

'Good.' She sat down on one of the wrought-iron chairs adorning her balcony – clearly not placed there by the designers of unit 287 Bella Tuscana. 'Tell me about Jenny,' she said. I sat on the other chair.

'There's not a huge amount to tell really. We have quite a lot of fun together but it's all very relaxed. She makes me laugh which is excellent.'

'You don't do relaxed, Angus.'

'Perhaps I've changed.'

'In some ways maybe, but not like that,' she said looking at me. 'Be careful about this, you're probably still a bit raw after Anna.'

I changed the subject, 'And you? Seeing anyone?'

'I've been on a few dates with a young partner from another of Satan's workhouses as you would put it. It genuinely isn't anything serious but he's a nice guy.'

We then had a good laugh about the email SB had sent us earlier in the day.

To: Angus, Jules
From: Hugh MacNaughton
Subject: F%&*ing baboons

Hey Guys,

Julia, I hope it's pleasant having Angus in Joeys for a few days.

Angus, apparently you walked through the main reception area at Jefferson's covered from head to toe in mud and bits of grass – in the middle of a group check-in! Thankfully the GM has a sense of humour but Johnny did phone to tell me, so I think he was slightly embarrassed. Why, for God's sake?

I'm well back into the swing of things here. Guests are coming in and out and the team is operating like a well-oiled machine (with Incredible as the obvious exception). He came to me two days ago with a 'plan' to get rid of the baboons – two more break-ins this week. He arrived with a huge grin on his face. Breakfast was in full swing and he was wearing a piece of greasy cloth around his head.

'Mr Hhyoo,' he called – he says my name like 'phew' without the p and a lot of air. 'A idea, I have a clever idea for to get those littlee ones!' I excused myself from the company of Gerald and Cynthia to whom I was chatting over a lightly smoked ham and cheese omelette and dragged Incredible to the back of the camp.

I began by making him remove the oil-stained sweat band and then asked what his plan was. What came out of his mouth pushed the limits, even for Incredible.

'Last night, I am watch Rambo on the TV and get idea!' By this stage, I understood why he was wearing the sweat band and I also knew that whatever came next was going to involve explosives. When he got to the part about disguising hand grenades as oranges, I stopped him and told him to keep trying.

That afternoon, they ransacked Rooms 2 and 5. We've had to buy ten new crystal decanters, lots of new sheets and until we have managed to sort the problem out we are not even putting nuts and rusks in the rooms. The stinking creatures are now starting to affect my Guests.

Then, yesterday morning, Baboon Destroyer-in-Chief, Incredible Mathebula, arrived at work in a camouflage uniform. I think it belonged to a family member who fought in the Mozambique civil war (someone who wasn't very good at dodging bullets because the uniform is full of holes). After I'd conducted a thorough search for explosives, he headed off into the bush around the camp. Believe it or not, his camouflage stealth approach worked for a while – we had a totally baboon free day. Today at lunch, however, in typical Incredible style, he took it too far.

The rest of the butlers and I were serving lunch under the trees around the pool. It was a hot day but there were some thick clouds and the huge mahogany tree next to the pool makes this area one of the coolest places to be. It was a very peaceful scene as Redman and Nora served the gazpacho with cream and chives and I topped up glasses with bitterly cold sauvignon blanc. I could vaguely hear the sound of rustling in the thick bush below the pool but didn't worry about it as I described the estate from which the wine had come, to Clarisse and Benny from Auckland.

Suddenly, there was a loud, rubbery snapping sound, followed quickly by a dull thud and then...absolute pandemonium. Baboons started screaming in the vegetation below the pool. They exploded off in all directions. An enormous male burst out of the bush onto the pool paving at full speed. By the time he noticed the water, it was too late. With his powerful arms flailing in an attempt to slow down, he tripped over a chaise longue and flew, head-first, into the depths with a huge splash. Clarisse screamed and, in her attempt to flee, kicked over her table, sending soup all over the place. The rest of the guests either ran or froze.

The vile primate soiled the water, swam quickly to the edge of the pool, hauled himself out, grabbed a basket of rolls from one of the tables and ran off.

Just as things calmed down, who should emerge from the bushes but Incredible, dressed in his uniform and armed with a lethal-looking homemade cattie. He grinned stupidly, walked over to me and whispered in my ear – thinking that this would minimise the disturbance of our peaceful lunch.

'I shoot him,' he whispered, 'that littlee one!' With that, he disappeared into the undergrowth while the rest of us attended to the mess and the terrified guests. Incredible's absence from butler duty has made a negligible difference to the service efficiency at Tamboti.

On the people front, Amber, despite her obvious stunning hotness, has zero self-esteem and is convinced that Jonesy is going to be seduced by Kerry. When she saw Kerry laughing while Jonesy told a story at the lunch table, she nearly went into shock and came over to Tamboti in a state (she sees me as some sort of mentor since I trained her). Redman asked her if she'd been bitten by a snake because she was hyperventilating so much. I sat her down in the kitchen and put a cold towel on her head.

She calmed down eventually and I tried to assure her that Jonesy had, on more than one occasion, commented on how satisfied she made him. (I neglected to mention that this was during particularly explicit descriptions of his endless sexual conquests.)

Off to prepare a bush drink's stop for a honeymoon couple!

Lots of love,
Your 'mentor-to-the-young-and-sexy' brother,
Hugh

Week 4

Metrosexual lawyer and misappropriating hound

It was Mum's birthday on the final day of my measly leave so Dad decided that we should all go out to dinner at the Local Grill that evening. By all, I mean the Major, Mum, Dad, Julia and me. (Jenny was invited but she had a girls' dinner). Julia, bravely or stupidly, decided that she would use the event to introduce her new love interest, Phil, to the family. They arrived half an hour late, by which time the Major and I had already consumed two double Jamesons each. My grandfather was at his belligerent best and apparently I wasn't far behind.

Phil, the legal partner, is tall and has brown hair coiffed to a perfect, angular parting. He was dressed in an exquisitely tailored suit and smelled of expensive aftershave – which he obviously keeps handy (probably in a man bag). I'm sure he works out in expensive, branded gym kit. In short, he is the quintessential Johannesburg metrosexual. The Major took an instant dislike to him. It took me about three minutes.

'Good heavens boy,' the Major bellowed on being introduced, 'men don't wear pink shirts!' Two or three tables stopped their conversations and looked round. Phil was knocked slightly off his stride but recovered quickly – as only a smarmy lawyer can.

'Ha ha,' he chuckled, 'Julsie told me her grandfather had a wonderful sense of humour!'

Conversation at dinner was not up to its usual robust standard. This is because Phil knows more about every subject than the Creator himself. He is an expert on wine, food, politics, quantum physics – you name it. It seems to me that young professionals of this ilk think that they have reached the end of history – they pass their bar or board exams and then they know everything there is to know about how the world works. Phil is even an authority on the natural world.

'I do enjoy going to the bush for a few days,' he began. 'I can't be away from the office for more than two days at a time but I find that sufficient to recharge me.'

As we left the restaurant the Major said, 'What a pompous arse that boy is! Needs a bloody good belting!' Of course, Julia and Phil were about two metres behind the rest of us. Mum went bright red and started walking quickly. Dad gritted his teeth and I smiled.

I don't know what Julia sees in him – probably blinded by his good looks and ambition.

Jenny came round for tea on Sunday. It started off rather well. Great Aunt Jill (GAJ) thought she was marvellous and suggested I marry her on the spot (in front of her). Julia and Mum also seemed to like her and the Major has a crush. Trubshaw leapt onto the sofa and made to steal her cheese scone. Regrettably, AIDS Cat was sitting on her lap at the time and jumped up to attack the hound. This sent Jenny's scalding tea all over the place and soured her mood a little. She is not fond of Trubshaw.

Week 5

Summer's caress and caterpillars

The return to Sasekile was pleasant, although it was without Jenny (who still has ten days of leave). I drove via Pilgrim's Rest – not the quickest route but I wanted to see the place so central to Percy Fitzpatrick's *Jock of the Bushveld* which I re-read on leave. It filled me with happy anticipation for the lowveld. There's been a lot of rain so the view stretching east from the escarpment was lush and endlessly green. It reminded me of my first impressions of the low country when SB and I (squabbling over driving duties) came over the mountains early last year.

As we drove into the town, I was laughing as I envisioned Trubshaw attempting (and failing miserably) to match the feats of South Africa's most famous staffie.

My good cheer was tempered a bit by the sense of decay that now seeps through Pilgrim's Rest. It's a huge pity because you can see the town was probably once really attractive. After a lunch at the hotel – a meal that rivalled sandstone in blandness and texture – I made my way back to the lodge.

Jeff was sitting on my doorstep when I arrived. He insisted on taking my bags and I had to forcibly stop him from trying to unpack for me. My new charge then gave me a detailed if garbled account of what he'd achieved in my absence and then handed me the worksheets I'd given him. Initial impressions are that Jeff has made a huge effort in my absence but that his ability to order his thoughts is about as appalling as his grasp of written English. A good example was the following answer to the question, 'Describe the similarities and differences between the social behaviour of wild dogs and dwarf mongoose'. Jeff replied, 'Mongeese is sumtimes like wild dogs because they can live in a groops but sumtimes if everiwun els is getting sick and dies then a dogs can live on his own but a mongoose is getting lonely and can be dead soon.'

That evening SB and I went for a jog. He hasn't done much exercise since school so he ran out of puff pretty quickly. We found a rock on the river bank and sat (lay panting in SB's case) on it in the shade of an apple-leaf tree behind us. I told him about my time in Johannesburg and he brought me up to speed on things at the lodge. He spent a good deal of time complaining that Simone was behaving out of sorts.

'She says she's tired of looking after kids,' he explained.

'What does she want to do?'

'I don't know.' He sat up and leant forward to stretch his hamstring. 'She says she likes being in the bush but that the children of the world's rich and famous are frustrating her.'

'I'd have killed a few by now.'

'Yes, well, that's not really allowed. Frankly, I'm getting tired of her bad moods and she's being so needy at the moment.'

'Well, while I'm not one to talk about patience, I think she's a special girl so try to be sympathetic.'

'No, you are definitely not the one to be giving advice on patience.' He stood up and we jogged slowly back to the lodge.

Unlike SB and Simone, Jenny and I seem to be getting on rather well and I often spend the night in her room. I wake early (careful not to disturb her as she's not a great morning person) and head to my room in the half-light to shower and shave before the game drive.

A few nights ago, after a frustrating evening of going over mammal facts with Jeff in the rangers' room, I headed to Jenny's home hoping she'd be finished with dinner at Main Camp. She was lying on her bed in a dark-green summer nighty, reading a magazine. There were candles lit on her bedside tables and a claret scarf was thrown over her lamp. The windows were open and the call of a white-faced owl floated in on the summer breeze.

I stood in the doorway for a while observing – the high arches on her elegant feet, her smooth legs, covered to halfway down the thighs in silky green. Her blonde curls were tied up neatly, showing her unusually long neck. She carried on reading, pretending not to notice me appraising her. After a minute or so, she dropped the magazine to the floor carelessly. She turned her wide hazel eyes to me and grinned.

'Are you gonna stand there all night or come over here and kiss me?'

A while later we lay peacefully, her head on my chest, her pretty face illuminated by the half-moon outside. A rain locust was stridulating on the red ivory tree at her window. She lifted her head, smiled, leant forward and kissed me. Then she sighed and returned her cheek to the nook below my sternum.

It would have been perfect but as I drifted off to sleep, my hand in Jenny's hair, I dreamt of Anna – a horrible image of her final moments. I jolted awake, my heart pounding.

'What's wrong?' asked Jenny.

'Nothing, just a twitch. Sorry.'

Dreamless slumber arrived slowly as my heart rate returned to normal.

I spent most of the rest of the week trying to drum information and a sense of acceptable human behaviour into Jeff. All in all, I think his knowledge is improved but he lacks any kind of social grace (not that I'm known for my social skills). It both amuses and scares me to think of him in charge of a real game drive. On the positive side, my trials with Jeff have meant spending mornings and afternoons discovering new bits of the reserve without the irritation of demanding guests. I'm not receiving much in the way of tips but given the generally appalling gratuities I earn, my bottom line is not too adversely affected.

Notwithstanding his infinite shortcomings, it dawned on me that Jeff is an excellent and natural storyteller. We are thus concentrating on his genial personality and storytelling abilities – not his aptitude as a naturalist or functional member of society. We've created a repository of anecdotes for him to tell while on game drive and the major task at the moment is to make sure that he tells the right story at the right time. I offer the following as an example of the magnitude this task presents. A few afternoons back, we were walking along a drainage line, identifying various trees. It was a beautiful late afternoon with long shadows criss-crossing the sand and a myriad birds calling in the leaves above the cooling afternoon. Suddenly, a squirrel started alarm-calling in a jackalberry tree across from where we were standing.

'Chip, chip, chip, chip,' it shouted, its tail flicking in time with its voice. We both froze. Well, more accurately, I froze and grabbed Jeff by his collar before he could blunder into something lethal. I searched the undergrowth for a predator – a leopard perhaps. Then, I spotted a Verreaux's eagle-owl on the leafy bough of a weeping boer-bean tree not far away – the source of the squirrel's consternation. The situation presented the perfect opportunity for Jeff to practise telling a story.

'Jeff,' I whispered, 'pretend we're on a walk with guests and tell me what you'd tell them.'

He looked confused.

'About the owl and the squirrel,' I hissed. He raised his binoculars first to the bird and then to the rodent. There he fixed his gaze.

He should have launched into an animated discussion about Africa's biggest owl and its feeding habits while linking these to the squirrel and its other potential predators.

However, Jeff chose to say, 'Oh my sack, look at the size of the giant balls on that tiny guy!' I stared at him, understanding that he wouldn't think twice about using this as his opening gambit with paying guests. Apart from the slightly inappropriate way of pointing out the enormous testicles, he shouted it so loudly that the owl flushed and the squirrel disappeared into a hole. The void in Jeff's head made a sucking sound.

I had one set of guests this week – an English family called the Ponsonby-Smythes. Jeff accompanied me on all game drives – with firm instruction not to speak without my express permission. Unfortunately during one morning drive, Elvis did something that I really wish my pupil, given his almost complete inability to filter the inappropriate from the appropriate, hadn't witnessed.

February is the time of the mopane worm – a large and colourful caterpillar which eventually pupates into an emperor moth. The worm is still a very important source of protein for rural people from northern South Africa all the way into southern Zambia. On the first morning drive we followed a herd of elephants into a stand of mopane near the north of the reserve. The pachyderms quickly disappeared and we found ourselves surrounded by tall trees. It was late in the morning, the shade welcome in the heat. Elvis turned to the guests and put his finger to his lips – they went silent. As we sat there, I noticed a soft crunching sound coming from all around us. It was emanating from millions of chewing mouthparts devouring the surrounding leaves. Elvis grinned and looked into the branches above his head. He reached into the tree and retrieved a huge caterpillar. He held the trophy up to show our guests.

'Elvis, that's disgusting!' said Sally, aged fifteen.

'Quite disgusting!' agreed her mother.

What my illustrious partner did next wasn't from the manual of 'Guest Delight'. In full view of the Ponsonby-Smythes, he held the head of the larva with his right hand and with his left he squeezed its guts out with a squelch. Then, as the gasps of revulsion reached a crescendo, he popped it into his mouth, chewed a few times and swallowed with a satisfied sigh.

'My God, man!' bellowed Gerome Ponsonby-Smythe covering his mouth with a silk paisley handkerchief.

Elvis doesn't say much but he is scrupulously polite in his own way. He quickly reached into the tree and drew another five caterpillars.

'Can you wanting eat?' he offered. This drew howls of protest from the family. Sally and her brother Jonathan retched and their mother covered her eyes. Elizabeth, Gerome's mother, aged 84, looked coldly at Elvis shaking her head.

'I see the civilisation of empire didn't quite reach these parts,' she snorted.

In a place where money is short and diets poor, the mopane worm is a crucial source of protein. Travel guides call it an 'African delicacy' which implies some kind of rare and delicious flavour. It's a welcome source of food in hard times but its flavour if not fried with onions, salt and tomato is questionable.

PJ, quite against local reserve rules, allows the staff at Sasekile a day to harvest the worms from the patches of mopane that dot the property. They go out in groups of ten or so and each person is allowed a small shopping bag full of larvae. These are then brought back to the staff village where they are gutted, boiled in brine and left to dry in the sun. This preserves them almost indefinitely. I was offered a dry one on my return to the village after the Ponsonby-Smythes refused Elvis's gesture. Gladys Khoza, she of the appearance and age of weathered shale, handed me one with such aggression that I couldn't refuse. I examined the shrivelled corpse.

'*Dyana!* [eat]' shouted Gladys.

I popped it into my mouth, intending to swallow very quickly but it was too prickly and my mouth went dry. There was nothing for it but to chew. I bit gingerly through the spiky exoskeleton, expecting there to be a surge of moist innards. Instead, there was sensation akin to chewing slightly gamey sawdust. There was virtually no flavour, save for the liberal amounts of salt Gladys had added.

I thanked Gladys and went on my way, trying to think of a way to expunge Elvis's example from Jeff's memory.

While in my room, the taste of dusty worm repeating on me, I heard the sound of stones smashing into tin cans. From one of my room windows I have a view over the soccer field. The pinging was coming from Incredible who was engaging in some target practice. He had lined up some beer cans and was shooting them from all angles with his cattie. String Bean informs me that, with some fine-tuning, Incredible's stealth and missile techniques are paying off – there've been no baboon break-ins and no guest assaults for a week. On the back of the Tamboti success, interviews are being conducted for a permanent baboon guard. This man's sole function in life will be to track the troop from dawn till dusk, making sure that the grey gangs don't ever come near the camps.

I received my second email from Arthur this morning.

To: Angus MacNaughton
From: Arthur C. Grimble
Subject: Hello!

Crocus Cottage
West Road
Wragby
Lincolnshire

My dear Angus,

Thank you so much for your last letter and my apologies for not writing sooner. It has been difficult learning to use this machine but I think I am finally getting the hang of it. This whole email and interworld business has been a revelation! I am really enjoying the regular contact I now have with friends all over the world.

Did you know that I can read the news on the interworld without having to buy a paper? Astounding! I have no idea how it all works but I am thoroughly enjoying it, especially as the winter here drags on seemingly indefinitely.

Your news was most interesting to read. I particularly enjoyed your descriptions of the African veldt so please keep those titbits from warmer climes coming.

I am also most pleased to hear that you have a new girlfriend. I'm sure it wasn't easy for you to open yourself up again, so good for you and well done. Anna would be proud of you. Life, as you have probably come to realise, is rather too fleeting to live in brooding regret.

On that subject, Mavis and I are going to the pub this evening. Mavis is much younger than me (aged 75 years) and lost her husband a year ago. She agreed to accompany me on the condition that I do not 'try anything'. My goodness, what she thinks my Zimmer frame and I are going to attempt I cannot imagine but I am flattered she even thinks me capable of it.

Keep well and do write soon.

My very best wishes,
Arthur

I'm not sure what Jenny would think of being described as my girlfriend. We haven't had a formal discussion about what our status is – I find such conversations most embarrassing.

Week 6

Sludge and St Petersburg

The volcanic ambient temperature at present necessitates that I spend much of my down time in the small staff pool. This cool but less-than-crystalline water body is situated at the southern end of the staff village, underneath a giant old boer-bean tree. After lunch every day this week, Jenny and I have made our way to this secluded spot and spent half an hour lounging in the cool, shaded water, making idle banter and laughing about the antics of our guests and colleagues. Our little dalliance has increased my enjoyment of the Sasekile summer a great deal.

The heavy summer rain has rendered the bush a hundred shades of luxuriant green. The cuckoos, particularly the Diederiks, are in full cry. The light is harsh in the middle of the cloudless days but sunset softens all the colours and if there's a storm brewing in the west, the dusk sprays the sky with endless shades of red, auburn, ginger and gold.

The rain hasn't only affected the vegetation.

The seeplines offroad are inundated and driving into them is to be avoided at all costs – this is not as easy as it might seem. Carrie finally gave me a succinct geological answer as to why these bogs occur. I asked her predecessor once but because his interest in the bush was limited to large mammals and how best to kill them, he wasn't able to answer me.

I remember him saying, 'Shark Crap,' as he was wont to address me, 'seeplines is things that you mustn't get your vehicle stuck in. How they is made you must look up, I'm not here to feed you with a spoon.' I quickly realised that 'I'm not here to feed you with a spoon' was Anton's way of saying, 'I haven't the foggiest idea.'

Carrie, on the other hand, explained that seeplines are areas where there is a sub-soil barrier. Water bubbles to the surface and quagmires result. During the rainy season, these sodden areas are capable of miring even the newest Land Rover. Because I am still the newest ranger, I drive the oldest, most buggered Land Rover.

Outwardly, the machine used by me and Elvis gives the impression of youth. The Land Rover Defender (aka brick-on-wheels) has enjoyed precious few design modifications during the 60 odd years that it's been breaking down around the world. For blinkered Land Rover loyalists, this is evidence of the success of the design rather than indolence and a complete absence of creativity in the design department of this once-British and now-Indian manufacturer. The dearth of design modifications means that with the application of a little paint, it's easy to create the impression of a spanking-new vehicle.

Bertha (the name I have given her) has just been re-sprayed. Beneath her gilded sheen, however, lies a hunk of rusting and pirated parts tied together with wire, string and God-knows-what-else. She is loud, noxious and disturbing and I do not believe that she retains even one original part. Bertha is tended by the two-man workshop team. This crack squad of mechanics consists of Oscar who is old, bored and tired, and Donald, a young and enthusiastic fellow. A complete lack of formal training in the workings of the internal-combustion engine is the one thing these men have in common. Their skills seem to be loosely based on the Law of the Instrument. (If the only tool you know how to use is a hammer, you tend to treat every problem as a nail.)

Three afternoons ago, Elvis, Bertha and I were following a young male leopard offroad. He was very relaxed and the guests were all snapping away with their cameras as the late afternoon sunlight reflected gold off his pelage. I was transfixed by the scene and Elvis, sitting next to me, was leafing through my bird book. No one was looking where we were driving.

A seepline sort of sneaks up on one.

Bertha's front wheels sank slightly and suddenly we weren't moving forward anymore. I looked out of the door and saw the tell-tale grass species that grow in seeplines.

'*Yima*! [stop]', said Elvis looking up from the page on lovebirds. He looked over the passenger door and clicked his teeth. 'Back,' he said. I engaged reverse and pressed the accelerator gently. Bertha wheezed and her wheels turned. This served to dig us in up to the axles in record time. I turned round to face six expectant expressions.

'Vye ve haf storp to forllow leppaard?' asked Igor from St Petersburg, his giant camera lens pointing at the thicket into which his subject had just disappeared.

'We're stuck,' I replied.

'Oh my Gaaad!' said Loraine, one of Florida's most-botoxed retirees.

'Why are we stuck?' asked Charmaine, a beautiful but dim resident of Brakpan, here as the sex companion of Josh the gym-owner, displaying a pseudo-Celtic tattoo on a his massive right bicep and a thick silver S chain round his neck.

'Because, I failed to notice the quagmire underneath us,' I said, removing my shoes, climbing out of the car and sinking to my ankles in grey mud. Elvis and I examined the extent of the problem. He told me in Shangane that the only option was to have the guests climb out of the car and then, preferably, help us push.

Guests who are paying in excess of R10 000 a night for their holidays react variously to being asked to wade about in evil-smelling bogs. To some, this sort of thing is a huge adventure, while others assume it's a deliberate attempt by the ranger to make life unpleasant. Igor fell into the latter category; Loraine and her down-trodden husband, Dwight, were too clueless to have an opinion. Josh thought it an excellent opportunity to show off his muscles.

'Not a problem, boet,' he said rolling up his Adidas track pants, 'we'll just push this puppy out.' He was in the mud before I could finish asking. Charmaine took her high heels off and gingerly eased herself off the middle seat.

'Thees ees reedeecooluss!' shouted Igor.

'Well, Igor,' I replied, '*reedeecooluss* or not, if you don't climb out we're not going to escape before the ravenous creatures of darkness descend. So if you'd be so kind, please alight. You don't have to push . . . if you feel it's beneath you.'

He and his wife/girlfriend/prostitute (WGP) then climbed out. She spoke not a word of English. In fact, I don't think she spoke at all.

Loraine and her doormat, despite being older than Methuselah, took to the task with relative gusto. They just needed instruction. Elvis assigned everyone a position, with him and Josh in front. Igor and WGP stood off to one side. The problem for the ranger at this point is that he has to drive and therefore cannot help with the pushing – while his guests are knee-deep in sludge, he watches from the driver's seat.

When everyone was in position, I shouted, 'One, two, three, puuuuuush!' Bertha belched, Loraine and Charmaine squealed and Josh shouted, 'Come on team Sasekile!' With this encouragement, Bertha slowly moved. Everyone heaved and then, just as we were almost out, the wheels began to spin again. Elvis yelled at me to turn the wheel right and put my foot down to maintain momentum. Thus, despite her slipping wheels, Bertha continued her crawl backwards. I was concentrating so hard on the pushers and what was behind me that I failed to notice Igor and WGP come into the firing line of the rapidly spinning and angled front wheels.

As soon as the ground firmed, I turned the engine off and looked up. Team Sasekile was staring at the Russians. They were plastered in thick grey mud. The silence was broken by a 'plop' as a dollop of seepline mud fell from Igor's nose. A high-pitched giggle then burst from Charmaine. Elvis disappeared behind the back of the Land Rover and the rest of us became mildly hysterical. Igor and WGP failed to appreciate the humour.

Dinner was awkward that night, especially after Igor demanded he be given another ranger.

Don't they have mud in St Petersburg?

Week 7

Jeff and justice

As I write this, the senior rangers and PJ are locked in the General Manager's office debating Jeff's assessment drive and his inevitable ejection from the world of ecotourism (and my consequent bankruptcy as a result of The Legend's bar bill). They've been there for over an hour.

My ex-neighbour and I have spent every waking minute of the last week together. I can safely say that we've done everything possible to make him into something resembling a ranger. I didn't tell him that if he failed, I'd be feeding The Legend's expensive cognac tastes for the rest of the year.

Jeff came to me late this morning. I was outside my room constructing a bookcase from some bits of scrap I'd found in the workshop. He sat down on my neighbour's rickety cane chair and sighed.

'I'm a bit nervous about tonight Angus!' he said.

'I'm sure you'll be okay,' I lied. 'Is there anything specific you're worried about?'

'Well not pacifically but maybe I should make a special cocktail for people to drink at drink's stop.'

I told him I thought that was a great idea and asked what he had in mind. He suggested a series of cocktails, some named after oral sex.

'Yes, well why don't you ask Hugh to make you something a bit more traditional, say some cosmopolitans and mojitos?' Jeff looked muddled and sad. 'Don't worry, I'll talk to him. All you'll have to do is pour them. What about snacks?'

'Yes, I like snacks,' he replied cheering up a bit.

'No, what snacks are you going to offer your guests tonight?' When he suggested peanuts, raisins and dried apricots, I realised he could perhaps have benefited from some time with Jenny or SB learning about hospitality. I went to speak to O'Reilly a bit later and he agreed that he would do everything he could to help Jeff.

This afternoon, on my way to the deck, I went past the digs I used to share with Jeff, intending to deliver my version of a pep talk. The Bat Cave still lives up to its name — the odour of droppings and urine singed my nasal passages as I walked in and if the bowing ceilings are anything to go by, the population of flying mammals residing in the roof has increased.

What I found in my old home was predictably farcical. As I arrived, Jeff came haring out of the bathroom sopping wet and buck naked. His levels of anxiety were so elevated that he could easily have been mistaken for a man about to attempt a world record base jump.

The idiotic Melissa was sitting on his bed in tears.

'Prethis prethis Jeff,' she wailed, 'pleath, you have to path your drive!'

My arrival served to drive the trainee closer to apoplexy. He put both of his legs into one trouser leg and then fell over.

'Melissa, if you value your life, you'll bugger off now,' I said to the slobbering wench.

'But Jeff needth me!' she was becoming hysterical.

'Jeff needs you as much as he needs a piano to land on his head.' I took the end of her collar and expelled her from the room. There was a bottle of Klipdrift brandy on Jeff's sparse bookshelf.

'Here,' I said taking the lid off as Jeff sat up, 'drink a good long swig of this.' He looked at me wide-eyed. 'NOW!' I yelled. He grabbed the bottle, took a long drink and spluttered.

'Now calm down. Let's concentrate on one thing at a time.' I handed him a towel and he dried himself. Then I made him have another long drink. The alcohol worked its magic on his large, unwieldy frame and he started to relax, sitting on the floor against his bed.

'Let's be honest, Jeff,' I sat down next to him, 'you are not exactly an academic.' I stopped short of adding that I've seen more academic pond algae. He looked at me blankly. 'But of the many things you lack, courage isn't one of them. You know that you have done all things possible to prepare for the drive this afternoon. Now, you have to forget about the outcome, gather your considerable bravery, go out there and, I hate myself for saying this, be yourself.'

I made him have one more swig of brandy and then waited outside while he dressed.

While I was waiting, Matto emerged from my old room, an iPad in his hand and some expensive, bright-green Sennheiser earphones around his neck.

'What are you okes so worked up about?' he asked.

I looked at him. 'Presumably you realise your neighbour is about to take his final assessment drive?'

'Ja, but shit, how hard can it be...? Taking a game drive's hardly rocket science.' As Jeff emerged from his room, Matto turned and walked back into his room with a perfunctory, 'Good luck bru.'

I accompanied my charge onto the deck.

The 'guests' on the drive included Carrie, Jonesy, Mango, Sipho and me from the field side of things. PJ, SB and Amy (PJ's wife), came along to monitor hospitality. I was only allowed on the drive because Duncan was sick. Normally only senior rangers are invited.

Jeff's hosting on the Main Camp deck during the tea was genuine – if slightly clumsy. He managed to slosh tea or coffee on three saucers. Jenny arrived just in time and took over from him before SB and PJ could see what he'd done. He then gave his orientation talk but unfortunately there was a fair amount of chocolate icing covering his two big front incisors. This smeared over his lip as he spoke. His delivery was passable and he even made a little joke which, although less amusing than the chocolate icing, lightened the mood a bit.

Then it was out onto the drive. I sat in the back row of the vehicle and offered the odd question that I knew he'd be able to answer. There were some lions close to camp so we went straight there. The pride was lying in the late afternoon sun and gave Jeff the opportunity to showcase what he knew about them without having to concentrate on following or tracking them. The sighting was entertaining but in some cases for the wrong reasons.

PJ asked, 'How much do lions eat?'

'Yes,' replied Jeff, 'they sleep for up to twenty hours a day.'

All thought this was hilarious – all except me. I shut my eyes, placed my thumb and forefinger over the bridge of my nose and breathed deeply. Jeff smiled along with the rest but clearly had no idea why they were laughing. PJ asked again and received a passable, if slightly far-fetched, answer.

It is when Jeff has to multitask that the potential for disaster increases to the point of inevitability.

The Legend told Jeff that he wanted to see a leopard. With the sun almost setting and after a great lion sighting, it would have been completely reasonable for Jeff to explain that he would try and find a leopard in the morning when the light makes it easier to follow tracks. Jeff, however, became flustered. He looked round to me and I shook my head violently at him. This didn't help.

'Sure, no problem Jonesy!' he replied, grinning inanely. Elvis, who was tracking for him, spun round in his seat on hearing his ranger make this cheerful assertion in the rapidly growing dusk. 'We find leopard, Elvy!' he said to my friend anxiously. No one has ever called Elvis Elvy before – and if they have I suspect they're long dead. Elvis looked at him for a few moments, the disdain on his face filling the short silence.

At that moment, the gods intervened and Jamie's voice came over the radio. He called in a leopard not too far from where we were – somewhere on the banks of the Tsesebe River. A little while later, Jeff was driving us offroad trying to find Jamie and the leopard which was on the move. When viewing a predator, the tracker sits inside the vehicle – this is for the sake of the predator (who feels less threatened) and the tracker (who also feels less threatened). Elvis was therefore sitting next to Jeff as we blundered through the thick riverine bush. We could hear Jamie's engine revving fairly close by but of the leopard, there was no sight.

'Jeff, come in,' said Jamie on the radio. Jeff, whose adrenaline levels must have been dangerously close to giving him a heart attack, dropped the radio mouthpiece, retrieved it, tried to speak into the back of it, turned it around and eventually said, 'Go ahead.'

'She's heading towards the river so you'd better move it up a bit.'

Jeff, in an effort to satisfy his guests, began driving like a madman. The vehicle bumped and thrashed through the bush as we took cover in the back. Sipho and I began to giggle at the ridiculousness of the situation. When The Legend was smacked in the forehead by an overhanging jackalberry branch, Amy, PJ and Carrie started laughing too. Jeff took the laughter as a positive sign and started to drive even faster. After ten minutes or so, we broke through the vegetation and onto the bank – a very steep part of the bank. There was a short grassy stretch heading towards the river and then an almost sheer drop over some rocky cliffs. Jamie was parked on top of the bank to the west and his guests were staring down over the rocks and into the river below. The leopard had disappeared into the reeds.

'Ah, sorry guys, eh, the leopard has gone away,' the crestfallen trainee ranger announced. I watched him carefully. He had turned the engine off and we were perched on the edge of the slope of the cliff. The car was in gear but he hadn't pulled up the handbrake.

'Perhaps we should go and have a drink,' suggested PJ.

The Legend looked round at me. 'I like drinks,' he said.

'Ja, okay good no okay cool,' replied Jeff as he depressed the clutch.

The car lurched forward towards the cliff, inexorably hauled by gravity. SB and Amy screamed as they beheld their impending doom. Elvis reacted like a cat. He grabbed the handbrake, hauled it up and then, with his giant hands, squeezed Jeff hard just above the knee. This made the trainee lift his foot off the clutch. The heavy Land Rover shuddered to a halt about a foot short of the cliff. It was about a ten-metre drop to the riverbed – plenty to wipe out a Land Rover full of people. There was a collective sigh as Sipho, who had had the presence of mind to leap off the back seat, climbed back onto the vehicle.

A white-browed scrub-robin made its evening call next to us. 'Chrrrrrrrr,' it said, admonishing Jeff.

'I think we'll have that drink now,' said PJ wiping his brow.

A little while later we were standing in a clearing, drinking strong cocktails. SB's creations were delicious and O'Reilly had supplied some spectacular snacks – beef chipolatas wrapped in bacon, bite-sized fresh asparagus quiches, almonds roasted in honey and mustard and a small wheel of camembert with preserved dates. Elvis ensured that service ran smoothly.

Everyone was most impressed with the effort the trainee had gone to for the sundowners and the atmosphere of the assessment relaxed as we appreciated our near escape.

It was as we were leaving that Jeff, quite by chance, pulled a masterstroke that will be, if he is not fired in the next 24 hours, the thing that saves him. It was almost dark as we were about to climb back onto the Land Rover for the night drive. There was a medium-sized, scraggly tree growing alone in the clearing.

'What's that tree?' asked Carrie. Something clicked in Jeff – like I've said, he can be a wonderful storyteller.

'That tree,' he said mysteriously, 'that is one of the most interesting trees in all of Africa.' With this line, he had us hooked. He walked to the thorny plant and, ignoring the spikes, broke off a small leafy branch. He beckoned for us to gather round. 'Feel the thorns! One pointing forward and one hooked back.' He made us all touch the needle-sharp things. 'Take a leaf and eat it!' As we chewed on the spinachy leaves, he continued.

'Notice the crooked way the branches grow! This is one of the most spiritual trees in Africa. It is used by many cultures from South Africa all the way to Ethiopia.' We all looked at him as he waved the branch around, passion for his story building.

'In many African cultures, it is very important that when someone dies, they are buried at home. It is even more important that the spirit of that person is brought home to rest. But, I ask you, what happens when someone dies away from home?' He paused for effect and a square-tailed nightjar called at the eastern end of the clearing. 'It is one thing for a relative to go and fetch the body but it is another thing to fetch the spirit.' Jeff's voice rose to a crescendo. 'How does a person bring the spirit of a loved one back home? How is it possible?'

Silence. Everyone held their breath. Jeff held the branch aloft.

'This is how you would bring the spirit home.' He cleverly switched the story to a very personal one by addressing Carrie, whose grandmother died a few months ago, directly. 'First you must find the tree closest to where she died.' He led her over to the tree. 'Then you must break off a branch.' He took Carrie's hand and pushed it up towards the tree. She broke off a thorny branch. 'Then you must stand very quietly and ask the spirit to come and sit in the branch.' Carrie stood silently with her branch. Jeff let the moment hang for almost a minute.

Then he grabbed her by the elbow and led her hastily towards the vehicle, straight through the rest of us who jumped out of the way to let them through. 'Quickly, you must carry the spirit and take her home but she must have her own space to sit.' He tapped Carrie's seat in the Land Rover. 'You must buy her a ticket, a separate ticket for the spirit of your grandmother. Now you must place her carefully in the seat next to you.' Carrie, mesmerised by the story, climbed into the Land Rover and placed the branch gently next to her while Jeff rushed around to the driver's seat and climbed in. He started the engine and drove off around the clearing, with us standing there in the middle, coming to a halt 180 degrees from where he had started.

He ran around to where Carrie was sitting, took her hand and she climbed down, carrying the branch with her. Now, it must be understood that Carrie is about as feminine as Bakkies Botha, but she stepped from that Land Rover under Jeff's guidance like a dainty fairy, totally focussed on her branch. I looked around at the group and they were all as mesmerised as the head ranger.

Jeff then led Carrie to a small pile of stones. 'When you have arrived home, you must place the spirit of your grandmother on her grave and she will be happy, she will bless you and your family all your lives.' Carrie placed the branch gently onto the pile of stones and stood there.

By now it was completely dark. A scops owl called in a tree towards the river as the waning moon rose. After a minute or so, Jeff led Carrie back to the group. I looked at Amy and saw a tear making its way down her cheek. Elvis was smiling broadly.

We made it home without incident after that – perhaps the spirit of Carrie's grandmother was protecting us from Jeff.

I have just left the Avuxeni Eatery where Jeff is sitting looking terrified. Many of the staff who aren't working tonight are waiting with him for moral support. Melissa is beside herself with worry; so much so that September had to go and run her camp tonight. We're all holding thumbs.

I am going to have a scotch with Jenny at Main Camp now. The suspense is killing me.

At 00h00 I was lying on Jenny's bed with her curled up next to me. Despite the slightly obscene amount of whisky I'd drunk, I was still unable to sleep.

There was a knock on the door. Jenny woke immediately.

'Who is it?' she asked sleepily.

'It's Carrie,' said a deep voice, 'is Angus in there?'

I shot out of bed and in one bound ripped open the door.

'Ah, there you are,' she said, her expression inscrutable.

'Well?!'

'You're quite worried about him, aren't you?' she said. 'Cynical Angus concerned for another human being – surely not?' Jenny giggled behind me.

'If you weren't a woman, I'd probably have a swing right now.'

'We all know you'd lose that fight,' she said flexing a big bicep.

'Can we discuss your cage-fighting prowess some other time? For God's sake tell me what happened – I'm going insane.'

'Look, there was a lot of strong debate on both sides – I mean it took us three hours to come to a conclusion so it's by no means unanimous. We've decided that Jeff must go . . .' she paused, '. . . on to taking game drives himself. He's passed. There are certain provisos but the long and short is that he will stay and begin driving guests. We haven't told him yet and I thought you might like . . .' Without waiting for her to finish, I hurtled out of the room and to the Bat Cave.

Jeff was sitting on his bed, his bags all packed around him and Melissa mewling softly next to him in the foetal position.

'Jeff,' I began.

'No, I know, I'll have to leave. You don't need to say it.' There was a loud and soggy sniff from beside him.

'Jeff, unpack your bags and tell that snivelling crone next to you to cheer up. Despite odds greater than those of a three-legged horse winning the Grand National, you have passed your drive.'

In less than a second, I was enveloped in a giant bear hug – from Melissa, and then Jeff joined in.

I may have smiled.

I was just about to go back to bed when I remembered my little wager with The Legend.

I wandered up to the admin office. From Jeff's pigeonhole and mine, I removed our bar bills and put them in an envelope. On the front I wrote, '*If you would be so kind as to look after these. Regards, Angus and Jeff. P.S. These will be best enjoyed with liberal servings of humble pie.*' I placed the envelope in The Legend's pigeonhole and walked out into the night feeling like a million bucks.

The next morning, SB, who wasn't in on the final deliberations, told me that he didn't want Jeff driving out of his Tamboti Camp.

'Frankly, I don't think he has the class to be a Tamboti ranger,' he explained.

'Who the hell made you an arbiter of class?' I felt bloody irritated that this was all he had to say about a situation that took a great deal of effort from Jeff and monumental patience from me.

The rest of the camp was far more positive and Jeff has been embraced, patted on the back and had his hand shaken by everyone at least twice. PJ and Carrie called me into the office just after breakfast. The General Manager bade me sit. He finished at his computer, stood and came around to the front of his desk. He smoothed back his neatly cut, dark hair and leant on the corner of his desk.

'Angus, we both want to say how amazed we are with what you have achieved with Jeff and to thank you for what you've done for him.' I felt a bit embarrassed by this but honoured at the same time. PJ doesn't throw praise around unless he feels it's deserved.

'Thanks,' I said, 'I don't think I did anything out of the ordinary – probably just made a few connections.'

'Rubbish,' said Carrie, 'you did a phenomenal job and you need to pat yourself on the back for it. You'll also be glad to know that Jeff will take Bertha from you.'

'I don't know how much you know about Jeff's background,' said PJ, 'but he hasn't had it easy. I'm sure you know that he comes from a very wealthy family but that hasn't made life rosy for him. He's the youngest of four brothers and the others are all super achievers – bright, sporty and now making their way in the family coal business. From what I understand, Jeff has been treated as something of an embarrassment by the family – he failed two years at school, has no ability at ball sports and then, in matric he was expelled because he was put up to stealing some booze from the school kitchens. He was caught and left to take the fall. Anyway, while he's never had to worry about money, I think he's always been an outcast and that's why I've kept him on here for so long – I mean we should have fired him a year ago.' He paused and shook his head as memories of Jeff's time at Sasekile flashed through his mind. 'Anyway, you have made a huge difference to him because he feels like he belongs for the first time in his life.'

While this speech explained a whole lot, it made me feel like a heel because despite all the time I'd spent with Jeff, I'd never once asked him about his family or anything else personal.

Week 8

Imbecile and impala

SB is on leave and, according to our sister, not behaving with a great deal of decorum.

To: Angus
From: Julia MacNaughton
Subject: What's up with our brother??

Hey Angus,

I hope you are well. Very glad to hear that your protégé passed his drive.

I just have to ask what is going on with Hugh? He's behaving like a boy on matric rave! I invited Simone and him round for dinner last night. It was supposed to be a dinner party (the first in my new spot!). I was thinking of a civilised evening with a few friends, edible food (I'd promised not to try my hand at any form of paella after what happened last time) and some decent wine. Hugh staggered in late and already somewhat sozzled – apparently he'd had a few drinks with the 'boys' beforehand. Poor Simone arrived on time (a good half an hour before her drunk boyfriend). I coul[d] see her cringe, absolutely mortified, when he walked in slo[

His behaviour did not improve from there. He complained incessantly about the wine – which was particularly embarrassing because Pen had made a huge effort to select it. However, the disdain he showed for the wine did not appear to reduce his appetite for it?! Simone had to drive him home after two of my friends helped him into the car.

I phoned him this morning to give him a piece of my mind. He offered a non-committal and pathetic apology and informed me that I could not possibly comprehend the pressure that he's under at work.

Well, is he under a tremendous amount of pressure or he is just being a tosser?

Love,
Jules

I replied with the following.

To: Julia MacNaughton
From: Angus
Subject: String Bean – probably needs a slap

Dear Julia,

String Bean is a camp manager here. This means that his main functions are speaking to guests, checking them in, eating and drinking with them and making sure that they don't run off into the bush and get killed. His job is about as intellectually ch⌐   as breathing. While he is very good at his occupation, ⌐   out from where the pressure of such daunting tasks

s ego is simply gaining an advantage over
will acknowledge, this won't be the first time
ened.

He's probably in need of a slap and I suspect Simone will give it to him in the not-too-distant future.

Bye bye now,
Angus

The highlight of my week was Jeff's destruction of one of the reserve's impala and consequent elevation to the rank of ranger. Brimming with new-found confidence tempered with moral conflict, Jeff went out into the wild with three rounds of ammunition and a rifle. His instructions, like mine of a year ago, were to go and shoot an adult male impala at least two kilometres from camp and then carry it home.

He came to my room on the eve of his hunt. Jeff is an oaf but he's no killer.

'I don't think I can shoot something that is still alive,' he said. I stopped myself from telling him that my days as his mentor were, praise the gods, over.

'Jeff, you have to know if you can kill an animal should the need arise one day for you to defend your guests. Make sure you treat the impala with respect and appreciation.' He looked mortified. 'I can't tell you anything else,' I continued, 'it's a very personal experience. I hated it but it was one of the most important things I've ever done.'

His visit gave me cause to reflect on my own hunt: missing with my first round; the frustration of trying to stalk the wily things; the terror of missing as I aimed my second shot; the mixed emotions when I finally killed my ram; the relief, then the tears; the mental struggle to cut him open; and finally the elation and exhaustion when I dropped the carcass at Anton's feet.

While Jeff was out overcoming his ethical dilemma, I was driving an 'interesting' couple. She was an American-educated Iranian human-rights lawyer working in Botswana on a project for the Kalahari Bushmen. She was 'hot' as opposed to beautiful. He was a filthy-rich London investment banker of indeterminate ancestry. His accent came from the sewers of London's East End. They were in their mid-30s and hadn't seen each other for three months – three painfully celibate months. I picked them up from the airstrip yesterday around lunch time. On the way back to the lodge they insisted on sitting in the back seat, despite the emptiness of the front two rows. It didn't take long for muffled moans to emanate from their perch during the ten-minute drive to Tamboti Camp.

I turned around, to check that the noise hadn't been caused by a spider or perhaps some falling vulture guano. I needn't have worried because the long-separated couple was fastened at the face. It was with great pleasure that I handed them over to Amber at Tamboti Camp a few minutes later.

When I arrived at tea that afternoon, Incredible was at the entrance to the deck looking agitated.

'Mister Angus!' he pulled me aside into the shade of a sausage tree, 'those guest of you in Room Siggis [6], is,' he looked around, 'very much of STRANGE!' he hissed.

'Strange, you say? How so?' I asked, knowing that what I was about to hear was going to be from the top drawer. He pulled me closer into the shadows. 'I am refill the ruskies in Room 5 when I am hear a screaming like when a buffalo is making killing of someone. That screaming is come from Room Siggis. I am run to see what is matter. The door is open and I am see ...'

I shall not delve into the details of what followed but it involved a broken description of an enthusiastic Briton and a Persian bent into what Incredible thought an inappropriate shape.

The couple did not arrive for game drive until 17h00 and when they did, they looked like they'd been mauled by the Granite Pride. Ten minutes out of camp, they were staring at each other with a great longing and not listening to a word I said. Elvis suggested we park them under a tree and go tracking. I concurred and stopped under a secluded jackalberry in a leafy drainage line. As I took the rifle off the vehicle I said, 'Excuse me.' This had no effect. 'OI!' I yelled. They looked round. 'Elvis and I are going to track a leopard. We'll be back in half an hour ... I tell you this in the hopes that you'll be decent when we return.'

About 20 minutes later, from the direction of our Land Rover, the report of a .458-calibre Winchester Magnum shattered the afternoon.

Jeff had fired his first round.

This, even by Jeff's standards, was asinine in the extreme.

It was dusk and therefore he'd never have been able to carry the ram home (assuming success) before sundown. Dragging a bloodied carcass around at night is a poor idea in a wilderness infested with lions and hyenas. Also, finding out if there are game drives in the area is considered polite before loosing off high-calibre hunting rifles. Elvis and I hurried back to the vehicle to find the lovers looking terrified.

'Something the matter?' I asked.

'P...p...p...oacher!' Miss Persia stammered pointing across the drainage line.

'Ee wen' tha' way – wiff a fuckin 'uge gun!' added East End. 'Ee was chasin a buck or somefin. Ih was limpin!'

As I tried to decipher this, another shot rang out, no more than 30 metres from us. The couple dived under the seat. (Taking cover as bullets whistle through the leaves is an activity lower on the 'Guest Delight' list than gutting and eating fresh mopane worms). The shot was followed by a loud whooping noise.

'Ge us the ou' of ere!' screamed East End from under his seat.

I realised that trying to explain the situation would be pointless – firstly because they were too panicked and secondly because if Jeff fired his last round, I genuinely thought we could be hit. I drove quickly out of the drainage line towards a clearing. Elvis was all but paralytic with laughter.

When we stopped, I calmed the guests down with heavily-poured scotches. I then explained the delicate situation of the impala hunt. They seemed to appreciate the principle of this rite of passage but it was much harder to convince them that Jeff hadn't nearly ended their love/lust holiday. They complained to Amber back at Tamboti. She was horrified but she is terrified of me, so she told no one.

Jeff returned to camp at 21h00 – his impala slung over his broad shoulders. (Nhlanhla followed him home in a Land Rover in case a thieving lion, leopard or hyena came ascavenging). Sasekile's newest ranger had half-gutted the animal and was thus covered in blood and the remaining offal. This did not deter Melissa. As the ram was placed at Carrie's feet, just outside the office, the simpering wench (Melissa, not Carrie) flung herself at the intestine- bespattered object of her affection.

The impala party followed a few nights later. Jeff told the story of his hunt with brutal and gory honesty. I managed to convince him to leave out the bit about firing rounds within 30 metres of my guests – although he really struggled to understand why his infant ranging career might be cut short by this revelation. He did, however, have everyone retching at his description of removing the alimentary canal. Jenny had to leave the room. I suspect Jeff has Asperger's syndrome combined with smatterings of Tourette's. This is an unfortunate combination, especially if your brain case has a smaller volume than a tot measure.

I sent SB a message to let him know of Jeff's success. He sent the following, swollen-headed reply to me, indicating that he hasn't come down to Earth yet.

To: Angus
From: Hugh MacNaughton
Subject: Paaarty in the home town

Hey Angus,

Nice to hear that Jeff has shot his impala although, like I said, I wouldn't be happy with him driving my guests.

I've been having an awesome time here and I have to say I think it's because Simone is away at the family farm. We really haven't been getting on and when she suggested the farm, I think the lack of enthusiasm was obvious on my face. She lost her temper completely.

'You never suggest that we do anything! And you hate my family!'

So that was that. She left yesterday and I went out to the Baron with Micky, Jakes and Bomber. We had an awesome night and rolled out of there at 1 am, in the company of three female friends from varsity, straight to the Colony Arms. About 46 cane and cream sodas later we all piled into a taxi to Bomber's place. I woke up this morning at elevenish – on Bomber's couch. I can never have a night like this with Simone. Perhaps we are just outgrowing each other.

Anyway, I plan to skop it real hard during the next seven days of freedom.

Cheers, your party-king, happy-to-be-free-for-a-while brother, Hugh

---

There are bits of that letter that remind me why my male sibling and I have endured a relationship of conflict for most of our lives. He becomes especially offensive when riding the crest of a social wave. Simone's not perfect but she adores SB and that's not to be sneezed at.

I was free the other morning so Jenny and I went out in the pre-dawn for a little game drive and coffee before the work day began. Jenny struggles to extricate herself from her bed so I fetched the Land Rover and the coffee and then half-dragged, half-carried her into the car. We drove out to a koppie not far from the lodge and then walked (staggered in Jenny's case) up onto a flat rock that looks east over the Kruger Park. There, as the francolins, cuckoos and sparrows sang the sun over the horizon, we sipped steaming mugs of coffee and ate rusks.

When she'd finished her mug, Jenny lay down with her head in my lap and I shared the contents of SB's letter and my related sentiments with Jenny.

'Simone is probably one of the nicest people I've ever met. Hugh is very lucky to have her,' she said. 'But,' she added, 'I don't think there's anything wrong with wanting emotional freedom.' A bearded woodpecker landed on a dead leadwood tree nearby.

'TA tatatatata TA.' He smashed his beak into the hollow trunk, his territorial tap echoing through the dawn.

'What are you going to do when you finish in the bush?' I asked her when the woodpecker flew off.

'I don't really know,' she said. 'I guess I'll probably travel. I'm feeling pretty confused about things at the moment – like there's more I want to be doing. I reckon I've got what I'm going to from being a camp manager.

'I made an attempt to delve further into this but Jenny's very good at being evasive – she has various brilliant techniques for ending conversations that might explore her too deeply. She changed the subject by saying, 'I wanted to tell you that I think you did an amazing job with Jeff. You're a very clever man, Angus.'

Week 9

Bertie and brains

Jeff is now firmly into the swing of being a ranger. As yet, he hasn't killed anyone and his feedback from guests has been officially positive. I say officially because while no one has taken the time to write anything bad about Jeff, I have witnessed a few bizarre things out in the field.

I was in a leopard sighting with him the other day; he had six guests on his vehicle. There was a mating pair of leopards resting, post-coitally, on the cool sand shaded by an old Ana tree. The subject of sex makes Jeff's mouth twitch and his ears turn bright red. When the carnal act is on display in front of him and he is supposed to explain it, he becomes catatonic with embarrassment. Mating leopards are something to behold. The female behaves like a roaring harlot, lifting her tail and rubbing her nether regions in the male's face until he, apparently reluctant, stands up to satisfy her. A great deal of noise follows as he bites his mate on the back of her neck. This biting can become quite vicious because his penis is barbed and so withdrawing it is a painful process for which he, seemingly, blames her. The reproductive act is repeated up to an astonishing fifteen times an hour.

Jeff's guests were obviously fascinated by what they were seeing and wanted their guide to explain. The new ranger just sat there during the first two mounts. The third time the female impressed her ravenous hind end on the male's nose, Jeff went puce.

One of his guests, a jovial Willy Nelson lookalike, asked, 'What's going on here, Jeff? Why does he keep attackin' her while they're makin' love?'

I thought Jeff was going to explode. He answered by listing a number of textbook facts about leopards, none of which had any bearing on the situation.

'Male leopards weigh up to 90 kg, females, up to 60. They have a variable diet ranging from amphibians and reptiles to large antelope. They are highly territorial; male territories can overlap about three female territories. They become independent at two years.'

All of this, he blurted out in less than two seconds, while looking away from the copulating cats and his guests. There was a confused silence on his vehicle. Elvis, who was sitting next to me leafing through my tree book, shook his head and chuckled.

At least the information he gave was relatively accurate.

A few days ago, I received my second training assignment. PJ has decided that the conservation team needs to start sorting out their own admin – currently run ineptly from the reception by the hussy Candice. The only thing Candice is good at is ambushing unsuspecting rangers at the Twin Palms.

Jacob 'Spear of the Lowveld' Mkhonto is a man of great skill but his interest in administration is non-existent. He is also illiterate. Bertie has therefore been earmarked as the man for the job because he is young, clever and ambitious. That said, he has no idea how a computer works so PJ has asked me to teach him to use Excel so that he can start keeping work records, budgets, equipment records, etc. He sweetened the deal by offering me a mentorship fee – not a large sum but an improvement on my pitiful remuneration.

Our first training session began with learning how to turn a computer on – Bertie mastered this task relatively easily. The mouse was a bit more challenging however and for about ten minutes the pointer was moving contrary to the way he thought it should. He got the hang of it eventually and then it was onto some rudimentary typing exercises which took a painful amount of time. I explained the filing system to him and when he'd saved a document titled 'Angus is my lord and master' we moved onto a basic spreadsheet. It quickly became apparent that although Bertie cannot spell at all, his aptitude for numbers is excellent. It's going to take a little while for him learn how to draw up management accounts but he'll definitely succeed.

When he'd learnt to shut down the compyoot (as he calls it with an exaggerated accent), I asked him about his education. Bertie told me about his schooling and then suggested that we go and visit his old high school in Hluvukani village. When I returned from game drive the next morning, we drove into Hluvukani to investigate Mangonzwana High.

The school forms a quadrangle centred on an old marula tree. The classrooms are in an L-shaped building forming two sides of the quad with the administration building and a library (I use the term loosely) forming the other two sides. We arrived at 10h00 and one might be forgiven for thinking that there would be an academic hush over the place – what with it being a Tuesday morning in the middle of term. Instead, what we found rivalled a medieval battleground for chaos. The racket emanating from the classroom block gave the impression of an unlicensed drinking house rather than a place of knowledge acquisition.

Bertie and I wandered over and peered into one of the classrooms. What I saw inside would have been amusing had I not seen the school's matric results from last year. Bits of scrunched-up paper, textbooks and fruit peels filled the air. In one corner, there was a large boy standing on his desk, shouting at anyone who'd listen. As I stuck my head in the door, he was hit squarely in the nose with a book bearing a geometric shape on a torn cover. He jumped hurriedly off his perch only to be replaced by another who also found himself pelted at his first utterance. In the middle of the class there was a skinny chap, attempting to write something in a school book.

The recently pelted fellow saw us and came over.

'Hello,' he said, 'can I help you?'

'Hello. Where are your teachers?'

He pointed over to the admin block. 'Are you having break now?' I asked.

'No no no, this is maths,' he replied heading back into the fray. That explained the trapezium on the cover of the book that had knocked him off his desk. I'm not sure how many budding engineers are going to emerge from Mangonzwana High School next year. We set off across the dusty quad towards the admin block.

As we approached, a man emerged into the sun. He was carrying a pile of books, sweat dripping into his eyes. He greeted us swiftly and then asked us to help with his load. We followed him over to the library building. We set the books down on a lopsided old tin table and then Bertie introduced Mr Mthabini, the maths teacher. Despite the heat, he was wearing a moth-eaten tie.

I asked him about the mayhem in the classrooms and where all the teachers were. He sighed, shook his head and loosened his tie.

'Most of the teachers are in the administration building discussing their pay demands with the teacher's union.'

'During school time?' I was incredulous.

'Yes, of course during school time.'

'What about the kids?'

'That is a good question. There are some teachers in there who would rather be teaching but intimidation from union members is so bad that they go along to the meetings and the pupils suffer.' He wiped the sweat from his forehead with a grubby handkerchief. 'Of course we don't have the books we ordered so teaching is not easy anyway.'

'How long do these meetings go on?' I asked.

'Sometimes days. I tried to teach yesterday but the headmaster came and told me I was becoming an *impimpi* [a sell-out or snitch].'

'So?' I asked.

Bertie gave a rueful laugh.

'You know what they do to *impimpi*?' he asked. I shook my head. 'They beat him up or burn his house or threaten his family.'

We continued chatting for a while and I began to feel really sorry for Mthabini who was clearly extremely dedicated to the cause – as evidenced by Bertie's relatively advanced numeracy skills. As we drove back into the reserve, it became obvious to me why a bright man like Bertie struggled with concepts I just took for granted. The countless others not fortunate enough to have work on reserves like Sasekile must be faced with a grim future.

That evening, I picked up a Portuguese family who spoke virtually no English so I was spared sitting with them at dinner. We were late arriving back from game drive so by the time I arrived at the Avuxeni Eatery for supper, there was no one around – the camp managers were in camp, the chefs were cooking dinner for the guests, the housekeepers were doing turndowns and the others had retired.

All that remained of the staff supper was an emaciated drumstick wallowing in oil, some wilting veggies and a potato that wouldn't have satiated a gerbil. As I considered my dinner, Matto arrived. He's recently completed his written knowledge exams and apparently grossly underestimated what Carrie expected of him so she's grilled him for a few hours every evening this week. It would seem that Matto is not used to being treated in this fashion. He stormed into the eatery. Without greeting me he looked at what was left and said, 'Ag fuck this man, what is this shit?' He slapped the counter, which made the chicken bowl jump, sending oil spattering onto his shirt. 'Fuck sakes!' he shouted before helping himself to all the remaining food.

As he sat down to eat, I said, 'No, thank you, I couldn't possibly ingest another morsel.'

'Huh?' he looked up, the drumstick in his hand.

I shook my head and wandered off towards the Main Camp kitchen in search of nourishment. O'Reilly was bellowing instructions at the chefs who were charging about – it looked like relatively controlled disorder. Kerry spotted me standing in the doorway. She wiped her hands on her apron and came over.

'Hello snake man,' she said.

'Good evening ginger chef.'

She smiled. 'Can I help you with something specific?'

I explained the meal on offer at the Avuxeni Eatery and asked if she could solve my problem.

'I'm busy with a chocolate soufflé, I'm afraid.'

'That'll do nicely,' I replied.

'Yes well, it's not for you,' she said as O'Reilly came over.

'Ungus,' he said. 'How urr ya? Kerry dat soufflé need soom attention,' he said gently. She saluted and left us. I explained my predicament and he was mortified by the thought that I might go hungry.

'Oh, dat'll never do. You go sit under de tree dere and Oi'll rustle you someting up.' He pointed out of the door to a sleeper-wood table situated beneath a low-hanging blue sweet berry tree. I told him a sandwich would be fine. He went off to the fridge and I wandered out to the table and sat down. It was bright outside, the moon near full, its soft light mottled by the branches over my head.

About ten minutes later O'Reilly emerged with a large tray. He placed it on the table. 'Rustle something up' was a poor description of his efforts. There was a small asparagus and cheese quiche to start, a little pottery pot filled with steaming venison stew, a plate with four different cheeses on it and some homemade oatcakes. He placed the tray down and scuttled back to the kitchen, re-emerging a few seconds later with two bottles of wine.

'Troi dis whoit one wit de ceech,' he said pouring two glasses.

'Thanks,' I said, 'I really didn't expect all this.'

'Don't be ridiculous,' he admonished, 'pens me te tink of people not eatin properly. Cheers!' He took a sip of his wine. 'Muurvellus stoof – French, friend of moin joost sent it.' I took a sip. It was freezing cold and delicious.

O'Reilly put the glass down, excused himself and returned to the kitchen. I sat in the moonlight savouring the meal. The red, also French (apparently a Bordeaux blend), was equally enjoyable. As I was about to tuck into the cheese, Kerry and Jane emerged from the kitchen, the former bearing a pudding plate. She placed it on the table and they sat down opposite me. I filled O'Reilly's empty glass with some of the red and handed it to them.

'Thanks,' Jane said.

'Duties complete?'

'Yes, you're about to eat the last of my duties,' Kerry replied.

The chocolate soufflé was incredible. I finished it quickly and then we shared the cheese and the remaining wine. I told them about my visit to Mangonzwana High School while we emptied the bottles. The two trainee chefs are good company. Then, feeling thoroughly satisfied, I wandered back along the path to my room.

I didn't have a torch with me so I walked slowly; listening carefully for any sign of the two buffalo bulls who like to hang about in the camp at night. The sky was clear, there was a gentle breeze and a honeyed smell wafted off the long Guinea grass lining the path. I inhaled deeply and relished the sense of peace and warmth that enveloped me.

It's about a five-minute stroll to my room at the far end of the village and there are two routes there; one through the middle of the village and the other goes through the bush to the back. The camp gives a very false sense of security to the staff, most of whom do not bother to carry torches. While the noise and activity of Sasekile lodge operations do deter some animals, there is no physical barrier preventing entry and there are often a few buffalo bulls, the odd hippo and, normally in winter, elephant bulls looking for greenery. Leopards and lions are also fairly regular visitors – although normally when the camp is sleeping in the dead of the night.

About halfway home the atmosphere changed. I froze as the bushes about ten metres in front of me rustled. I stopped and peered towards the source of the noise, grateful for the moon but silently cursing my lack of a torch. I sniffed the air – buffalo smell like a dairy, but there was no such scent. The bush was too short to be hiding an elephant. I hoped to God it wasn't a hippo because they can be very nasty and very fast and there was nothing for me to climb. But again the shrubbery was too short to conceal a big hippo. I could hear my heart thrashing in my chest. In hindsight, I could have just walked backwards and then turned to use the other route but I didn't. I just stood and watched.

The rustle came again. Because I was standing still, I could make a more accurate assessment of the sound. It wasn't a rustle so much as a gentle brush of hair or grass. Eyes, about two feet off the ground, reflected in the moonlight as a young (about two years) male leopard emerged from behind a round-leafed teak and onto the path to face me. I've no doubt that he'd been watching me for some time. There was no menace in his eyes, just some curiosity. We looked at each other for about a minute and then he took a step forward, sniffing the air.

'Hello boy,' I said quietly, feeling life coursing through my veins, my senses fully alert. He sniffed again and then sneezed. This gave me a fright and I started which made him do the same. Then calm returned. 'Bless you,' I said.

He turned and walked off north towards the river.

I couldn't wipe the smile off my face – it was still stuck to me when I woke up the next morning.

Hugh sent me another Johannesburg update yesterday. Our grandfather continues to struggle to come to terms with the new South Africa.

To: Angus
From: Hugh MacNaughton
Subject: The Major's marbles

Hey Angus,

Spent most of the last week doing just about nothing. The Major had a bit of a fall last weekend so he's been immobile. Nothing too bad, he's going to be on crutches for the next week though. The two of us (and Trubshaw) have watched TV and DVDs most of the week. The Major sits on the sofa either with his head snapped back and his mouth open, fast asleep, or he stares at the screen shouting comments about the incompetence of the actors or sportsmen. It's been good to spend some time with the old boy but I think he's really starting to lose his marbles now.

His relationship with Francina is worse than ever. He's started calling her 'Darkie Francie' and this makes her very angry.

'Darkie Francie,' he said yesterday morning, 'bring me some tea – in a pot, not like you people make it in a tin cup.' She looked up from the vacuum cleaner with contempt and pointed a finger at him.

'Mr Major, the time for speaking like that is finished a long time. When you can learn to ask nice, I will make.' She kicked the cleaner back to life and I had to go and make our grandfather a pot of Earl Grey.
Do you need anything from the big smoke while I'm here? Back in the next few days and looking forward to it. Also, I've managed to organise Julia some bed nights so she's coming end of next week which will be fun!

Cheers,
Hugh

I'm really looking forward to showing Julia around the reserve.

Week 10

Violence and visit

The highlight of the week was Julia's visit. That said, before she arrived there was some conflict with one of my favourite Sasekile employees.

Whenever a new girl (bed-night or staff member) comes to Sasekile, there is excitement among the men. This can spill into some fairly crude but generally harmless banter. When this sort of talk is directed at your sister by the likes of Matto, it becomes deeply offensive.

I arrived back from game drive the day of Julia's arrival looking forward to welcoming her and her friend Penny. Just outside the rangers' room there is a whiteboard which the rangers are obliged to check every day. It contains instructions and information about pick-ups, drop-offs, walks, guest requests, etc. I normally studiously ignore the latter but the rest I need to know so I can plan my day. While reading the mundane tasks for the morning, I heard a few of the rangers talking about Julia and Penny's arrival. It was pretty innocuous stuff. Then Matto waded in.

The arrogant little prick, despite the fact that he's the most junior member of staff here, struts about like he owns the place. He crossed the line with an intimate description of what he intended to do with Julia and Penny at the same time. I stepped into the rangers' room.

As I walked in, everyone went silent. Matto was sitting on the back of the sofa in the middle of the room. I saw him shoot a glance at The

Legend – looking for reassurance. I walked to the rifle safe, opened it and replaced my rifle slowly. As I relocked the safe, I heard Carrie's office chair swivel. I turned to face Matto who was pretending to read a magazine.

'Would you like to say that again?' I asked through gritted teeth, taking a step forward. Jamie and Duncan looked up from their magazines; The Legend just leant back and watched proceedings.

'Hmm?' said Matto feigning surprise.

'I said would you like to repeat what you just said about my sister?' Matto looked towards his cousin and then to me.

'Just a joke bru, don't take it personally,' he said and returned to the page. I could feel Carrie watching me and I knew that she would try to stop me doing something stupid and that she would deal with Matto in her own way but I really didn't want that. I took a deep breath and removed my hat slowly. Then, quite suddenly, I threw it hard at Matto's head. As the hat flew, I took two quick steps forward and swung my open right hand at the trainee ranger's left ear. It connected with a satisfying slap.

When you are a man of my proportions, shock and awe in the first assault are essential in order to avoid being beaten senseless in the reprisal. If you get it right, cuffing someone over the ear leaves them stunned with a horrible ringing. My accuracy was perfect and Matto slumped back onto the sofa behind him, holding his ear. As I did it, The Legend, Carrie, Duncan and Jamie leapt from their chairs. The Legend tried to climb over the coffee table at me but Duncan and Jamie grabbed him. Carrie inserted herself between Matto and me.

'I'll fuck you up!' yelled The Legend struggling against Duncan and Jamie.

'Let your shitty cousin fight his own battles,' I said lifting my middle finger at him.

'Angus, get out right now!' shouted Carrie.

I picked up my hat and walked out into the lowveld mid-morning feeling quite pleased.

About an hour later, I was reading in my room when the door flew open. Carrie burst in, incandescent with rage.

'Angus, for God's sake, what the hell do you think you are doing? Do you think this is a high school? You are 27-years old now, not 18! You don't deal with insults using your fists! I will not tolerate that sort of behaviour!'

I sat up.

'Did you not hear what he said?' I asked, feeling the blood rush into my face. 'What did you expect me to do?'

'Of course I heard him. He's a spoilt child who I'd have dealt with later. You behaved like a savage and I won't put up with it. There are ways of dealing with him and while I sympathise with you, I cannot allow this to pass. I cannot allow myself to be seen to be allowing rangers to throw fists at each other.'

She handed me a piece of paper.

'I really hate having to do this but, your inability to control your temper leaves me with no choice.'

A familiar document.

DISCIPLINARY PROCEDURE

NOTICE TO ATTEND A DISCIPLINARY ENQUIRY

EMPLOYEE'S NAME: Angus MacNaughton
DATE & TIME & PLACE: 16/03, 14h00, Meeting Room
ALLEGED MISCONDUCT LEVEL: Level A – violence against
   another member of staff

You are accused of assaulting another staff member (Matthew Ivey)

NOTE:

AT THE ENQUIRY, YOU WILL BE ENTITLED TO:
1. Be represented by a fellow employee of your choice
   (STRONGLY SUGGESTED)
2. Call witnesses to give evidence on your behalf
3. An interpreter (YES/NO)

SIGNATURE OF MANAGER _____

If the person handing the piece of paper to me had been anyone other than Carrie, I reckon I'd have tried to cuff them too. Carrie is a reasonable and consistent person who I respect and that is rare – so I just took it from her.

Ain't life just a peach? And this just after my epic salvation of Jeff's ecotourism career. The universe is clearly averse to my existing in anything resembling a comfort zone, and has defecated on me again. I could well be fired in the next week or so.

Just over a year ago, I managed to insult Jenny so severely (unintentionally dredging up painful memories of her teenage struggles with bulimia) that I ended up in my first disciplinary hearing. On that occasion my brother took pity on me and made an effort to defend me – citing my ADD as the excuse. His defensive strategy made me cringe to the core of my being but it was very effective.

This time, String Bean was less accommodating. He was just back from leave so I went off to find him – to ask if he'd like to repeat his performance as my representative. I expected a slightly more enthusiastic response especially given that we now tolerate each other.

He was at the Tamboti bar when I arrived – conducting some whisky service training with Redman, Nora and Incredible.

'A word if you don't mind,' I said to him as he explained the peaty nature of an Islay malt – likening it to the licking of an old piece of leather.

He wrapped up and indicated a white sofa next to the fire place.

I sat down with a sigh and explained my situation.

'Angus, I can't believe this. Now I have to get in the middle of things. These okes are my mates. I know Matto's a bit full of himself but he's just young. Come on man … you can't just go around slapping people.'

This response irritated me.

'Julia is your sister too, you know!' I snapped.

'Ja, but he's just a young oke shooting his mouth off.'

'Look, will you help me or not.' After some huffing and sighing and asking me if there was no one else, he agreed. It seems he doesn't want to upset the apple cart filled with his friends – even if there are a few rotten ones.

The hearing is next week. I'm something of a veteran now.

Jenny's reaction to the incident was also not encouraging. I found her in the Main Camp bar doing a stock take.

She rolled her eyes at me and said, 'Angus, you have a really nasty temper and it's unattractive. Guys are such idiots sometimes.' At which point someone called her on the radio before I could ask her if she meant me, Matto or both.

Despite the threat of the disciplinary hanging over my head, the day improved a lot after that – Julia and Penny arrived just after lunch. They were hugely appreciative of their Tamboti Camp suite complete with personal plunge pool, fully stocked minibar and bathroom fit for royalty.

I was afforded lunch with them on the Tamboti deck. I didn't have guests so we had a fairly boozy meal. After a brief kip, I took them out into the bush with some staff – Jenny, Bertie, SB, Simone, O'Reilly and Jamie (who also didn't have guests). The idea this morning was for Matto to take them out and practise his game-driving skills but after our little contretemps, Carrie changed the plan.

We had a really pleasant afternoon, not looking for anything in particular. I turned the radio off and made for a special tree in the far north of the reserve where the rangers seldom take their guests because it's so far from the lodge. The gnarled old nyala tree grows in the middle of a long-dry floodplain. I parked the Land Rover nearby and carried a cooler box over to the old giant. It's a fairy-tale tree, almost six metres in diameter and we positioned ourselves in the little hollows and holes amongst the roots around one side of the base. There, we sipped on milk stout (Bertie, O'Reilly and me), Hunter's Dry (all the girls) and Heineken (SB and Jamie). O'Reilly raided his supply store and provided us with a huge brown bag of biltong.

While we sat there sipping our drinks in the gathering dusk, O'Reilly and Bertie told us childhood stories of Rosegreen in Tipperary and Hluvukani village respectively, which had us chuckling away with a flock of grey helmet shrikes settling in the branches above. Penny and Jamie hit it off immediately and managed to position themselves next to each other in a hollow made for two.

On the way back to camp, Jenny sat in the passenger seat next to me, shining the spotlight. Jamie and Penny sat in the back seat giggling.

O'Reilly and SB occupied the middle making increasingly lewd comments which made us all laugh. Bertie, Julia and Simone sat on the front bench. Halfway home, Jenny spotted a leopard and we watched her for a while as she marked her territory along the track.

The next morning I took Penny and Julia (Jamie also came along) for a walk and the four of us tracked a herd of buffalo for most of the morning. Eventually we heard them in front of us, their tracks heading towards a well-used waterhole deep in the middle of a mopane forest. We moved quickly downwind and skirted the herd in order to reach the water before them. As we arrived, I indicated a huge mopane tree at the edge of the pan and told everyone to climb into it. We could just hear the approaching buffalo.

In my backpack, I had a flask of tea and some rusks. When we'd settled, about ten metres off the ground, I carefully handed out three tin mugs, poured the tea and shared out the rusks. And there we sat, sipping our tea and taking in the herd as they arrived to drink – totally unaware of us watching them from above. We drank gingerly to keep as quiet as possible and also to avoid plummeting into the middle of the buffalo.

Fifteen minutes later, the herd began to move away. The cows at the front sniffed the air, slightly uneasy, clearly able to smell where we'd been but they had no inkling of us watching them from high above. The leaders soon decided there was nothing amiss and belched and burped off to snooze in the shade somewhere. It was fantastic sitting up there watching 250 or so buffalo grazing slowly by.

That evening I was driving real guests so Julia and Penny went on a drive with Carrie who was trialling a new tracker. The Legend went along – without Amber. I didn't think too much of it at the time but it would seem that the romance of the bush worked some of its magic on my sister and The Legend.

I wasn't sitting with my guests that evening and when I arrived at the Avuxeni Eatery for supper, The Legend and Julia were sitting talking to each other at one end of the long table – seemingly oblivious to any of the ten or so people eating around them. This made the bolognaise I was about to consume totally unpalatable. The situation was made more unpleasant by Brandon who looked from me to them and then made lewd signals with his hands.

The next morning, I went to the car park with Jamie (who was bleary-eyed after 'talking' to Penny in the Tamboti boma until the wee hours) to say goodbye to Julia and her friend. SB was helping to pack the boot of Penny's Polo while The Legend was talking to my sister. She was leaning against the bonnet of the car, chuckling and pushing her light-brown hair back behind her left ear. She saw me coming over The Legend's shoulder and their flirtation ended abruptly. I had to fight back the urge to throw up my breakfast.

We said muted goodbyes while Penny and Jamie went behind a spike thorn bush to 'look for a bearded robin that had just called'.

That evening, the weather turned foul. A front came over, accompanied by a gusty wind and intermittent drizzle. It's almost impossible to take a good game drive in conditions like that. All the animals run for cover. The guests only go on drive because they feel obliged to given the number of organs many of them have had to sell to afford being here.

After the deathly quiet game drive, the sparks flying between Julia and The Legend, the imminent disciplinary hearing hanging over my head like a guillotine blade, and a vile dinner at Rhino Camp where Amber was hosting, I wasn't in a great mood. I hoped to find some cheer with Jenny so I went to her room when my guests had gone to bed.

She was pulling on a shapeless nighty as I walked in. She climbed into bed and picked up her book as I sat on the bed next her.

'How was dinner?' I asked.

'Fine thanks,' she said and opened the book. I took my shoes off and told her about The Legend and Julia. 'Well?' I said as I finished.

'Hmm?' she said, not looking up from the page.

'What do you think?'

'Not much. Jonesy's really not that bad and your sister's definitely leagues cooler than Amber.' She closed the book, placed it on the bedside table and sighed heavily. 'I'm really tired.' She sat up, kissed me on the cheek and then lay down, pulling the covers up tightly. She was asleep before I could climb under the covers next to her.

Week 11

Discipline and dilatoriness

A few days after their departure, SB and I received thank you messages from Penny and Julia. The former I appreciated (despite the unjustifiable use of exclamation marks), the latter made me nearly send my laptop through the window onto a flock of babblers squabbling on the grass outside my room.

To: Angus Mac; Hugh Mac
From: Penny Johns
Subject: Thank you both so so so so much!!!

Hi Guys!

I just want to thank you both so much for the most super two days at the lodge! It was one of the most incredible 48 hours of my life and I feel so privileged! It was really rough coming back to work with thoughts of the beautiful bush so fresh in my mind – my boss thought I was sick and suggested I take the rest of the day off!!

You are so lucky to work where you do – the people, the bush and the animals make it so extra special and I'm really starting to question my office job! Perhaps I'll have to take some time out one day and spend a year or two working in the bush.

Thanks again and tell everyone I say hi! Especially Jamie (!!!!) ha ha!

Lots of love and see you soon!
Pen xxx

So that from sweet Penny. Jamie, by the way, cannot stop talking about her. He is her newest Facebook friend and he spends hours trawling through her pictures despite the glacial speed with which the Internet works here. He acknowledges that this is stalking but says he can't help himself.

I was in a foul mood in the lead up to my disciplinary and Julia's letter sullied my disposition even further.

To: Angus
From: Julia MacNaughton
Subject: Thanks.

Hi Angus,

Thanks so much for the effort you made making our stay such fun. That buffalo walk was just incredible, a truly memorable experience [so far so good]. It was also great to meet the people that you work with – I knew they must be quite something to put up with your antics. I know you don't always see it like this but you really do work with some very interesting people indeed [building up for the clanger].

I really don't think that Alistair is such a bad guy, I think you should give him a chance. Just because he's not like you doesn't make him a bad person [the clanger].

Anyway, I look forward to seeing you next week. Any plans for your leave?

Lots of love,
Jules

Despite her obvious intellectual abilities, my sister lacks judgement when it comes to men – she always has. My reply . . .

To: Julia MacNaughton
From: Angus
Subject: Some immutables

Dear Julia,

It was a pleasure taking you and Penny around the reserve. It is always fun to show the wild to people who appreciate it.

I know that not everyone sees the world the way I do but certain things in life are immutable. These things include: death, the speed of light, the criminality of Johannesburg taxi drivers and the fact that Alistair 'The Legend' Jones is a cock.

See you next week,
Angus

I have not heard from her since. Worryingly, Amber told SB the other day that The Legend was being distant. I don't know what I'll do should my sister choose to engage in some sort of romance with him. SB thinks they would make quite a nice couple but his ability to judge character is poorer than that of those who propelled Zuma to power.

My disciplinary hearing took place a few days after Julia left. PJ presided, Carrie prosecuted and Jamie (sheepishly) acted as witness for defence and prosecution. I was in a state of high anxiety beforehand. SB said almost nothing at all, ostensibly leaving me to conduct my own defence. Matto was not present but I saw him lurking outside with The Legend – clearly chuffed that I was suffering such humiliation. PJ sat and listened to Carrie as she repeated her speech about the necessity for control and following the correct procedures. SB then gave a half-hearted speech during which he stated that while my behaviour was not from the top drawer, there were extenuating circumstances. He failed to mention what these were and when PJ asked, I stepped in and gave him a precise and graphic description of what Matto had said. The General Manager looked across to Jan for corroboration and he simply nodded.

PJ gritted his teeth, took out a form and filled in a(nother) written warning with my name on it. He handed it to me.

'Sign this and we'll hear no more of it,' he said. I took the paper and signed, relief washing over me. He could easily have fired me. Despite the fact that it's virtually impossible to dismiss someone for gross incompetence in South Africa, our labour laws frown upon assaulting colleagues. I handed it back to him. 'Angus, your temper has been the undoing of you before. You've had a good run for a while so don't spoil it now.' He dismissed us all but held Carrie back. I'm not sure what he said to her but Matto spent the next week helping the maintenance crew unblock the septic tanks in Main Camp.

A few days later, Bertie and I took some of my guests on a trip to Hluvukani village. Martha Allen, her husband and two of their Texan friends are of the firm opinion that they can save Africans from themselves. They are the sort of people who think we should all aspire to a world of V8s, four-bedroom mansions, shopping malls, church on Sundays and carefully planned families. My intention was to give them some Hobbesian rural African truths.

Our first stop was Mangonzwana High. Unlike the last time we arrived, there was relative quiet at the school. We climbed from the air-conditioned Land Rover Discovery into the brutal midday. Mthabini emerged from one of the classrooms, tie firmly in place. He walked over and greeted the guests warmly.

I asked after the headmaster and the maths teacher told me he was probably in his office – there was an almost imperceptible roll in his eyes as he said it. Bertie and Mthabini then took the guests off to the classrooms and I went in search of Mr Ndlovu, the headmaster.

I walked to the administration block, turned left down the narrow, dusty passage and came to a door marked 'Principal'. The 'c' and the 'a' were hanging upside down, barely clinging to the tiny nails holding them in place. I knocked and walked in to find myself in a windowless waiting room. It was separated from the office beyond by a wall of thin, unpainted

nously fat woman sat at a tiny desk. She was writing
I'm not sure how she saw what she was writing over
ns spilling onto the desktop. She looked up without

_, I said smiling.

_es, she replied.

'I'm well, thank you,' I said, 'and I hope you are too. I'd like to see the
principal please, I have some potential donors from overseas waiting
outside.'

'Do you have an appointment?'

This was a stupid question as she was staring at a diary page with the
day's date. It was blank.

'I don't.'

'You must make an appointment and come back,' she said, 'Mr Ndlovu
is a very busy man.'

I disregarded this obvious lie and walked through the door in the
chipboard.

The principal was sat at his desk, his balding head resting gently on his
folded arms. Dribble darkened a shiny ice-blue shirt sleeve.

'AHEM!' I cleared my throat. He sat bolt-upright. Before he had a chance
to say a word I told him I had some visitors waiting in the heat outside. Mr
Ndlovu sat back in his chair and considered me, his face inscrutable. He
picked up a pair of thick spectacles from his desk and pushed them on.

'What do they want?' he asked.

'They are potential donors,' I replied. This galvanised the man.

'Come, I will show you around,' he said shooting out of his chair.

Mr Ndlovu led me outside and we found the Americans in the 'library'.
I introduced the headmaster who, once he'd admonished Mthabini for
neglecting his teaching duties, became an obsequious toad. The headmaster
indicated some old plastic chairs and we all sat down. Martha – the self-
appointed leader of the group – began by asking Mr Ndlovu (or Indi-
loe-voo as she pronounced it) what he felt the major challenges of the
school were. (It was clear to me that Mr Ndlovu was probably the greatest
challenge the school faced.)

What followed was a twenty minute diatribe of complaints. The highlights of this litany included his salary, his housing allowance, the lack of a government car, the lack of computers, lack of books . . . and so the list went on. Some of these would have been valid had he been making the most of what he had. It was an impressive performance.

Mrs Allen let all of this wash over her. With a concentration span of three seconds and a complete inability to climb out of her hair-breadth view of the world, she announced that the school would receive computers. Forty of them.

'The kids here need INNERNET, can't learn without INNERNET these days.'

'Martha, there are no telephone lines here, wired or otherwise,' I said.

'Angus, your problem is negativity – where you see problems, I see solutions and with Mr Indi-loe-voo in charge here, I'm positive he'll implement my INNERNET solution.' With that she rose. 'It's gettin' really hot here, let's get back to the jeep.'

The snivelling Ndlovu bade us farewell although his enthusiasm waned considerably when he heard he'd be receiving computers and not the money to buy them.

The arrival and implementation of the INNERNET system will be fascinating – for all the wrong reasons.

Our next stop was the home of Thobela 'Sox' Siwela, aged about 80. Elvis introduced me to this remarkable man at the end of last year and I spent a fascinating afternoon talking to him. Thobela is a repository of Shangane oral history and philosophy. He also has some fairly strong views on land redistribution and redress in South Africa. In the late 1930s when Thobela was a boy, his family (mother, father's second wife, four siblings, six cattle and some chickens) were forcibly removed from their property when it was incorporated into the greater Kruger National Park. Despite this traumatic childhood experience and a complete lack of formal education, Thobela Siwela is one of the wealthiest businessmen in the area. He owns a large chicken farm and a string of local panel beaters that double as driving schools.

Thobela bade the Allens and their friends sit on chairs under a large marula tree. He placed himself on a weathered stump and then, with his hands resting on a stick, polished with age and use, narrated the history of the Shangane people. He has a tremendously deep voice and a pure white goatee. The Allens, for the first time on their four-night stay, were mesmerised. They forgot about the heat and shut up for a full half hour. When the old man told of his family's removal from their homestead, Martha had to blow her nose.

Thobela drew me to one side when the Allens went off with Mrs Siwela to look at the chicken coops.

'How is my boy?' he asked in Shangane. His son Abbot works at Sasekile as the store manager. I haven't had much to do with him but he is renowned for being smart, lazy and not particularly fond of Caucasians.

'I think he's doing okay,' I replied. 'I don't really work with him.' Thobela shook his head.

'I worry about that boy,' he said. 'He is always angry. Angry with me, angry with his mother, angry with the world and, of course, with you guys.' He drew a circle around my face with his hand.

'Why, do you think?' I asked.

'Ag, he was a happy little boy but he was always looking for shortcuts. He never did a good job of anything. He also had some bad friends at school and they did naughty things. I remember once when he was a teenager, he and some friends were caught stealing oranges. One of the farmers nearly beat him to death with a sjambok.'

'That's horrible! When was it?'

'He was eighteen at the time. But he was stealing. You think a Shangane farmer would have treated him differently?' He looked at me wide-eyed. 'Of course not! He'd probably have killed him.' He sighed heavily. 'To be honest, I think his big problem is that he knows his brother will take over the business from me.

'Abbot is just one of these young guys who thinks the world owes them something. He is lazy and because I have some good businesses he doesn't think he has to work hard. I just can't trust him with my business and Abbot knows this. Also, his ambition is much greater than his work ethic.' Our conversation ended as the Allens returned from the chickens.

I told Jenny about the school visit on the deck before tea, thinking she'd be interested and that it might cheer her up a bit – her mood has really dulled over the last week. She gave a forced chuckle at the end of my description and stared out over the Tsesebe River.

Her behaviour is particularly annoying given my increasing desire to open up to her – she's become something of a companion to me as well as a lover (although there's been precious little evidence of the latter recently). We are going on leave next week and she's going overseas with her family so perhaps that will knock her out of her funk.

I had a conversation with Simone about it last night when I took the Allen children over to her before dinner. She was waiting at the Warren (kiddies area) where she'd prepared some sort of papier-mâché modelling experiment for them. While the kids set to soaking old newspapers, Simone turned to me and said, 'How're things with Jenny?'

'Why do you ask?' I replied. It was unusual for Simone to initiate a conversation like this for while we have a civil relationship it's not as if we are best buddies.

'Because I know she's just not very happy at the moment.'

'And you think I'm the problem?' I asked, my hackles rising.

'No no no,' she soothed. 'I don't think you're the problem at all really.' There was a silence.

'Well, I have no idea what the issue is so any light you could throw on the situation would be appreciated.' I sat on a kid-size chair next to the door.

'I had a drink with her last night and we got chatting about life and the future. She says she's feeling restless. Like she wants to achieve so much more than she is right now – I guess she feels like she's wasting herself here.'

'So why doesn't she try and achieve something – do a degree, teach some staff? Or why doesn't she leave?'

'She hasn't really got a clue what she wants to do. She told me that her friends are all in careers or overseas travelling and she feels stuck in a rut.'

There was silence for a little while.

'And me … what did she say about me?'

'Nothing – you didn't really come up.'

'Well that speaks volumes. Why doesn't she tell me this stuff?'

'I don't know, Angus, maybe because she knows you're a logical, black-and-white person and maybe she thinks you wouldn't get it.' She paused. 'I'm not sure,' she shrugged; there was sympathy in her eyes.

'Great,' I said looking at my watch. 'Why are you telling me this?'

'Because I know her well and I know how closed she can be and I think you quite like her.'

'I better go.' I stood and turned to leave, then paused and looked at Simone. 'Thank you,' I said. She smiled.

Week 12

Mutinous Major and seething sister

It's been good to be home for a while. Weather-permitting, Trubshaw and I have walked along the Braamfontein Spruit every evening. Obviously he can't be taken from the house without a lead and choke chain. Watching dogs, people and children scatter as he strains against his bonds is very amusing. He looks terrifying but given that he has slept through two Kenton burglaries, the potential harm he poses to humans is negligible. The same cannot be said for other dogs. Being a Staffordshire bull terrier (and a particularly gormless example from a breed known for its lack of intelligence), he has no concept of his own size.

I've also spent some time with my relations. I decided to treat the Major and GAJ to lunch yesterday. (The meal was essentially courtesy of The Legend – I'm saving quite a lot of money with his looking after my bar bill.) Taking them together was ill-considered. My mother's father and my father's retired older sister do not hold an enormous mutual affection. GAJ thinks the Major is a foul-mouthed old racist, which of course he is. The Major thinks that GAJ is a reprehensible liberal lesbian communist. I'm not sure if she's a communist and she's definitely not a lesbian. She did, however, spend many years as an active member of the Black Sash and was arrested once by the security police in the eighties.

I took them to JB Rivers in Hyde Park. Everything was going fine until the Major, after his second Castle Lager, accused the waiter of stealing his cellphone. Sandile, a very well-spoken and educated student paying his way through a BCom, took this accusation in his stride. He pointed out the fact that the Major's phone was under his napkin. GAJ launched a scathing attack.

'My God, Henry, how dare you! You'd never have accused a white waiter like that! You're the absolute limit!'

'Bloody right I wouldn't,' snapped the Major leaning forward and whispering, 'he wouldn't have had long dark fingers!'

GAJ stood and picked up my pint glass of Windhoek draft.

'You are a beastly ... bloody ... dinosaur,' she hissed before emptying the glass onto the Major's bald head. So ended the lunch. GAJ stormed from the restaurant and I was left to take the soused and muttering Major home.

That evening I took Jenny to the airport. She was to fly out to Rome and then the Amalfi coast to join her family who left last week. I'd hardly seen her since we arrived in Johannesburg – she'd had a succession of 'girls' dinners'. Whatever one does at a girls' dinner seems to have cheered her up a bit and she was particularly affectionate on the way to the airport. She laughed at my jokes and, after two large drafts in the Keg & Aviator, we had a long and probably slightly inappropriate kiss in front of the security gates.

I was relieved things finally seemed to have improved between us.

That said, I have heard precious little from her during the rest of the week. Her phone is apparently on roaming but perhaps signal on the Amalfi coast isn't great. She sent one message on arriving in London but there's been nothing since.

SB sent an update from the bush midway through the week.

To: Angus; Jules
From: Hugh MacNaughton
Subject: My New Wine Cellar!

Hey Guys,

The first highlight of the week was the completion of the Tamboti Camp wine cellar. I've been talking to PJ about various improvements to the hospitality of the lodge for a while now – we need a spa with a therapist and a great wine cellar. On Monday, quite unexpectedly, a crew of builders arrived to fulfil my second wish – the wine cellar.

As you know, the Tamboti deck is set on a very steep part of the Tsesebe River bank so there is quite a lot of space beneath it. Under the highly capable leadership of Gert van Schalkwyk (a two-toned Hoedspruit local) they turned the river bank under the deck into a cool haven for viticultural appreciation.

The other notable news from the week is a bit more disturbing. Three days ago, the staff wage negotiations started. I didn't even know what that meant. Apparently a new union has managed to sign up most of the local staff during the last few months – the Millennium Solidarity Union, militant as they were, is out. The new union's shop steward is Abbot Siwela (ironic given that he, as head of procurement and stores, is one of the best-paid people here). He is the Workers' Association for National Comrades of the Revolution's man on the ground (quite a mouthful hey?).

These guys arrived in a black BMW 535i – with windows so tinted I'm not sure how they could see out of them. They were all dressed in black suits with Police sunglasses. PJ has been stuck in meetings with them ever since. They were apparently so rude in the first meeting that he refused to let them stay on the property. He is looking super stressed at this stage.

Other than that, all is well here. Amber came to see me again about Jonesy – he is still being distant to her (any messages coming your way, Jules? Ha ha – Angus won't like that). Whatever his problem is, it must be serious because Amber is hotter than ever.

Anyway, send some news from home and see you soon Angus.

Lots of love,
Hugh

I phoned Julia immediately on reading this. The receptionist at her firm told me she was meeting a client so I told her there was an emergency of sorts (well I did consider it an emergency). She put me through.

'Julia MacNaughton speaking.' Very formal, probably in her black power suit; hair tied up aggressively.

'Julia, its Angus, have you read Hugh's latest email?'

'Priscilla told me there was an emergency; what's the problem?'

'You and Jonesy is the problem ... are you and he in contact?' There was a silence, gravid with steaming anger.

'Is that why you dragged me out of a meeting? Is this what you consider an emergency?!' She was hissing down the phone.

'Of course! If you're considering The Legend as a prospect, it's most definitely an emergency!' There was stomping of high heels in the background, an opening and then closing of a door.

'Angus,' brief loss for words, 'Angus, who the hell do you think you are? This is the first client I've ever been trusted with alone and you are screwing it up. Now piss off and grow up.' The phone went dead.

She didn't speak to me for four days and could barely look me in the eye at Sunday lunch. This means two things: she is still filthy mad with me and, far worse, she is in contact with The Legend.

Shit.

Week 13

Choir and complaint

Jenny returned from her trip to the UK and Italy three days before we had to go back to work. It was a Friday morning and I'd had one SMS from her during the time she was away. It surprised me how often I checked my phone in the hopes of receiving some sort of communication from her. I was, as can be imagined, beginning to doubt her fealty. We'd been invited to her cousin's wedding on the Saturday.

I saw her briefly for coffee the morning she returned and met her parents and younger brother. They were very warm, interested and interesting. Their daughter, however, was on her phone for most of the time I was there. She kept apologising as it rang and then rushed out of the room to answer it.

'Sorry,' she'd say as she'd came back in, 'so many bridesmaid's duties.'

I could hardly be angry but the fact that Jenny sat at the other side of the table from me during the entire visit disturbed me somewhat. Her father, brother and I spent most of the time talking about the Super 15 – they wanted all the news from the last two weeks. Her mother wanted to know all about my family and she ejected a mouthful of coffee when I told them about the time Trubshaw pulled Dad off the jetty in Kenton.

I left sometime during the 150th phone call/What's App/SMS.

The next I saw of her was at the church – St Martin's in the Veld. Her family had kindly kept me a space. I was positioned on the aisle about four rows from the front. The bride wasn't a particular beauty and her choice of dress was odd for someone of her rotund proportions. She gave the impression of a corpulent albino penguin as she waddled down the aisle.

Her bridesmaids (six in all) looked very attractive, Jenny especially. They were in pale pink dresses of varying designs.

The music and readings were profound in their lack of originality, the low point being the bride's entry to Pachelbel's *Cannon in D* (puke). The last hymn, however, was one of my favourites – *Cwm Rhondda*. I gave both verses stick (especially the bass bits at the end, 'Want no more!'). I was feeling quite good after it and Jenny's mother complimented me. Her daughter wasn't quite so impressed.

'Why didn't you just sing normally?' was the first thing she said to me when I saw her at the reception.

'Yes, good afternoon and may I say how beautiful you look,' I replied, sipping some Veuve Clicquot.

'Seriously Angus, you sounded like an opera singer. Everyone heard you, it's embarrassing.' I found this quite difficult to stomach. Of the many talents I'm short of, singing is not, never has been and never will be, one. Apparently I should have just whispered half-heartedly along like the rest of her friends.

'With due respect, you and, I wager, most of your peers, wouldn't know an opera singer if he sat on you.' I drained my glass and stalked off.

Jenny was fairly rat-arsed by the time the dancing began so my rendition of the bass part of the Welsh rugby hymn was forgotten and we all had a pretty good party.

I'd love to have told Julia about it, but she's still a bit irritated with me. I mentioned it to Mum and Dad while we were having coffee and croissants on the morning of my departure.

'But Angus you have a beautiful voice!' said Mum, clearly shocked that anyone might think otherwise. Dad looked up from the *Sunday Times* and frowned.

'That is a great pity,' he said.

Week 14

Run and rhino

My return to the lodge was very pleasant in that I didn't have guests on my first night. Jenny and I arrived back just after 14h00. She had to go straight into Main Camp to meet a whole lot of new arrivals – a responsibility which made her sigh and wheeze a lot. Her doldrums have returned.

Bertie came to see me as I walked into my room. He delivered the three computer assignments I'd given him to do while I was away. He was so excited by his efforts that he wouldn't let me unpack until I'd examined them. Their standard was fair to middling but he is making very good progress – in fact astounding progress for someone with such appalling high schooling who, until a few weeks ago, had never turned a computer on.

Once I'd unpacked and sent Bertie off, I went to see Elvis. He was sitting under a mopane tree outside his room – his vast frame supported by a beaten-up old wire chair. He was staring absently into the branches, his hands cupped behind his head.

'*Avuxeni* [hello] General,' I said. (I have taken to referring to him as the General.)

'*Ahe* Angus!' he said looking up. I pulled over an upturned crate and sat down. We sat in comfortable silence for a while watching an orange-breasted bush shrike searching for morsels in the branches. We asked after each other's families and then went over the highlights of the last fortnight.

For him it was the fact that his daughter, aged seven, had just learned to read. He was amazed.

'Me, I only learned to read when I was 22!' He was glowing.

I went to the rangers' room a little while later to see what guests I was picking up the next day. Carrie was in there labelling the library books. She was very welcoming in her butch way. I sat on one of the sofas and picked up the latest edition of *Africa Geographic* magazine. As I leafed through it, Carrie invited me to join her and a few others for an evening drive. I wanted to have a run so we agreed to meet at a river crossing.

Just after 17h00, I headed out west along a road that runs parallel with the Tsesebe River. The edge has come off the summer heat so it was warm but very pleasant. As I ran along, listening to birds, the river and my footfall on the earth, I felt my body relax. I didn't realise I was tense but perhaps the time in Johannesburg and Jenny's distance had wound me up. My shoulders and back eased into the movement, my lungs opened up and my heart beat reassuringly against my ribs. The smells of the end of summer – dry elephant dung, dust and muddy wallows – added to the full-body smile that developed as I ran. I stopped to watch a herd of impala scattering into the mopane trees fringing a clearing. A little further on some kudu fed in a thicket of buffalo thorn trees. It never fails to astound me that they are able to eat from plants with thorns vicious enough to tear canvas.

Just after the kudu, the road dipped through a dry tributary of the Tsesebe and then rose onto an old flood plain. On the northern side of the plain, flanking the river, there are enormous trees – mahoganys, jackalberrys, large-leaved albizias and one huge Ana tree. I spotted a rhino and her calf ambling down to the river bank. I snuck up behind a wide, low termite mound to watch. The rhino were totally oblivious to my presence and came within twenty metres of my hiding place. As is their wont, the calf walked in front; the cow gently setting her offspring on the right path.

As the rhino disappeared over the lip of the river bank, I walked out from my hiding place and continued west through the floodplain. I arrived at the rocky drift where Carrie was supposed to be waiting about 45 minutes after I set off. There was no one there so I sat on a well-sunned flat rock and watched a green-backed heron fishing under a low-hanging brak thorn tree. Without wanting to sound twee, I felt a genuine connection with the stone under me, the water flowing past and the buffalo bull watching me quietly. I hadn't noticed him as I sat down – chewing his cud on a flat, shady piece of the bank about 40 metres to the east.

After ten minutes or so I heard the sound of an engine and presently Carrie drove down the northern part of the crossing. In her Land Rover were Jane and Kerry, O'Reilly, Bertie and Nhlanhla (he with the glass eye). They parked off to one side and a little while later we were drinking our tipples of choice, chatting on the rocks in the last of the day's light.

I haven't had a lot to do with Jane – but it seems to me that Carrie might have. The two of them sat close together. I happened to look at them as O'Reilly commented on the beauty of the light reflecting off the water. Jane shot out an elegant hand and squeezed Carrie's thigh quickly. Chickens roared home to roost. While Kerry has been flirtatious with the male staff since her arrival, Jane, while always pleasant, has not. I've never seen Carrie as relaxed, sitting on that rock knocking back a Black Label quart as Jane sipped a Savanna next to her.

O'Reilly was as amusing as ever. He described the trials of teaching Rufina, the aggressive scullery lady seeking to become a chef. She speaks not a word of English and O'Reilly isn't exactly easy to understand.

'She's a little ting and trois really hurrd but her hands ur loik fekkin rock crushers. I usked hurr to fillet a piece o' fish dis mornin – turned me back for two seconds and she'd made fekkin fish mince.'

This little vignette had us all giggling as his pale chubby face contorted expressively with the effort of telling the story. His performance was mainly for Kerry's benefit and he watched her with poorly disguised yearning as she laughed, tossing back her thick, dark, red hair. She really is a stunner with her wide smile and button nose; a few freckles dotted across the bridge. Her boss is helplessly in love with her and it was plain to see that although she clearly finds him amusing, she doesn't find him remotely attractive.

Bertie and I discussed the stars and the planets on the way home – he struggled to understand the Copernican universe so I'm going to add that to his computer training programme.

It felt great to be back but for one thing.

Jenny has hardly said a word to me since I carried her bags to her room the day we arrived. Three times I've been to see her after dinner and the lights have been off each time. I went in the first night but she complained about being woken up so I haven't tried again. She hasn't come to my room at all and I'm going through a fair amount of internal turmoil as a result. I wish she'd tell me what the hell is wrong.

Arthur was slightly distressed about my being reprimanded for my singing at the wedding.

To: Angus MacNaughton
From: Arthur C. Grimble
Subject: Sing sing sing!

> Crocus Cottage
> West Road
> Wragby
> Lincolnshire

Dear Angus,

I so enjoyed your last letter – especially your story about your family pet. He does sound like a remarkable beast.

I was slightly distressed that your singing was not entirely appreciated. How sad. I belonged to a choir for many years; in fact most of us sang in the choir and played cricket for the village. It was wonderfully social. Anyway, I say anyone who is unable to appreciate that beautiful Welsh hymn sung well needs his or her head examined.

The weather has warmed a bit now and all my crocuses are in full bloom. A few swallows have returned and there is a pair building a nest in my little garden shed. I do so enjoy it when these special birds return.

Mavis is coming around this evening and I have cooked a roast chicken. Spring is in the air etcetera!

Best wishes and you just keep singing your heart out.
Arthur

He has such a refreshing view on life.

Week 15

Anger and annulment

The relations between men and women have confounded the greatest philosophers since the beginning of our species. While I'm not an idiot, I can't lay claim to being any sort of Descartes or Aristotle. So it was with profound irritation in my heart and deep confusion in my head that I ended my daliance with Jenny on a windy evening three days ago.

Things have not been ideal between us as I have chronicled over the last few weeks. She has been increasingly distant although not unpleasant. The uneasy feeling that started to develop a few weeks ago became something of an ache. It was a familiar sensation – one that I remember feeling the week after my matric dance. When Elizabeth Harrington told me she was confused; that she liked me a lot but wasn't ready for a relationship, could we just be friends and see what transpired?

Of course, Gary Weston, the 1ˢᵗ XV hooker, assuaged her confusion beside a clump of azaleas about ten minutes later.

Unlike Elizabeth Harrington, Jenny just let things ride for weeks. Neither here nor there. She talked with longing about her friends working in London and having fun there. She spoke like she was stuck on a prison island which I began to find rather pathetic.

Three nights ago, I went to her room, looking forward to seeing her but with a sense of apprehension growing in my belly. She was reading a travel magazine and didn't look up as I walked in.

'Hi,' she muttered.

'Hi.' I took my shoes off and sat on her bed. 'How're things?'

'Cool,' she said turning a page. The silence hung as my irritation began to build.

'Jen, what's going on with you?' I asked.

'What do you mean?' Still not looking up.

'Look at me a second.' I took the magazine gently from her.

'Not now Angus.' She turned her head to the open window. I thought about just leaving it but I was too irritated.

'Yes, now,' I said. She just lay there, the chilly frontal weather rustling the leaves outside. A hippo called from the river. 'Jen, this is obviously not working for you – have you had enough?' Her answer to this question was one of those unfathomable female answers that even girl friends of mine cannot explain.

'I don't really mind,' she said sadly. The muscles of my jaws clenched.

'You don't really mind what exactly?' I snapped.

'I said not now Angus, please, I don't want to talk about it.'

'I don't give a shit whether *you* want to talk about it or not. There are two of us involved in this. It's not like there is some great personal tragedy that's taken place in your life, so turn round and at least have the grace to look at me.'

She slowly turned. There was a real distance in her eyes.

'Now what the hell does "I don't really mind" mean?' I knew then that there was only one way the conversation was going to end.

'I don't know. I feel numb. I feel like I really don't mind what happens with us. I'm just so unmotivated with life. I feel like I'm missing out.' She looked at me blankly. There was no softness in her brown eyes – just an indifferent distance. It was difficult not to take this personally.

'For God's sake. You feel you're missing out on what exactly? You're living in one of the most beautiful places on planet Earth, with people you like and one in particular who likes you more than a lot. You're hardly burning in the sulphurous fires of hell.' My temper was starting to get the better of me.

'Angus, you don't understand,' she rolled her eyes heavenward and turned back to the window.

'You're bloody right I don't understand. But you've made a piss-poor attempt to explain it.'

The tension of the moment slowly dissipated and was replaced by a lingering heaviness. 'Well I need some sort of clarity on this because I'm going slowly mad.'

'I don't know what to tell you,' she replied.

'Tell me how you feel about me!' I almost yelled.

'I don't know how I feel! I don't know what I want!' she shouted. Tears of frustration started to leak from her eyes as she turned back to me and sat up.

I picked my shoes up and stood. 'Well, I refuse to deal with that. I can't deal with your being indifferent to me after four months. So I'll do what you should have done a while ago. We'll call it quits.' I moved to the door and turned. She just looked at me with a horrible blankness. I shook my head and walked out.

Although I did the breaking up, it feels like it was the other way around. I suppose I could have carried on living in the greyness that Jenny and I were, but I've never been good living in anything other than black or white.

My game drive the next morning was less than entertaining, I fear. I drove around the reserve with a thunder cloud over my head and gave one-word answers to the over-enthusiastic young Americans who asked me endless questions, most of which I'd answered the afternoon before. The ability of some Yanks to ask a question and then pay absolutely no attention at all to the answer is astounding. God, it was irritating.

Unfortunately, the guests were in Main Camp so I was unable to avoid seeing Jenny after game drive. I walked onto the deck and there she was, talking to a young (clearly-in-love) couple. I managed to escape without being spotted but she saw me about half an hour later. I was eating some toast on the veranda at the Avuxeni Eatery, alone but for a little bearded robin. He was hopping about in the shade of a fig tree, picking insects off the ground. I was momentarily absorbed in his robin world.

Jenny arrested my attention as she arrived to fetch some milk. I looked up at her.

'I feel like I've been punched in the stomach,' she said.

'Me too,' I replied matter-of-factly.

She took her milk and went away again. While it was nice to think that she was also hurting a bit, the way she said it indicated that she wasn't about to come rushing into my arms and tell me she loved me. I looked back to the robin, which carried on with its breakfast, unconcerned. I watched it for a while and then left, my toast half-eaten.

One of the worst parts of a break-up in this place is the fact that nothing is private because people are around all the time, watching and listening. I was spared having to tell anyone because I chose to skip lunch, but she must have told someone there.

I was lying on my bed staring at the ceiling around lunch time. There was a knock at the open door and in marched Jeff. He pulled my desk chair out and sat next to my bed, staring at me like one might a friend in a coma.

'What the hell do you want Jeff?'

'I'm so so so so sooooooo sorry!' he said.

'About what exactly?' I asked him.

'You and Jenny. You must be sooooo sad.'

'Jeff, as Boris Becker said after losing at Wimbledon, no one died. Now go away.'

'But ...'

I cut him off. 'Not another word. Get out.'

Week 16

Surly and sarcastic

One positive of the break-up is that I don't have to be around Jenny as she mopes about like a downtrodden cotton slave. Also, The Legend's bar bill is taking a greater hit than usual as I attempt to lift my mood through the medium of fine malt whisky. Sometimes, however, I feel like I'm slipping into the void and it would seem my guests are suffering. My game drives continue to barely scrape the barrel of acceptability and, not for the first time in my career, there has been a complaint. Carrie summoned me to the rangers' room after lunch the other day and told me to shut the door.

She gestured to one of the sofas and then sat on the other. There was a piece of paper in her hand.

'I'd like to read something to you,' she said without preamble. At this point One-eyed Joe opened the door. 'Not now please,' said Carrie. Joe disappeared quickly. She turned back to me, read the email and then handed me the piece of paper. 'I want you to read it again please.'

To: Sasekile General Manager; Sasekile Head Ranger
From: Sandra Janse van Rensburg (Black Eagle Travel – Senior Consultant)
Subject: Fw: Ranger at Sasekile Private Game Reserve

Dear PJ and Carrie,

As you are knowing Black Eagle send to you a lot of business. We send so much pax to you because the standard of your accommodations and staff is very good. Therefore we are not happy with the letter that is forwarded below from a Australian pax and his family. Please can you assure this is not happening again.

Kind regard,
Sandra

To: Sandra Janse van Rensburg (Black Eagle Travel – Senior Consultant)
From: Bryan Rafferty
Subject: Ranger at Sasekile Private Game Reserve

Dear Sandra,

Thank you for organising our trip to Africa which, for the most part, was exceptional. There was, however, one part of the experience that was simply not up to standard and was, in fact, just insulting on a number of levels. I am referring to our ranger at Sasekile Private Game Reserve.

The ranger in question, Angus MacNaughton, is possibly the most sarcastic, surly, impatient and downright unpleasant person I have yet encountered in my long life. That he is employed in the hospitality industry is bizarre given that he has no people skills whatsoever. I am not sure if you are familiar with the television series *House* but Hugh Laurie's character is like a kitten compared with the offensive Angus MacNaughton.

I offer the following as a few examples of the abuse my family and I were subjected to during the course of our two-night stay with him.

My daughter is an eager twelve-year-old and she loves animals. At a sighting of three giraffes one morning, she asked him how fast these animals can run. Without saying a word, Angus climbed from the vehicle and ran at them, clapping his hands and shouting. The startled creatures took off – ruining the photograph my wife had been setting up for ages.

He returned to the vehicle, looked at my daughter and said, 'Well, Sheila,' (my daughter's name is Sarah), 'apparently a lot bloody faster than me.' Without another word he climbed into the driver's seat and we drove off.

We were also unfortunate enough to accompany him on a walk after breakfast one morning. During his introduction talk to the four of us and a number of other guests, he said, 'Stay behind me and the rifle at all times. If you fail to adhere to this, I will have to put a gory hole in you before engaging whatever murderous beast is trying to kill us.'

One of the guests on this walk, an old French woman with a nasty cold, stopped to tie her shoelace and consequently fell behind the group. When Angus noticed, he turned around and said, 'Madam, the predators out here instinctively look for three things: the infirm, the aged and individuals at the back of the herd. You fulfil all three of these criteria so might I ask that you keep up. Your demise would be a blight on my otherwise-sparkling record.'

These are just three of the belligerent things said during our stay. I am not in the habit of complaining but I am also not in the habit of being insulted by people for whose company I have paid handsomely. I feel it is my duty to let you know that Angus MacNaughton is out there ruining safaris for any number of high-paying tourists.

I would appreciate your forwarding this to the relevant management at the lodge. You may also let them know that, but for the ranger, our stay at Sasekile was wonderful.

Sincerely,
Bryan Rafferty

I looked up.

'Anything to say?' asked Carrie.

'Not really. Bruce and his family were painful. They didn't stop asking questions the whole time they were here and the old French bat wouldn't listen to instructions on the walk.'

'Bullshit Angus!' she snapped. 'His name was Bryan, and he paid exorbitant rates to stay here and it is your *job* to answer questions. It is your *job* to be polite. It is your *job* to take people on walks and make them feel comfortable.'

There followed an awkward silence. I knew she was right but I couldn't bring myself to apologise.

'I know you and Jenny have broken up and that a lodge is a shit place to be with both of you working here but if you can't be an adult about it then you can bugger off and work somewhere else. I'm taking you off the road for a week to think about it. You can go and burn firebreaks with Jacob.'

I wondered what PJ was going to say about it. He was on leave so, although the department heads looked after themselves, Carrie was *de facto* Commander-in-Chief. As if reading my mind she said, 'I'm checking PJ's mails while he's away. I don't think he needs to know about this. So don't let it happen again.'

This was most reasonable of her. I look forward to spending a bit of time away from guests and out in the bush all day. I can't really afford to be without gratuities but I'm unlikely to be making anything substantial in my current state of mind.

Arthur's advice on my situation went as follows.

To: Angus MacNaughton
From: Arthur C. Grimble

Subject: Chin up, forge ahead!

Crocus Cottage
West Road
Wragby
Lincolnshire

Dear Angus,

I am sorry to hear that your relationship with Jenny has ended. I am sure you are feeling thoroughly miserable. I must be honest however and say that although I am sure she is a perfectly pleasant young woman, your descriptions of her do not indicate a huge commonality. I may be wrong but give that some thought.

In the meantime, keep your chin up and try not to take it out on anyone.

All the best,
Arthur

Clearly I'm already failing miserably at his last piece of advice.

The other 'enjoyable' part of the week was a brief altercation I had with Thobela Siwela's son Abbot, the new union shop steward. I went to the stores to fetch some white paint at the behest of Jacob – for painting the rocks that will mark out the corners of the firebreaks to be slashed by the tractor.

Abbot Siwela is a corpulent man with a severe bray (he has never been to Malmesbury). He therefore sounds a bit like the wookie from the *Star Wars* films. As I told his father, I hardly had anything to do with him last year. What I didn't tell his dad was that I did notice that although he was courteous and sometimes shared a joke, there was always something bitter behind his eyes. He was promoted to his current position when

putting spy cameras in the guest showers. Abbot has
_and of English and this combined with his devious
_red him promotion to the position of storeman and head
_. Since signing up most of the staff to the new union – the
ociation for National Comrades of the Revolution – he has
be_ _easingly belligerent.

I had fully intended to be polite – my purpose being to keep my nose clean for the next little while. So it was that I arrived at the stores to collect the paint for Jacob. Abbot's fiefdom is a warren of rooms added to each other haphazardly over the years as the lodge has grown. There is no natural light in it and I suspect that not even Abbot knows the full extent of what's in there. He has selected the most inaccessible room at the back of the maze for his office. I found him staring at his computer.

'Good afternoon Abbot,' I said.

'Come back at two o'clock; it is actually lunch break now.' He did not look up. I looked at my watch – it was 13h55.

'It's almost two,' I replied mustering a smile. 'I just need the white paint Jacob uses.'

'Actually, come back at two o'clock,' he snapped, clicking his teeth. 'It's lunch break now. I'm not a slave whatsoever.' Behind his chair on the wall was a certificate headered: 'Workers' Association for National Comrades of the Revolution – Official Shop Steward'. I looked at the certificate closely.

'Abbot, you know why I wouldn't sign up to your union?'

'Because you are actually not believing in our revolution.' He still didn't look up.

'No Abbot, it is because the acronym of your union alludes to masturbation.' This got his attention.

'In so forth as whatsoever are you saying?' he leapt out of his chair.

'W...A...N...C...R?' I spelt it out to him. Steam built in his head.

'I'll help myself to the paint. I saw it as I came in. Do have a nice day.' I walked out.

Dad just mailed to tell me that he, Mum, Dad and the Major are going to be in the area next week. They are staying with some friends on a citrus farm close to the mountains. Apparently Trubshaw has also been invited. They're going to come through for lunch before heading home, which should be fun.

Week 17

Ginger beer and gammon

For most of the week I was relatively at peace, this mainly as a result of full days out on the reserve marking, cutting and burning the firebreaks with Jacob, Bertie and Nhlanhla. This task, I have discovered, is one of the most important ones the conservation team performs. If it's done poorly, fires could threaten the lodge anytime from midwinter to the first rains. The near disaster we had last year was partly because Anton took it upon himself to do the firebreaks. Thankfully Jacob is in charge of this job now.

Creating effective firebreaks involves securing a 20-metre strip on the fringes of the borders that separate us from neighbouring properties. Then similar strips are created along a few strategic roads in the middle of the reserve. These strips provide safe points from which to start back burns or coordinate fire fighting (like we had to last year).

The first thing we did was drive the boundaries and place stones, painted white, at strategic points for Timot to follow with the tractor and mower. It took us the best part of two days to place all the stones. The first morning, we left the lodge just after the game drives, Jacob at the wheel, Nhlanhla next to him with Bertie and I in the load bin of the battered old Land Rover. We had the paint I had secured despite Abbot, pangas, lots of water and some packed lunches from O'Reilly.

'Good furr you guys goin out dere te protect the ludge,' he said handing us a large bag of goodies.

Normally the conservation guys just eat a huge meal on return from the field but I, not being made of such Spartan stuff, convinced O'Reilly to pack us some food. I think the other three were very pleased with my contribution to the day.

I'm not often out all day. In summer it's just too hot to be out at midday but come the autumn, temperatures are very pleasant at noon. The relative cool allows animals to move around during the middle of the day, more than they would do in summer. We had some wonderful sightings of general game and a really good view of a kudu bull posturing on a termite mound as Bertie and I painted a little cairn.

Lunch was consumed in the shade of a brown ivory tree, growing from a giant termite mound. We sat around the base and shared out sandwiches (roast beef and mustard, chicken and mayonnaise, ham and Swiss cheese), fruit (first oranges of the season) and bottles of O'Reilly's homemade ginger beer. This drink is probably the most refreshing thing that's ever passed my lips. After lunch Jacob informed us that we'd be having a rest for half an hour – this is very unusual and I can only put it down to the kick in O'Reilly's ginger beer.

We all found a patch of shade to settle in – some against the trunk of the tree and others just laid down in the grass. I chose a tall stand of Rhodes grass and watched as the tall inflorescences danced against the sky. A vulture scudded overhead, so high I could barely make it out. I felt nostalgic – remembering being a little boy, walking through the bush with my father one day, on a reserve not far from Sasekile. It was afternoon and the rest of the family was sleeping, much like the men around me. Dad and I went out to find a baobab tree that we'd seen on a drive that morning. We crossed a dry river bed and found the time-worn giant, perfect for climbing. It was probably the first time I noticed the peace of the wild infuse me.

After lunch the team continued, all still slightly light-headed from the ginger beer and I suspect wishing there'd been a lot more of it. We returned to camp just as the game drives were going out.

Once the mowing was complete, we had to burn the strips. The task is laborious at this time of the year because, while there hasn't been rain for about three weeks, the ground is still moist and the grass doesn't burn easily. We singe it by walking in zigzags with special dispensers that drip lighted paraffin onto the grass. I'm not skilled enough for this job so a few others and I walked slowly along behind the fire lighters beating out any logs or smouldering pieces of elephant dung.

During the burning, a tractor pulling a water bowser moves with the line. Jacob sits imperiously on top spraying out errant bits of flame. He also sprays members of the conservation crew that he doesn't believe to be pulling sufficient weight. There is much good-natured howling in protest when he does this – thankfully it's still hot in the middle of the day.

I had a really good time out with the conservation team. I can be as quiet or as chatty as I want and no one seems to mind – as long as I do my bit. Yesterday morning, I was leaning on my beater, trying to identify a firefinch I'd heard calling when a jet of water caught me in the middle of the back. The rest of the conservation crew thought this was thoroughly hilarious. None more so than Bertie who fell about until he too was blasted.

In the afternoons, Bertie and I continued with his lessons. On the day of our drenching, we went to the rangers' room via the Main Camp deck seeking a slice of cake. The guests were all out on drive so the staff were cleaning up the remnants of tea and setting the tables for the evening meal.

As we arrived, I saw the toadying Matto helping Jenny carry a buffet table into its position for dinner. Matto is possibly the most unhelpful turd I've ever come across. It was clear his only motive was Jenny. A certain amount of jealousy – okay more like a lightning-strength surge of anger – flashed through me. September was standing just near me.

'Angus, are you sick?' asked the portly Shangane with genuine concern.

'Quite possibly,' I replied. I left and Bertie fetched the cake.

The next afternoon did not improve my chances of regaining Jenny's affection. Mum, Dad and the Major arrived for a brief lunch at Tamboti Camp. I met them in the parking lot as they arrived. The back of Dad's Subaru Forester was misted up. As the car stopped in the shade of a mopane tree, two black nostrils pressed up against a side window, splitting the precipitation. Then they exhaled, re-misting the glass.

Trubshaw.

The back right door opened and the Major clambered out as fast as his ageing bones and muscles could propel him.

'My God, that bloody dog! He's a scalding nightmare!' he bellowed, causing Precious the chamber maid to drop her laundry as she walked past.

'Oh, he's not that bad!' said Dad climbing out.

'Dear, we all know he most certainly is that bad,' said Mum shutting her door. 'Darling, how are you?'

'Fine thanks Ma,' I said.

'Hello boy,' said Dad, 'we'll have to make this quite quick I'm afraid, don't want to leave T-man in the car on his own for too long.'

'Didn't you give him his tranquilisers?' I asked.

'Enough to knock out a hippo,' said Dad.

I climbed into the back seat to greet the over-excited staffie. He was separated from the back seat by a grill. I shut the back door and opened the little hatch to the boot. Trubshaw shot through it like a cannon ball and covered me in saliva and scratches. My plan was to say a quick hello, stuff him back through the hatch, open the windows a bit and then go and have a bite to eat.

At this moment the Major, alas, remembered he had forgotten his arrhythmia pills in the car. He pulled the door open, unaware that the hound was free in the back seat. A new world opened up to Trubshaw and he had no intention of missing out. He barrelled out over the Major, knocking him to the ground and exploding into the lowveld.

'Trubshaw!' screamed Dad as his best friend disappeared like a bullet down the path towards the Main Camp deck. 'Oh shit, TRUUUUBSHAAAAW!'

'Oh God,' said Mum, holding her hand to her mouth.

'Bloody foul animal!' yelled the Major from the dust.

I turned and ran down the path, which was littered with a trail of destruction. The first victim was Precious. I found her halfway up a tree, her laundry spilled on the floor covered in muddy paw prints. I didn't stop to help because I could hear startled shouts coming from the deck. I ran over the small bridge that crosses a stream feeding the Tsesebe. Glass and sliced lemon covered the wooden slats; Calvin the butler was just clambering out of the mud below. I continued down the thick tree-lined avenue; the Main Camp deck's double doors in front of me. When you emerge from the trees onto the deck, the effect is startling because you are presented with a stunning view north over the Tsesebe River.

I wasn't concerned with the view, however. I was rather more concerned with the fact that Trubshaw had chased a tree squirrel onto the deck. The rodent could find nothing to climb so it leapt onto the buffet table. Trubshaw followed at top speed and I watched in horror as the dog and his quarry ran the length of the table. The squirrel dodged neatly between the bowls, glasses, cutlery and crockery. The hound didn't bother. Salads, loaves, cheese, rolls, jams, jugs of juice and a bowl of fruit flew into the air and over the side of the table as the unstoppable cannon ball careened after the alarmed squirrel.

At the end of the table the squirrel leapt across to a wooden pillar and then onto a cross beam above the deck. Trubshaw followed at ground level, scattering screaming guests, tables, chairs and glasses. A few of the butlers who, up until this point, had been too startled to move, gave chase. This only exacerbated the situation. The dog forgot the squirrel and engaged fully in the new game with the butlers. Clifford tried to flick him with a dish towel but the dog was too fast. He swung round, grabbed the towel and yanked. Clifford, who is a tiny man, was jerked clean off his feet. He was summarily covered in slobber.

Jenny and September emerged onto the deck at a run, drawn by the commotion. As I saw her, Trubshaw returned to the destroyed buffet table and helped himself to a side of gammon.

Jenny was speechless for a few seconds. She recognised the dog and then saw me. This galvanised her.

'Angus! What the f...?' She remembered her guests. 'What is that goddamn thing doing in here?'

'Yo yo yo yo!' said Clifford pointing. Trubshaw, atop the table with the gammon in his jaws, stepped deftly into the strawberry pavlova (the only untouched item on the buffet), ran the length of the debris-strewn table, jumped off and made for the entrance he'd come through. Dad, Mum and SB arrived in time to grab him as he emerged from the doors. My father then tried to pry the gammon from his dog's mouth but all he succeeded in doing was suspending the animal from his jaws. A brief wrestling match ensued – in full view of the Main Camp guests.

'Leave, Trubshaw, LEEEAVE!' said Dad. He had the gammon at both ends with the dog's jaws clamped around the middle. 'Oh for God's sake let go!'

'Grrrrrrr!' said Trubshaw, his tail wagging like a propeller.

Eventually, SB took the hound's back end and they manhandled him to the car. Dad was puce with rage. Mum was the same with embarrassment.

'Jenny, hello...um I'm so dreadfully sorry,' she said and disappeared quickly after the others. I was standing next to the buffet table. Silence descended. September had his hands on his head. The Main Camp deck looked like a bomb site.

I looked at Jenny who was shaking her head, wanting desperately to explode at me. It was the creamy tracks leading from the pavlova to the end of the table that set me off. A terrible case of the giggles began in my belly until I could hold it no longer. Tears started streaming down my face. The more I tried to stop, the more I laughed.

'Angus, no! Not now! It is not even a little bit funny!' Jenny shouted. This, of course, made it twice as amusing. I wanted to apologise to the guests. I turned to face them.

'I'm so s...' but I got no further. I had to just walk out, howling all the way back to the car park. As I left, I heard an English guest say, 'Not funny, Jennifer? That's the funniest thing I've seen in ten years! Bravo!'

Mum, Dad and Major didn't stay for lunch. Trubshaw had his meal in the car. I'm told that the gammon-fuelled gas that came out of him on the way home singed the remaining hairs off the Major's head.

PJ had just arrived back from leave so SB and I went to confess Trubshaw's sins to him before anyone else could. He found the story hilarious but cautioned that we had both better go and apologise to September and Jenny. He said he would deal with any guest complaints.

We chose to split that responsibility, knowing that Jenny would probably stab me. I collected a bottle of Jameson from my room and took it to September as a peace offering. He accepted my apology graciously. He then asked that I tell my parents that they were welcome on his deck at any time but that their dog was not – ever. I said I thought this was very fair and we parted on good terms.

Apparently SB's meeting with Jenny was less cordial. She blamed me for the incident and said that my conduct afterwards was 'immature, rude and unacceptable'. I seem to have become the chosen vector for the venting of her frustrations. Funny how that works.

Week 18

Cooling and courting

The weather is cooling and most of the migratory birds have left or are in the process of packing their bags. The cuckoos, the Wahlberg's eagles and the diminutive willow-warblers are heading north for the winter. There's much of me that would like to be heading out with the last of the bee-eaters despite the pleasantness of the 'cold season' here. I am profoundly irritated with my inability to forget about Jenny – even writing her name irritates me.

The general blackness of my mood is not being helped by the insufferable Matto. He went on his second assessment drive early yesterday morning and passed. I wasn't part of the assessment team so I'm not sure how good or bad he really is. Although already pushing stratospheric levels before the drive, his arrogance is now reaching for the boundaries of the known universe.

I was in the rangers' room cleaning my rifle on the morning after his drive. He strutted in like a peacock, smelling of Hugo Boss, blond hair perfectly styled, uniform spotless, face immaculately shaven and moisturised, jersey tied around his shoulders. He reminded me of one of those pristine but plastic-looking men in a 'Nivea for men' commercial.

'Morning Mac,' he said slumping down on one of the sofas.

'Morning Nivea Man,' I replied. Carrie's office chair creaked, I looked over at her and she lifted an authoritative finger at me. Without taking my eyes off her I continued, 'and may I offer my heartiest congratulations to you on this the morning of your assessment drive success.' I smiled at Carrie who turned back to her desk.

'Like I said, not rocket science,' Matto replied, ignoring my sarcasm and picking up a magazine. At this point Jeff the Genius walked into the room from his game drive, full of gormless bonhomie and enthusiasm.

'Hey Matto! Well done man! Super cool that you passed!' he walked over to the reclining Nivea Man and slapped him heartily on the shoulder. 'Can't wait to work with you out in the field!' Matto muttered perfunctory thanks and returned to the *Men's Health*.

I left soon thereafter as Jeff launched into an animated and confused monologue on the behaviour of the rutting impala he'd seen on drive.

The loathsome Nivea Man is now courting Jenny. This is driving me slightly mental. Of course, there's no reason that they shouldn't be together but the thought of being passed up for that conceited trust-fund chop makes my heart rate increase to dangerous levels. The day after he passed his drive, he was given his first real guests. They were operating out of Main Camp where I had also been assigned the responsibility of driving a surprisingly pleasant old Scottish couple on a private Land Rover.

I met my guests, served them some tea and a large slice of carrot cake each. I took them over to a table in the corner of the deck and asked them why they'd come to Africa and what they wanted to see. As Fergus began to explain, his voice floated off. I watched Jenny arrive on the deck. She was dressed in a white Sasekile shirt that hugged her figure and a pair of shorts that showed off her legs. Her hair was tied up, accentuating her gerenuk neck. I put my fork full of carrot cake down and swallowed.

'...So we do like to see birds...' Fergus's words wafted back into my consciousness and then out again as the Nivea Man emerged onto the deck. He strutted over to the tea table where Jenny was serving his guests and confidently introduced himself. He said something that made them all chuckle. In that moment, Sasekile's newest ranger deftly moved his hand into the small off Jenny's back – just for a second. I nearly puked onto Fergus's plate.

That night, I lay in my bed staring at the ceiling, heart thrashing in my chest as images of Matto and Jenny entwined rushed to mind. Eventually I had to get up and take two (maybe three, okay four) large gulps from a bottle of Famous Grouse. This calmed me slightly and I eventually fell into a fitful sleep.

Mine has not been the only emotional turmoil in camp this week although the latest incident did worsen my mood. Amber and The Legend have officially broken up. The former is utterly distraught. The Legend on the other hand appears to be rather too chipper with life and the fact that he's heading to Johannesburg for his leave in a few weeks' time instead of on some exotic holiday is not good news. I strongly suspect that he's going to meet with my sister.

Nivea Man courting my ex-girlfriend and The Legend courting my sister – brilliant.

Julia, of course, will tell me nothing. This was the response she sent to my last email.

To: Angus
From: Julia MacNaughton
Subject: Mind your own business

Hello Angus,

Thanks for your last mail – well, most of it anyway. I still really enjoy hearing about your experiences in the bush and I am really sorry that things with Jenny are the way they are. It must be just horrendous for you to, as you put it, 'witness the coming of her inevitable violation by the Nivea Man'. That said, I really think it's more a case of a bruised ego than anything else – but perhaps I am wrong. She's great but really not your type. I think you were in love with the idea of it all; you're sore about not having been able to make the idea work, not sore about her.

I did not, however, appreciate your digging for information about my interactions with Alistair. Because you are so completely biased in your judgement of him and cannot mention his name without some sort of childish dig, I do not feel the need or desire to tell you anything about my conversations with him. I'll thank you not to ask me about any potential liaison until you can be a bit more mature about it.

I believe you're on leave soon … any cool plans?

Love,
Jules

Bloody annoying. Something is going on and it's made more obvious by the fact that my brother and sister are clearly in cahoots. Shortly after receiving the above I went to Tamboti Camp to find my other sibling.

The camp was quiet as the guests were in their rooms sleeping off the effects of the early morning and some giant breakfasts. The butlers were just clearing the last of the buffet.

'Good morning Redman,' I greeted the man I consider to be the finest butler in the lowveld.

'Yes, indeed, how are you Angus?' he asked. We exchanged a few pleasantries and I asked the whereabouts of SB. Redman shook his head sadly.

'Eish – in the wine cellar with that girl, crying crying crying!' I thanked him and made for the hatch leading to the sub-deck cellar.

Snuffling sobs floated up to the top of the steps. I wandered down to find SB and Amber sitting on one of the old leather sofas. She was leaning forward, hands over face, elbows on knees, howling as if she'd just witnessed a massacre. I enjoy her about as much as I might a rabid puff adder in my bed so I didn't feel a great sense of empathy. The same cannot be said for my soft-headed sibling. He was sitting next to her, his hand on her shuddering back.

'… It's okay. I know it's shitty now, but you'll feel better soon. You just need to stay positive and focus on your work.'

SB has clearly learnt little during his relationship with Simone. There is one thing that I have garnered in the time I've spent with women – it is unwise to ever offer practical advice to a distraught female. Solutions are best discussed after tears.

Anyway, Amber was wallowing too deeply in her misery to notice.

'String Bean,' I said. This gave him a bit of a shock and he took his hand off Amber.

'Angus,' he said, standing up. The guilty look on his face reminded me of Simone's jealousy of Amber's apparent designs on SB when the she arrived late last year.

'Could I have a word?' He nodded and we left the cellar as the pathetic sobbing continued with renewed vigour. 'What's going on with The Legend and Julia?' I came straight to the point as we topped the steps onto the Tamboti deck. SB looked awkward for the second time in less than five minutes.

'Nothing that I'm aware of,' he said pretending to search for the black-headed oriole that was calling in the sausage tree below the deck.

'String Bean, you are a terrible liar. Now tell me what the hell's going on?'

'I don't know Angus, why don't you ask her?' he snapped. 'It's none of your business anyway,' he continued.

'I have asked her but she's being cagier than a Russian spy and I now know that you know something.'

'Angus, I've got stuff to do.' He looked back at me impatiently, arms folded. I raised my eyebrows and looked down to the cellar.

'Really?'

'Really,' he said.

That afternoon, a certain amount of peace returned. I was still driving the two Scots for whom I'd developed some affection. They were fascinated by everything that I told them and they loved walking. We drove out after tea and found some fresh rhino tracks at a muddy waterhole. I suggested that Fergus try to track the rhino with Elvis's help and he thought this a wonderful idea. Fergus and Alisa are both in their early 80s so it was a bit of a risk but they were pretty fit if not particularly supple.

So we began; Elvis and Fergus walking slowly in the front, then me with the rifle and Alisa just behind me. Following rhino after they've been sleeping in a wallow is an excellent way to learn how to track because they leave mud everywhere. Elvis silently put Fergus to the task. He pointed out the direction and Fergus then attempted to follow. After a few moments the old man stopped. Elvis pointed at a fallen trunk, there was fresh mud scraped along the bark-stripped wood.

'Touch,' Elvis whispered beckoning Fergus and Alisa. They did as they were bid and ran their fingers over the mud. A large strip came off in Fergus's hand and he balled it in his fingers, grinning.

'It's still wet!' he said.

'Hush Fergus,' hissed his wife, looking around.

Elvis put his charge back on the tracks. After about an hour of very slow tracking we came to the top of a gentle slope. Elvis and I spotted the rhino bull grazing some way down the slope but our guests were so enthralled by their searching for signs on the ground that they failed to notice the two-tonne animal standing out in the open. I tapped Fergus on the shoulder. He looked up.

'There it is!' he whispered.

'So it is!' said Alisa.

There was no wind to speak of and the setting sun was behind us so we remained out in the open, the bull grazing slowly away from us, the warmth on our backs. I breathed in deeply, absorbing the atmosphere. I smelled the touch of autumn in the air and listened to the diminuendo of evening birdsong. I reached down to touch the long grass at my knees, picked a culm and chewed it, savouring the salty sweet sap.

Life's not all bad.

As soon as the sun went down, a distinct chill wove through the air and I had to pull a jersey on for the first time this year.

Marx and moron

I am going on leave tomorrow and I have agreed to go on a trip down the Orange River with a few of the staff (Sipho, Duncan, Kerry and Brandon). That will take a week and I'm then going to visit Uncle Charles and Aunt Bridget in Hermanus for the remaining seven days. I am really looking forward to it.

Jenny arrived at my room a few days ago just before lunch. I was doing my press-ups in some aged Woolworths cotton briefs – with holes in the crotch. She knocked once and just walked in. I was facing away from the door so she received a view of my nethers she wasn't expecting.

'Angus!'

I flopped onto the floor, turned over and sat up. 'Yes?' I said, the irrational part of me convinced she'd come to suggest we give it another go.

'That's so gross!'

The rational part of me bashed its irrational counterpart out of the way. 'This, I believe, is *my* room in which I am allowed to dress as I please,' I snapped, standing up and reaching for a pair of shorts. 'Can I help you?'

'I'm looking for Clifford. Just thought I'd come and say hi on my way past.' She leant against the door frame and pushed her hair back over her right ear with the aerial of her radio. 'How're things?'

'Alright thanks. You?'

ɔol,' she replied with a shrug.

suffering under the immeasurable strain of living in Hades I see?' I picked up a bottle of water and took a long sip. Before she could reply, I saw Clifford walking past behind her. 'Clifford's behind you.' She looked over her shoulder and called him. He bustled over and the two of them engaged in an increasingly animated discussion until she moved out of the door with him.

'Thanks for the chat,' she said and they disappeared. I struggled to continue with my exercises after that. I've been waiting for a knock on my door ever since. Yesterday, it came – at around the same time and my heart beat a bit quicker but the knuckles were too heavy to be Jenny's. Instead, my alcoholic neighbour, Petrus, appeared as I opened the door. His breath smelt like rancid milk stout. He looked at me blearily and asked if he might 'borrow' ten rand.

'Petrus,' I replied, 'borrow implies that you have some intention of repaying me. Given that this is the fourth time you have *borrowed* money, I'm going to decline your request.' He stared at me. 'But I'll *give* you ten rand and then I can live next to you without expectation leading to resentment. How's that?' The confused stare remained. I went over to a drawer, pulled a note from it and handed it to him.

'Thenk yhooo!' he said exhaling heavily into my face. My eyes stung.

The afternoon after the Scots left, I had my second altercation with Abbot Siwela.

I had the afternoon off so Carrie asked me to help her hang up a new whiteboard – she promised to buy me a beer afterwards for my troubles. So at 16h30 I met her outside the rangers' room. She was measuring where to drill the holes. I held the enormous board while she drew on the wall with a builder's pencil. (Carrie is the only woman I know who owns a builder's pencil – well, she might be the only person, full stop.) It was bloody heavy and I was shaking by the end of it.

'Hold it still, Angus!' she admonished.

'Yes ma'am,' I replied, teeth clenched. 'I'm trying!' Eventually she finished and helped me lower the board.

'I have to make a quick phone call, would you mind going to fetch a drill and some screws from Abbot?'

'Sure,' I replied and headed off towards the stores – fiefdom of Abbot Siwela.

I found Abbot in his office on the telephone, his feet up on his desk. He has painted his command centre pristine white and there is now a drawing of Karl Marx next to his shop steward's certificate. I don't recall ever seeing pictures of old Karl looking quite so dark-skinned.

Abbot hastily removed his feet from the desk and his tone became extremely official as I walked in. I waited patiently for him to end his conversation which was very clearly of a personal nature. After five minutes, I walked out and eventually found the cage where the tools are kept. I was helping myself to a drill when Abbot stormed up behind me.

'What are you doing?' he screamed, his fat cheeks wobbling. I turned to look at him.

'Why are you shouting?' I said, trying not to laugh.

'Actually this is *my* office and no one can in so forth as come in here and take *my* equipment whatsoever!' Sweat formed on his brow as he ranted. I sighed.

'Abbot, you were on the phone, I'm in a hurry. I need a drill.'

'Actually you must wait for me to finish on the phone! I am the boss here!' I picked up the drill and brushed past him.

'Get out of my way you absurdly-stupid little man,' I said and left. There was a lot of shouting after that but I didn't hang about to hear the words.

'What took you so long?' asked Carrie as I arrived.

'Abbot,' I said. She nodded.

As I was fixing the bit into the front of the drill, Kerry and Jane arrived with a small cooler box and a packet of biltong.

'We'll go into the bush as soon as we're finished here,' said Carrie. Jane then helped me hold the board in place while Carrie drilled the holes and knocked the self-tapping screws into the wall. Kerry sat on the stair next to the door and lit up a cigarillo.

'Angus, why are you not drilling the holes?' she asked as Carrie moved her ladder.

'Because the strongest labourer in the workforce always operates the power tools,' I replied. She laughed.

Satisfied with our work, Carrie suggested I fetch a Land Rover so that we could head into the bush to consume the contents of the cooler box. A little while later I parked the vehicle on a dam wall not far from camp. Kerry was sitting next to me while Carrie and Jane sat on the seat behind us. There was a pod of six hippos in the water below with a tiny calf standing on its mother's back. On the other side of the dam, a grey heron waited patiently in the shallows and a little covey of crested francolin pecked about in the short grass and dry elephant dung.

We sat drinking in silence, listening to a flock of babblers in the bush below the dam wall and the 'pppffff' of the hippo as they opened their great nostrils. The only other sound was the rustling of the brown bag as we removed chunks of biltong. After a little while Kerry asked, 'So Angus, what's the vibe with you and Jenny?'

I turned to her. 'What are you talking about?'

'Its okay dude, don't get mad. What's going on? Have you moved on, still upset, found another bird, crying yourself to sleep at night...? Tell us, we're your friends.' Although there was teasing in her voice, I realised that she was right. Carrie – although there are lines that may never be crossed – has become a friend. So too have her lover (with whom she was being openly but subtly affectionate in my presence) and Kerry.

'Jenny and I are best friends for life,' I muttered pulling the lid off a fresh Heineken.

The babblers landed on the road in front of us, squabbling.

We sat in silence for the next half hour as the darkness gathered and the hippos slowly emerged from the safety of the water to graze; the calf in the middle of the group.

The next morning, I went for a walk on my own. I took a flask of coffee and some rusks and headed out into the dawn; crossed north over the river and spent an hour sitting on a koppie reading a book, looking at the birds and drinking my coffee. It was blissful if a little chilly.

When I returned to camp, I noticed the black BMW of the WANCRs waiting outside the office. As I walked past PJ's door, it opened and he beckoned me.

Shortly thereafter I found myself sitting in a meeting with two shiny-suited WANCRs and Abbot. PJ looked extremely uncomfortable. He introduced me to the suited officials and then sat down. He explained that there had been a complaint of racism against me which he was obliged to clear up.

'Racism towards whom exactly?' I asked.

'Against me!' yelled Abbot.

'Be calm, my comrade,' said Suit 1.

'I'm sorry, I'm deeply confused,' I said. Suit 2, who had more oil in his hair than a V8, sniffed.

'Comrade Abbot, our shop steward, actually tells us that you made a racist remark to him yesterday afternoon. The attack took place in the afternoon. It is not acceptable to be a racist in the workplace.'

PJ said, 'Could we just come to the point? What exactly is Angus alleged to have said?'

'He tells me I am stupid!' yelled Abbot again. 'I'm not stupid! I'm a shop steward.' The suits looked at me.

'Is this true Angus?' asked PJ.

'Almost,' I said, 'more precisely, I think I called him an absurdly-stupid little man.'

'You see!' Suit 1 leapt out of his seat. 'We demand this man be dismissed!'

'Please remain calm and sit down,' said PJ. I could see the General Manager was tired and irritated but in a difficult position because the WANCRs have signed up more than 50 per cent of the staff. He is therefore obliged to take them seriously. I felt no such obligation.

'Abbot, I call people stupid all the time – white and black. I may be an offensive person but I'm not a racist. Perhaps I was just put out by your generally foul and unaccommodating disposition. I'm sorry I called you stupid, for this is probably inaccurate.' I let the silence hang before continuing. 'I should perhaps have called you an unhelpful, fat shithead instead, but that still would not constitute any form of racism.'

'That's enough Angus!' snapped PJ.

'You must show respect for our shop steward!' bellowed Suit 1.

When everyone had calmed down, PJ asked me why I had said what I had and I gave my side of the story. He told the WANCRs that he could find no evidence of racism. He also told them that a number of staff, black and white, had complained about Abbot. There was some officious jargon spoken and then, eventually, they all left when PJ assured them he'd talk to me about the way I address other staff. He asked me to remain behind.

'Angus, please, I'm staring down the barrel of a wage strike right now. Don't stir up any more trouble, especially with Abbot.' The tension made him look older than his 43 years – a bit jowly and drawn. I left as he returned to his computer with furrowed brow.

Other news from the week is that Simone is moving into camp management. She has had enough of looking after kids and Amber is not coping – especially since The Legend gave her the boot. This means we're on the lookout for another childminder. Perhaps I should volunteer.

Now I shall pack my bags and prepare for my trip down South Africa's longest river. I'm looking forward to it but I believe it'll be freezing at night. We're all travelling in Brandon's double cab. My role on the trip is to bring music. I've appointed myself to this task because everyone else here thinks that music is what is played on Jacaranda FM.

Week 20

River and relaxation

It has been a blissful week, paddling gently down the Orange River, flopping into the water during the heat of the day and negotiating some good rapids. There isn't the same sort of white water that nearly drowned me on the Zambezi at the end of last year but it was great fun. I managed not to fight with any of my travelling companions – once we'd established that I was not, under any circumstances, going to wear 'Team Orange' gear or be referred to as a 'Team Orange' member.

The trip there was torturously long with five of us in the double cab and all our clobber in the back – a full east-west traverse of the country. We left at dawn, passing through Johannesburg to pick up a few supplies around mid-morning. I had a brief tea with Mum during which time she lamented the state of my relationship with Julia.

'Angus, I do wish you'd make up with your sister, you know I hate it when you fight,' she said, taking a bite of her anchovy toast which AIDS Cat had just licked.

'Mum, she has taken offence to my prying into her affairs,' I replied, 'she can't see that I'm doing it for her own good.'

'Darling, it might occur to you one day that Julia has her own best interests at heart.'

'If that were the case Mother, Alistair The Legend Jones wouldn't be having a look in. She has a generally appalling taste in men. Just look at that bloody awful metrosexual she was seeing earlier this year.'

I changed the subject after that and then went to find my sleeping bag in the garage. Unfortunately, it reeked of cat's pee. When I told Mum she said, 'Oh, I thought I saw the neighbour's cat wandering in there a little while back.' Then, before I could say anything, she added, 'And don't you dare think about blaming Phoebe – and I wish you'd stop calling her AIDS Cat. It's not good for her self-esteem.'

The upshot of this was that I was forced to take the Major's old sleeping bag – probably last used just prior to the Napoleonic Wars. It was so threadbare that it fitted quite comfortably into a shopping bag. The rest of 'Team Orange' (can't believe I've just used the term), thought my equipment was hilarious.

From Johannesburg we travelled through some lesser-visited South African towns. These included the late Eugene Terre'Blanche's backwater of Ventersdorp, then Kuruman, Upington, Pofadder (always wanted to go there) and Springbok. We spent the night at a B&B in Upington – a sparse affair that Brandon found. I slept in a room with Sipho and Kerry. The former made constant jokes about that fact that Upington is not a place for people of his skin tone. Every time he went near the window, he ducked down citing a fear of separatist Boer snipers.

At breakfast the next morning it was clear that Sipho's fears were not necessarily misplaced. The looks our little group received from the mostly large and two-toned shirted residents of the B&B weren't entirely welcoming.

After an ice-cream in Pofadder, we pushed through to the border and arrived at the base camp by mid-afternoon. The old place was constructed of stone and had a fully-stocked bar which we decided to make use of almost immediately. Then we sat on the banks of the river, looking at the South African side where a similar canoe safari operation was situated. Brandon and Sipho tossed lines into the water and we all drank a great deal of beer.

During the afternoon, two other groups of intrepid paddlers arrived – two couples from Saldanha Bay and seven first-year students from Stellenbosch. The latter brought enough turbo-lettuce to supply the population of Kingston for at least a year. They were, therefore, thoroughly stoned for most of the trip.

We went to bed fairly early mainly because we'd been [in the] sun from 15h00. I say bed but we actually just lay under [our] sleeping bags. The temperature plummeted during the n[ight. I] put just about all my clothing on as the Major's sleepi[ng bag proved to] be somewhere between useless and pointless. My rest was not aided by Brandon from whose adenoids a sound like the chainsaws of the apocalypse emanated.

The next morning it was out onto the river in inflatable canoes – two people to a boat with their belongings in a large waterproof bag at the front. We had two cooler boxes with us that carried our booze supply and some of the food for the group. Our guide, Livingstone, was a wiry man with a brilliant sense of humour – he could not explain how his Xhosa parents came to name him. His sidekick, Jacobus, was a slow-witted fellow of few words. I wasn't surprised to hear that his parents are the owners of Orange River Tours – our hosts for the week. I'd have been equally unsurprised to find that his parents were closely related – such was the faraway look in Jacobus's eyes.

I shared a canoe with one of the students. Francis was comfortably the laziest boatman on the water that week. She was a thin girl with a pretty face, an attractive figure and some nasty blonde dreadlocks. A slight wiff of BO surrounded her. She also had four holes in each ear, one in her tongue, one in her left eyebrow and, she told me, one down there. Predictably she is studying fine art and considers herself a modern-day flower child. She was pleasant enough despite squealing loudly all the way down every rapid.

We capsized into the first white water because Francis dropped her paddle, leaving the front part of our craft without steering. Team Orange thought this very funny especially when I fell in again while trying to haul my partner and her bedraggled dreadlocks back into the boat.

The best thing about Francis was the fact that she was happy to be silent for long periods (she lay in the front of the boat while I paddled). I really enjoyed moving gently down the river, looking at the rock formations and the scree-covered hills. On the first day, I spotted a pair of black eagles which I pointed out to Francis. She was most impressed until she heard that they kill dassies by dropping them onto the rocks from a great height.

In the evenings we simply stopped and camped on the bank under the clear (cold), starry sky. Livingstone cooked us a basic but tasty meal and then we all sat around the fire talking and drinking. The students were entertaining and jovial (possibly because they were stoned). The two couples from Saldanha Bay were Cape Afrikaners, and very pleasant. Willie, a coastal engineer, might be the most sarcastic person that I've ever met so we played off each other to the hilarity of the others.

On our second morning, we discovered that Jacobus has at least one talent – the baking of bread in a subterranean oven. Every morning he woke up well before dawn, set a fire, dug a special hole and then, while the coals were forming, he made the dough. The product of his labours was, without question, the best bread I've ever tasted.

And so the days went lazily by and I thought about Jenny a bit and Anna was also in my thoughts often – completely different people. Melancholy seldom overtook me because the company was good, the scenery beautiful and the atmosphere totally relaxed.

We passed a few diamond mines (some deserted, some almost intact and others still active) and a few fruit farms that survive only because the river is there – rainfall is extremely erratic and minimal. We also passed a number of local fishermen, one of whom had caught himself a catfish six-feet-long. We moored our boats next to him and all had pictures taken with the giant fish and its captor.

Each evening, when we'd moored the boats and helped gather wood for the fire, Sipho and I headed up into the scree-covered hills to find a high spot from where we could look into South Africa and Namibia. The river is a ribbon of green in a barren land. I particularly enjoyed this time with Sipho. My view of how other people see the world has changed so many times since moving to Sasekile and working with such a wide cross-section of South African society.

Sipho, aged 29, is remarkable. He has little formal education but with a determination that beggars belief he re-did his matric via correspondence a few years ago and, at the end of this year, will write his final exams for a diploma in conservation. He's done all of this while working to support eight relatives and two children. He hopes one day to move into research but I think he's making a better living as a ranger than he ever would as a researcher – Sipho is one of Sasekile's highest tip earners (the opposite of me).

On our last night, Livingstone prepared a delicious potjie and we sat around the fire chatting for hours after eating it. It was the coldest night that we'd experienced and the thought of climbing into the Major's sleeping bag wasn't comforting, so I had no intention of leaving the fire before I absolutely had to. So it was that I found myself sitting with Jacobus and Kerry by the time everyone else had retired. We tried to engage the cretinous fellow in conversation but he had little to say, and was only allowed to sleep when the last of us laid our heads down, so eventually Kerry and I wished him a good night and left the fire.

'You're going to freeze tonight,' she said as we began climbing into our sleeping bags.

'In all likelihood, yes,' I replied pulling a beanie onto my head.

'You can share my sleeping bag if you like,' she said, 'it's quite roomy in here.'

'Really?' I replied, not sure if she was being serious.

'Your choice.' She lay down and zipped up. I attempted to do the same but when my foot went clean through the base of the Major's ropey bag, I climbed out and rolled over to where Kerry lay.

'Open up,' I said. She giggled and the zip opened. I moved in next to her and she re-closed the zip behind my back. In the confined space, we moved about until we were spooning.

'This arrangement is out of concern for your health only,' she said.

'Your magnanimity knows no bounds. Night night,' I replied.

'I don't even know what that means. Sleep tight.'

It was marvellously warm in there and I fell asleep almost instantly, waking just before dawn with dark red hair tickling my nose, my right arm numb under Kerry's shoulder. I lay there for a few minutes considering my position. Kerry is a beautiful girl, no doubt, but I can't see us ever in a relationship and I'm pretty sure she feels the same. Still, it was very comfortable having her lying there next to me.

Eventually I climbed out of the bag into the chill of the dawn. At a secluded part of the river, I cleaned my teeth and then decided to brave the water. I removed my warm clothes and stepped through the undisturbed surface. Gritting my teeth, I descended slowly into the liquid which was surprisingly warm given the outside temperature. I swam out into the thin mist hanging over the water. When I'd had enough, I dried quickly, revelling in the numb warmth that envelops the body after a cold swim. Back in the dawn-lit camp the others were just stirring as the aroma of Jacobus's wizardry began to waft out over the camp.

I felt thoroughly content at the thought of some coffee, the best bread on Earth and a day on the river.

We crossed the border back into South Africa late this afternoon and we're currently holed up in a B&B in Springbok. Sipho and I are sharing a room and he is currently giving a loud rendition of *Umshini Wam'* from the shower – he seems to have forgotten his fear of separatist militias.

Tomorrow we're driving through to the Cape. Sipho is going to stay with some guests of his who live in Bishopscourt, Kerry is staying with her family and the other two are being put up by Duncan's friends on a wine farm while I head for Hermanus.

Week 21

Train and tears

My second week of leave was, on the whole, extremely enjoyable. Uncle Charles and Aunt Bridget treated me royally. Each morning, Walter and I went down to the beach (regardless of weather) with their beautifully-behaved retriever for a brisk walk and a quick swim. Trubshaw could learn a lot from this dog; sadly Trubshaw is incapable of learning.

During the week, we visited some of the wine farms in the area and walked most of the mountains flat. Aunt Bridget is a wonderful cook and I'm not sure that I've ever eaten quite as much as I did during the five days I spent with them. Nor have I engaged in so much exercise – wind, rain or sun, we were out on the mountains or the beach.

Just after lunch on my first day in Hermanus, I received an email from SB.

To: Angus
From: Hugh MacNaughton
Subject: Bits and pieces from Sasekile

Hey Angus,

Hope things are good with you – that you didn't drown anyone on the Orange.

Simone's camp management training is going pretty well but she doesn't like Amber much. PJ has decided that they will both run Kingfisher Camp, with Melissa moving to Rhino Camp. I'm not sure how well they're going to work together with Simone as the junior. She's due to start there pretty soon. My girlfriend is convinced that Amber is after me and that I don't think it's a bad idea. Well, Amber has been quite flirty but she sees me as a mentor so I can't tell her to stop coming to see me given her very tender emotional state at the moment.

PJ has finally convinced the owners that it's time we built a spa and hire a massage therapist. Not having this facility has meant that we are seriously falling behind our competitors. Allegra is the new employee. She is a qualified therapist and arrived this week. She's going to help with the set up and design of the new facility and until it's built she'll double as the childminder now that Simone is in camp.

Allegra is about 24 and has dark shortish hair – I think she's only about five-foot-three. She arrived yesterday and takes no nonsense. Matto sat down next to her at dinner last night and started talking immediately.

'How you settling in, Allegra?' he said.

'Fine thanks,' she said bluntly.

'Cool, nice to have you with us. Let me know if there's anything I can do to help settle you in.' She laid down her knife and fork and looked up at him.

'Who are you again?' Matto looked a bit surprised that she hadn't remembered him from lunch.

'Matthew, Matto to my mates,' he said.

'Oh yes, the junior ranger.'

'Ouch,' said Jamie.

'Matthew, thank you for the offer, loaded as it is, but I'll be just fine on my own.' She carried on eating next to Matto who didn't say anything after that.

Other than that, the big news of the week is that we've started planning for the owners' visit at the end of June. It's Nicolette's 60th birthday and she's taken out all four camps so there's lots of excitement. After the success of the YMS group last year, I've been put in charge of planning with Jenny again so there is much to do!

See you soon,
Hugh

I was delighted to read that Matto was put firmly in his place. I think Allegra and I will get on famously.

The highlight of my second week of leave was a train trip up from the Cape. Brandon, through a guest connection, managed to wangle us some special rates on South African Railways Premier Classe. We drove down to the station, parked Brandon's weathered double cab, handed the keys over to a valet and climbed aboard. Duncan had flown home a few days earlier so it was just the four of us in a family compartment – a bit cramped but very comfortable.

When we left the Cape there was a storm blowing in but as the train forged into the Karoo, the weather cleared and I spent many hours alternating between reading and staring out of the window. We ordered our first G&Ts at about 12h00 which made the scenery outside even more impressive. Lunch, with two bottles of First Sighting shiraz, was a tasty affair and by the time we rolled back to our compartment, we were ready for a snooze. The beds weren't made up so we just sat and dozed with our feet on the benches opposite.

I woke up at around 16h30 and took myself off to the dining car to have some tea and scones; I sat there reading until the sun set as we rolled into

Beaufort West. For dinner, we donned the best outfits we could muster and headed through to the dining car for an excellent meal of fillet with fresh veggies, a bottle of Secateurs red and some Glenfiddich afterwards. Kerry excused herself as the second whiskies arrived and went off to ready herself for bed.

The nightcap drained, Brandon and Sipho went off to check on the double cab and I went back to the compartment. I opened the door and saw Kerry staring at the rising half-moon, dressed in a huge old T-shirt making do as a nighty. The window was open, the freezing air filling the compartment. She didn't hear me come in for the noise of the air rushing past.

'Is hypothermia not a concern to gingers?' I said. She snapped out of her funk, pushed the window closed and then turned around wiping her eyes, which were swollen and red. 'What's the matter?' I asked.

'Oh, not much,' she said, 'I don't want to talk about it.'

'Okay,' I said. Suddenly she came across the compartment and put her arms around me. I felt a bit awkward as she started to sob.

'What's it?' I asked, reciprocating her embrace. She didn't say anything; she just stood there and wept. Eventually the sobbing subsided. She pulled away from me, climbed into one of the beds and I tucked her in. She turned to face the bulkhead and fell asleep almost instantly. In the morning she was back to her cheerful self and I didn't have a chance to ask her about it again as the other two were with us until we arrived at Park Station. She was picked up by a friend as soon as we arrived.

I felt thoroughly rested and relatively happy after my time away. Trubshaw was ecstatic to see me and we had a good wrestle on the lawn as I arrived home.

'Darling, I do wish you wouldn't rile him up so! The family's coming for lunch!' complained Mum.

Sunday lunch with the Major, GAJ, Julia and the cousins was great until the subject of boyfriends came up. Mum asked Al about her new boyfriend. She gushed about how wonderful he is – a jewellery designer who she's branded 'The One'. GAJ approves of him thoroughly so perhaps wedding bells are on the horizon for Al. Andy then asked Julia whether she was seeing anyone. I stopped chewing and looked up as a nervous glance shot from my sister to my mother and then they both looked at my father. There was silence.

'Yes, Julia,' I said putting my knife and fork down, 'are you seeing anyone?'

'Not really, no,' she said laughing nervously.

'Oh don't be so coy!' said Andy failing to pick up the tension. Uncle Ant joined in.

'Come now Julia, tell us all, why so cagey – who's the lucky chap?' There was a pregnant silence.

'I'm not *seeing* anyone,' she said taking a gulp of wine.

'But you might be next week? Right?' I said recalling that The Legend will be coming to Jo'burg on leave. Again silence. 'Right?' I snapped. Julia looked up at me and shook her head.

'Angus, it's none of your business,' she said through gritted teeth.

I slapped the table in front of me, 'I've warned you about him.'

'Angus!' bellowed my father from the head of the table, 'that's enough! You have no right to pontificate to your sister. Julia is not a child and I'm sick and tired of your harsh judgements on just about everybody you meet.' He sat up and breathed heavily. 'I'm sorry to shout, everyone.'

Conversation slowly resumed as Mum and I rose to clear the main course. Dad arrived in the kitchen as Mum was whipping the cream and I was packing the dishwasher.

'Angus, you've got to take a hold of yourself. I won't tolerate the way you are treating Julia. I hope I make myself very clear,' he said and then stomped out. It astounds me how much it still stings when he talks to me like that. I distracted myself by watching Trubshaw who was snuffling about in the bottom of the dishwasher licking the gravy off the cutlery. AIDS Cat was trying to stick her paw into the whipping bowel.

'Darling, I know this is not easy for you to hear, but try to remember what Anna said to you, about being open and trying to see the world through other people's eyes.' She finished with the cream and walked back through to the dining room. I picked up the apple crumble and followed her.

After everyone had left, Julia included, I sat down to watch TV. Dad came through bearing Trubshaw's lead (which he had to hold above shoulder level as his hound was trying frantically to grab it.

'I'm taking this thing for a walk if you'd like to come,' he offered. I sighed and stood up. We walked, in silence mostly, through the sunny, wintry suburb and down towards the river. The dog played his part in mending things with my father by being hilarious. Two unleashed Boston terriers came charging over; their owner, a pretty blonde with short hair, failed to see the threat posed by Trubshaw's jaws.

'Hey, call your dogs off!' shouted Dad, gathering up Trubshaw's lead. She called but the yapping little things didn't react. When, however, Trubshaw nearly pulled Dad over in his attempt to have an early supper, they received the message loud and clear. We laughed as they scuttled back to their owner.

Tomorrow I return to the lodge.

Week 22

Potions and pilfering

Travelling back to Sasekile was relatively enjoyable. There were just three of us in Brandon's double cab – Kerry stretched out asleep in the back, and Brandon and I in front arguing most of the way about his appalling taste in music. I say relatively fun because we stopped in Dullstroom for a coffee and there we came across Jenny and a friend of hers who I don't think ever liked me much. Lesley was coming up to spend a few bed nights at the lodge. We exchanged some fake pleasantries but my mood was sullied slightly.

Back at the lodge, I took note of the fact that my welcome-back card had far more greetings on it than at the same time last year. As always, however, the drink that it came attached to was empty. Petrus no longer even bothers to hide the fact that he pilfers my welcome-back beer – the bottle top was resting on his doorstep.

While I was packing, he arrived back from his shift in the kitchen. He popped his head in and said,

'*Avuxeni* Angus.'

'Yes hello, you thieving alcoholic wretch,' I muttered and then added more clearly, 'how are you?'

'Aye yes, I am fine thank you, but not so good.'

'What is ailing you Petrus?' I enquired, 'Hangover or guilt?' I turned to look at him. His face was a bit gaunt and there were sores on his lips. 'Yes, you don't look well.' He took a swig from a small brown bottle. 'What's that?' I asked.

'It is my special *muthi*,' he replied. I was immediately suspicious. There are any number of quacks out here claiming to be able to cure troubles ranging from unfaithful wives to job prospects, the common cold and all the way to HIV. That is not to take away from some of the traditional herbalists who play a valuable role in local health care.

'Where did you get it?' I asked, referring to the bottle's contents.

'I bought it from Abbot,' he answered, 'it can help all kinds of sickness.' I held my hand out and he handed me the bottle. On the label appeared the sickle and hammer that make up part of the WANCRs logo. Apparently the union won't stop at just making money out of monthly subs. The *muthi* inside smelt horrific. The label explained that the tonic was available exclusively from the union and that '*All illness of the body, spirit and mind is cured*'. I handed it back to Petrus.

'You need to see a doctor – a real one,' I said to him. From my limited experience in rural Africa, I'd have to say that Petrus has HIV. He is of the opinion that he's been bewitched by a jealous neighbour (he was unable to say why such neighbour should be jealous). After my interaction with him, I finished unpacking and went to see PJ and explained Petrus's predicament. PJ was most concerned and promised to take it up with the union immediately and also to send Petrus to see a professional at a clinic.

So my neighbour is going to have his HIV tests tomorrow. He has had the process explained to him and seems calm. That may also be a result of the four quarts of Black Label that he drank this evening.

I've seen quite a few people walking around with little brown bottles since then and so I think I might have to go and have a word with Abbot.

As usual Bertie came to say hello upon my return. He handed me a wad of assignments that I'd set him. Next week he's taking over the admin of the conservation team from Candice. Carrie was welcoming and shook my hand viciously. I found Jacob and Nhlanhla fixing a bowser pump in the workshop. Jacob waved and nodded, which is like being hugged by most people. Nhlanhla started the pump and tried to spray me. I heard Jacob yelling at him as I left.

I also met Allegra on my way to see SB in Tamboti. She was supervising operations at the building site of the new spa. The spa will fit snugly between Tamboti and Main Camps. She heard me approaching and turned round, her hands on her hips. She flicked the fringe of her pixie-styled dark hair out of her eyes.

'You must be Angus MacNaughton,' she said without preamble and with a slight Edinburgh lilt.

'No, I'm the ghost of Robert the Bruce,' I replied.

'You can't be, he was taller than you,' she said without missing a beat or smiling.

'Age has shrunk me. You must be Allegra,' I said.

'I suppose I must.' She extended a firm hand and looked up into my eyes. I shook her hand and moved on, feeling her eyes boring into my back as I went.

SB was at his desk in the corner of the Tamboti main area. There were two files and bits of paper all round him.

'Good day, String Bean,' I said. He didn't look up.

'Hello Angus, how was your leave?'

'Very good thanks.' I sat down in front of him. 'How're things here?'

'Manic, just manic…completely manic in fact – Nicolette's birthday celebrations have to be perfect and it all rests on my shoulders.'

'Surely you have help?'

'Yes, but it's all on *my* shoulders.'

'How's Simone?'

'Fine. Listen I can't talk now, I'm too busy.'

I left after helping myself to a crunchie in the kitchen.

On my way back past the building site I saw that Allegra, in her capacity as the new childminder, had enlisted four of her charges. Two of them (roughly six years old) were helping the building crew mix cement and the others were carrying bricks in oversized rubber gloves. They were filthy dirty but seemed to be enjoying themselves.

My first guests were a varying bunch of Europeans – three couples – Italian, German and Welsh. The Italians spoke no English, the Germans spoke a bit of English and some Italian and I've no idea what the Welsh spoke – although it may have been English. Somehow between the six of them they managed to translate what I said and relay their requests and questions. Dinner in the evenings was a frustrating process because they insisted on sitting together and so conversation, although friendly, was painfully slow. I had to drink heavily to survive the meals.

The guests were operating out of Kingfisher Camp, where Simone has just been installed as the assistant camp manager – under Amber. This, as SB predicted, is not a match made in heaven. Amber is still devastated by the demise of her relationship with The Legend (almost as much as I am). She demonstrates this by walking around like a morose blancmange – shoulders stooped, lip on the floor. Everything is too much effort. Simone, on the other hand, is enthusiastic about her new designation and does not tolerate people wallowing in self-pity. The tension between them was palpable from the moment I stepped into the camp. Even the butlers were on edge.

It reached a head the other night. The Welsh woman wanted an Irish coffee after dinner. It took me about ten minutes to figure out what she was asking for because all of her Ls were prefixed with shh and suffixed with litres of spittle. Once I'd figured it out with Joachim von Vivenot's help, I hailed Simone and she said she'd gladly sort it out. Twenty minutes later, there was no Irish coffee and I went to see what was going on.

The kitchen is separated from the dining area by a narrow flight of stairs. As I climbed these, I could hear muffled shouting and the clattering of kitchen equipment. I pushed open the swing doors. Standing at the far end of the kitchen was Auto the butler, a look of amused astonishment on his face. In the middle of the room, Amber and Simone squared off. Simone was holding a bowl of whipped cream, destined for the Irish coffee. At her Amber pointed an open bottle of Jameson.

'I'm in charge in *my* camp; you are *my* assistant. That means you have to do everything I say with *my* guests!' squealed Amber.

'Ladies . . .' I began.

'Fuck you, Amber! All I *have* to do is make sure *our* guests are happy! This isn't *your* camp and I'll never be *your* assistant!' What followed occurred in about ten seconds. Simone scooped out a handful of cream, walked over to Amber and flung it in her face from point-blank range. Amber screamed like a banshee and tipped the bottle over Simone's dark blonde hair. Simone dropped her mixing bowl and grabbed Amber by the shirt collar. The whisky bottle crashed to the floor as Simone pushed Amber into the kitchen counter. As Amber hit the wooden surface, her right hand flew back and landed squarely in a wheel of soft gorgonzola. She removed a fistful and pushed it into Simone's face.

'Auto,' I shouted, 'get Amber.' I pulled Simone off while Auto grabbed Amber as she came forward. The two women strained to have at each other again. Auto started giggling first and then I started. The girls didn't find it funny so I escorted Simone out and told her firmly to go home. When I was sure she'd gone, Auto released Amber and we sent her home too. Auto finished making the Irish coffee and I returned to the guests. Luckily for the two girls, neither Auto nor I saw any reason to report the incident to the powers that be.

The arrival of Allegra has necessitated a shift in staff housing. She has moved into Kerry's old place and the red-headed chef has moved up into the block of four rooms close to mine. Her room is next door to Bertie's. She hasn't been a particularly happy camper since we arrived back. I returned from the Irish coffee dinner to find her sitting on her little veranda in the cold, staring into the moonless night, smoking a cigarillo.

'What's up?' I asked. She looked up and smiled.

'Not much. You?' She looked like she needed some cheering up so I told her of the incident in the Kingfisher kitchen. Halfway through my story, Bertie's light came on and he opened his door, dressed in long-sleeved flannel pyjamas big enough for Elvis. He thought the story thoroughly amusing.

I was about to leave when Kerry said, 'Have you seen these little brown bottles of *muthi* people are carrying about?' I explained that I had and Bertie said there were at least 30 people taking the stuff. He added that it cost R100 a bottle and explained that people were taking the stuff for everything from colds to virility. By the time he'd finished, I was riled up and determined to do something about it. I knew that talking to Abbot would be a waste of time.

'How about a little adventure?' I suggested. They both nodded so I outlined a makeshift plan and told them to meet me at my house in ten minutes. They arrived at the appointed time, dressed for the occasion. Bertie was outfitted in black pants, a black leather jacket and a navy balaclava (topped with a pompom). Kerry was in long, black spandex running pants, a black polar neck and a black beanie. I emerged from my house with a torch, some rope and my Leatherman, but dressed normally.

'People, we're not about to burglarise the Louvre,' I said as we set off.

We snuck through the staff village to the storerooms. It was late, the camp was quiet and despite the fact that the security guards are supposed to patrol every half an hour, I was pretty sure they'd be snoozing on the job. We circled round the warren of rooms looking for a way in but there were no open windows. There was, however, a ladder leaning against the wall. I climbed it and eased onto the corrugated-iron roof. It creaked loudly and I froze. A hippo called from the river and there was silence again. A few seconds later Kerry and Bertie were seated next to me. I looked at Kerry who was grinning. All I could see of Bertie through his balaclava was his teeth.

Because the rooms have been added onto each other haphazardly over the years, many of them don't have windows but Abbot's office has a skylight. We crawled achingly slowly across the creaking rusty roof until we came up against the Perspex dome. It was screwed into a wooden frame. Bertie examined the skylight.

'Phillip's head,' he whispered holding out his hand like a master carpenter to his apprentice. I unfolded the Phillip's head from my Leatherman and placed it in Bertie's gloved hand.

With practiced skill, he removed the four screws and the two of us slid the dome off to one side. I shone my torch down into Abbot's command centre.

'It's quite a drop,' I said. Kerry looked down and without a pause, elegantly lifted her long legs through the hole and dropped soundlessly to the floor below. Bertie went next and I was just about to follow when I realised we'd never get out again.

'Wait for me there,' I said and inched back across the roof to the ladder. There I fastened the end of the rope to an exposed roof beam and crawled back. I tossed the rope into the darkness below, eased myself through and dropped to the floor, over-balancing and falling into Kerry.

'Angus, I had no idea you felt like that about me,' she said.

'Shut it,' I hissed. Bertie flicked my torch on and the search for the WANCRs *muthi* began. It took us about ten minutes to locate a huge stash of the quack medicine in the back of the paint store. There were twenty boxes, each weighing about ten kg. Bertie opened one of the boxes and we peered inside, there were 40 little plastic bottles per box.

'Shit,' said Kerry doing some mental calculation, 'R4 000 per box!'

'Enough here to swindle the staff out of R80 000,' I said.

Bertie pulled his balaclava up off his face and shook his head. The silence of his anger was broken by the sound of a key turning in a lock, the main door opening and then the unmistakable sound of Abbot's bray. He was talking in Shangane to his latest victim – promising that the *muthi* she was about to consume would ensure a salary increase and cure her plantar warts.

'The ancestors are in the bottle!' he concluded.

'What now?' whispered Kerry. Abbot was heading our way and the other two were looking to me for some sort of plan. There was only one door leading to the room we were standing in and virtually no space with all the paint and boxes of *muthi*. To make matters worse, Abbot had flicked on the lights in the main area. I silently leapt onto a huge drum of whitewash, reached up and twisted the bulb from the light socket.

'Kerry, get into the corner there,' I whispered. She moved to the corner furthest from the door and folded into it, I moved a twentyt-litre drum in front of her. 'Bertie: next to the door.' He moved swiftly into the corner behind the door. That left just me exposed. Above me there was a bracket normally used for storing planks. With seconds to spare, I jumped up, my fingers just closing around the bracket. I hauled myself up and then swung my feet forward to rest on the oversized lintel above the door just as Abbot and Rufina, from the kitchen, came in. Abbot flicked the light switch at the door – the bulb felt comfortingly cold in my pocket. The store man clicked his teeth and moved over to the boxes.

Thankfully Abbot loves the sound of his own voice or he and his victim may well have heard my feet slipping and straining for purchase on the lintel. My shoulders and arms burned with a hellfire as I hung above him while he jabbered on and on, taking an age to select a bottle for Rufina. Eventually he removed one and they walked out. He pulled the door shut behind him and as it banged to, my legs gave way and I fell to the ground, panting.

'Feels like we're in a Bond movie!' said Kerry, emerging.

'Yes, Fields, it does. Don't relax yet. If Abbot goes into his office and sees a rope hanging from the skylight, things are going to get ugly.' I snuck my head through the door as Abbot flicked off the light and closed the door. I sighed. 'All clear.'

'Well, we've come this far, so we might as well get rid of this stuff somehow,' Kerry said. Bertie picked up a box and carried it through to Abbot's office. We followed suit and, in no time at all, we had a pile of boxes below the skylight. Bertie climbed the stack and pulled himself out of the hole. Kerry and I tied the rope to a box, Bertie pulled it up slowly.

'Why Fields?' said Kerry as the rope returned.

'She's a ginger Bond girl,' I replied. 'Now you climb up and help Bertie.' She climbed neatly out. It took us about 30 minutes to remove all the boxes. I then used the rope and a lot of help from Bertie to extricate myself from the skylight. Once on the creaky roof, Bertie re-attached the Perspex cover.

'Let's empty the bottles here,' suggested Kerry. The roof sloped off to a gutter that flowed into a subterranean drain. We sat for a further hour whispering to each other and emptying all 799 bottles. Ridding ourselves of the empty bottles and boxes wasn't hard. We moved them easily off the roof to the enormous skip that lives next to the stores. Obviously we couldn't just leave them on top of the other rubbish so Bertie and I climbed into the stinking mass and made sure each box was well-covered as Kerry tossed them up to us.

With that we went quietly back to our part of the village. I was in a great mood and found it difficult to sleep after the excitement of the evening's mission and I was nervous about the boxes being found.

The next morning Abbot stormed into PJ's office as I returned from morning drive. I didn't hear what he said as I cleaned my rifle but it wasn't hard to imagine and it was with profound relief that I saw the waste-removal truck arrive at lunch time.

Week 23

Elevation and elephant

This week Matto was sent out to shoot his impala. With typical arrogance, I heard him telling Jamie that he thought he'd have it back by lunch the next day.

'Just take it easy out there,' said Jamie, 'it's not as easy as it might seem.' Matto snorted and walked off.

To my great delight, he's been unsuccessful for seven days now. He's fired two rounds so only has one left. At dinner he is hangdog and silent – like the spoilt brat he is.

The very faint whiff of rotting *muthi* is the only evidence of our escapades last week. PJ held an open house meeting a few days after the incident. He spoke of various issues that concerned the staff and then brought up the fact that something had gone missing from the stores and asked that everyone keep a look out for 'a few boxes of tonic'. He didn't seem at all perturbed. I'm sure Abbot didn't give him the full story of how much he was storing for his union mates or the full details of what it was being used for.

The store man has been in a foul mood ever since. Bertie has heard that the WANCRs are holding him personally responsible for the loss. Despite the paltry cost price of the *muthi*, I'm pretty sure he'll be in their debt for some time.

I broke our team secrecy vow and informed Arthur of the great heist. His reply went as follows.

To: Angus MacNaughton
From: Arthur C. Grimble
Subject: Jolly Good Show!

Crocus Cottage
West Road
Wragby
Lincolnshire

Dear Angus,

What a wonderful story you told of your burglary last night. I am so pleased that you and your friends took it upon yourselves to do something so courageous about what seems to be an appalling situation. On the other hand I think you are quite lucky that you were not caught. I fear if you had been it would have meant the chop for all of you. While you and the young girl would no doubt have found employment elsewhere, I suspect it would have been a lot more difficult for young Bertram given his lack of education. Still, as the proverb adopted by The Bard says, *All's well that ends well'*!

It is wonderfully warm in Lincolnshire now and the garden looks magnificent. The big news is that I have asked Mavis to make our arrangement more permanent. In other words she has moved into Crocus Cottage. After so long alone it has been a bit of an adjustment but I do find life easier having someone I am so fond of around all the time. Perhaps we shall marry in the future but there are no wedding plans at present

Next weekend we are going through to London where I shall meet her children and grandchildren (eight in all!). I am looking forward to it immensely as we are going to see a few shows and a performance of Beethoven's *Choral Symphony* at the Albert Hall. Keep well and write soon.

Your friend,
Arthur

I hadn't really considered the consequences of our actions on Bertie (or anyone for that matter) but I'm still glad that we did it.

While I was engaged in activities that could have ended my employment, the other MacNaughton brother received a promotion this week. PJ has given him the title of hospitality manager. His inflated sense of self-importance, however, might lead one to believe that he'd been promoted to the position of Lord High Commander of the Universe (LHCU). From what I can gather, his new job includes directing hospitality across all the camps while retaining his responsibilities as the Tamboti Camp manager.

He came to tell me while I was adding some grass samples to the plant press I've just built. I was kneeling outside my room, in the shade of the leafy mopane tree, tightening the wing nuts on the clamps.

'Good news, Angus,' he said.

'Don't tell me, The Legend's been arrested for drug trafficking in the Far East and is shortly to be incarcerated for the rest of his natural life?' I said finishing and looking up.

'No. I've been promoted.'

'To what?' I asked, slightly incredulous.

'I'm the new hospitality manager.'

'Who was the old one?'

'You could congratulate me.' He sighed.

'I'm sorry, yes, well done, that's great. What does it mean?' I stood up and shook his hand.

'There wasn't an old one. PJ has created the position. He says I'm a bit young and inexperienced but as the only one with formal training in hospitality he says he'd like to try it out. Apparently there've been some complaints about some of the service and the lack of attention to detail in the camps.'

That afternoon, I was driving out of Kingfisher Camp with Sipho. When the two of us arrived at tea, SB was there talking to Simone and Amber (they are still 'working' together). He was pointing at things on the tea table with his radio aerial. Amber took notes and Simone stood with folded arms.

'…Take this iced coffee,' he pointed at the jug, 'it is simply not up to standard. Look at how the ingredients have separated; imagine a guest having to drink this? Can you? Huh? Then there is the cake. It should be neatly cut and the correct number of forks and napkins need to be over here.' He thumped his hand on the heavy yellowwood table. 'Come on guys, we are supposed to be a world-class establishment!' He then turned and pranced out of the entrance.

Simone looked mortified while her new best friend Amber wrote in her notebook. I've thankfully never had to manage people – much to the world's relief, I suspect. I'm therefore no doyen on inspirational leadership but I fear SB's first attempt at Kingfisher is perhaps not the way to build positive team spirit. Perhaps I shall buy him one of those putrid self-help leadership books.

Simone wandered over to me as four guests walked through the entrance SB had just vacated. She introduced them – a family of South Africans (lots of them in winter) – mother (Miranda), father (Oliver), recently-affianced daughter (Kelly) and son-in-law to be (Neil). Miranda was a jolly-hockey-sticks sort who believed meals are earned by regular exercise and that afternoon sleeps are an enormous waste of productive time. Kelly was almost pretty if slightly androgynous. Neil, her fiancé, was of the opinion that bankers know all things worth knowing. He was astounded to hear that a commercial qualification wasn't firmly on my horizon after my 'time off in the bush'. But on the plus side, the family had travelled to game reserves regularly so they knew the drill and it wasn't a dreadful trial hosting them.

On their second morning, I took them for a long walk instead of a drive. O'Reilly packed us a picnic breakfast, which Elvis loaded onto his broad back and we headed out north. First, we picked our way across the river. The water is low so it's possible to pick a careful crossing over the rocks and through the reeds. It's a little risky given the thickness of the vegetation and the number of hippo around. Halfway across, in the middle of a fairly thick stand of reeds we came across a wide flat rock and I told everyone to sit down. We sat there, the reeds stretching up over our heads into the brightening sky.

As we were about to leave, a red-faced cisticola landed on a reed close by.

'Click click click twit twit tweet tweeeeet,' he said. It was one of those moments where all seems right with the Earth; a moment for the ranger to be silent and allow the world to speak for herself. When the little bird flew off, we continued onto the northern bank and out into the open. Elvis and I then set a fairly brisk pace due north, which warmed us all up.

We walked mainly through bushwillow woodland; the yellow leaves falling from the trees and crunching underfoot, giving the air the distinctive dry leaf-litter smell that I associate with this time of year. We passed through a few stands of mopane that will stay green until the very end of winter.

Apart from the wonderful scenery, the smells and the atmosphere, this part of the walk was made infinitely more entertaining by Neil. He might be a wealthy banker but his physical abilities have waned in inverse proportion to his income. About twenty minutes after we crossed the river, he was panting ferociously and asked if we might have a rest. Miranda was unimpressed.

'What's the matter with you, Neil? I'm 35 years older than you and I'm hardly breathing. Don't you do any exercise at home?' His sagging physique bore testament to an answer in the negative.

'I ... don't ... really ... have ... time,' he gasped flopping down onto a low termite mound.

'Rubbish,' snapped Miranda, 'just a lack of discipline and application. Come on, we're not waiting around.' Neil staggered to his feet. Elvis didn't have much more sympathy than Miranda and we continued at the same pace. Another twenty minutes passed before I thought to check on Neil – so enjoyable was the warming morning. The sight that met my eyes when I did turn round was shocking and I called a halt.

'Now what's the matter?' Miranda swung round to face her daughter's fiancé. Neil had removed his shirt and his puce face was sweating onto two impressive man boobs and a sagging belly – both pasty white and dotted with sparse hair. I'm not sure she'd ever seen him with his shirt off but the sight of the physique he was about to bequeath on her unborn grandchildren upset her.

'Good lord...that's disgusting!' exclaimed Miranda, staring. Neil, apparently close to death, flopped down onto another termite mound. Unfortunately for him, this one wasn't unoccupied and the top of his corpulent plumber's bottom covered an active entrance hole. It wasn't long before the worker termites, no doubt almost as offended as Miranda, had hailed their soldier brothers and sisters. With their powerful biting mouthparts, the defenders of the mound started savaging the exposed skin on Neil's backside. He leapt up with a yelp, swatting at his attackers. Miranda just stared, shaking her head. Before anyone could aid the man, he tripped and fell backwards – into a woolly caper bush. These are not plants one would ever choose to engage with a naked torso and it took us a good fifteen minutes to extricate his flabby body. When the banker eventually stood up, his sweaty skin was covered in dust and little red welts from the sap and thorns of the bush.

I gave him some water and tried hard not to laugh. Elvis stared at his shoes and pretended to cough.

When Neil had recovered sufficiently, we continued the walk.

Ten minutes later, Elvis found some elephant tracks...and a pile of steaming dung.

Elvis stopped and stooped to examine the ground while I scanned ahead of us, listening, looking and smelling. I checked the wind with my ash bag – there was an almost imperceptible breeze blowing from behind us.

'One bull, fresh,' said Elvis. He looked at the little ash cloud, glowing in the early sunlight, floating slowly towards where the tracks were heading. The tracker looked a little uneasy as he scanned the bush in front of us. Elvis very seldom looks uneasy. The source of his concern was the fact that with such fresh signs, we should at least have been able to hear or see the big bull. The thing with elephants is that they can hide astoundingly well and be utterly silent. This meant one of two things. Either he was moving quickly and was out of earshot or he had smelt us coming and had 'gone to ground' in order to evaluate us and our intentions.

Despite what some might say, elephants have eyesight probably as good as humans, excellent ears and sharp olfactory senses. Until recently, I'd have laughed at someone who said what I am now going to, but here goes: elephants also have a way of communicating their presence through, shall we say, non-traditional methods – i.e. extrasensorily. People like Elvis, who are in tune with the natural world around them, understand this (although he might struggle to explain it). I suppose the New Agers would call it 'picking up on the elephant's energy'. Whatever the case, the fact that Elvis felt uneasy meant the elephant was close and that it knew we were there.

Guest reactions are interesting in these situations. Some, Kelly and her father for example, immediately feel the change in their tracker. They instinctively went silent. Neil, now fully dressed, was too tired to say anything. Miranda tapped me on the shoulder and asked what was going on. I gathered them, pointed out the very fresh tracks and then shook my ash bag again to show them which way the wind was blowing.

Elvis indicated a giant termite mound about 30 metres to the east of us and perpendicular to the tracks. I told the guests to be completely silent as we walked quickly over to the mound. We climbed up and scanned the area north and west of us. Elvis looked more relaxed and I saw a smile develop on his face as his eyes fixed on a point. Then I heard the whoosh of an elephant's ears flapping. An enormous bull appeared from behind a stand of false marula trees about 60 metres off. He walked slowly round the thicket until he was side-on. Although not looking at us directly, his trunk kept lifting and turning towards the termite mound. I told the guests to sit down.

We watched him for a few minutes and then he turned to face us – a bull in his prime, the undisputed King. No one who has ever seen an elephant like this could ever consider the lion as monarch. He had an enormous right tusk that curved up; the left one was snapped off halfway down. He eyed us for a minute or two and then took a few steps forward, his head held high. I looked at Elvis who was watching the elephant with a slight frown. Then, the great grey frame began plodding slowly towards us; I looked behind the mound – there wasn't much cover. I reasoned that it didn't actually make a huge difference because he'd seen us and it's almost impossible to lose an elephant bent on finding you – especially with four guests. As if reading my mind Elvis said in Shangane, 'We're staying, tell the guests.'

'Everyone, just sit still,' I said looking round at them. They looked relatively relaxed. In hindsight, I think they probably thought the elevation of the mound would give us some sort of protection but elephants are incredibly agile for their size. When I looked back to the bull, he'd closed the gap to about 30 metres. There he paused, picked up a round-leafed teak branch and popped it into one side of his mouth. It emerged from the other side, stripped free of bark. All the while he watched us.

An elephant with malicious intent often gives indication of his displeasure by folding his trunk onto one of his tusks or walking with a distinctive rocking of the front shoulders. If he's uncomfortable he'll often rock on three legs and if he's going to warn you, he'll shake his head. This bull just chewed his twig and then stepped slowly forward again. By this stage my heart was hammering. I'm not nervous on my own in the bush anymore but the fact that I was responsible for the four people behind me suddenly hit home. My mouth went dry and I looked again to my tracker who, although far from panicked, wasn't quite his normal, unruffled self. The guests were also starting to look nervous.

'What's he doing?' asked Miranda. I didn't know what to say.

'Please, everyone just be very quiet and completely still,' I whispered. 'Everything is fine,' I added, hoping to sound more confident than I felt.

I was sitting, my rifle pointing into the air, the butt tucked in between my legs. My left hand was sweaty on the cold steel barrel. I couldn't shoot from the position I was in and I needed to make sure that if the worst scenario played out, I was in a position to do something about it. Ever so slowly, I swivelled my legs around until I was on my haunches. Elvis glanced back at the guests.

The bull had closed to twenty metres.

Elvis edged closer to our charges so that, if need-be, he could grab any of them who took fright. We tried to do all this without alarming them but by this stage it was clear that we were all a little perturbed. My right hand went to the bolt as the elephant closed another five metres. Sweat poured into my eyes as I squatted there. I knew instinctively that pushing a round into the chamber might well escalate the situation to a point of aggression beyond which a battle to the death would be the only outcome.

154

Instead, I started whispering to him as he closed the distance once more to about ten metres. I don't remember what I said exactly but they were words as calm and soothing as I could manage in my adrenalised state. 'It's okay, boy, we're just sitting peacefully.' I may have even told him I loved him. The mound was so big that we were sitting level with the top of his head.

There he remained for another five minutes, just looking, his trunk lifting to smell us every so often. It felt like six weeks on that mound. Then, without warning, he turned to the north and walked away, disappearing into the woodland in less than two minutes.

I sat back down, my shaking and sweating right hand rubbing my face. Then I looked around to see Elvis, woolly hat in hand, doing the same. He sighed. The guests were grinning from ear to ear.

'That was the most amazing thing I've ever experienced,' said Miranda. Her husband, who was breathing heavily, agreed loudly. The other two sat in stunned silence. There wasn't much to say so I unpacked our breakfast. While we ate, the adrenaline levels slowly ebbed and conversation began to flow as the guests all went through what they thought was going to happen. Neil was convinced that when I moved onto my haunches, I was going to shoot the bull. Then Oliver asked me what my plan had been.

'To be honest, I didn't have one,' I replied. 'I don't believe that it's possible to plan a situation like that because there are so many variables and they're changing all the time. The only training for those situations is experience; that's why having Elvis with us is so important.' I took a sip of coffee. 'There was something about his behaviour that guided my reaction. I didn't ever seriously consider aiming at him. It felt like…like he was testing us. He was showing his dominance and I felt like as long as we sat here and acknowledged it, we were always going to be fine.' Everyone nodded. Elvis smiled. 'Of course,' I added, 'I may be entirely wrong and we may have been in mortal danger.' Nervous laughter.

My neighbour's test results from the clinic came back positive. The bad news is that Petrus has HIV and a dangerously low CD4 count. The good news is that he's been put on anti-retrovirals with immediate effect and thus stands a chance. I found him outside his room just after the elephant walk, sitting on an upturned crate and staring out into the middle distance somewhere. There was a tear running down his right cheek. I realised without asking what must have happened.

'Are you okay?' I asked lamely in bad Shangane.

'Ai ai ai,' he answered, fresh tears filling his bloodshot eyes, 'I'm going to die.'

What do you say to that? I pulled up a crate and sat down next to him and for about twenty minutes he cried intermittently. One of the women in the kitchen is a diabetic who has to take insulin all the time, so I tried to explain that his illness just needs to be treated in a similar way. I also tried to impress on him that if he was disciplined about taking his medication and changed a few things about his lifestyle, he'd live for a very long time. This seemed to cheer him up a bit.

The next day, however, I had to have another gentle conversation with him after I found four empty quarts outside his room. I'm not sure how he's going to stop drinking.

Week 24

Megalomania and misery

The week began with O'Reilly planning to set himself up for what, in my opinion, will be an epic disaster. He has decided that his love for Kerry cannot go unannounced any longer. Short of shouting it from the treetops, I'm not sure he could have made it any clearer – he talks about her non-stop, goes bright red in the face when she's around and always sits next to her at meal times. She's good-natured about it because he doesn't overtly hassle her and he's a generally pleasant fellow.

I was driving some guests who were celebrating their 30th wedding anniversary and they wanted to take some special snacks and champagne on a game drive for the celebration. So it was that I went to see the head chef in his kitchen office. The place is a like a mad scientist's laboratory. There are mixing bowls full of experimental recipes, bits of paper, books and cutlery all over the place. Given the standard of the food he cooks, I suppose he must actually know what's going on in there.

I knocked on the door and walked in. He was standing in the far corner with a stainless-steel bowl, frantically whisking something.

'Mornin Angus, have a seat. Be wit ya now.' He ceased whisking, put the dripping implement on a scrawled piece of paper and pushed the bowl towards me. 'Have a test of dat den . . .' I put my finger into the bowl and licked it. 'Me new crem brulee . . . muurveluss isn't it just?' And it was spectacular. Before I could answer, he put the bowl in my lap.

'Ting is,' he walked conspiratorially across to the door and shut it. 'Ting is, Oi got ta do someting about dis predicament Oi foind meself in.'

'Your predicament?' I asked, spooning some more of the mixture into my mouth.

'Yes, me predicament regardin dat gorjiss ting, Kerry.'

'Ah,' I said, 'do go on.'

He explained that the torment of being around Kerry and not declaring his love for her was slowly killing him. He then went on to outline his plan of action which, at some point in the not-too-distant future, involves him serving a special dinner to her (the details of which he gave me down to the mixing techniques) in his fairly palatial staff house. He finished with, 'After dat, Oi suspect we'll mek lov into de urrly hours.' He looked dreamily out of the window. I didn't tell him I thought this idea to be the most poorly conceived plan since Napoleon invaded Russia in mid-winter. Instead I just wished him luck and then asked for what I needed.

A few days ago, SB who was back home in Jo'burg on a few days' leave, sent me the following message. It would seem that Simone is not taking kindly to her boyfriend's new role as the LHCU.

To: Angus
From: Hugh MacNaughton
Subject: STRESS!

Hey Angus,

I need some help please. I haven't had much of a holiday as I've been trying to organise things for Nicolette's visit. There's a file I left behind and it has a list of decorations that I need to buy – it's either in my room or with Jenny, I can't remember exactly.

Simone is not helping me much. She says I've become 'a nasty megalomaniac'. I had to look up what that means but I think it's a bit unfair – she doesn't understand my stress levels since the promotion. Imagine how bad it will look if Nicolette arrives and the camps are not all up to scratch. I'm determined not to let PJ or myself down and I'm not going to let anything get in my way.

Anyway, if you could find that list for me I'd be grateful.

Cheers,
Hugh

When placed under stress, my brother tends towards self-involved melodrama. I went to look for the file in question. It wasn't in his house so I knocked on Jenny's door after lunch.

'Who is it?' she asked.

'Me,' I said flatly. She invited me in so I opened the door and stuck my head in. 'Hello, I need String Bean's file on some group or other that the two of you are working on.'

'Fine thanks, how are you?' she said.

'Yes, good, fine, how are you?' I forced a smile.

'Ja, okay,' she replied.

'Do you have the file?' I said after an awkward silence.

'Yup, what does he need?'

'A list of decorations or something.'

'It's here, I'll scan and mail it to him just now.'

'Thanks,' I said. A slightly awkward silence followed and then I said goodbye and left, feeling irritated.

Then, last night, came the colossal lowlight of the year.

The impala party of Matto.

He shot the poor beast two days ago, arriving home around lunch time. Rangers are supposed to shoot a ram that is at least two-years old. Matto's had horns that were suspiciously inward-curving for a two-year-old ram. He placed the animal at Carrie's feet and the usual congratulatory crowd of rangers and other staff gathered. PJ shook the new ranger's hand. Matto was sprayed with champagne and then, unlike me, managed to down a quart of beer in less than five seconds to rapturous applause. While all of this was going on, I watched the head ranger as she examined the murdered antelope – clearly she had suspicions about its age but there was enough doubt in her mind to let it go.

The impala party followed yesterday evening. It was similar to the usual format – lethal punch in abundance, new ranger's hunt story and then drunken dancing till the wee hours. Matto told the fable of his hunt making it sound like he'd spent five minutes as opposed to almost two weeks completing the task. There is no disgrace in taking a long time over it – Carrie took three weeks to kill hers. Apparently she just really struggled to justify taking the life of an animal that bore her no ill-will. She eventually shot hers at 60 metres – with one round. Matto, judging by his vile mood during those two weeks, saw it as extremely ignominious to have taken longer that Jeff the Genius.

I found it difficult to believe 50 per cent of what the great hunter claimed, but the booze flowed and no one really minded as long as he was downing punch fast. Candice played the role of dead impala, no doubt hoping to be carried back to Matto's quarters at the end of the evening. In that, however, she was to be sorely disappointed.

After the story, the music began and the crowded room began to heave. The punch was bottomless and free and a pleasant numbness came over my body as we all danced. At one stage I spotted Kerry in the crowd so I took her hand and swung her round the limited space. She's an excellent dancer and taught me a whole suite of new moves – some of which were a bit dangerous for her given that she's taller than me – I nearly smacked her head on the floor a few times while she was spinning around my arm.

After my dance, I met Allegra at the bar and even managed to elicit a smile from her.

'Good evening,' she said formally. I turned and bowed deeply.

'Good evening lady.' The corner of her mouth turned up almost imperceptibly as I assumed the ponciest accent I could muster. 'May I ask if your card is yet full?' She looked a bit confused, then light dawned.

'No sir, I do not have a card. I'm not a dancer.' Almost smiling.

'Not a dancer? My lady, next you'll be telling me you do not play the pianoforte!' That did the trick – the corners of her huge grey eyes turned up and she giggled. 'She smiles!' I shouted. We then had a drink together and she told me a bit about herself. Allegra is actually a very pleasant woman, despite her reserved nature. She's what I'd describe as a seeker – someone on a very serious mission to find the ultimate reasons and mechanics for our existence. My enjoyment of Allegra's philosophy on the universe was soon to be shattered, however. As she was about to explain the link between the latest thinking in quantum physics and its relationship to Tai Chi, I turned to see my worst fears being realised.

The music changed to *Wherever You Will Go* by The Calling – Jenny's favourite song. Over Allegra's shoulder, I saw Matto make his move. The chorus began as the new ranger appeared behind Jenny, he put his left arm round her belly and pulled her into him. She closed her eyes and put her hand onto his, their fingers entwined. He kissed her neck and she reached up to put her left hand over the back of his head while his right hand explored the outside of her right thigh. As the chorus reached a crescendo, the crowd closed around them but parted just enough for me to see Jenny turn around to face Matto. Then as the lyrics said 'I'll be with you for all of time' their lips connected.

Adrenaline surged through me. My face went hot, I couldn't breathe and I had to lean on the bar for support. Allegra, who hadn't witnessed the foul deed, frowned.

'Are you alright? You've gone ghostly pale!'

'No, feeling a bit sick,' I said. 'Excuse me.' I pushed past her and made for the door, the room spinning around me. Halfway across, a powerful hand gripped my elbow and supported me steadily towards the door. I looked to my right to see Carrie moving people out of the way and then I was out in the cold winter air. Carrie kept pushing me until we were well away from the Twin Palms. When she let go, I bent over, my hands on my knees. I thought I was going to be sick.

'I'm sorry,' said Carrie. 'That's really shit.' I stood there, doubled over for a minute or two

'God, I'm pathetic,' I said.

'Ag, it's perfectly natural – we all want what we don't have, etc. I think you'll find it's only your ego that's a bit bruised. Will you make it to your room okay?' I nodded, breathing deeply.

'Yes, thank you ma'am,' I replied and walked slowly away.

The freezing night filled my lungs with cold spears and the darkness closed around me. I took the back route home, half hoping to be murdered by a buffalo or a hippo. I saw neither but as I was about to reach the village, there was a familiar-sounding swoosh off towards the river. I stopped to look. There was no moon but the camp cast some light and the white of an enormous tusk reflected in the darkness. I stood looking for a few minutes, listening to the elephant breathing. Then he went silent, obviously picking up my presence in the dark. I saw the dark shape turn to face me – one enormous right tusk pointed up and the left one broken off halfway down. I shivered. We looked at each other for a few minutes; he was about 30 metres away. Then I turned and walked into the village.

Predictably, slumber didn't come for many hours and I had no whisky to help me. When fitful sleep did come, I was tortured by images of the night's events and at one stage Anna came vividly to mind – I was chasing her across a green floodplain, but she was too fast. By the time I climbed into the shower at 05h00 to ready myself for game drive, my eyes were bleary and my head ached. Mercifully, there were animals in abundance on the drive and I didn't have to say much to the family of Americans unlucky enough to have been saddled with me.

I'm driving out of Tamboti Camp at the moment where Amber is relieving SB on leave and I saw her on the deck on return from drive.

'How are you, Angus?' she asked, head cocked to one side. A mixture of fear and fake sympathy made a poor attempt to cover her thirst for gossip.

'Fine and you?' I said pouring myself a glass of orange juice.

'No really. *Are* you okay?'

'Amber, I assume you are making reference to the fact that Jenny and Matto engaged in a public display of affection last night?'

'Well…' she began. I held up my hand.

'Amber, I am not in the habit of sharing my feelings with anyone, least of all with women whom I consider to have tongues which wag almost as frequently as their unfettered legs swing akimbo.' I downed my juice and then reached behind the bar to help myself to a full bottle of Famous Grouse. 'Add this to Jones's bar bill,' I said to her and left.

When I arrived in the rangers' room, Jeff was being subjected to a verbal savaging by Carrie. While I cleaned my rifle, I gleaned that he had lost five rounds of ammunition. He swore blind he'd put them in the ammunition safe but Carrie was having none of it. Jeff, for his sins, will be working with the conservation team for the next week while he thinks about his actions.

Week 25

Car and clues

It was inevitable that I would see Jenny again after the mincing my heart took the other night. I managed to avoid her for the whole of the day after the heinous event but the day after that it happened. I was in the workshop attempting to persuade Jackson that it is not acceptable for my Land Rover to be belching acrid fumes onto our guests and, more importantly, the animals, every time I start the engine. He eventually agreed to have a look and set to bits of the engine with a small hammer.

I watched in bemused fascination for a little while and then Jackson asked me to fetch him a number ten spanner. I wandered over to the tool room where Oscar was fiddling with a gearbox – also making liberal use of a hammer. I greeted him and asked for the spanner. He smiled and pointed a greasy finger at the wall where the spanners live. I retrieved the tool and as I stepped out into the sun, there was Jenny.

Fresh waves of adrenaline were released into my body. We just stood and looked at each other for an awkward moment.

'Hi Angus,' she said.

'Hello Jenny.' She looked at her feet and over my shoulder. I nearly puked.

'Howzit?'

'Fine and you?'

'Fine – my guest left something on Sipho's Landy. I'm trying to find it.'

'Oh.' I looked at my feet during another uncomfortable silence.

'Listen,' she said, 'I was really drunk the other night and I . . .' she paused.
'You . . .' I prompted.

'I don't know,' she said abruptly, 'I'm sorry you had to see it. It wasn't
ideal.'

'Oh that,' I said, 'right.' I managed to look up. 'Oh well, you don't owe me
anything. Oscar's in there; he'll tell you where Sipho's vehicle is.' I walked
past her.

SB sent me the following comforting mail at the beginning of the
week – this after I had informed him of the impala party and asked if The
Legend was in Johannesburg and, if so, whether or not he was meeting
with Julia.

To: Angus
From: Hugh MacNaughton
Subject: Time to move on

Howzit Angus,

Thanks for organising that list for me. I now have to come back
to work early because there is too much to do with Nicolette and
co. arriving next week. Simone is really irritated because we were
supposed to spend two nights near Sabie on the way back. She
still doesn't get that my work is a priority now that I have so much
extra responsibility.

Sorry to hear about Jenny and Matto but it's time you moved on.
You weren't with her for that long and they are better suited than
the two of you. They have lots of the same friends and similar
interests. I know that's a bit harsh but sometimes it helps to hear
the truth.

I may as well tell you that Jonesy and Julia have been seeing
each other quite a lot. Again, I really like Jonesy so I don't have a
problem with it. We all agree that you need to grow up a bit and
stop judging him – not that he really cares.

See you tomorrow,
Hugh

The LHCU has spoken. I must remember to thank him for his pearls.

I'm not in the least bit surprised that Simone is ready to kill him.

He arrived back the next day and didn't bother to come and say hello. When I saw him at lunch he was sitting with all the camp managers explaining *his* strategy for the group – *his* ideas for the menu, *his* plans for the entertainment and even *his* desires for the game drives, with special snacks, etc. Taking a break from delivering plans he considers worthy of Trevor Manuel, he managed to tell me that he is 'sick and tired' of the Toyota Tazz that we share.

'I've decided to upgrade. I looked at an Audi A3 in Jo'burg which I really like and I can probably now afford. The money you pay me for my share of the Tazz will be enough for a deposit.'

'String Bean, I'm sure you know what's best,' I replied suddenly feeling immensely weary.

O'Reilly has yet to act on his desire to woo Kerry. I fear for the poor man's sanity should it not go according to plan – and there's no way it will. I also felt a twinge of guilt that I'd spent the night in Kerry's sleeping bag not too long ago but it's not like anything happened, or is likely to.

I arrived at my room after dinner a few nights ago and saw a glowing red cherry on the end of one of Kerry's cigarillos. She was sitting on her veranda, silhouetted by yellow light from her window. I wandered over and sat down next to her. She looked round as I approached, wiping a tear from her right eye. I didn't feel like engaging but also didn't really feel like lying sleepless, staring at my ceiling again. So I just put my arm round her; she put her head on my shoulder and started crying softly.

As I sat there, moisture seeping into my right shoulder, I considered the fact that whatever is making Kerry so sad must be substantially worse than watching a girl who doesn't care for me much kissing an asshole like Matto. The emotions poor old Petrus is experiencing as he contemplates his mortality must also be much nastier.

'Whisky?' I asked Kerry. She nodded. I rose and fetched two glasses and my bottle of Famous Grouse. It was cold so ice wasn't required; we just drank it neat, staring out at the night.

'Come on, Ginger, what's going on with you?' I asked eventually.

'Ag man. Talking about it makes me too sad,' she said. 'This time of year always makes me very sad. It brings back some horrible memories of childhood and my mom. But it's really difficult for me to talk about.' She sniffed.

'It's okay, don't worry about it.'

'I want to tell you about it but it's just too difficult right now. Thanks for asking though, I appreciate it.'

When we'd finished half the bottle, I no longer felt the cold and Kerry had ceased her tears. I led her into her room and we both passed out on her bed.

I woke around 02h00, dreaming of Matto and Jenny. My head had a demon in it and my mouth was stuffed with sawdust. Kerry was lying on her front, her head away from me. I covered her up and walked back to my room with another slight pang of guilt for sleeping next to the object of O'Reilly's affection.

Game drive in the morning was a trial – my headache was improved slightly by the frigid air blowing on it.

After drive, I planned to go to sleep for a number of hours but it was not to be. All of the front-line staff were instructed to meet at the Avuxeni Eatery for a briefing on the birthday of Queen Nicolette. I staggered down at 11h00 and found a spot between Kerry and Jane. Jenny was at the other end of the table. Matto arrived late and sat down next to her, making sure to look over to me as he did it, at which point Kerry laughed loudly at nothing and said, 'Angus, you are soooo funny!' and then rubbed my arm. I smiled. Jane giggled. Jenny looked up and Jane kissed me on the cheek.

PJ, O'Reilly, Carrie and SB came in presently, the latter frowning deeply and bearing a large lever-arch file in one hand and his new iPad in the other. PJ sat at the head of the table and explained that Nicolette's visit to the lodge was extremely important and that we needed to make a good impression. He then handed over to Carrie who explained who would be driving out of which camps (I am driving out of Tamboti with my boss, which will be good). She also explained that the evening drinks stops will have to be coordinated.

Then came the turn of the LHCU. His plans took twenty minutes to explain. The monologue was delivered with breathtaking pretentiousness. That said, it was meticulous and I felt a sense of sadness that my brother was unable to elucidate his clearly well-coordinated ideas with more humility and with more credit given to the other people involved. When he'd finished, the meeting broke up and we dispersed – me to my bed.

The next day, however, there was already trouble. You see, the programme of events for the group will require quite a lot of extra effort from all staff. Duncan, Jamie, Sipho and I, for example, have been assigned the task of creating an adult orientation-course-cum-treasure-hunt – with clues, maps and various prizes that will take the guests all over the reserve. Every Land Rover full of guests has to have a different course to do so it's been quite a task but great fun.

Abbot, however, has demanded that he be paid extra for every second over his normal working hours. This wouldn't be so unreasonable if PJ wasn't so lenient about giving people unrecorded leave when they have issues at home to which they need to attend. Because Abbot runs the stores, just about everyone needs him to complete the extra bits and pieces they've been assigned.

SB and Abbot had an enormous and public blow-out at lunch time today. My brother arrived while the store man was feeding on a vast plate of food.

'Abbot, I need to talk to you please,' said String Bean.

'After lunch, at two o'clock,' he replied, jettisoning a large piece of carrot from his stuffed buccal cavity. He replaced this with his fingers. 'Actually, no, come tomorrow morning, I'm very busy today, no time whatsoever for meetings.' Now the new LHCU is not used to this sort of response – especially where Nicolette's birthday celebrations are concerned.

'Abbot,' he said, 'I know you are busy but I really need to tell you what room amenities must be ordered for the group. That cannot wait for tomorrow because the stuff needs to be ordered today otherwise it won't arrive in time.' Other diners at the Avuxeni Eatery stopped eating.

'I will not be exploited. Actually this will take some overtime and management is not paying overtime,' replied Abbot sucking on a chicken bone. SB's temper and glaring lack of experience just escalated the situation.

'Abbot, I am running this group and you have to do what I tell you!' This was a match to the tinderbox. The shop steward stood up.

'You can't tell me what to do! You are not better than me whatsoever. Actually I am more higher than you in this lodge! In so forth as you are a little boy, just a little boy. Don't come to tell me what to do!' By this stage bits of food were coming out of Abbot like machine-gun bullets and his fat chin wobbled. People hurried to move their plates from the line of fire.

I was about to say something but as I stood, PJ came round the corner.

'The two of you will come with me now and we will sort this out in my office,' he ordered.

As they disappeared, Bertie explained that Abbot is rather in need of extra funds because the WANCRs have added a hefty interest to the money he owes. Apparently they took possession of his furniture a few days ago. His father has refused to lend him the money so it's not exactly surprising that the shop steward is grasping at straws for overtime pay.

This afternoon the lodge was virtually empty as we prepared for the imminent arrival of the owners and their group. The four of us in charge of the orientation course went out to check that our clues made sense. We left just after 14h00, and were driving out past the Main Camp entrance when Allegra hailed us from the newly-completed Sasekile Spa. Duncan stopped as she made her way over.

'If you are going out into the bush, I wonder if I might accompany you,' she said.

'Lady, we are indeed going into the veld,' I replied, climbing out of the passenger seat and indicating for her to climb in. Her eyes twinkled.

'Thank you,' she said. I hopped into the middle seat behind Jamie and Sipho.

Off we headed for an afternoon in the wild. It began as a clear warm winter afternoon and we chatted amiably as we drove, following the clues we'd written. Allegra held the clipboard and read out the clues while the rest of us suggested modifications and spotted birds. At each drop-off point we stopped to investigate the places where the clues and prizes would be stashed. At about 17h30, Duncan revealed a large cooler box hidden in the back seat and we all gratefully accepted a drink. Allegra leapt into a Heineken with gusto and this loosened her up a bit.

A little while later, we arrived at the last place indicated on the clue sheet. The clue had to be placed in the nook of an easily-climbable Natal mahogany tree, sitting alone in a dry floodplain. Everyone climbed into the boughs while I waited below. When they were settled, I tossed up another few drinks and climbed the trunk. We perched in the ancient tree, still leafy in the winter, and watched the sun disappear. A flock of white-faced ducks flew overhead in perfect formation, whistling as they went. We remained there until it was completely dark and the stars had showered the night sky.

A little while later, Jamie decided to try a long exposure with his camera. He climbed down the tree and drove the Land Rover a little way off in order to capture the tree silhouetted against the starry sky. While he set up the shot, we remained in the tree chatting. Allegra, after three beers, wasn't nearly so serious. My spirits lifted as I leant against the gnarled, old trunk, the smell of the fresh winter hanging in the air.

A lion roared in the distance.

'Hmmm, about two kilometres,' said Sipho. There was a brief silence and then another lion roared, his great voice exploding the clearing around us, echoing down the river and reverberating through the leaves.

'Oh!' said Allegra. 'How close do you think that one was?' At that point Jamie turned on a spotlight. It silhouetted a big, blond-maned lion striding across the clearing between the vehicle and the tree. He must have known we were there but he didn't even look up as he headed for his companion or rival. He did us the honour of calling again and as he began, Jamie turned off the light and the awesome thunder of his grating roar shook our bones. When he stopped all I could hear was Allegra breathing heavily. We let the moment hang for ten minutes.

'That was extraordinary,' Allegra whispered in my ear.

'So it was,' I replied.

'Do you think he's gone now?' she whispered again.

'Why are you whispering?' I whispered. There was a pause.

'I don't really know.' Still in hushed tones.

'Yes, I think he's gone.'

We drove home feeling very satisfied.

Week 26

Clout and chaos

The week began with The Legend's return from leave. I had to meet the insufferable git at a ranger's meeting just prior to picking up Nicolette's group at the airstrip. I bumped into him at the door and he stuck out a hand. 'Hello, Angus,' he said, the satisfaction behind his eyes sickening.

'Jones.' I shook his hand quickly and walked into the room.

Most of the group arrived in two airplanes and the rest made their way by road. Carrie drove Nicolette and Dennis Hogan, their two daughters (mid-to-late twenties), and another couple, down to Tamboti Camp. I followed with six others – two couples about the same age as the birthday girl –and two young guys, apparently there as companions to the daughters. They were both dressed in fading skinny jeans, checkered shirts and shoes that I assume they thought to be trendily scuffed. They also had haircuts and facial hair in the fashion of Caleb from the Kings of Leon. I therefore referred to them as Caleb 1 and Caleb 2 – I've no recollection of their real names.

The Calebs spent the week taking artful pictures with their iPhones and then editing them on their MacBook Pros – which went everywhere with them. I'm being a bit ungracious – they weren't entirely unpleasant but the young Hogans didn't seem much enamoured with them. The guests in the other camps were a collection of family, friends and sycophants – the latter obvious by their constant references to being the Hogans' friends for 'the longest time'.

The group was there for five days and we had planned various daily activities, most of which went off pretty well. The highlight was a mini-ranger's course which Carrie organised. We cycled all the guests through a number of ranger activities, including shooting, 4x4 driving, guiding and tracking. I helped out at the shooting range where Brandon was in charge and Melissa was serving refreshments. Brandon delivered a brief explanation of how to use a hunting rifle and then, with military discipline, we allowed the guests to shoot at targets set fifteen metres away. Caleb 1 refused to shoot more than one round after the recoil of the .458 cannoned into his shoulder.

'Shit shit shit shit . . .' he said, dropping the weapon into the dust. The young Hogans fell about laughing and Caleb 2 took an Instagram photo with his iPhone. Dennis Hogan (wild man extraordinaire) shouted, 'Struth, that's pathetic', in his nasal Australian twang. He then took the rifle and put five holes in the middle of the target.

'Howdja loik that then?' He winked, walking up to the refreshment table, slapping Melissa on the arse and taking a drink.

SB's plans worked out for the most part although he was thoroughly painful while it was all going on. He ran about officiously with his clipboard delivering orders without a touch of modesty, or thanks for the enormous effort everyone was putting in. Dinners were combined for the four camps, alternating between the Main Camp deck, boma and a bush dinner which was a pleasant if slightly frigid affair. The new spa was a massive success and Allegra was inundated from the outset. Guests emerged from her rooms looking dazed and glowing.

On the third night there were special bush drinks organised for sunset. The plan was for everyone to arrive on a crest that overlooks the western mountains just before the sun disappeared. There, special cocktails and canapés would be served.

I was late, arriving about ten minutes after the sun had disappeared. A while earlier Elvis had found a young male leopard quite far from the designated drinks stop. My guests, which for that drive were the two

Calebs, the daughters and another couple, were completely enthralled by the sight of the young cat trying to chase a squirrel into a spindly mopane tree. It was hilarious watching him trying to figure the problem out. First he tried to climb the tree but soon realised that wasn't feasible. Then he shook the base hoping the little rodent would fall out – again to no avail. All the while the squirrel was alarm calling frantically – 'chi ch ch ch ch ch ch ch' and flicking his tail. A flock of magpie shrikes also yelled at the leopard from a leafless tree wisteria nearby.

I reasoned, given that the guests were enjoying the wildlife, that being late for more drinking and eating wouldn't constitute a problem. The Lord High Commander of the Universe did not share my view. He started hailing me on the radio at 17h20, demanding to know where I was. When I arrived, he was puce. He welcomed the guests and they wandered off to join the others. While I packed away my binoculars, he raged.

'Angus, who the hell do you think you are? Everyone else got here on time and you...well, you just think you can do what the fuck you like. Have you any idea how hard I've worked to make this work?' A cool anger developed as I turned to face my kin.

'String Bean, everyone knows how hard you have worked because you keep telling them. I am late because the guests were enjoying a leopard. I'm sure you'll agree that their desires must surpass yours in importance – or perhaps you've forgotten that.' He stared at me. 'One other thing,' I continued climbing from the car, 'if you speak to me like that again, regardless of who is here, I will clobber the teeth from your skull.' I pushed past him.

The evening went well after that. Sipho gave a superb star talk while we sipped our drinks. I was sitting on the grass off to the side with a glass of O'Reilly's superb glühwein, watching as Sipho's green laser pointer cut the sky and his rich, theatrical voice filled the air. Kerry and O'Reilly, their duties complete, wandered over and sat next to me – she in between us.

'Ah Kerry, isn't dis just de morst rormantic ting in de world.' It was cringey, but said with genuine feeling. Kerry prodded my thigh as she said it and raised her right eyebrow to me in startled amusement.

Our treasure hunt was a roaring success. On the evening afterwards, Nicolette pulled me aside in the boma and said, 'Well Angus, it would seem that you've come a long way since our last meeting.' She looked at me sternly, her once-pretty face almost smiling.

'I like to think I've grown up a bit,' I replied.

'Not too much I hope,' she winked, 'my congratulations on that wonderful treasure hunt; sophisticated and a lot of fun. I believe you were largely responsible.' SB's voice, taking credit for all things, popped into my mind and out again.

'I had a lot of help,' I replied, sipping on my scotch.

'Well, please extend my thanks to the others.' She made to leave, then turned back. 'I was devastated when I heard about Anna last year. I believe you and her were very close.'

I nodded, 'We were.' She gave me a genuine smile and walked off to join her husband at the fire.

The final dinner, the night of Nicolette's birthday, was a black-tie affair on the Main Camp deck – the culmination of their week in the bush and a glorious celebration of the lodge and its owners. To the guests it was just that. Behind the scenes, however, chaos normally associated with an episode of *Fawlty Towers* reigned.

I arrived back from a spectacular drive during which we'd seen a pack of wild dogs fight off a ragged band of hyenas that was trying to steal its freshly-killed impala. The sighting was close to camp so I was the first ranger back by about twenty minutes. I dropped the guests off at the Tamboti car park and then went to my room to change. We'd been instructed to dress as smartly as possible. For me, that meant a pair of clean uniform slacks and a new, white Sasekile shirt. I put a bit of aftershave on my face and wandered down towards the Main Camp just as the other rangers were arriving back.

Instead of heading straight to the deck, I wandered into the kitchen to see what O'Reilly and his team were conjuring up for the grand affair. An unfamiliar smell of burning emanated from the kitchen as I approached. Inside, there was a scene of some confusion. Richard, Petrus, Rufina, Gift, and Jane (the chefs) were all standing at the door to O'Reilly's office, which was firmly shut. Jane and Richard were knocking gently on it.

'Come on, you can't stay in there all night, we need you out here,' coaxed Jane.

Kerry was standing off to one side looking shocked, chewing a fingernail.

'What's going on?' I asked of the redhead.

'He's gone completely crazy!' she said.

'Why?' I asked.

'I don't know!'

'Tell him, Kerry,' said Jane before returning her attention to the door. Kerry groaned.

'Well, this afternoon he came to my room and just blurted out that he was in love with me and that he couldn't live another day without me.'

'And then?'

'Well, I mean, what could I say? I was shocked so I sort of thanked him and then said I was sorry but that I don't feel the same way!' She stopped attacking her cuticle. 'Then he went pale, said he understood, and left. That was at about five o'clock.'

Jane continued the story: 'We all arrived here about half an hour ago and he was locked in the office.' At this point there was a loud bang as some sort of kitchen implement slammed into the door from the inside.

'Fek uhf de lotta ya!' the Irishman bellowed.

'The big problem is that the food is ruined. It was all prepared and ready but he's gone and put it all – everything we had prepared – in that giant pot over there and turned the heat to high. It's all completely inedible!'

'Well, has anyone thought to tell PJ or, I hate to suggest it, Hugh?' I asked. Blank faces stared back at me. 'Okay,' I said, 'we need PJ. Richard, go and look in his house. Rufina, you check the office. Tell him to come to the kitchen, now. Gift, Kerry, Petrus, get into the fridge and see what else is in there.'

'And me?' said Jane looking for a task.

'Um … you help me with him,' I said.

'O'Reilly,' I shouted, 'get out of there now! This is ridiculous.'

'Fek uhf!' Another bowl crashed into the door. It was a flimsy door, so I gave it a good kick and it swung open. The executive chef was lying on an enormous, open bag of flour. Next to him were four bottles of wine – all empty. He was clearly rat-arsed, his head and face covered in flour. He tried to get up and attack me but slipped, cracked his head on the desk and slumped back into the flour.

'Oh God, he's dead!' said Jane.

'I doubt it,' I replied as a loud snore emerged from his nostrils, sending a cloud of flour into the air. 'Right, well, he's useless tonight; we'll have to do without him.'

Simone came rushing into the kitchen. 'Guys, the guests are coming through and there are no snacks!' She paused as she beheld the recumbent, flour-covered form of the Irishman. 'What happened?'

'Long story,' I said, 'Everyone out.' I shut the office door behind me. 'Where's String Bean?'

'I don't know,' said Simone. Richard and Rufina arrived with PJ tucking in his shirt. I gave him a brief summary of events and, like the captain of a ship in a storm, he took control of his crew.

'Okay, Richard, you're in charge in the kitchen now,' PJ said. 'We need snacks in ten minutes. Can you do that?' The old Shangane's chest swelled with pride.

'Yes, I can do it!' he shouted. He beckoned Gift and Jane and they went to help him.

'Angus, I need you to find Hugh, and get him in here – quick as you can, please.'

Simone and I dashed out of the kitchen and onto the Main Camp deck. There were a few guests there, quaffing champagne and being attended to by the butlers and a few camp managers. SB, however, was nowhere to be seen. I hailed Clifford who came jogging over.

'Hello Clifford, have you seen Hugh?'

'Oh yes, hello, there are no snacks.'

'Yes, thank you, we're taking care of that. Where is Hugh?'

'He go to fetch some more champagne in the bar store.' Simone and I ran for the little bar store between the boma and the deck. I kicked open the swing door and walked in, Simone close behind. The sight that greeted us was, shall I say, unfortunate.

There were two people in the bar store 'fetching champagne'. Amber was pressed up against the white wine fridge with her stocking-covered legs wrapped around the rear-end of the missing LHCU. Mercifully, they were both fully clothed although the straps to Amber's yellow dress were round her shoulders.

As we walked in, they split apart and faced us, Amber replacing her straps and SB staring, lipstick all over his face.

'This is … um … not what it looks …' That was as far as he got before a stainless-steel ice bucket came flying over my left shoulder, clattering into his face. The language that then came from Simone Robertson's mouth is not repeatable but was directed at Amber and String Bean. The latter bellowed loudly trying to stem the blood flowing from his ruined nose which was no longer facing front. Simone stormed out.

'String Bean, you utter turd,' I said. Amber made to have a look at my brother's nose. 'You,' I pointed at the girl through gritted teeth, 'you fuck off and don't let me catch sight of you again tonight.' She hesitated for a second. 'NOW!' I yelled. She grabbed her pashmina and ran out. LHCU was whimpering in the corner. I gave him a brief highlights package of the disaster occurring in the kitchen. 'You go and see PJ,' I said.

'I can't go like this …' he whined. He had a point. There was blood all down the front of his shirt and his nose was badly out of shape. If he wasn't my brother (though I struggle to acknowledge our genetic connection at times like this) I'd have left him there or dragged him to the General Manager.

'Your only hope,' I said, seething, 'is to get into that Tazz you feel is so beneath your station and drive to the hospital. I'll tell PJ you've tripped and broken your nose – at least one part of that isn't a lie.' More groaning.

'Okay, I'll do it,' he snuffled, realising the hopelessness of his predicament.

I returned to the deck with a case of champagne and handed it to Clifford as three butlers emerged from the kitchen bearing platters full of Melba toast and various pâtés. The Melba toast looked suspiciously like it had originated as thinly sliced and stale government bread. I ran into the kitchen where PJ was having a conference with Richard and Kerry.

'Where's your brother?' he asked.

'I'm afraid he's had to drive into Hoedspruit. He tripped on the stairs into the bar store and smashed his nose.'

'When?' asked PJ, suspicious.

'Um … five minutes ago,' I replied, shoulders shrugged.

'Dammit.' The General Manager scowled as Carrie walked in. PJ turned to face her.

'I've just seen Simone ru…' Behind PJ I waved my arms and shook my head.

'Simone what?' asked the GM.

'Oh, never mind,' replied Carrie.

'Fine,' said the GM, 'now we've got a crisis here. There's no meat – I mean none. O'Reilly's burned the lot.'

'What about venison,' I ventured.

'Aren't you listening? There isn't any!' shouted Kerry.

'We're sitting in a game reserve full of the stuff!' I said.

'He's right,' PJ's eyes shone. 'I reckon we've got, at an outside maximum, an hour and a bit before we have to serve the main course. Who's the best shot in the ranging team?'

'I am,' said Carrie without arrogance.

'Radio Jacob and Elvis to help you get out there and fetch us some venison. You've got less than half an hour because we'll have to skin, fillet and then cook it.'

Carrie ran out, talking to Jacob on the radio.

'How are we going to cook meat that needs to hang for days?' PJ asked the *de facto* head chef, Richard. He held up his knife and pulled a whetstone from his apron.

'We slice it very, very thin!'

'Okay, but we can't just serve venison – some of the guests here specifically don't eat red meat,' said Jane.

'Gladys Khoza's been poaching fish from the river for years,' said PJ. 'Angus, go and find out what her stock is looking like. Threaten her with arrest if she gives you any trouble.'

I hurtled out of the kitchen and up to the village. As I ran past the staff shop, another disturbing sight greeted me. Abbot was standing at the head of a group of people holding placards – he was yelling at the top of his voice. I didn't hang about to see why.

I found Gladys outside her isolated house at the top of the village – cooking a fish on a little open fire. She glared at me, then the fish, and covered it with a pot. The following interaction took place in Shangane.

'What do you want?' she asked, her single yellow tooth bared.

'Fish,' I replied without preamble.

'I know nothing about fish. It is against my religion to eat fish,' she replied.

'Mother, that is not a steak on the fire,' I said and pushed past into her room. In the corner there stood a small chest freezer.

'Get out of my house!' she yelled, coming in behind me. I pulled open the lid – about a dozen tilapia, three enormous catfish and even a few small tiger fish stared up at me from the freezer.

'Where did you get these, Mother?' I asked grabbing an empty plastic bag and packing the fish into it.

'Um, I buy them!' she said. By this stage she was slapping me on the back.

'Gladys!' I shouted. 'We need to feed these to the guests. If you want to argue then we can call the police about poaching.' She backed off, snarling. I felt a bit sorry for the old duck – she's had a bloody tough life. 'I'm sure you can catch some more, but please, there is a big problem in the kitchen and we need them.' She moved out of my way.

I ran from the house, very glad not to be responsible for having to make something edible out of the plastic bag's contents. The little crowd at the staff shop was singing (very nicely – if a little aggressively).

I arrived at the kitchen just as Jacob, Carrie and Elvis skidded to a halt in the conservation Land Rover; the horns of a massive impala ram protruding from the back. Inside the kitchen, there was furious activity – slicing, mixing, tasting, and a lot of shouting. Richard was firmly in charge and his team included a number of rangers who were doing menial tasks like washing and chopping. I spotted Matto, tears streaming down his face, ineffectually hacking at an onion with one hand.

I handed the fish bag to Jane who emptied it onto a spare surface.

'Oh!' she said, 'um, well I guess we'll have to make a stew of some sort – and spice it very heavily.'

Melissa came running into the kitchen. 'Thit thit thit thit!' she screamed. 'Guyth Nicolette wantth to bring a whole lot of guethtth through to the kitchen to meet O'Reilly!'

'Oh thit indeed,' said Jane hacking the head off a slimy catfish.

'When?' said PJ emerging from a cloud of steam at the stove.

'Now!' shouted Melissa.

'Get out there and stall her,' said PJ.

'How?'

'Just go and tell her that O'Reilly will be ready in a few minutes.'

'O'Reilly won't be ready for another week,' said Jane. Thwack went her knife, severing a tail.

PJ and I went round to the office and opened the door. The Irishman had shifted about a bit and there was flour everywhere. He was still snoring.

'Well, she can't meet him,' said PJ.

'No thit,' I said.

'You'll have to do it,' he looked at me. I smiled and then frowned, realising he was being serious. 'She's never met him; you're about the same height.'

'She's met me, though! Get one of the other chefs to do it.'

'Angus, I hate to point out the bleeding obvious here but, all the other chefs are either black, female or both and she knows O'Reilly isn't either!'

Melissa ran in.

'We can't hold her anymore, thee's getting angry. They're on their way from the deck.' As we stood there, the sound of singing touched our ears.

'What the hell is that?' asked PJ.

Carrie came into the kitchen through the back door, carrying a freshly-butchered impala fillet.

'Abbot Siwela seems to be leading a small *impi* towards the kitchen,' she said handing the meat to Kerry and disappearing back outside. PJ's relatively calm exterior cracked.

'Fuck!' he barked.

'What about Nicolette, they'll be here in a minute!' Jenny wailed.

'Angus, please, you have to do this!' he said. 'I have to go and stop Abbot murdering someone. Melissa, get out there and tell her O'Reilly will welcome her in two minutes.'

'Okay, okay!' I snapped. I looked over at O'Reilly – he's about my length but his girth is vast. 'Kerry, help me out here.' She tossed the bloodied loin straight across the kitchen into Richard's waiting hands. Then she grabbed two aprons hanging from the office door, folded them up and pushed them up under my shirt.

'It's my face she's going to recognise,' I said unbuttoning O'Reilly's chef's jacket. Kerry pulled off his pants. 'He'll wish he'd been awake for that,' I remarked.

'Shut up and put them on, I'm coming now.' I donned O'Reilly's less-than pristine uniform and then covered my face in flour. I grabbed the chef's hat off the desk and pulled it as far onto my head as it would go – it was big and hung half over my eyes.

Jenny and Kerry arrived at the office simultaneously. Jenny beheld the comatose form of the head chef, covered in flour and dressed in nothing but a pair of holey Y-fronts. Her hand went to her mouth.

'I found this in the dustbin outside,' said Kerry, holding up a dust mask, 'the maintenance guys left it after the freezer paint job.' I pulled the mask on.

'Nicolette's at the kitchen door with four people! She wants O'Reilly, and Richard is just staring blankly at her with a piece of bleeding meat in his hands! She'll never believe you,' wailed Jenny. Kerry threw more flour at me. Jenny's lack of faith filled me with a desire to prove her wrong.

'My dear, this is no time for your whining. Now, step aside.'

I walked out of the office towards the door where Nicolette waited. The kitchen went quiet as I passed through the team of chefs. All eyes moved with me.

'Tanks Richard, Oi'll tek it frum here.' Richard's mouth opened, I put my hand on his shoulder, turned him and said, 'Do dat lot medium rare.' He walked off dumbfounded. I swung to face the owner. 'Mrs Hogan, happy burrthday and welcome to me kitchen. It's a real honour!' She glared at me.

'O'Reilly, is it?' she said curtly.

'At yurr surrvice, madam!' I held out my hand. 'Please excuse de mask boot Oi've got a corld and Oi'd heht tu infect ya all!' She shook my hand while holding my eye.

The moment of truth.

'Quite, well, show us round. My friends here would like to see where the exquisite food they've been eating is prepared.' While this was going on, Jane subtly moved all the rangers out the back door.

I took the little group round the kitchen, introducing all the chefs by name, my face reddening as each of them looked from me to her. All the while, the singing from outside became louder and louder until it couldn't be ignored any longer.

'What's that singing?' asked Stephanie, Nicolette's sister.

'Um, it's the staff choir warming up for their performance,' said Kerry quickly.

'Wonderful!' exclaimed Stephanie, 'I love African singing!'

Thankfully they weren't able to understand the militant nature of the lyrics that, from what I could make out, had a lot to do with the violent overthrow of oppressive regimes.

As I introduced Gift, the last chef in the kitchen, loud shouting came from the back door and then some banging. Nicolette spun round.

'Bluudy hyenas, always trooin to get in de kitchen!' I said loudly.

'Hmm,' said Nicolette, 'are they indeed? I don't recall any mention of a choir before.'

'A surprise!' I said.

'Well, I don't normally like surprises,' Nicolette turned to the door and then back again. 'I thought you were from Tipperary?'

I looked at her. 'Oi am,' I replied.

'You've obviously spent time in Belfast then.' Her eyes bore into mine.

'Oi...um...yas, soom toime in de nort! Indeed!'

'Hmm...well...thank you for the tour. I look forward to dinner.' With that she swept out; friends and Jenny in tow.

Pandemonium resumed in the kitchen as the manic attempts to ready an edible meal on time continued. I pulled the mask off and rushed out of the back door where I bumped into Elvis, Carrie and Jacob as they finished butchering the carcass hanging up outside. Beyond them, there were some 30 men, some with sticks and others with placards. They were leaping up and down as they sang. Abbot stood at the front, brandishing a panga and railing at PJ. The GM drew him away from the crowd to where we were standing.

'Actually, we are tired of exploitation. We demand 100 per cent increase in salary or we are marching to the deck to show the guests in so forth as the workers are very angry!' he shouted. I looked over the group of singers. There were at least twenty young men at the front of the phalanx that I'd never seen before. Behind them, there was a group of staff, some singing enthusiastically, and others standing about looking bored.

'Who are these people?' asked PJ.

'The workers!' yelled Abbot.

'I've never seen half of them,' replied PJ.

'It is a solidarity from workers all over!'

'Well, they're trespassing,' said PJ. 'I shall be forced to call the police if they don't leave.'

'You can't threaten us whatsoever. Actually, we are not afraid!' PJ looked at the group.

'Okay,' he said, 'you ask them to be quiet for a few minutes and then you and I go into the kitchen to talk.' Abbot agreed. He walked over to the band of singers and they quietened down.

As he was doing this, PJ whispered something in Jacob's ear. The big man nodded and moved inside, Elvis close behind him. Then he turned to me: 'What you're about to witness you will not find in the labour-relations handbook.' Abbot walked over and we returned to the kitchen.

'If you'd just step into the office,' said PJ to Abbot. The shop steward walked in. As he saw the naked head chef lying on the ground, he spun round to be faced, not with the GM but with Jacob 'Spear of the Lowveld' Mkhonto, and Elvis.

You have no permission for a demonstration, so unless you want to spend this night and a few more in jail, you'll sit on that chair and not leave it until I tell you to.

'Sit down,' Elvis instructed. Abbot began to remonstrate as PJ walked in behind them. 'Shut up,' said PJ, pointing at Abbot with menace. 'If you say another word, I will have you arrested and charged for inciting a violent riot on private property. You have no permission for a demonstration so unless you want to spend this night and a few more in jail, you'll sit on this chair and not leave it. Abbot realised he was defeated and slumped into the chair.

I walked back outside to see PJ talking to the protestors. The twenty or so trespassers stood up presently; their sticks and placards left on the ground.

'Jenny,' he called over the radio, 'would you please come to the kitchen and escort the choir onto the deck. They are ready to perform for the guests.'

As we walked back into the kitchen, PJ explained that he'd simply offered them a meal and a hundred bucks each – double what Abbot had offered.

So, as the 'choir' gave their performance, I ordered a triple of the most expensive malt on offer, added it to The Legend's tab and watched as plates of venison and powerful fish curry were distributed to the guests.

The deck looked spectacular. It was closed off by thick blinds to make it cosier. There were braziers all around and a large fire in the hearth off to one side. The tables each bore a large silver candelabrum and were set with crystal glasses, silver cutlery and new, white table cloths. LHCU, before his spectacular fall from grace, managed to organise lilies for each centrepiece so the air was sweetly perfumed.

The atmosphere was amplified by the elegance with which the guests had all dressed – bar the Calebs of course. They were, predictably, in black suits, their pants tapered and jacket sleeves too short. Stringy black ties hung loosely from their necks as they looked through the photographs on Caleb 1's MacBook. The young Hogans looked like two goddesses and one can only hope that they don't turn out quite as severe as their mother.

I wandered back into the kitchen as Richard and Gift pushed a malva pudding into the oven. The rest were standing about looking shell-shocked. They all started laughing as I walked in and their mirth increased exponentially as O'Reilly staggered out of the office in his Y-fronts.

'Whut de fek is goin on in here?' he slurred. He then leant against a wall and passed out again, sliding gently to the floor.

The next day, the group left and Nicolette gave PJ a sterling review of the week. Her only complaint was that she found the venison a bit gamey on the last night. Dennis, who had the fish, said that eating the curry was like putting a blowtorch in his mouth – rather that than the taste of muddy catfish, I say.

Week 27

Apologies and au pair

After the excitement of last week, there has been relative calm at Sasekile. If you delve a little below the surface, however, there are deep scars from the Hogan visit – mental and physical. SB is sporting a thick plaster over his nose and the flesh under his eyes has gone from angry black to jaundiced yellow. He hasn't said anything to me all week, which is good because I'm still so irritated with him that I'd probably re-break his recently-set beak. Simone is not talking to him or Amber. The latter is on leave presently so Simone is alone in Kingfisher Camp – I think she's thriving in the absence of her home-wrecking 'superior'.

Rumours abound amongst the staff as to the reason that String Bean and Simone are on no-speaks. The story that he fell on the steps and smashed his nose has been greeted with scepticism but there seems to be no knowledge of what went on with Amber.

I've been driving out of Kingfisher Camp for the whole week so I've seen quite a lot of Simone. She's not happy but has stoically kept busy, which I'm sure is helping. At tea the other day I asked how she was doing as I helped myself to some iced coffee.

'Not great,' she replied, 'but I'll survive. I'm really enjoying the work here but I don't know what's going to happen when that bitch comes back. There's no way that I can work with her.'

I replied, 'Well the way I see it, you have two choices. One, you tell PJ that you can't work with her but he's going to ask why. Two, you tell SB that he had better move things around in his capacity as Lord High Commander of the Universe or you'll be forced to ask PJ. I reckon that'll terrify him enough to make a plan.'

'I'll think about it but I'm really not sure I can ever talk to him again – especially as my boss!' She spat *boss* out.

'I know what you mean.'

O'Reilly went to PJ the minute the Hogan group departed. Word has it that he went with a resignation letter, apologised profusely and said he'd be off the property within the hour. PJ, wisely, accepted the apology and not the resignation. Kerry also received a letter from him asking for forgiveness and swearing he wouldn't bother her again. She says he can't bring himself to actually speak to her yet.

As for Abbot, his life became nastier before it improved. Two WANCRs arrived the day the Hogans left, this time in a black Audi A5 (and shiny suits of course). I was sitting in the rangers' room reading an article about the wildlife of South Sudan when I heard Abbot's obsequious bray, welcoming his masters. I assumed they were here to help defend their shop steward in the wake of his failed protest march. I looked out of the window in time to see the store man being grabbed by the throat and thrust onto the bonnet of the dusty car. He started flapping like a flipped tortoise. I rose from my sofa and hailed Jeff who was reading a *People* magazine next to me.

'Action stations, Jeffrey.' We walked to the door to see the second WANCR flapping a piece of paper in Abbot's face.

'You are late with your account! You want to me to kill you like a little beetle!' yelled the WANCR with the paper.

As we stepped outside, PJ burst from his office across the way. 'What is the meaning of this?' he shouted.

'It is none of your business monopoly capitalist,' said the WANCR, brandishing Abbot's account. Jeff and I joined the General Manager.

'You are trespassing. Let him go right now!' he yelled.

'Actually, this is the business of the union!' the WANCR responded.

'I will have you forcibly removed if you don't leave in the next three minutes!' replied PJ.

'Are you threatening me imperialist?!' He moved forward and prodded PJ in the chest. By that stage the commotion had drawn interest from a number of other staff – among them Elvis. The tracker moved to the front of the group and without hesitating, clattered his plate-sized hand across the WANCR's face. His knock-off Oakleys went flying into the dust. Jeff grabbed the WANCR holding Abbot on the back of the neck, wrenched him off and tossed him into the dirt like a shiny-suited ragdoll. The store man rolled onto the floor spluttering.

Not long after that, the WANCRs drove off. PJ gritted his teeth, helped Abbot to his feet and pulled him into the office. Carrie says Abbot broke down during the meeting and confessed to trying to trick the staff with the *muthi*. PJ agreed to pay the debt and deduct instalments from his salary on condition he never tries to be a shop steward again. I don't think we'll be seeing the WANCRs again any time soon.

There was some more conflict this week, but this time from some slightly more junior members of humanity. Allegra has been inundated at the spa so there's been no one to look after the kids for most of last week. This means that the rangers have had to cover the childminding duties in the middle of the day. Children are not my forte.

A few days ago I was on duty at the Warren when seven beastly little spawn ranging in age from six to ten arrived. Two of them came from the loins of a couple of my guests. Candice and Britney were six-year-old twins with the manners of warthog piglets. The other five were begat by other rangers' guests. Their names I did not attempt to remember. There were three Germans (two boys, around six or seven and a girl, a bit older) and two Dutch boys (seven and ten).

This merry crew was my responsibility for two hours after breakfast. Normally, the kiddies' programme consists of story-telling, face painting or something else that adults think small humans enjoy. They all arrived at the Warren around 11h00 where I was waiting and wondering what on Earth to occupy them with. The twins immediately set upon the little table filled with wax crayons and colouring books. It took them half a minute to start fighting over a red crayon. Before I could intervene, the Dutch boys arrived whereupon the small one picked up a wooden giraffe next to the door and bashed his brother on the knee. The wounded one started howling and then picked up a tiny plastic chair with which he tried to take his revenge.

While I stared at the growing anarchy, the German mother arrived with her three children. She regarded the others with distaste.

'Vot iss going on here?' she asked as her youngest ran to join the fray at the colouring table.

'Isn't this normal?' I asked.

'Not in Chermany!' She then said something to her two remaining offspring. They walked meekly over to the Lego table and their mother departed. As the stern fraülein disappeared, the two Lego Goths launched into the melee at the colouring table. The twins forgot about the red crayon as an international conflict over the entire box of pastels ensued.

'I was here first!' screamed Britney.

'No, I was,' yelled her sister, grabbing the handful Britney was holding.

'*Meiner!*' shouted the smallest Goth trying to remove the whole box.

The female Goth then took a fistful of crayons from the box and was about make an escape when the younger Dutchman made good his sibling vengeance. He dispensed with the little chair he was wielding, picked up a world globe and flung it. It collected his brother in the chest and sent him reeling backwards onto the female Goth who fell on the colouring table.

Being plump to the point of obesity, her mass buckled the little plastic table legs and it crashed to the floor. Candice ended up under the table and Britney finished perched on top of the round Goth. There was silence for about five seconds. This blissful but brief period was followed by a great wailing and gnashing of teeth.

I lost my temper.

'Right, that's it!' I bellowed. 'Shut up, now – all of you!' The Germans hardly spoke English but the tone of my voice contained all the meaning I wished to convey. 'Stand up,' I commanded. They stood and looked at me, lips quivering. 'If you do not all do exactly as I tell you, I shall feed you to the lions.' More lip quivering and a sniffle or two.

I lined them up like a platoon and made them hold their hands out. They obeyed wide-eyed, probably expecting a smack. I fetched a giant bottle of sunscreen and squirted a dollop onto each outstretched palm.

'Put that on your faces.' They obeyed instantly. I found a pile of Sasekile hats in the corner of the room and placed one on each of the little heads before handing out an assortment of butterfly nets, collecting jars and water bottles. The twins looked like they might start squabbling again so I glared at them and they resumed their lip quivering.

'Come,' I ordered and walked out of the room. They followed and we marched towards the kitchen in a neat line. Jane was standing outside the kitchen drinking a mug of tea. She smiled widely as the platoon come into view.

'Halt!' I shouted. The group came to an immediate standstill in front of Jane.

'Ah, the Pied Piper!' she said.

'Yes,' I replied, 'with the rats. Please would you watch them for a second?' She smiled and nodded. I turned to the kids and lifted a finger at them. 'Don't any of you move an inch – understood?' They all nodded.

'Shame!' said Jane.

'Shame, nothing,' I snapped and walked into the kitchen. Inside, I found O'Reilly in his office, working on a recipe. He went red.

'Ungus, how are ya? Just so dreadfully surry about de udder noight. So so surry!'

'Fear not, O'Reilly, things turned out fine. You've obviously taught your charges well because they handled things with aplomb.'

'Well, dat's a very gracious ting of ya t'say. Whut can I do fur ya?' I explained my predicament with the kids and he ruffled about in a drawer and produced a packet of cherry Fizz Pops. 'Deese'll do de trick!'

I thanked him and walked out with the bag.

The kids were standing around Jane, telling her their names and where they were from.

'Attention!' I shouted. They went silent and stood stock straight.

'Angus! Be nice!' said Jane.

'I am being nice. Forward, march!'

We walked out of the delivery entrance and on to a clearing about ten minutes from the camp. There, I lined them up again and made them drink some water. Then I split them into non-sibling groups and told them there would be a prize for the group that collected the largest number of insects. They stared at me briefly.

'Now!' I yelled. They wandered slowly out into the clearing and I removed myself to a termite mound not far off to observe. Initially the language barrier and the unfamiliar surroundings made for an awkward time but eventually they were leaping on grasshoppers and running about trying to net the few butterflies flying about. There wasn't a huge amount to catch with it being winter but the game removed them from the painful squabbling and, no doubt, the fresh air worked wonders.

I relaxed beneath the deep-blue, warm winter sky. A flock of Senegal lapwings flew off in protest as the female Goth and Britney made to catch a beetle near them. A tawny eagle watched proceedings from a dead leadwood at one end of the clearing.

After 30 minutes or so, I called them to me. Candice and the older Goth had done a remarkable collecting job and they'd even made an attempt to provide food for their prisoners. In the interests of peace, however, I judged that there was no clear winner so we all had a sucker and wandered back to camp, the kids chatting amiably amongst themselves. In the end, I was late for lunch and felt pretty good as I lay down for a brief kip before game drive. Thankfully, that has been my only childminding duty this week.

Leave starts tomorrow – it's been a busy cycle so I'm looking forward to some rest but the thought of winter in Johannesburg doesn't fill me with glee.

Week 28

Family and frost

Like I said last week, while I was tired from the long work cycle and I'll never be one to complain about having time to myself, Johannesburg is not a holiday paradise in the winter time (or any other time for that matter). Julia and I are still barely talking to each other and I haven't made an effort to contact her for our usual dinners and lunches because the subject of The Legend is bound to come up – they are having a dalliance of some description. I'm trying to avoid a massive intra-family feud – with me on one side; father, brother and sister on the other; and Mum desperately trying to make peace in the middle.

I saw Julia at lunch this afternoon but we hardly said anything to each other and the subject of significant others was studiously avoided by all. She left early to go and study some documents for a case in the morning. What a shitty way to spend a Sunday afternoon – for her, I mean.

Of course, the Major now lives at home so I've spent a lot of time with him, which has not been entirely agreeable. His levels of cantankerousness are increasing in inverse proportion to his tolerance of other races, religions and nationalities other than the British (specifically excluding the Northern Irish and lowland Scots). Francina will no longer talk to him. He also doesn't have much affection for Trubshaw but the dog is far too dim-witted to notice and still greets the old man with the same fondness that he does the family, its friends and the two sets of burglars who cleaned out the Kenton house under his watchful eye. The Major's olfactory sense is obviously not functioning as it should because he tolerates AIDS Cat on his lap. This animal, despite being given three months to live when Mum adopted her, shows no signs of throwing off her mortal coil but her odour continues to offend.

It's become profoundly embarrassing to take my grandfather anywhere because he can't contain himself. I took him out to lunch in the middle of the week and he managed to have us turfed out the restaurant. We went to Parkhurst and found a table in the winter sun. I ordered two large beers and we soaked up the rays, enjoyed our drinks and watched the world going past for a little while. Halfway through his beer, the Major began haranguing me about the state of the country and the people that purport to run it.

He concluded his treatise with, 'Mark my words – we're on a slippery slope! Just look at the appalling state Rhodesia finds herself in!' he shouted. The people at the tables around us stopped their conversations and stared.

Our food arrived shortly thereafter; a burger for me and bangers and mash for the Major. The Major devoured his sausages like a starved refugee and then set to his remaining gravy with two arthritic fingers.

The manager, an Indian man called Pravesh, arrived to check if we were enjoying our meal. The Major scarcely looked up, so intent was he on hoovering the last of the gravy. I told the manager that our food was excellent.

Pravesh then looked to the Major and said, 'And you sir, may I fetch you a beer?' The Major ceased his slurping and glowered at Pravesh. I answered for him quickly and told the manager we'd appreciate two more drinks. As he left, the Major leant over the table, gravy spread about his lips. At a volume I assume he thought to be a whisper but which more accurately approximated that of an erupting volcano, my grandfather said, 'Never trust a wagon burner – diddle you out of the last coin in your pocket before you can say Mahatma Gandhi.' The restaurant went deadly quiet again as the patrons (inside and out) turned to stare at us.

Pravesh stopped midway back to the bar and turned. He lifted his index finger and waved it at the Major as he strode back to the table.

'No no no no no sirs, that is not acceptable at all. I must ask you to leave immediately. That sort of the language will not be tolerated!'

'I'll tell you what won't be toler...' the Major began but I grabbed him by the elbow before he could continue and we left. I returned later that afternoon to pay and apologise to Pravesh. He was very gracious but obviously deeply insulted by my aged relation.

The highlight of the week was a bachelor party I attended for Donald Gilbert. Unlike most affairs of this nature, this was not just a drinking competition. We went to a spot near Rhodes to do some fishing for two days. I'm comfortably the worst fisherman ever to grace the crystalline waters flowing off the Eastern Cape highlands and I was required to pay for this deficiency in my talents by drinking shots of neat scotch. I didn't mind at all because the whisky was generally excellent and the temperature so cold that downing neat alcohol was virtually the only way to stay vaguely warm.

There were ten of us wandering the hills alone or in groups trying to pull trout from the frigid streams. Despite the temperature I had a fantastic time walking and tossing my line into the water (and the vegetation behind me). The rivers are pristine and I had forgotten what a rare privilege it is to drink water straight from a river, unafraid of picking up amoebic dysentery, courtesy of indiscriminate abluters upstream. The air was also so crisp and clear I could almost taste it.

We stayed in a little stone fishing lodge with very few creature comforts but there was a huge fire place and we burned a lot of wood at night. There was even some snow on our second night. The next morning, Donald incurred a black eye and a number of welts all over his body as he was forced to stand in the snow, dressed in only his boxers, while being pelted from all angles. His brother, Richard, has a powerful but wayward throwing arm and he managed to collect Donald just below the right eye with a giant snowball. Of course we all thought this hilarious, especially after we realised Donald would have to walk down the aisle with a miscoloured eye.

On my return to Johannesburg, Mum showed me an email from SB.

To: Mum; Jules
From: Hugh
Subject: Troubles

Hi Mum and Jules,

Thanks for your last message. I'm glad that you have enjoyed having Angus at home – although I'm sorry that he couldn't stop the Major creating an enormous incident.

Big news from here is that Simone and I have broken up. I'm sad about it but frankly she really didn't seem to understand the extra work I now have on my plate as the Hospitality Manager and I always felt under pressure to give her more of my time. I need someone who can support me and not harp on and on about how they need more of my time.

On a positive note, I'm going to be retraining all of the butlers from the camps because some of them have never had any kind of formal training. I'm really looking forward to it and I've created what I think is an inspirational course on silver service. I've put together a plan that goes all the way from basic table cleaning to advanced wine service. I think the course will make a huge difference to general hospitality here. Operation Service Fantastic starts next week!

So that's my news. Please give the Major my best regards and tell him his favourite grandson will be back to see him in a few weeks!

Lots of love, your trainer-of-the-stars son and brother,
Hugh
P.S. There's been an elephant in the camp eating the greenery around the lodge because the bush is so dry. He's causing havoc with the gardens.

SB obviously took the calculated gamble that I wouldn't spill the beans on the notorious ice-bucket incident. I would ordinarily have shared the story with Julia but I'm not sufficiently well-disposed to her at the moment. I suppose Simone and SB must eventually have had a conversation about ending things officially.

I sent him the following on reading his less-than-frank letter to our mother and sister.

To: Hugh MacNaughton
From: Angus MacNaughton
Subject: Yellow Belly

String Bean,

Blaming Simone for the demise of your relationship instead of your own gargantuan failings as a human being is a cowardly cop-out.

I submit the following as an example of what would have been a more accurate representation of the situation.

Dear Mum and Julia,

Simone and I have broken up because she caught me trying to have sex with a slut against the white wine fridge in the bar store. She has also objected to the fact that I treat her and the people I am managing like a bunch of ignorant peons.

I'm sorry for soiling the family name and being such a complete arse.

Yours in deep personal regret,
Hugh

There it is.
Angus

P.S. History is littered with examples of people who have risen to great heights, turned into despots and then fallen spectacularly from grace. Hospitality Manager of a small reserve in the lowveld is hardly up there with Richard III, but I suspect if your giant ego isn't brought under some semblance of control in the near future, you too might feel much like the last of the Plantagenets did.

I have yet to hear from him.

Week 29

Rubbish and rest

Week two of leave in the chillsome climes of Johannesburg has been relaxed if somewhat unspectacular. The Major continues to say outrageous things to Francina, Trubshaw continues to knock him over at every available opportunity and AIDS Cat sleeps on his chest every night.

I finally received a reply from String Bean.

To: Angus
From: Hugh MacNaughton
Subject: Mind your own goddamn business!

Angus,

I don't have to justify myself to you for a few reasons:
1. You are a ranger. You just drive around the bush and people think you are a hero. You have no idea of the strains that a Hospitality Manager experiences.
2. I thought you were beginning to understand me but I was obviously wrong.
3. Simone has been very difficult and unsupportive during this very pressurised period that I'm experiencing and Amber has been very supportive.

4. My position as the Hospitality Manager puts me in a difficult position. I have to manage my friends and give leadership to people who normally see me as the party animal.

PJ has given me this responsibility because he trusts me and I have no intention of letting him down, and, I don't mind saying, I think he's made the right choice.

Regards,
Hugh

P.S. I will be doing hospitality training with the rangers over the next few weeks so please don't be difficult when your turn comes around.

I have not responded to this putrid litany of absolute tripe.

Tomorrow I shall be driving down to the lowveld with Kerry who has just flown in from Cape Town. She is staying the night here in the guest room.

The sadness that enveloped her during the train trip up from Cape Town six weeks ago has returned to her eyes. When I picked her up from the Gautrain station she hugged me hello but said virtually nothing on the way home. She looked tired and her dark-red locks seemed to have lost their lustre.

'How was your leave?' I asked, trying to be cheerful.

'I love going back to Cape Town but there is a lot of sadness there for me.' I was about to press her for more when she switched the topic, 'Jeez, its cold up here!'

This evening we had a pleasant supper and Kerry lapped up the family atmosphere and laughed at almost everything the Major said. Most people find initial conversations with my father like being hauled in front of the Spanish Inquisition but I think she was particularly appreciative of the interest he took in her views and aspirations. Every time the subject strayed to her family or past, however, she skilfully evaded the questions or gave one-word answers. My parents are thankfully intuitive enough not to pry too much.

After supper, my mother said she had a 'surprise'. She'd had all the old home videos put onto DVD. The first thing she played was my performance in the school play, aged twelve – dressed as a girl. Any residual sadness immediately left Kerry's face as she beheld me prancing around the stage in a dress singing Gilbert and Sullivan.

When everyone else had gone off to bed, Kerry said she wanted to smoke, so we went outside into the cold highveld air. Trubshaw joined us and while Kerry drew on her cigarillo, the dog and I fought over his favourite toy – a deflated old rugby ball – to keep warm. After that, we returned to the warmth of the house and Kerry said she was ready for bed. She went to the bathroom while I gave Trubshaw his biscuits, put him to bed in the laundry and switched off the lights.

Kerry came into my room while I was packing the last of my things for the new work cycle. She was dressed in the same old T-shirt she'd had on in the train.

'It's freezing!' she said looking at the photographs of my life that Mum has hung on the walls.

'Well, it would be remiss of me not to offer you the same courtesy you did me on the Orange River. You are welcome to share my bed.'

She laughed and replied, 'I think I'll just borrow a jersey.'

I pointed at my cupboard. 'Help yourself.'

As she rummaged through my clothes she said, 'You have such a special family. You are so lucky.' She selected an ancient and shredded woollen jersey my mother knitted for me at least a decade ago.

'Don't you?' I asked, hoping for some insight as she pulled the stretched and faded garment over her head.

'Oh they're special alright, just not in the same way as yours.' She walked over and put her arms round me. 'Night night Angus, I'm really happy to be here.' She kissed my cheek and walked out.

It's now 06h00 and just about time to leave. I'll have a quick coffee with Dad and Trubshaw and then it'll be back to the wild. I'm looking forward to the relative warmth of the lowveld. Winter's nearly done – I always feel like we're on the home stretch come the end of July.

Week 30

Departure and damage

The big Sasekile news of this week is that Jenny has resigned.

She came to my room almost immediately after she'd been to hand PJ a letter. I was removing grass samples from my plant press on the lawn outside – readying them for mounting. I didn't notice her arrive.

'Hi Angus,' she said. The fizz that used to course through my nervous system on hearing her voice has all but gone.

'Hi Jen.' I looked up and then placed *Eragrostis superba* onto its mounting board.

'What you doing?' she asked.

I looked at the grass. 'Baking a cake,' I replied.

She ignored that and continued, 'I've come to tell you something.'

'Oh yes?' She waited for me to give her my attention.

'I came to tell you that I've resigned. Not sure why I came to tell you but I just thought I should.'

'When?' I asked.

'About five minutes ago.'

'Wow ...'

'Anyway, just thought I'd tell you.' She turned round to leave.

'Jen,' she turned back. 'I'm not driving this evening. Do you want to go and have a drink in the bush?' I'm not sure why I suggested it but it probably had quite a lot to do with the confusion I saw in her eyes.

'Ja, that'd be nice,' she replied and went on her way.

At about 17h00 that evening, we headed out away from the river to a dolerite outcrop in the south of the reserve. We didn't say much as we drove but it was a beautiful crystalline afternoon. I led her to the top of the rocks and we sat down looking east into the Kruger Park.

She opened a Savanna and I a milk stout.

'So what are you going to do?' I asked to break the silence which was becoming a little awkward.

'I'm going to travel to start with,' she answered, 'but I'm not really sure after that. I'll probably start off in London.'

'Startlingly original decision that,' I thought but didn't say out loud. I just nodded as a white-backed vulture shook itself in a dead knobthorn tree just south east of us. A piece of bark dropped to the ground and the silence grew again.

'Angus,' she said, 'I wanted to say that I'm sorry if I hurt you. I just genuinely don't know what I want. You were so intense and I guess it just kind of freaked me out a bit.'

'It's okay, Jen,' I took a sip of my drink. 'I only think of suicide once a week these days.'

She laughed. 'Despite how things have turned out, I hope we'll still be friends.'

'I don't see why we shouldn't be,' I paused, 'but for the fact that I've been passed up for a man possessed of the same qualities as a septic tank.' She chuckled again.

'Everyone has some redeeming qualities,' she said.

'Not him.'

'Maybe you're right,' she replied.

'Not taking him with you then?'

She sighed. 'No – he's not really what I expected or painted in my mind.' I didn't push the subject.

We sat there till it was almost dark, talking about this and that, but nothing of much substance. As we drove back to the lodge I was really glad for the time that we'd had to clear the air. I'm not sure we'll ever be great friends – mainly because out of the bush we have virtually nothing

in common. Of course, my ego also felt much better at the thought that she
and Matto would be separated and that she wasn't in the slightest bit cut
up about it. I stopped the Land Rover outside her house.

'Thanks Angus, that was very cool.' She smiled at me and went off into
her room. I now have closure on the troublesome affair.

I was driving out of Kingfisher Camp the next afternoon. Simone is doing
a great job there and seems to be enjoying herself.

She greeted me with a smile and said, 'That was big of you to take Jenny
for a drink last night; she really appreciated it. Even though things didn't
work out between the two of you, I think you should know that she has a
lot of respect for you.'

This made me a bit embarrassed so I changed the subject. 'How are you
doing?'

'Ag, I'm okay. I had a good leave and spent some time with my family
and at the farm. I thought about resigning,' she paused and then her voice
crescendoed, 'but then I thought, fuck that, I'm really enjoying my work
so I'm not going to let that shithead ruin things for me!' She took a deep
breath. 'Sorry, I don't mean to get all worked up.'

'Not at all – good for you. I'd say you're absolutely right.'

The other major, although less-surprising news of the week is that Julia
and The Legend are now officially 'together'. I know this because she sent
me the following mail yesterday.

To: Angus
From: Julia MacNaughton
Subject: Alistair and I

Hi Angus,

This mail serves to inform you that Alistair Jones is now my
boyfriend. I'm letting you know this for two reasons. Firstly, I don't
want you to hear it from someone else. And secondly, despite how
incredibly unreasonable I think you have been throughout this, I
know (or at least hope) deep down (very deep) that you in fact

care about me. Please trust me on this, Alistair is not the asshole you think he is.

Anyway, I look forward to seeing you soon. I hope that things can return to a semblance of normal between us.

Love,
Jules

P.S. I don't enjoy writing emails to my brother that open in a similar fashion to that of a legal summons.

Return to normal?

She must be bat-shit crazy. Does she imagine us having a cosy little dinner for three in the boma or, God forbid, Sunday lunch with The Legend? I can just see him sitting next to GAJ, gloating as I'm unable to force the roast lamb down my throat for the bile coming up the other way. Perhaps the worst scenario is the thought of The Legend coming to Kenton and violating my happy place (and my sister).

No, not now, not ever. Julia is being a fool and so is anyone who doesn't see what a jumped-up chop he is.

I read the offending mail in my room after dinner one evening and became so incensed at its contents that I picked up the cricket ball that lives on my desk, stood and flung it at the wall behind me. Of course, it bounced straight back at me. I ducked ungracefully and the ball smashed through the large glass pane above my desk.

There was a mighty crash as shards of glass exploded out into the night. A gust of winter came in, carrying with it a familiar winter smell around the camp – the unmistakable scent of grey skin – like a mixture between sweaty horse and fresh beer. The mopane tree outside the window shook and grey wrinkles, illuminated by the light from my now-smashed window, moved off towards Bertie and Kerry's block. I opened the door and looked out. The elephant bull ambled slowly over to a knobthorn tree next to their veranda and began picking at the bark.

I watched him for a few minutes and then he froze. As he did, I heard the sound of human feet on sand from behind my room. I stuck my head out of the door and looked round the frame. Kerry was returning from the kitchen – sans torch and looking at her feet. She had no idea the elephant was there.

'Psst,' I said, clicking my fingers. She was lost in thought. 'Oy!' I shouted. She looked up.

'Hi,' she said maintaining the momentum towards her room. 'Can't stop, need to pee!' she said.

The elephant, no doubt astounded that she had failed to see his six tonne bulk, swung round and shook his head. This arrested her movement. She squeaked and then, with the agility of a genet, darted for the safety of my door.

'You'll have to use mine,' I said as she ran past me and slammed the bathroom door. She emerged a minute or so later and dried her hands on the towel hanging from my chair.

'That was close!' she said.

'The elephant or an accident?'

'Both!' Then she noticed the glass strewn about the place. 'What happened to the window?'

'Cricket ball,' I replied.

'Oh,' she said, letting the silence hang as the bull turned back to his knobthorn tree. 'Any idea how it got through the window?'

'Evidence suggests it was either thrown or struck within this very room – see, the glass is mostly outside.'

'Ah...ja...I see.' The bull crunched on a branch. 'Any idea why it was thrown through the glass?'

'Indeed. It would seem that the sister of the ball's owner has taken up with an unsuitable partner.'

'Oh, right...you don't think the ball's owner might be overreacting just a little bit?'

'The chances are miniscule.' I turned back to the elephant and changed the subject. 'You know this is the third time I've had a close encounter with this fellow. So I've decided to name him. I shall call him Mitchell henceforth.'

'Explain...'

'See how his left tusk is broken off halfway down? It's his incisor – worn in similar fashion to the incisors of many of the residents of Mitchell's Plain.'

Kerry thought this poor joke was rather funny.

'What news of your suitor in the kitchen?' I asked. She laughed again.

'Oh he's finally managed to speak to me but he looks at the floor and says please and thank you a lot. Shame, he's a good guy and he's teaching us all so much – he's the most skilled oke I've ever seen in a kitchen.'

While we waited for Mitchell to eat his fill, Kerry kindly helped me pick up the glass that littered the desk surface under the window. As we were about to finish, there was a mighty crack and we looked up in time to see a huge branch from the knobthorn crash onto the roof of her veranda and then roll off onto the ground.

Bertie's light came on and he exploded from his room.

'Hey, *voetsek*,' he shouted. The elephant turned slowly and walked back towards the river. I felt a bit sad to see him go.

In the morning, we discovered that Bertie and Kerry's veranda roof is badly damaged. Mitchell meted out similar treatment to a few of the other trees in camp – one of which was in Tamboti Camp. SB arrived at lunch complaining loudly that *his* best gardenia in *his* camp had been destroyed.

On the subject of SB, it would seem that he and Amber are making a poor attempt to conduct a secret affair – poorly secretive that is; I'm not sure of its merits otherwise. She is still fawning over her Lord High Commander of the Universe and he is deeply impressed with the fact that such a looker, albeit one with the disposition of Lucifer, has taken a shine to him.

Tossers and tumble

It feels like winter might just be coming to its end – there's a hint less bite in the morning cold. The stars also herald the far end of the cold season. Scorpio had disappeared over the western horizon by the time I made my way home after dinner last night. The feeling that spring is not too far off fills me with anticipation.

I've been driving more or less flat out this week, initially at Rhino Camp. The management team has been restructured temporarily by the LHCU, given the conflict between his ex-girlfriend and his new lover. I'm not sure what he told PJ but, until she leaves, Jenny will be in Kingfisher with Simone. Allegra is looking after things in Rhino Camp (Melissa is on leave) for the moment and Amber has been sent to Main Camp to work under September.

My first lot of guests, two forgettable South African couples, felt their game ranger to be well below their exalted stations. Brett Jacobs owns an executive car dealership and lives in Dainfern with his wife Bernice. Storm van Schalkwyk and his wife, Chantel, live three houses down from the Jacobs in the same gated community. I cannot fathom why some people are named for weather systems – it's not like the Van Schalkwyks come from a long line of Red Indian shamans. I doubt I'll ever name my progeny Cyclone, Tornado or Cumulonimbus.

The Jacobs and the Van Schalkwyks spent a lot of time telling me about the exclusivity of their neighbourhood. This, despite the fact that the Fourways area has nothing to recommend it whatsoever. In fact I believe that were a neutron bomb to land squarely on that architectural blight, the planet would be a far safer and more attractive place.

'You, know, Dainfern uz so great bucoz uts only for the upper clors,' said Bernice just after admonishing Themba the butler for not filling her glass to the brim with Waterford shiraz. 'Also, not a lot of them,' she pointed with eyes at the retreating butler.

'Butlers?' I asked. The sarcasm wafted over her head.

'No, bleks!' she hissed.

Chantel waded in, 'Ah mean, uts not laak we racialists or anything laak that. But uts naas to know you safe un your bed at naat.'

'Very new South African of you,' I said, taking a sip from the giant scotch that was helping me cope.

'My brutha,' said Storm, a hint of menace in his voice, 'uts a kull or be kulled wirld out theh. Faan foh you yah un the bush but for us running the ucononmy from the city uts diffrnt.'

Mercifully, dinner arrived just then and I excused myself and wandered into the kitchen to let the steam from my ears recede. Allegra was in there directing service on the pass. She was dressed in a navy-blue, knee-length dress and a pair of black pumps. Her chocolate fringe has grown a bit and she'd clipped it back onto her head. The dress was quite tight and her boobs are not small for someone of five feet and three inches.

'Dress shrunk in the wash?' I asked as the butlers took the last of the starters out to the tables.

'It did actually...probably hugs my chest a bit closely,' she replied candidly. 'Do you think it's a bit slutty?'

'No, I'd say more courtesan than hooker.'

'I see.' She paused and almost smiled. 'How are your guests? I find them pretty awful to be honest.' (I suspect she struggles to be untruthful.)

'Yes, they are somewhere between painful and torturous.'

Storm and Brett had enough photographic equipment to launch a small international surveillance operation. They each had two camera bodies and about a dozen lenses. With these, they took rank average pictures lacking

any form of originality or artistic character – full-frame phot
regardless of lighting.

As they departed, Brett shook my hand and said, 'Left a little son...
for you gaas wuth the cemp meneger.'

'Thank you, I think,' I muttered as they drove off in a cloud of Mercedes-Benz ML63 dust.

I wandered down into the camp and asked Allegra about our gratuity. This time she did laugh.

'They left you and Elvis twenty rand . . .' she paused, aiming for some sort of comic timing, 'to share!'

I stared at her.

'Allegra, why is it that you don't laugh at my jokes but you find my pitiful financial situation thoroughly amusing?'

'Well, to be honest, I often don't know if you are joking or not,' she replied, 'but I knew your face would be a picture when I told you this.'

My next lot were out of Main Camp. Amber doesn't feel her position as September's assistant is befitting of someone who has made the efforts she has to sleep her way to the top. I imagine that SB is receiving endless complaints from her. Her face is almost always like thunder and it's amazing to me how such a physically beautiful woman could be rendered so enormously unattractive by such a defective personality. Unfortunately for Amber, September is not a man who will tolerate a bossy little city girl simply because she looks like a ramp model.

On the first afternoon in Main Camp, I picked up six Brazilians. I arrived on deck early – hoping to sit peacefully and watch goings-on in the river below for a little while. I poured myself a cup of coffee and retired to a comfortable armchair in the corner of the deck to contemplate the almost-dry Tsesebe meandering slowly past. A grey heron fished in a pool deep within the browning reeds. A flock of Cape turtle doves drank at another pool and a water monitor basked on a rock nearby – grateful for the warmth of the winter sun.

I was soon distracted by the sound of September's barely-controlled voice as he spoke to Amber.

'Amber, I asked you very nicely to cut some lemons for the lemonade.' She began to make some sort of half-arsed excuse but he stopped her. 'Not time for talking, time for cutting lemons,' he said firmly. She wheezed and I heard her drag her feet off the deck.

The Brazilians arrived a few minutes later: two couples and two preteen boys belonging to one of the couples. Carlos was the *de facto* leader of the group by virtue of the fact that he was the only one who could speak any English. The introductions complete, I asked Carlos what they all wanted to see.

'The Beeg Five of course!' he answered. I gritted my teeth and then Carlos added quietly, 'And I like to see the birds.'

This pleased me no end. When people ask to see the Big Five (Bug Faav as my residents of Dainfern referred to it) it tells me a few things. Mostly it says that they have a terrible travel agent who hasn't bothered to convey anything about the vast array of wildlife we have on offer out here.

Carlos drew me over to where the family had placed its belongings. He pulled a brand-new *Newman's Birds of Southern Africa* from his bag and handed it to me. I leafed through the pages and noted that he had circled all the birds he might be able to see at Sasekile.

'I like to make collection of bird photosgraph,' he said beaming. 'But family is not so very much to be interested.'

That afternoon we saw a pride of lions, some elephants chasing a rhino out of a waterhole and a buffalo bull. With the Beeg Five almost complete and most of the group suffering horribly from jet lag, I suggested that Carlos and I go birding the next morning on our own. He thought this a grand idea and explained it to the rest of the crew who wore expressions of extreme relief at not having to rise before the sun came up.

I went through to the kitchen to organise a snack for the pre-dawn departure. O'Reilly was sitting in the bomb site that is his office. There was a glass of red wine on his desk and he was reading through the menu for the next day.

'What ho, O'Reilly?' I said.

'Ah yes, good Angus. Whut aboot you?' I told him I was fine and then explained my needs, which he said he would sort out for me.

Just before leaving, I said, 'Everything good with you and Kerry now?' His body shuddered with the memory of the Hogan visit.

'Oh Gud, dat was a terrible noight,' he took a sip from the wine. 'Boot, Oi'm orkeh now. Joost managed te bring meself te talk te hurr. She's still sooo byootiful – ah boot wut can Oi do? Joost haf to be a bit machoor aboot it.' He sipped his wine and I left as his eyes glazed over.

The next morning, Carlos and I headed off before first light. I drove to a clearing where I knew we'd catch the dawn chorus and the first avian risers trying to find a high spot to catch the warming rays of the morning. Carlos was a twitcher in the true sense of the word – far more concerned with the number of birds he saw than with the specific biology of each species.

I turned the engine off in the frigid darkness and poured us each a cup of coffee. Then, like the beginning of Brahms's *Academic Festival Overture*, the dawn chorus began – quietly at first but with an unmistakable intensity building to an enormous crescendo – as the eastern horizon changed from black to purple.

Carlos became insanely excited as I began rattling off the names of the birds as they called:

'Doo du du du du du' – ground hornbill in the distance;

'Chip chip chip prrt' – I clicked my fingers and pointed at the silhouette of a grey-headed sparrow calling in a dead tree;

'Chick cha chick cha chick cha chee chee chee' – crested francolin;

'Pirripup pirripup' – dark-capped bulbul;

'Proo pro pro pro pr pr pr' – green pigeon;

'Doo doo da do da do' – red-eyed dove;

'Kokokokokokoko' – yellow-billed hornbill.

As I called the names, Carlos, flicked through his book and ticked off the birds. He was frantic with joy.

We sat there as the sky slowly brightened and the birds sang to us. There were a few calls I heard but couldn't identify in the cacophony around us but Carlos was none the wiser. Then, as the sun peeped over a marula-strewn crest in the east, I started the car and made slowly for the river.

We stopped halfway across an almost-dry ford with a view into the vegetation that grows in the middle of the Tsesebe. There, we saw red-faced cisticolas skipping through the reeds like mini fighter jets; a patient malachite kingfisher waiting for prey, perched on a reed overhanging a small still pool that reflected the orange dawn; and a fish eagle surveying the new day from high in a jackalberry. Just onto the northern bank, in the boughs of a huge torchwood tree, a bird party was underway led, as is often the case, by a southern black tit. He was aided by two long-billed crombecs, a yellow-bellied eremomela, a chinspot batis, a green-backed camaroptera and any number of others.

Then we drove onto a crest to warm ourselves in the sun. There we found a red-billed hornbill with the same idea. He was facing the new sun, feathers all puffed out, his eyes half shut. A flock of Retz's helmet shrikes squabbled in a marula off the side.

Just after 09h30, as the thermals started to waft upwards, the raptors took to the skies. A male bateleur skudded low over the treetops; a gabar goshawk chased a sparrow-sized quarry into the boughs of an apple leaf tree; a pair of African hawk eagles – one high, one low – scoured the ground for a francolin or guinea fowl not paying sufficient attention. The highlight was a pair of white-headed vultures soaring miles overhead as we drove back into camp. All in all, we saw 60 birds, which is pretty good for a winter's morning.

I felt very satisfied until I arrived at the rangers' room to find that the time between drives was not to be my own. For the next three days, the rangers were to be subjected to hospitality training.

This grandstanding opportunity for the LHCU began at 11h00 and ran for two hours. I surprised myself by actually being quite impressed with some of the things SB said – I even learned a thing or two. He explained wine service in painful detail but gave some pretty interesting information on pairing wines with different foods. Again, however, it was the breathtaking levels of arrogance that angered me – and not only me.

'Guys,' he began, 'you are ruining wine service by not pouring wine at the right temperature and in the wrong glasses. It's not acceptable at a five-star place like this. I felt the group around me bristle. SB pointed at Brandon who has the sophistication of a horny tree frog.

'Brandon, just last night I heard you recommend a shiraz to your guests. They were eating yellowtail for heaven's sakes!' I saw Carrie reach over and touch Brandon on the wrist as he fought the urge to stand up and clock the lecturer. SB turned to his computer and popped a slide of various pairings onto the screen in front of us.

'Now,' he said, 'I want you to all look at this slide and then we'll have a test to see if you remember it.' He left the graphic up for a few minutes and then flicked up another slide that had the wines and foods all jumbled up.

'Right,' he began, 'Sipho, what would you pair with this Salmon?' Sipho considered the slide. 'Quickly, quickly!' our instructor snapped.

'Chardonnay,' said Sipho.

'Correct. Brandon, what about this beef?'

'Sauvignon blanc,' said Brandon – pronouncing the words phonetically.

'Nooo!' shouted SB. 'Matto, you answer.'

'Shiraz,' said Nivea Man.

'Correct. Angus, what about this lamb?' I looked at SB and felt any semblance of brotherly love desert me.

'String Bean,' I began, 'I find that lamb goes best with cane and creamsoda mixed in a one-to-one ratio.' This broke the tension and everyone started laughing – everyone except SB that is. He glared at me. As the laughter died down I added, 'With a chaser of who-the-fuck-do-you-think-you-are-talking-to.' A few nervous giggles. I thought SB was going to explode but he realised the crowd, for the first time during our stay at Sasekile, was with me and against him. Carrie rescued the situation.

'Angus, that's enough. Guys, this stuff is important. Please make an effort to take it seriously.'

The rest of the 'course' proceeded without incident and would have been pretty edifying but for the attitude of the teacher.

Unfortunately for SB, his complete failure to grasp basic leadership principles has not gone unnoticed by the General Manager. This man misses almost nothing. I received the following from my parents yesterday evening.

To: Angus
From: Mum
Subject: Hugh's troubles

Hello Angus,

I hope this finds you in good spirits.

Your father and I received a very angry email from your brother this afternoon. He says he has been demoted from his position as hospitality manager. He feels victimised and that you, through jealousy of his success, might have had something to do with his demotion.

I do not wish to pass judgement on the situation without your side of the story but your father and I are desperately worried that Hugh seems so unhappy. You know how prone he is to moods when things aren't going his way. We are also very worried that things between the two of you seem to have deteriorated again – we were so hopeful.

Please could you send word of his condition and what is happening.

Thanks and love you,
Mum

I replied:

To: Mum
From: Angus
Subject: Re: Hugh's troubles

Dear Mother,

This is the first I have heard of your son being stripped of his title as Lord High Commander of the Universe. I can only assume that he's too ashamed to tell me. Rest assured that his demotion had nothing to do with me but that, despite our brotherly connection, I have not the slightest bit of sympathy for him.

Do you remember when SB was put in charge of directing the house plays? The actors went into revolt on the night of the performance because he called them a 'bunch of ingrates with less talent than his bowel movements.' Well, the same approach to his leadership role here has precipitated this.

Love,
Angus

This morning, my brother arrived at my room in a foul temper. He barged in as I was adding some labels to my grass collection (an exceptional piece of work, if I say so myself).

'Angus,' he exhaled, his top lip curving down like it always does when he's really cross. 'Thanks a lot, I suppose you were the instigator of this!'

'String Bean, do not shout at me. I've had nothing to do with anything.'

'I've been demoted!' he yelled and then all the bluster went out of him and he slumped onto the bed, putting his head in his hands.

'This comes as something of a shock to you?'

He ignored me.

'I can't believe it. I was working harder than ever. I can't believe how ungrateful everyone is being. Apparently a whole delegation of butlers and a few others went to PJ to complain about me!'

'I'd have to say that Jacob Zuma apologising for trying to return us to the 17th century would be less surprising,' I said sticking the label for *Hyperthelia dissoluta* to its card.

'PJ told me they said I was rude, pompous and disrespectful and I was making everyone upset!'

'Yes, well I'd say that's probably about accurate. Although I would summarise by adding that you have been a prize-winning knob for the last few months.' This brought the rage back.

'Angus, why is it that no one understands? Huh? Why is it that I am so alone in this? I'm doing my best!'

'String Bean, you clearly aren't going to learn from this. Why don't you go and tell Amber your troubles?' I asked. 'I'm sure she'll be sympathetic. Now bugger off, I'm no longer interested.'

'No one gets me!' he shouted and then left.

Week 32

Snobs and sympathy

SB is on leave recovering from his demotion. He is doing this in Cape Town with some friends of his from hotel school who have put him up at one of the five-star guest houses where they're employed. I have heard nothing from him this week and he failed to say goodbye to me when he left – he wangled a flight out citing once again how much he hates the Tazz.

I still can't bring myself to reply to Julia's mail about The Legend but I did hear from Arthur this week.

To: Angus MacNaughton
From: Arthur C. Grimble
Subject: Summer Fun

L'Escaladieu
Vien
Provence
France(!)

Dear Angus,

You will see from the address above that I am not in England but having a wonderful summer holiday in France. Mavis's daughter and her family kindly included us in their holiday plans so here we are enjoying *le bon vivant*! It is very hot indeed but I am surviving by lolling about in the pool. The hills are covered in lavender, the food is exquisite and the wine is chilled and plentiful.

I am most sorry to hear that your brother and you are not really talking. It seems to me that you might like to provide some sort of brotherly leadership to him. I do not wish to interfere but it may be worth considering this approach. I remember when my late brother took me in hand as a young man and while I cannot remember if I listened to him or not, it felt good to know that he was on my side. Perhaps the same might be said for your relationship with your sister.

Anyway, I do not mean to dish out advice.

Send news soon and I will send you some pictures (apparently that is possible on the interworld) when I return to Lincolnshire.

All the best,
Arthur

Well, the old boy does provide a certain clarity of thought and his advice is remarkably similar to that lavished on me by my father over the years. I'll have to give it some thought but this week hasn't left me with more than a few seconds to think about anything except my job.

The camp is packed and many guests are South Africans on their winter breaks. I've decided that my countrymen are both my favourite and my worst guests. In the case of the former, they are amateur naturalists interested in the smaller things and deepening their ecological knowledge. In the case of the latter they're arrogant know-it-alls. They either tell me how to do my job or, if they are sharing the Land Rover with international guests, they take over the game drive by sprouting their meagre bush knowledge (much of it nonsense). Often they have their own hobby farms which they feel qualifies them as ecologists, rangers, trackers, hunters and generally exceptional men of the wild.

My first bunch fell into this second category – a family of four with two companions for the teenage kids – Basil and Sylvia Hilton (mid 40s), their son William (17), his friend Andy (17), daughter Caroline (18) and her friend Camilla (18). Despite the existence of any number of fine educational institutions in South Africa, the Hiltons chose to send their children to be educated in England – William at Charterhouse and Caroline at Ascot Girls College. Their slightly less well-heeled companions were being schooled in Cape Town.

Basil works for a mining company and he believes the wealth he's amassed qualifies him as a genuine Sloane. He speaks with a strong English accent despite the fact that until very recently, he had never lived in Old Blighty. Mr and Mrs Hilton talk of South Africa like it's a British colony and treat its inhabitants as inferior subjects of Her Majesty's. Just about every utterance that comes from their mouths is laced with patronising snobbery and normally contains a far-fetched name drop.

William is quite obviously gay and just as obviously in love with Andy (who is of the same persuasion). This plain truth has apparently escaped his parents entirely. Caroline, being much more liberal than her mother and father, is fully aware that her brother is queerer than an eleven-rand note – to quote Brandon. She finds it amusing to regularly insinuate as to his relations with Andy.

I picked the Hiltons up from the airstrip. This is a task I really enjoy in the winter because at 11h00, when most of the planes arrive, the temperature is perfect and the atmosphere at its most peaceful. I always head up to the strip a good half hour before wheels-down and spend a happy 30 minutes reading beneath a mopane tree on the southern end of the strip. There is always a bird or a pair of squirrels pottering about in the leaves above my head.

The Hiltons' plane arrived 25 minutes after I opened *Guns, Germs, and Steel* by Jared Diamond. The dim buzz of the engine grew louder as I reluctantly closed the book, rose and dusted myself off. I wandered over to the Land Rover as the PC-12 touched down, destroying the peace that had cocooned me.

Sylvia emerged into the light, a long white silk scarf streaming atop a chic, khaki safari suit and some ankle-length leather boots. I moved to the base of the steps to greet her, offering a hand.

'Sylvia Hilton, Johannesburg and London,' she said proffering a limp wrist. I looked her in the eye.

'Angus MacNaughton, bushveld and reality,' I replied. She frowned, handed me her hand luggage and wandered off to the Land Rover. The rest of them emerged presently and while the pilot and I loaded mountains of expensive matching luggage onto the Land Rover, Basil disappeared into a mopane thicket.

'Basil,' I called, 'could you rather not wander off? Your family would be most distressed to see you mauled at this early stage of your safari.'

He stopped moving and turned to look at me. 'I've hunted big game from here all the way to the Selous – don't you worry about me, sonny.' He continued into the thicket – and emerged less than a minute later at a gallop. 'Bloody great big buffalo in there!'

'No shit,' I muttered as he did up his fly.

We made for the lodge. The first sighting the Hiltons had was of Mitchell. The elephant was standing at the Tamboti Camp entrance. It's an inconspicuous camp in the trees – the idea being that guests hardly notice any structure until they walk out onto the deck. The car park is about 30 metres in diameter – just wide enough to turn a Land Rover in. Mitchell's vast form filled most of this space. He was feeding on a creeper entwined in the fringing bushes and trees. We watched for a little while as his dextrous trunk selected and then carefully gathered the single species he wanted. He took virtually no notice of us – his trunk once turned slightly towards the Land Rover and then returned to its task.

The Capetonians, despite having been on any number of exotic overseas trips, had never been to the bush. (Much like many of the residents of their part of the world, they hadn't realised that Africa has anything to offer beyond their windswept piece of coastline, its mountain, its frigid waters and its cliques.) In short, Camilla and Andy were astonished by Mitchell and our proximity to him. They stared wide-eyed at the enormous pachyderm until Incredible emerged from the camp entrance with a tray of champagne flutes to welcome them. He was concentrating so hard on not spilling the Graham Beck rosé that he failed to notice six tonnes of Mitchell.

'Welcome all everybody!' he yelled and then looked up to find his field of view filled with Mitchell's grey flank – paused not ten metres from him.

This outburst prompted the elephant to cease his selection of creeper and spin on his heel to face the butler. Incredible screamed and then tossed his tray of rosé into the air. The flutes clattered to the ground and the butler ran for cover. It soon became clear that Mitchell wasn't leaving his creeper any time soon so I reversed and we walked the Hilton party to their rooms via Main Camp. Mitchell spent much of the rest of the afternoon modifying the car park. His last act was to block access by breaking off a very large mopane branch and leaving it across the entrance.

Allegra is helping out at Tamboti with SB on leave. She didn't take to the Hiltons much but she was her usual professional self and made them feel welcome. Sylvia and Basil in turn enjoyed her formality and the slight Edinburgh lilt to her accent. In general, the Hilton stay was predictable – we had some pretty good sightings, Sylvia and Basil were painful to the extreme and Elvis spent as much time as possible tracking in order to avoid too much time with them. The last night was a bit different.

I have not induced khaki fever in many of my guests so it was with some surprise that I noticed Caroline Hilton catching my eye more and more as the three-day stay progressed. In character, Caroline wasn't much like her parents in that she didn't consider herself a subject of Queen Elizabeth II and conversation indicated that she rather resented being schooled in England. She was a pretty girl, if not stunning – very well turned out with dark blonde hair and a buxom figure.

She made sure she sat next to me on the last night of their stay and it wasn't long before I felt her leg touching mine under the table. I looked to see if it was perhaps a mistake but she caught my eye in a way that made it very clear there was no error. I shifted uneasily to my left and continued my attempt to listen to Basil dispensing advice to me on how best to further my career – in his opinion this should include becoming a professional hunter and bird-shooting guide.

'Basil, thing is, I'm just not really interested in killing,' I said as Caroline's left leg made contact under the table again.

'Pah, rubbish – bunny huggers. Never had time for them,' he snapped. 'Nothing wrong with ethical hunting – it's fair game going out on foot, tracking down an animal and shooting it. Fair game I tell you.' By this stage I was sitting on the far left of my chair – awkwardly close to Sylvia. I sipped my scotch.

'Basil, while I understand that some men feel a very real need to shoot things and that it's not always simple to hunt big animals, calling it fair game is simply far-fetched. I have yet to see a heavily-armed covey of francolin with a pack of pointers and gun dogs. I have also yet to see an elephant armed with a 500 Nitro Express capable of killing its quarry at more than 100 metres. In a fair game, the hunter would carry the same risk of being shot as the hunted, as opposed to being blasted out of the sky by birdshot while trying desperately to escape.' I was a bit heated by the time I'd finished this. There was silence round the table. Basil clearly wasn't used to being challenged.

Caroline, who had drunk at least four glasses of champagne, broke the silence with, 'Papa, not all people like the same things. For example, Mum likes gardening, you like hunting. I like taking cocaine and William likes taking Andy.'

'Oh Caroline! You are so embarrassing sometimes!' Sylvia cast a furtive glance at her spotty-faced son who went puce and fiddled with the asparagus on his plate.

'Caroline!' snapped Basil, forgetting me. 'That's enough! Why are you constantly casting aspersions on your brother's manliness and the family name!'

'Just facts, Papa and I mention them because he won't ever – and, by the way, they have nothing to do with manliness at all.'

'Well, I won't have it so keep your depraved ideas to yourself!' he bellowed and then gulped at his wine. I found it amusing that Basil and Sylvia were horrified at the thought of their son being gay but not in the slightest bit perturbed at their daughter's use of narcotics. I excused myself as the pudding arrived and went through to the men's loo for a breather. As I was about to shut the door it burst open and Caroline forced her way in. The speed of her entry forced me onto the wall opposite the door. She turned the key.

I looked at the shapely hips blocking my exit and said nothing.

'My father has some strange ideas about my brother and me,' she said. I didn't reply, knowing that I should tell her to leave but I was more tha little intrigued. 'He lives in the late 1800s.' She began unbuttoning her shirt and I held up my hand.

'That's definitely going too far,' I said.

'Relax. I want to show you something.' She undid her top halfway and then turned round as she pulled the shirt off her shoulders. I stared in fascination as an enormous tiger tattoo appeared on the exposed skin. 'Didn't expect that, did you?' she said turning back to face me and replacing the shirt – although not redoing the buttons. 'If my father saw it he'd be almost as upset as he's going to be when he finds out his son is a queen.'

'Why exactly are you showing me?' I asked.

'Because I've got a crush on you,' she giggled.

'I see. Well, we'd better get back to the table or there are going to be questions.' I made for the door and she moved aside but as I came near her, the scent of her perfume touched my nose and I paused, my face less than a foot from hers. Our eyes locked and before I knew it our lips were fixed in a hard (almost vicious) kiss. It only lasted about ten seconds but I knew we'd do something really stupid if I hung around so we left without another word.

I walked to the table through the back of the kitchen – hoping to compose myself before returning to the Hiltons. Allegra was there – just dishing the last of the pudding. She caught my eye and shook her head.

The corner of her mouth turned up. 'What have you been doing?' she asked.

'What do people normally do in the water closet?' I replied.

'Not what you just did, I suspect.'

'Oh? And what did I just do?'

'From your flustered disposition, the scratches on your neck and, of course, the lipstick on your mouth, I would say there is either an angry, make-up thieving genet living in the loo or you were just mauled by Caroline Hilton.'

'Allegra, that was dangerously close to humorous sarcasm,' I said. She ''ed over with a cloth and I submitted my face to be wiped free of
⸻ unlike you to be amusing – have you been at the brandy?'

⸻ d three gin and tonics.' The matter-of-factness had

⸻ re you?' I asked as she straightened my collar.

'Desperately,' she replied.

'Sarcasm twice? You should drink gin more often.'

'Who says I was being sarcastic?' She winked a grey eye at me, then pushed me out of the kitchen.

I moved back to the table where Caroline was already tucking into her chocolate mousse. I planned to complete the meal without further incident but it was not be. William decided, finally, to confront his father. His stand was precipitated by a gay couple who arrived with September from Main Camp (they'd asked to see Tamboti Camp). They came swanning onto the Tamboti deck and made a point of greeting everyone and then apologising for disturbing dinner – they couldn't have been more polite or pleasant.

As they left, Basil said, 'Oh God, nothing worse than a poof. So unnatural. Foul people.' William put his fork down gently. Andy played with the remains of his mousse.

'Papa, I've something to tell you,' began William, sniffing. Basil looked up as the tension built. Caroline stuck her fork in my ribs.

'Yes? Well get on with it, boy,' he knew there was something of significance coming.

'Papa, I too am gay.'

'No shit,' muttered Caroline.

Sylvia gasped, pulling her napkin to her mouth. Camilla looked up.

'Whaaat!' bellowed Basil dropping his fork and leaping to his feet. Allegra came running out of the kitchen. Basil was panting, his face reddening with every second. 'What did you just say to me?' he yelled. William found his courage at that point, the terrified little boy disappeared, and he too stood up.

'I am gay. I am a queen. I am bent. I bat for the other side. There is nothing I can do about it and I don't see why I should feel like I should do something about it anymore.' He met his father's gaze. Sylvia made a very poor attempt to calm the situation – by pushing things under the carpet which I suspect is her default response to emotional difficulty.

'Now now Will dear, sit down and finish your pudding, we'll talk about this later when we're all thinking clearly.'

Caroline waded in, 'Mum, for God's sake, there's nothing to talk about. My brother, your son, is gay and there is nothing you can do about it. We're into the second decade of the 21st century — it's really not a big deal.' Sylvia looked at her husband.

'This is intolerable! No son of mine will be gay — it's not right...it's...' Basil was shouting and bashing the table. Allegra looked at me and I realised she expected me to do something.

'Basil...' he didn't hear me as he railed. 'Basil!' I snapped. All six feet four of him turned to me.

'You stay out of this, sonny!' I stood up and faced him.

'Basil, you are creating a scene. What you and your family have to discuss has nothing to do with me or the staff here but I won't sit here and listen to you pontificating your Triassic attitudes. Either sit down and finish your meal or I'll have you escorted to your room.' Basil stormed off the deck and into the night followed closely by a security guard.

'Please not go walking alone in the night,' yelled the guard rushing after the guest. Basil's voice grew fainter as he disappeared towards his room and the remaining Hiltons resumed their seats. No one said anything for a little while and then Caroline spoke.

'Will, that was the bravest thing I've ever seen anyone do.' Her mother started mewling quietly and Andy smiled at his brave beau.

Kerry was sitting out in the cold again when I walked home after William brought his father's world down about him. The inevitable cigarillo was glowing as she looked out at the stars. I wanted to tell someone about my evening so I wandered over.

'Fancy some company?' I asked. 'Got a great story for you.'

'Ja sure,' she replied stubbing out the cigarillo and placing it on the stump next to her. I sat down and looked at her face which was, again, stained with tears.

'What's wrong, Ginger?'

'Same old, I'll tell you soon,' she replied wiping her eyes. 'Tell me your story.'

I related the tale of the evening and she was smiling at the end of it. Then she said, 'Angus, you are a filthy oke — she's eighteen!'

'I know but it was something about the tattoo.'

'You like tattoos?'

'Not generally, no.'

'Want to see another one?' she looked at me from the corner of her eye.

'Definitely,' I replied. She looked about to see that there was no one else around and then undid the drawstring on her scaffy old tracksuit pants.

'Where is it exactly?' I asked.

'Just look,' she replied pulling her pants down enough for me to see the silhouette of a bird just above and to the left of where things would have become awkward. 'What do you think?' I stared and then she let her pants snap back into place.

'What is it?'

'It's a swallow.'

'Why a swallow and why so close to your ... um ... jade gate?'

'My what!?' She thought that was hilarious.

'Never mind. Tell me about the swallow.'

'I like swallows because they follow the summer. There's no winter in their lives.' She pulled a cigarillo from the box and lit it. 'I'd like to be able to escape winter always.'

'I assume this is a metaphor for something else,' I probed.

'Perhaps. As for its position, I put it there so that people don't notice it and I don't have to talk about it. Also, only people I feel really comfortable with will ever see it.' We sat in silence for a few minutes while she finished smoking. Eventually I stood, put my hand on her shoulder, squeezed it and went to bed.

The Hiltons left in stony silence the next morning. When I dropped them off at the airstrip, Basil and Sylvia didn't say goodbye but the rest were very friendly. Caroline waited till last. She threw her arms round me and pressed her full lips to mine and there she remained for an inappropriate period. As she climbed into the plane, I saw her father glaring at me from his window. I grinned at him and waved – my middle finger ever so slightly further forward than the others.

My guests for the remainder of the week were mild in comparison.

Eggs and elephant

I saw my first Wahlberg's eagle today – one of the very first returnees of the new season. Together with this harbinger of spring, the weather is warming up and although it's very dry and windy I don't mind because winter is departing. The camp was a bit quieter on the guest front this week but Mitchell has been wreaking havoc. As the bush continues to dry all around us, the camp forms something of an oasis with its irrigated gardens and swimming pools full of clean water. Mitchell is clearly a fussy elephant who doesn't see any reason to be scraping dry bark from leafless trees and drinking from the muddy river when he could be satiating his needs on green camp plants and crystalline pool water.

Late in the afternoon a few days ago I was in the rangers' room on my first day off in the last two weeks. Carrie was putting the finishing touches to a new arthropod collection while I read some *TIME* magazine headlines to Bertie and he then tried to find the relevant location on the world map. As I was explaining where Palestine is, Jane burst into the room.

'That fucking elephant!' she panted. We all looked up.

'Mitchell?' I asked.

'Who?' said Jane and Carrie at the same time.

'The one with the broken tusk?'

'Yes, that one. He's tearing Rhino Camp to pieces. Allegra and I were busy setting up a private dinner on the Room 2 deck. She wandered off to pick some leaves for the centrepiece and that fucking giant emerged from the river and chased her. She jumped into the pool just in time. She's still there now, too terrified to come out!'

'Angus, please would you go down there and see what's going on. I'll try to think of a way to move him.' Bertie and I headed for Rhino Camp.

We walked through Room 2 and out onto the deck. The pool is set into the river bank a little way off the deck and is accessed by a narrow boardwalk. Mitchell was feeding on a gardenia bush to the left of the pool. I could see Allegra's head peeping over the rim.

'Bit early in the season to swim, don't you think?' I asked.

'It is not pleasant in the least,' she snapped.

'Well get out then,' I said.

'Not while that thing is standing there,' she said through chattering teeth. I looked at Mitchell who was paying us no attention.

'Oy!' I shouted and clapped my hands. Mitchell exhaled loudly and continued feeding. 'Would you mind moving off a little, please!' I yelled. He took no notice. I picked up a loose stick that had fallen onto the deck and flung it at the elephant. It caught him on his left ear and he spun round and shook his head at me. We were safe on the deck so I shouted at him again and he rushed a few steps forward and then trumpeted.

'Brilliant,' chattered Allegra, 'just brilliant.' The dust settled. Bertie tapped me on the shoulder.

'My uncle says that elephants hate eggs,' he said.

'Well thank you, Bertie, do they prefer kippers and croissants?' I looked at him. 'What am I supposed to do with that information?'

'No, they don't like eggs – I'll go and fetch some.' He ran off before I could question him further. I returned my attention to Allegra who was glaring at me from the pool.

'Angus MacNaughton, I don't mean to nag, but could you please get me out of here!'

Mitchell had meanwhile moved off to a mopane tree a little further from the boardwalk.

'Mitchell, I'm going to walk to the pool so you just stay where you are,' I said. He didn't react at all. So I stepped onto the boardwalk.

It creaked loudly.

The elephant stopped feeding for a few seconds and then resumed. I continued along the squeaky wood to the edge of the pool.

'Give me your hand,' I said, 'I'll help you out.'

'What if he charges again?'

'He's not going to,' I smiled. She regarded me with deep suspicion and then reached up to take my hand. I helped her out at the steps. She was wearing a white uniform shirt which had gone predictably see-through and I was momentarily distracted by the impressive sight beneath the stretched white cotton. It was a poor time to be side-tracked.

Suddenly eggs began raining onto Mitchell's back and sides from the direction of the deck. The elephant wheeled around as if stung by a giant bee and blasted out a deafening trumpet. Allegra screamed, and pulled on my hand. We both over-balanced and fell back into the water. I came to the surface, Allegra clinging to me like a monkey, in time to see Bertie, Jane and Carrie hurling eggs at Mitchell from the Room 2 deck. Each time a shell broke on his skin, he shuddered and screamed. When a full tray of 24 eggs had been dispensed, the elephant, his tail pointed out behind him and his head held high, crashed through the bush, back down the bank and into the reeds fringing the river.

'Allegra,' I said as the sound of Mitchell's departure died down, 'are you flirting with me or just afraid the elephant might come back?' She released her grip.

'I do not know how to flirt,' she said evenly, moving to the pool stairs, 'but I am well aware of what distracted you just before we fell in.' Carrie arrived a few seconds later with two towels and we climbed out of the water.

Social news on the lodge front is that Incredible is to marry in a few weeks' time. Incredible has done more half-witted things in his life than a large group of asylum residents, so his wife will need to be as severe as a bandsaw to keep him in line.

The afternoon after the elephant incident I was sipping some coffee on the Tamboti Camp deck when Incredible arrived bearing the lemonade.

'Mister Angus, I can tell something very much important,' he began with the breathlessness of someone who has just run the 800 metres in record time.

'Yes Incredible, what great exposition of groundbreaking importance do you have for me?'

'No I am not break anything. I am to tell you that I am like to get married.' I looked at him for a little while – various scenarios of the future for the object of his affection ran through my mind.

'Congratulations, Incredible, who is the woman – if she is indeed a woman and not a particularly vapid transvestite?'

'Her name it is Constance – I am pay *lobola* yesterday!' he replied. He was so excited I thought he might burst.

'Incredible, what did you pay for *lobola*?'

'Oh I am pay R15 000 and ten cows,' he replied with great pride. For the first time since meeting him, I stared at Incredible with something approaching a sense of admiration. For a man of his means to have saved that sort of cash (given that he already has two kids) is astounding.

'You must have been saving for a very long time,' I replied and then, with his next utterance, the seedling of respect withered.

'No, I am borrow that money.' He made to leave but I grabbed his elbow.

'From whom did you borrow the money?' I asked.

'It's a guy in Hoedspruit, he's got very good company called Shaya Madolo Cash Loans – it is owned by that union for us!'

'What interest rate are you paying on that money?'

'Yes, I am very interest in marriage – for long time with Constance!' I didn't push him further and he went about his duties. The problem of course is that there are dozens of unscrupulous loan sharks out here preying on people like Incredible who have all but the most rudimentary education and for whom the concept of compound interest at 45% is entirely meaningless. It will not be long before a member of Shaya Madolo Cash Loans arrives to confiscate the little that Incredible possesses.

At any rate, I have been invited to the wedding for some reason – it's almost as surprising as being nominated as Jeff's mentor. On the subject of Jeff, he seems to be going great guns and has yet to kill anyone and there have been no complaints to speak of. I suspect that has something to do with the fact that Carrie gives him all the guests that don't speak English or have never visited the bush before.

This is SB's second week of leave and he has returned to Johannesburg from the Cape. Of course I didn't hear this from SB as we are on no-speaks since his demotion – his choice not mine – but I received the following from Julia.

To: Angus
From: Julia MacNaughton
Subject: Don't know why I bother

Hello Angus,

I'm not sure why I'm bothering to write this to you given that you haven't made the effort to reply to my last mail sent almost four weeks ago! I have to say it hurts me quite a lot especially as I am now getting all of my Sasekile information from Alistair and not from you. I also wanted to inform you once again that I'm coming up there next week on bed nights. I hope you will be mature about the fact that I'll be staying with Alistair and not make it awkward for all of us.

Anyway, in the interests of peace and in the hopes that you give a damn, I'll give you an update from home...

Hugh arrived back from Cape Town yesterday, still in the doldrums about his demotion. It has really affected him badly; he's wandering around shrouded in a deep misery much like he did when I, as a knee-high toddler, accidently ate one of his limited-edition dinky cars. I'm also a bit suspicious about what happened with Simone. He's being very cagey about it and I strongly suspect he is hiding something about how events unfolded.

Anyway, write back if you like. It would be good to hear from you even if you don't like my boyfriend.

Love,
Jules

I shuddered when I read the word 'boyfriend'. I felt a bit bad about not replying to her but as the old adage goes – if you have nothing good to say … The Legend is simply the sort of man I'd emigrate to escape being around. Still, it was good of her to write – I penned the following reply.

To: Julia MacNaughton
From: Angus MacNaughton
Subject: Hi

Dear Julia,

I'm sorry for not writing back after your last mail.

I just cannot see anything positive in your liaison with The Legend. He is a quintessential jock with a trust fund who doesn't stand for anything of significance but himself and his social standing. I have failed to find anything to recommend him. The fact that you are coming up here is good news but that you are to stay with him makes me ill to the core of my being. I can taste bile as I type. I realise your face is reddening as you read this but I am not going to lie to you in the interests of peace – it's not my way.

With regard to our brother, I'm not going to 'rat him out'. Obviously by saying that I've already implied that there is something to tell, and there is, so I suggest you sit him down, ply him with liquor and make him tell you – it's a good story.

Winter is almost finished here, which is great. A few of the birds have returned from their wintering grounds, the temperature is up and the dryness combined with the August winds means it's fire season so we're all being extra vigilant.

Bye now,
Angus

I haven't had a response.

Mitchell and mortality

String Bean arrived back from leave and for the second time, he didn't take the time to come and say hello. That was the least of my concerns this week, however – survival was closer to the top of my priority list.

The week began with another elephant altercation. This time Mitchell picked on Hilda from finance, although Bertie and I nearly copped it on her behalf. I've stayed mercifully clear of this gargantuan specimen for most of the year but Mitchell conspired to bring us together. Hilda lives in a house specially constructed behind the offices for the finance controller. It's a pity her domicile is so close to her desk because with her physique she should be running at least 50 kilometres a day.

Mitchell chose this human's residence because she has a well-tended garden. She lavishes so much care on her horticultural exploits that she has none left for the Sasekile staff.

I had an afternoon off and again found myself in the rangers' room trying to explain some basic astrophysics to Bertie who was struggling with the concept of the speed of light. As I was about to draw a diagram of a photon travelling from the Sun to the Earth, some foul language shattered the peaceful sounds of the afternoon.

'*Ag nee, fokkit man!*' screamed Hilda in her gravelly baritone. 'Fokken doos elephant!' Bertie and I rushed outside and around the office to find the cause of her irritation. The sight that met us was amusing.

Hilda was standing on her raised veranda brandishing a long broom. Her multiple chins wobbled as she bellowed and swatted ineffectually towards the elephant. Mitchell, on the other hand, was a picture of calm bliss. He had discovered her potato and cabbage patch. One by one he was picking Hilda's vegetables from the ground and swallowing them.

Hilda eventually saw us watching her from the safety of our position and shouted, 'Don't just fokken stand there, fokken do something about this fokken elephant!'

'We'll be back now; stay where you are.' I turned to my companion. 'Bertrum, eggs are required here.' Bertie and I ran down to the kitchen where we found O'Reilly and Kerry in his office doing some sort of experiment with berries. She was standing with a mixing bowl and he was tossing things into it while she chuckled.

'Afternoon chefs,' I began.

'Yes welcome, Ungus and Bertie, troi dis!' Before we could ask him for the eggs he had shoved spoons of berry coulis into our mouths. 'Fresh berries at de end uf de winter – Muurveluss stoof for de poodins!' I extracted my spoon and while Bertie helped himself to another few mouthfuls, I explained what we needed.

A few minutes later, Bertie, O'Reilly and I stood at the corner of the office building where Hilda and Mitchell were in the same position we'd left them. The only difference was that Hilda's garden now looked like the wildebeest of the Serengeti had migrated through it. I stepped out from our cover with an egg in my right hand and a tray of 23 more in my left. Mitchell was standing about twenty metres away behind the flimsy paddock fence that surrounds the garden. He was facing me but didn't seem perturbed – a disposition that was about to change. I lobbed the egg in my hand and it looped up and then down onto the elephant's forehead. This inspired a reaction and as he looked up, ears splayed out wide, Bertie and O'Reilly let fly. Yolk, albumen and shells exploded all over Mitchell's skin, and he was not amused. He trumpeted loudly and then charged through the paddock fence.

'Feeekk! De fekker's comin!' shouted the chef, dropping his tray and running for cover. Bertie and I held our ground and loosed more eggs, which clattered into the face of the advancing elephant. Mitchell suddenly turned, his tail horizontal, and made for the Main Camp car park.

'We must chase him properly,' shouted Bertie and the two of us ran forward after the retreating Mitchell. We hurdled the shattered fence and ran through the destroyed garden.

'Watch my fokken beans!' screamed Hilda as we disappeared out of the other side of her plot and into the bush leading to the Main Camp car park. As we ran, we flung eggs. Some hit home and others cracked on the dry trees and grass. Our aim was less fettered in the clearing afforded by the car park and we became so enthralled by the egg tossing that we failed to notice our ammunition running out. Just as Mitchell crossed out of the car park and into the bush beyond, we ran out of eggs. He soon noticed the hiatus and stopped moving.

The energy of the situation then changed very rapidly.

Quite suddenly, Mitchell spun round and gave chase. Bertie and I chose discretion over valour and ran for our lives but we were some distance from the safety of the Main Camp deck, and an irritated elephant is not slow. We didn't look around as we hurtled back through the open car park and down the path that leads through the thick riverine vegetation towards the deck. Mitchell didn't bother about the path and all we could hear was the deafening noise of breaking branches and trumpeting as he closed in. We flew across the bridge that crosses a tributary of the Tsesebe and I chanced a glance behind us to see if the stream would halt our pursuer, but at the last minute he swerved and made for the bridge. He stepped straight onto the concrete structure and there was a mighty crack but his pace didn't abate as the bridge collapsed behind him in a cloud of dust. Bertie was in front of me by this stage and Mitchell about twenty metres behind. I had about 50 metres to go to the safety of the Main Camp deck. I was now terrified, my lungs heaving and legs burning. Up until then Bertie and I had been giggling as we ran, somehow thinking the charge wasn't serious but I realised as the bridge disappeared that Mitchell meant business of the worst kind.

The noise had brought September, the Main Camp butlers and Amber to the double doors of the A-frame and their faces fell as they beheld our impending death. I could hear the great thundering of footfalls on the ground about ten metres behind me, expecting a trunk to knock me from my feet and huge grey feet to trample me to death at any second. The Main Camp staff screamed encouragement.

Bertie made it through the doors in front of me and then I dived. As my feet left the ground, I felt hot hair on the back of my neck as Mitchell lunged for me, and then I was safe. Dust billowed through the doorway as the bull slid to a halt outside. The lintel came to midway up his forehead and he thankfully thought better of trying to crawl under it. I lay on the ground, the dust settling around me, looking up at Mitchell's brown eyes. He was so close I could see his eyelashes. He trumpeted once more and then turned and made his way into the river.

I sat up panting and put my head in my hands. I'm not sure how long I sat there but after a while September tapped me on the shoulder and said, 'Here Angus, drink this.' It was cold Coke and I had to hold it with both hands because I was shaking so much. I looked up and saw Bertie sitting on one of the sofas, also with a Coke in his hand.

The next day there was a full staff meeting about Mitchell. He is spending more and more time in camp and so there are plans afoot to remove him. In the meantime everyone has to be extra vigilant and cautious. SB spent a lot of time bemoaning the fact that the elephant is destroying the aesthetics of his camp and the other camp managers agreed. Abbot, who has been very quiet for the last while muttered something about danger pay but PJ shot him a look that silenced the once-belligerent shop steward. Then Carrie addressed everyone.

'People, the elephant, as far as I can make out, has only chased people who have thrown things at him. I've seen him a few times at fairly close quarters and he has not reacted to me at all. I don't believe he's dangerous unless he's startled or chased. I'd ask that no one throw anything at him and please carry torches at night so you can see him.'

The Legend then had to wade in. 'Ja, I disagree. He's got used to people and that's not going to change. He's a danger and we need to get rid of him and maybe that means permanently.' There were a few mutters of approval and I felt my blood begin to boil.

'I assume by permanently, you mean with the aid of a .458 brass slug?' The Legend looked at me. 'Well, that's just ridiculous. He's an elephant in a game reserve doing what elephants do. Just considering shooting him is plain wrong.'

PJ said, 'We're not at that point yet but we need some ideas quickly because he's tearing the place apart.'

I drove ostensibly from Tamboti Camp this week where SB is still moping about. That said, the butlers in Tamboti are definitely much happier with him since his return to planet Earth and continue, with the obvious exception of Incredible, to do a great job. Waiting for my guests a few afternoons ago and sipping some iced coffee, I watched as two squirrels chased each other round the sausage tree below the deck and a bushbuck fed on some of the diminishing greenery fringing the river. SB arrived bearing a jug of lemonade.

'Hello String Bean,' I said, 'thanks for coming to greet me on your return yesterday.'

'Hello Angus,' he said, 'thanks for telling Julia about Simone and me.'

'I said nothing but that she should ask you – did you fess up to your misdemeanours?'

'I told her about the strain I was under and that Simone wasn't supporting me and that I needed support.'

'So you didn't tell her you tried to bang Amber against the fridge and were caught red-handed?'

'Angus, it's not like that – you just don't get it.' It was all quite light-hearted until that point but his latest pathetic attempt to rationalise his behaviour angered me.

'String Bean, there is no justification for what you did to Simone. Everyone makes mistakes but if you can't be man enough to admit to them then you are just a coward. Have you even apologised to her?'

'Fuck you, Angus, I'm not talking to you about this,' he pointed his finger at my face, which enraged me further.

'Don't stick your skinny finger in my face you yellow-bellied turd.'

I grabbed his finger and he was about to take a swing at me when Redman and Carrie (also driving out of Tamboti) emerged from the kitchen with a plate of choc-chip cookies and a cake.

'No no no no no!' Redman shouted.

'Guys for God's sake don't be ridiculous! There are guests coming!'

We let go of each other and turned to face Carrie and my group of twelve antique Americans – all residents of a retirement village for the super-wealthy in Florida. This was their first trip to Africa, and in the case of four of them, their first overseas visit. They ate a truly obscene amount and consumed enough medication to supply a large pharmacy for months. For Carrie and me, their stay consisted largely of repeating the answers to all enquiries at least four times – not only because they couldn't hear properly but because, much like many of their countrymen, they were born without the ability to listen. I eventually started making stuff up.

When Nancy asked me for the fifth time what impala eat (despite a whole herd grazing in plain view), I replied, 'Nancy, impala live on a diet of frogs, mice, nuts and small children.'

'Right. Okay, thanks. And rhinos – what do they hunt?' This was the third repeat of this question.

'Rhino use their horns to skewer fish from waterholes and fledglings from their nests.'

'Oh good, that's nice,' she said as she re-applied some shocking pink lipstick to a large area surrounding her mouth.

On Friday morning, Julia arrived by plane – The Legend, being a legend, managed to wangle her a flight for next to no cost. Nancy and her friends had just left and I was looking forward to a few hours on my back before meeting my next lot. I was lying on my bed reading when Kerry knocked on the open door and walked in.

'Angus, your sister's here,' she said.

'Good morning,' I replied.

'Why haven't you gone to say hello?' She was upset.

'What are you talking about? Why on Earth does it matter to you?' I sat up and looked at her.

'Angus, come on, man. You're so lucky to have a sister. Don't be an idiot – whatever your issue is with Jonesy. Don't make a mess of things with her.'

'Why the hell do you care?' I was slightly dumbfounded.

'I care because I think you're being an idiot about all of this. Please go and say hello to her.' I was about to refuse when the fact that my brother and I are no longer speaking and a desire not to be completely alienated from my siblings came to my consciousness.

'Okay,' I said, 'where is she now?' I hoped fervently that I wouldn't have to go to The Legend's room to see her.

'She's having lunch on the Main Camp deck.'

I sighed, stood up and Kerry and I walked down to the deck together.

My sister was at the buffet table helping herself to some soup and fresh bread. I walked over and took the knife with which she was trying to cut a slice of bread.

'Hello Julia,' I said slicing a piece of ciabatta and placing it on her plate.

'Hello Angus,' she replied.

'How was your trip?'

'Very easy thanks – much nicer flying here than the long drive when I only have two nights to spare.'

'Do you want something to drink?'

'I'd love a glass of sauvignon blanc,' she smiled for the first time.

'Go and sit, I'll bring it over.' I went to the bar and asked Clifford for the drink and then took it over to Julia and sat down.

'How's work?' I asked.

'Insanely busy but I'm really enjoying it. I'm definitely in the right place at the moment – I find the people and environment so stimulating.'

'Well I'm really pleased for you.' Before I could say anything else, The Legend swaggered onto the deck and straight over to the table. Julia stood up and gave him what can only be described as a dazzling smile.

'Hi Baby,' he said and my throat closed. He then looked over to me. 'Howzit Angus.' I stood up, unable to be around them together.

'Jones,' I nodded and then turned to Julia. 'I'll see you later, Jules, I have a few things to do.'

The rest of her stay passed without incident although I hardly saw her. At least we're sort of talking again.

Week 35

Marriage and Mathebula

The week started with Jenny's farewell party. It was a typical affair – PJ made a kind speech, a gift was presented, and then there was a lot of drinking and some fairly wild animal behaviour. The next day Jenny left while I was on morning game drive. I felt a tremendous sense of relief when I returned to the lodge knowing she was gone but I'm glad we parted on good terms.

The universe has continued to spit on SB this week. It would seem that his sleep-my-way-to-the-top friend, Amber, is no longer prepared to be his lover since his fall from grace. I know this because I overheard them talking in the bar store (the same place it all began) a few nights ago. I was driving out of Rhino Camp and Melissa asked me to fetch some Strandveld shiraz on my way down to dinner.

I was outside the door when I heard my brother moaning, 'Come on, you know I can't do anything about it now!'

'Well, what am I supposed to do?' Her normally sickly-sweet voice had a nasty edge to it. 'I didn't come here to work for September! I was doing a great job as manager at Kingfisher and now I'm working for a dude who does not even have a matric!'

'There's nothing I can do about it!' wailed SB. 'It's not my fault that no one here sees my talents!'

There was a pause and Amber concluded icily, 'Well I can't be with someone who doesn't have ambition and isn't prepared to fight for me.'

'But . . .'

She cut him off. 'No, it's done. It's over.' The door opened and she walked out. She saw me standing there and was taken by surprise. 'Oh . . . um . . . hi Angus.'

'Hello you evil, gold-digging, slapper.' I smiled at her. Her mouth dropped and she thought about replying but I stopped her. 'Before you utter any more tripe – String Bean made one good decision regarding you. September may be uneducated but you work for him and not the other way around because he's infinitely more competent than you are. So why don't you try and learn something from him instead of whinging like a spoiled toddler?' I pushed past her and into the bar store.

SB was sitting on a wine barrel, head in hands. I still couldn't bring myself to feel sympathy.

'What ho, String Bean,' I said looking for the Strandveld section in the store. He looked up, his hair all over the place and his eyes bloodshot. He sighed heavily and said nothing. 'Your supportive mistress let you down?' I took two bottles of the shiraz from their designated spot. 'Just imagine how marvellous it would be to have Simone to comfort you at a time like this. Still, you know best.' I walked out.

String Bean's being slog-swept for six over the long-on boundary has, predictably, made his hang-dog expression move from beagle to miserable basset hound.

The highlight of my week was the wedding of Incredible to Constance. It was my first Shangane wedding and I was enthralled. The format was probably similar to most of the weddings out here but because the groom was Incredible, there were some bizarre moments.

There were about 40 of us from the lodge who went along – SB, as the immediate boss of the groom, was also invited and I suspect that my genetic relationship to him was the reason I was included. We drove out in a few vehicles, most of us on a flatbed trailer being pulled by the tractor.

I don't have a huge selection of clothes out here but I didn't want to make a *faux pas* at Incredible's nuptials. I therefore went to ask the groom about the dress code a few days before the great event. Typically, my conversation ended with my being none the wiser.

'Incredible,' I said as I spotted him walking past my home on his way to the staff shop a few afternoons ago, 'what should I wear to your wedding?'

'Yes, of course,' he replied.

'No, I need to know what kind of clothes for your wedding?' He looked at me as my words failed to penetrate his cranium – he wore a blank expression a bit like Manuel's in *Fawlty Towers*. 'Clothes – you know – shirts, trousers, socks, etc.!' A confused and slightly offended expression. I repeated everything in Shangane but it became clear that language wasn't the source of his consternation.

'Yes, of course definite. You must to wear the trousers to my wedding.' I gave up and sought Elvis who explained that Sunday best was the normal form. In my case that meant some khaki chinos and a fresh shirt – I don't have a jacket out here. Jeff offered to lend me one when he saw me climbing onto the tractor trailer. He rushed off to his room and returned bearing a maroon sports jacket that would have hung even on his substantial frame.

'Jeffrey, how tall are you?' I asked him as he tried to hand it to me.

'Almost 186 cm,' he said, pleased that he could answer.

'Jeffrey, I am just 172 cm. That is a 14 cm difference. While I don't wish to be ungrateful, wearing a dressing gown at Incredible's nuptial festivities may be frowned upon by the socialites of Gazankulu.' Jeff's eyes glazed over as the tractor spluttered to life and we headed off.

Elvis, Jacob, and I sat up against the back wall of the trailer and chatted as Timot drove us out. Bertie, who was in a group on the back of the trailer, fell off over a big bump and had to run to catch up while the rest of us had a good laugh. SB considers himself above such forms of transport. He managed to wangle a lift with PJ and Amy in the GM's Discovery.

The ceremony was held in a primary school hall and we were a little late arriving so there wasn't much room left. Elvis and I found ourselves standing against the side wall about halfway along the hall.

The outfits worn by the guests went from respectable and formal to totally bizarre. Most people (about 150 in all) arrived dressed to the nines. The young men went to town and the amount of bling on display, had it not been plastic, would have sunk an aircraft carrier. None was more resplendent than the groom himself. His attire consisted of a shimmering lemon-yellow suit. This tasteful faux satin garment was beaded with gold rope. The back of the jacket had an elephant embroidered on it – also in gold. His belt, which matched his shoes, was bright purple. The pants were a good three inches from the top of his shoes and their horizon was joined to the purple of the shoes by some garish red socks. On his bald head, the groom wore a hat (somewhere between a bowler and a top hat) the same sparkling lemon as his suit.

I took in the groom's outfit and those of his two groomsmen (satin white for both with enormous sunglasses – worn throughout the ceremony). I caught SB's eye, knowing that even in his current state of wretched self-pity, the sight of Incredible's suit would give him apoplexy. I nodded over at the groom and my brother, who was in the process of swallowing some water, choked and the liquid reversed back up through his nose. PJ had to pat him hard on the back.

A violent blaring of kwaito music from distorted speakers erupted as the bride made her entrance. It was at that point that I realised the couple would be perfectly matched. Her dress looked as if she had collected all the voile curtains and mosquito nets in Gazankulu and sewn them into her billowing nuptial garment. I looked over at SB, who had to look away again as he started convulsing from his VIP position in the second row. She could barely squeeze the folds of the dress down the aisle. There was great ululating as the bride shuffled down towards the Seventh Day Adventist pastor waiting at the front of the hall.

When she'd arrived next her lemon-bedecked fiancé, everyone, except those of us on the wall, sat down and the pastor began to speak – and speak and speak and speak. The service ground on – taking roughly the same length of time as the Israelites were in the wilderness. When the vows, three readings, some lengthy prayers and a few songs (beautifully sung) were complete, the bride and her lemon made their way down the aisle and outside to rapturous ululation. We were all swept along with the crowd and once outside, the lesser Sasekile staff piled back onto the tractor trailer for the short ride to Incredible's parents' homestead.

Not long after that, we were drinking quarts of beer, chatting to the other guests and becoming thoroughly mellow. While fetching my second quart, Bertie and I met Mr Mthabini, the maths teacher from Mangonzwana High School. We found a relatively quiet spot and I asked the dedicated fellow about the school. He shook his head and gave a wry smile.

'Those computers from your guest arrived. They were sitting in the library for a few months – getting a lot of dust. We have got electricity but there is still no phone line and no way of connecting to the Internet. Then, about two weeks back, I arrived at school one morning only to find that all the computers – 40 of them – had disappeared. I called the police but they didn't come until the afternoon. The principal – you know, Mr Ndlovu – he shouts at me for calling the police.' He took a sip of his beer, sighed and continued, 'You will not be surprised to hear that Mr Ndlovu was wearing a new suit the next day – if you know what I mean.'

'So is that it?' I asked, becoming worked up.

Mthabini smiled. 'Normally, that is the end. This time, I was too angry. I called a friend who is a detective in Phalaborwa. He asked around and, to make a long story short, the computers were found with a well-known fence in the area. My friend managed to pull some information from this man and he told us Mr Ndlovu had given them to him to sell.' Mthabini leant back on his chair. 'Mr Ndlovu is now out on bail awaiting trial but best is that he is no longer at Mangonzwana.'

Mthabini's wife, Prisca, arrived then and we moved on to more cheerful subjects.

The wedding food (beef, goat, pap and sheba) was served about an hour after we arrived. The beef, I was informed by Elvis, came from a bull slaughtered early that morning. It was clearly an animal that had spent much of its long life on foot in the harsh climes of the lowveld as its flesh was about as tender as barbed wire. I didn't sample the goat flesh but I saw Bertie feeding his to a hound outside so it couldn't have been much better.

Once the meal was complete, the dancing began in the middle of the marquee. It was started by some traditional Shangane dancing. There was some pretty impressive stuff until Incredible, dark stains starting to appear in the armpits of the lemon jacket, pulled SB onto the dance floor and then it became more amusing than impressive. My brother, even after three or four quarts, is not much of a dancer but no one seemed to mind and soon everyone joined in to the beat of the drums provided by three ageing but tireless women.

As the sun began to set, PJ gave us the signal and we delivered our wedding gifts, bade farewell to the party and thanked Mr and Mrs Mathebula for having us at their attractive homestead. We staggered onto the flatbed and Timot drove us east into the reserve as the first whispers of spring warmed the evening. I sat in a row with Bertie, Allegra and Elvis, our legs hanging off the back of the trailer, facing the blazing red horizon. As we drove, the three of us tried to teach Allegra some Shangane words. She was well mellowed after a few Black Label quarts and had us all giggling at her efforts to master the subtle whistling sounds that permeate the language.

By the time we arrived home, it was dark. Bertie, Elvis and the rest of the staff bade us goodnight and the tractor drove off, leaving Allegra and I standing alone beneath the crisp, late-winter sky. I didn't feel much like going to bed.

'Would you like a drink, little miss champion of the Shangane language?' I asked. Allegra turned her face to me, a strand of her lengthening fringe falling across a grey eye.

'Although I have clearly already had enough, I might be convinced to have a night cap.'

I thought about taking her to my room but realised there was nothing but brackish tap water to be drunk there.

'Excellent, let's go to Main Camp and have a good malt.'

'I have not yet developed a taste for whisky,' she replied as we turned onto the path that leads from the office area to Main Camp.

'Well madam, tonight is as good a night as any to become acquainted with the elixir of the Celts.'

About halfway to the camp, a rustle in the bushes about 30 metres south of the path made me freeze. Allegra bumped into me.

'Oh!' she said.

'Shh.' I turned to look at her. 'Elephant.' I assumed it must be Mitchell.

'How do you know?' she whispered.

'Smell.' A branch snapped and then all went quiet as the elephant either heard, saw or smelled us. I felt no threat – it was like he was inviting us to make the next move. I took Allegra's hand and pulled her forwards along the path. The elephant didn't stir until we had passed where I thought he was. Then we turned around as we heard him move again. A small piece of me expected him to come hurtling down the path at us – given our less than cordial previous encounter. Instead, he slowly crossed the path about twenty metres away, turning briefly to look at us, his broken tusk glinting in the moonlight.

Allegra gasped and I savoured the feeling of her pressed up close behind me, treating me as her protector as Mitchell disappeared into the night. I turned around as a cloud cleared from the moon rising behind her. We stood and I breathed in the coming season mixed with the smell of her dark hair and perfume.

After some greedy lungsful, I moved my head back and looked into her grey eyes. Then, obviously reading my urge, she took her left hand from my waist and placed the index finger gently on my lips.

'Do not move from where you are. I am already much closer to you than is appropriate right now.' She, sighed, pulled her hand away and took a step back. 'I suspect I have been lured into this position by the beer and the beauty of the night.' She paused. 'And possibly by you too.'

A thick-tailed bushbaby screeched down towards the river.

'What are you talking about?' I asked.

'Angus MacNaughton, I am not a free woman. You see I find myself in what one might describe as a long-distance relationship.' The bushbaby called again.

'Oh, shit,' I said suddenly deflated. 'Mired or happily ensconced?'

She chuckled but didn't answer directly.

'We have been seeing each other for about four years now. We met at university in Edinburgh.' I sat down on a flat rock next to the path and she sat next to me. A hyena whooped from a clearing north of the river.

'That sounds pretty serious,' I said.

'I suppose it is serious – whatever that means.' She didn't sound overly enthralled but I had no desire to engage in a heavy discussion as to the relative merits of her four-year liaison so I changed the subject.

'So does your Edinburgh lilt come from your university days?'

'Do I have a strong accent?'

'No, it's very subtle.'

'Well, I was born just outside Stutterheim in the Eastern Cape. We moved to Scotland when I was ten when my dad was transferred – he is an agronomist.'

'Why did you come back – especially given your relationship with what is no doubt a pasty-white Brit?' She chuckled again.

'I wanted some time in the sun after finishing my studies. I spent a few months at my aunt and uncle's lodge in the Drakensberg, worked for a medical NGO in the Eastern Cape and now I am here for a while.'

'Medical NGO? What did you study?'

'I am a physiotherapist,' she replied. The hyena whooped again, and another one answered, its voice echoing down the river.

We continued chatting amiably for a while until the night grew cold and then we returned to our respective homes.

The next afternoon, just before game drive, I bumped into Allegra outside the kitchen on my way to the Main Camp deck to meet my new group of honeymooning Americans. Things were pleasantly unawkward between us and after we'd exchanged friendly greetings, she said, 'I have just had a mail from my uncle and aunt. They need some hosting and guiding help over the next two weeks – one of the ladies is on maternity leave and they have just fired a guide. I know you are going on leave soon so if you would rather spend a couple of weeks in the KwaZulu-Natal Drakensburg instead of Johannesburg, they would love to have you.'

Well, that was a turn up for the books. Johannesburg is a poor option at the best of times but it's even worse for the next fortnight given that Mum and Dad are away with Trubshaw, and Julia and I aren't on the best terms.

'Thank you very much,' I replied, 'that would be really cool. I'll definitely take them up. Aren't you going on leave too – can't you help them?' She blushed a bit.

'I will be there too,' she replied.

This evening I wrote to Mum and Dad telling them that Francina would have to look after AIDS Cat and the Major on her own for the next fortnight. Tomorrow I head for the mountains.

My last order of business for the work cycle was to go and see PJ about a mail I received from Arthur.

To: Angus MacNaughton
From: Arthur C. Grimble
Subject: Celebration of life

Crocus Cottage
West Road
Wragby
Lincolnshire

Dear Angus,

As you are no doubt well aware, the anniversary of Anna's passing falls near the end of next month. I am writing to tell you that Mavis and I will be coming out to South Africa. I have secured a booking at Sasekile and I hope that you might be able to guide us while we are there. Mavis has never been to Africa and so we are both very much looking forward to being there.

I hope you are well and we will both see you soon.

All the best,
Arthur

I replied that I would absolutely be here to guide them and then went to see PJ. Arthur hasn't two pennies to rub together, so how he and Mavis have managed to book to come out here I cannot imagine. The General Manager was unaware of the booking but assured me that he would happily give them two complimentary nights given what Anna meant to Sasekile.

Week 36

Mountains and music

Hlolela Mountain Lodge – here be peace and quiet in natural splendour.

Mike and Liz Coach (Allegra's aunt and uncle), are in their mid-50s and inherited the place from Mike's parents, who also inherited it – it's really old. Mike grew up here, speaks Zulu like a Zulu, and the local people treat him as an *induna* rather than a boss.

There are ten little stone cottages on the property. Each one is a uniquely and tastefully decorated suite. It's not cheap to stay here but one doesn't have to sell a kidney to visit. The cottages have a bedroom, a sittingroom with a huge stone fire place, a good size bathroom and an outside shower. The chimney runs up between the bedroom and the sittingroom so when there's a roaring fire going, the whole cottage warms. (Unlike the lowveld, the rarefied air of the Drakensburg in early September is still cold at night and in the mornings). Because I am temporary and doing the Coaches a 'favour', I've been put in one of the suites for the duration of my stay. They treat me like royalty because they think someone who guides at famed Sasekile must really be something special. This illusion would obviously be shattered should they ever come across Jeff or that heaving knob, Matto.

My main functions here are to take guided walks and, since the Coaches discovered I'm no mean horseman, help out with the riding. Mike also saw my guitar on arrival and immediately expressed an interest in hearing me play. Allegra helps out with the admin in the office and also does some hosting duties at meal times.

Mornings at Hlolela consist of a walk, ride or cycle in the mountains surrounding the lodge. After lunch, the guests generally pass out and a lull descends. There is admin to do but I, thankfully, am not required for this so I head off to my cottage and read on the veranda from which I have an unparalleled view of the Main Berg.

Tea and fresh scones are served at about 16h00 and I then guide a short walk or play tennis with the guests. At dusk, people disappear to their rooms to shower and change for dinner. At 18h30 on most evenings, everyone gathers in the Stone Bar which might now be my favourite indoor place in the world.

It was the first building on the property, built in 1893. The thatch roof is low and I can just fit through the doorframe without stooping. The floor is stone, all the pieces cut by hand, so it's a bit hazardous after a few drinks. The counter and tables are all antique yellowwood, the planks cut from the trees that used to grow in somewhat greater abundance in the wetter parts of the mountain. The huge fire place is constructed from pale granite and the four low tables are surrounded by old leather sofas and covered with colourful throws collected from all over the world. The place smells like thatch, wood smoke and cigars.

Mike is a collector of fine whisky and the display of single malts (Scottish, Irish, some Canadian and even a few Japanese) is something to behold. He is always behind the counter when the guests arrive, always in a branded and faded green shirt, a red and white tea cloth over his left shoulder. He serves the drinks with the help of Portia, the bar lady and, if he thinks a guest is vaguely interested in whisky, he generously pours them tastes of his favourites for which he never charges.

On my second evening, all the guests (sixteen in all) and some staff sat at one big table for dinner in the diningroom annexed to the Stone Bar. It was one of those evenings when the atmosphere just clicks. Conversation flowed almost as fast as the great wine that Liz had brought back from a recent visit to the Rhône Valley. The guests were all fun South Africans ranging from an eighteen-year-old all the way to an 86-year-old who drank us all under the table. I watched as Mike cleverly guided the conversation to the positive; heated sometimes, but never negative.

After pudding, Mike asked me if I would like to play the guitar for the assembled company.

I was so swept away by the atmosphere of the evening that I replied, 'It would be my pleasure.'

Ten minutes later, we were packed into the Stone Bar, the sofas set in a semi-circle around the fire. I sat on an armless old chair off to one side.

'What would you like me to play?' I asked sipping on the Compass Box Peat Monster that Mike had set next to me.

'Do you play anything classical?' asked Graeme, a stout, hilarious and wealthy entrepreneur from Johannesburg.

My fingers felt out the soft but urgent opening notes to *Asturias* by Albeniz. The fire crackled as the music built to its tremendous crescendo. As I stroked the calm reflective middle section, the leather of the sofa creaked softly and my audience savoured their drinks. Then the passion built again as the earthquake-mimicking first section repeated before returning to the serenity of the end. I don't believe my fingers have ever flown across the fingerboard like they did for the few minutes it took me to play the piece – inspired as they were by the atmosphere of the room. As I played the last E minor chord, there was a collective sigh and then some soft but appreciative applause.

An hour later I played my finale. Graeme asked me to play another classical piece so I obliged with *Come Again* by John Dowland. I delivered the last verse *a cappella* with just the crackle of the fire to accompany me.

'All the night my sleeps are full of dreams/My eyes are full of streams/ My heart takes no delight.'

After that, the guests dispersed and Allegra and I were left to clear the remaining glasses.

'That last one was really beautiful,' she said as she locked the door and we walked out into the crisp, clear, star-sprayed night.

'Thank you,' I replied. We were standing looking up at the sky, arms folded, shoulders touching. Then we both sighed loudly which made us giggle.

'Goodnight, Angus MacNaughton.' She turned, kissed me on the cheek and left. I wandered back to my cottage.

I received my first message from SB in a long while this week.

To: Angus
From: Hugh MacNaughton
Subject: Some help please and Hanro

Hi Angus,

I need to ask a small favour. I know we haven't been seeing eye-to-eye for a while but I hope you'll help me out anyway.

I have ordered a whole lot of wine from a number of new estates in the Cape. The stuff is all in Johannesburg as the idiots sent it to our home instead of here. I suppose that could be my fault because I put our address on the delivery form without thinking it was for the lodge. Anyway, I need the three or four boxes brought here. I know you aren't in Jo'burg but perhaps you could make a detour on your way back. The Major signed for them and had already consumed two bottles before Francina discovered him – pissed and asleep on the lawn with AIDS Cat licking his face. Francina thought he was dead and called an ambulance but the paramedics confirmed that he was just wasted.

News from the lodge is that PJ has hired Jenny's replacement. Shit, you are not going to like her. Her name is Hanro and she comes with a wealth of experience from other lodges. She used to work for a large safari company with lodges all over the place – I think she looked after their food and beverage or something. She grew up in Potgietersrus, is the same height as me and weighs much more. She's pretty fat but she's also just huge. She sweats a lot too which is not very attractive (not that she would be attractive even without the sweat). PJ has hired her on the recommendation of a recruitment agency – he says she's got experience with 'systems'. As has become the norm, she came over to me for some training and orientation at the lodge.

She thinks she is much too good to be trained and she refused to listen to anything. I was pointing out the different wine blends that we have on offer and why I've selected them when she stopped me and said, 'Ag, no. I know everyfing about wines. I been working vis industry for longer van you been walking.'

'Hanro,' I replied, 'no one knows everything about wine, not even you. And, you're only five years older than me so I doubt you've been working since I was born.'

'Well I'm much more mature van you anyway.'

She's running Rhino Camp on her own now. (Melissa is now back on base at Kingfisher, and Simone is floating.) I hate to think about the experience the Guests must be having. She keeps referring to everything in the camp as hers – my staff, my camp, my bar, my rangers.

Anyway, if you can't get that wine for me, please let me know.

Thanks in advance.

Hope you are having fun there in the mountains,
Hugh

P.S. Other news from the lodge is that an elephant fence has been put up to keep that one-tusked bastard from coming in. It's a two-strand wire so not too unsightly. It's only been a day so we're not sure if it works yet.

Luckily for SB, I do have to pass through Johannesburg, so fetching his wine shouldn't be an issue provided the Major hasn't consumed it all by the end of next week. Hanro sounds like a real delight and I'll no doubt get along famously with her. It is interesting that dear SB is irked by her use of the possessive first person – I wonder if he'll hear himself doing it. Perhaps there's a hint of humility creeping into him, but I'm not going to hold my breath.

Week 37

Saddles and scotch

The highlight of my second week in the mountains was a ride a few mornings ago. It was highly entertaining but dangerous to the point of near mortality for at least two of the guests.

I met Thulani, the groom and horse guide, at the stables after an early breakfast. Thulani is about six feet tall and as wiry as a phone line. His bloodshot eyes bore testament to a big night of beer and turbo-lettuce. He has a huge gap between his front teeth and a wide mouth. While his odour and demeanour didn't inspire confidence, his way with the horses was something to behold.

The stables are a short walk down the mountain from the lodge. There are twenty horses and when I arrived, they were milling about in a paddock. I watched as Thulani greeted each one individually – all of them neighing softly as he approached – and fed them each a handful of horse cubes. He separated eight out from the group by calling their names and whistling, and moved them to an adjacent paddock to be saddled. I helped him tack up and he pointed out a bay of just under fifteen hands at the far end of the group, standing on his own.

'You ride Everett,' he said nodding at the stocky gelding. 'He is not for the guests. He will like you.'

The advert for the ride, posted in the main area of the lodge, very clearly states that the morning ride is not for people who do not have some experience on horseback. This was taken seriously by four of the guests and ignored completely by Conrad and Susan. On her left ring finger, Susan displayed a rock of at least 46 carats set in a platinum band thicker than a puff adder. Conrad, despite the chill of the morning, arrived in a T-shirt sized for a toddler. Conrad is a twelfth generation South African. His surname is Van der Sander. It is therefore difficult to fathom his obsession with Celtic art; a craft to which he is so devoted that he has pseudo versions inked along the length and girth of his substantial biceps.

The other four hailed from Johannesburg and KwaZulu-Natal: Samantha (17) and Andrea (17) – experienced show jumpers from Johannesburg, very hot in jodhpurs; Jonathan (40ish) – horse breeder from Natal, closet homosexual; and Yvonne (35) – lawyer from Johannesburg, bottom the size of the Eastern Buttress.

While these four arrived dressed to ride, Conrad had on a pair of True Religion jeans (which I later found out cost him R3 000) and All Stars. Susan's spindly legs were covered in black tights. She sported a pair of black, ankle-length boots with short pointy heels. If there was one thing in the world these were not designed for, it was riding horses. It was patently obvious that Conrad and Susan had no business being there.

Thulani's way with horses does not extend to humans.

He greeted the guests perfunctorily and muttered something about there being hard hats in the tack room. If anyone heard him, they didn't bother to take him up on the offer.

'You can ride?' he asked the assembled company. Everyone agreed that they could ride. 'You!' he pointed at Conrad and Susan. 'You are sure you can ride?' There was a smirk on his face.

'Of course, Ah can raad,' said Conrad. 'How hord can ut be? Raat babe?' He looked over at his lover who was smiling nervously. Thulani nodded and a mischievous grin spread over his gap teeth. He pointed to two docile-looking beasts and told the couple to mount up. He then divvied out the rest of the horses and in a few minutes we were on our way but not before Susan had placed her left foot in the right stirrup and swung up backwards.

It was magnificent riding east down into the valley in the early light, the sun warming our faces and burning off the light morning mist. Thulani instructed me to ride at the back and check on the guests. Everett was very relaxed in the initial stages as we walked slowly past fields of long, gold thatching grass. Andrea, Jonathan and I walked three abreast chatting amiably. After about half an hour, we turned through a gate into a fallow field.

Thulani turned to us.

'We go for little canter now', he said. He then placed his left hand on his Stetson and instead of heading off at a steady canter, he and his big black mare took off at a flat-out gallop. Conrad and Susan were just behind him. Their 'docile' beasts perked up instantly and tore after their leader. Conrad was holding his reins like one might hold a golf club. He hauled on these viciously but he was holding them so close to the buckle that there was no contact with his chestnut's mouth. He then let go and simply fell forward clinging to his horse's neck. Susan screamed as her mount bucked into a gallop. She whiplashed backwards but managed to jam her hand into the pommel of her saddle. This was the only thing that prevented her from bouncing over Buttercup's backside into the dust.

The rest all handled the situation with aplomb. They spread out and raced out across the field. I turned Everett's head to hold him back – I needed to see no one fell off. He started cantering sideways, snorting with each stride, his muscles coiled. When everyone was about 50 metres in front of me, I stood in the stirrups, leant forward and let the horse have his head...

There is very little to beat the thrill of riding a horse like that as he unleashes. With his ears pricked forward, and his black mane blowing, Everett was at a full stretch in about four strides. We gained on the others with ease and moved into the middle of the pack, charging eight abreast across the field. I looked to the side and saw the grins of complete bliss on the faces of Andrea, Samantha, Yvonne and Jonathan. I couldn't see Conrad's face because it was buried in the flapping chestnut mane of his mount. Susan's face was paler than hyena dung.

Thulani was out in the front, like the leader of a great cavalry charge. Everett passed through the group and we moved up next to Thulani and his mare. I looked over to him and he winked. Then we were both pushing our mounts on, as we raced for the end of the field.

What I didn't realise was that the field ended in a barbed-wire fence. The gap in this fence was just wide enough for one animal to fit through. This did not seem to perturb Thulani at all. He kept urging his mare on, her huge black nostrils flaring, her ears flat back. Everett was not to be held back at this point and he too careened hell-for-leather at the small gap. I wasn't too worried about the two of us but I feared for guests behind, even the ones that could ride. At the last second, Thulani swung right and brought his mare to a neat stop in a cloud of dust. I went left and reeled in the enthusiastic Everett. I looked behind as the four riders in the group followed us alternately left and right, stopping just short of the fence. The other two, however, had no chance.

Conrad didn't even see his imminent demise coming as he clung on like a giant monkey. His fiancée, however, did, and began to scream like a banshee as her horse and his friend galloped side-by-side towards the small gap.

'Waaaah waaah, fence! Fuuuuck! Conraaad!' This hysterical bleating only spurred her mount on, which in turn inspired Conrad's. I watched in horror as the two Basotho ponies flung themselves at the gap. Luckily for them, Conrad's bulk and 'riding' style made his animal marginally slower than Susan's and hers reached the tiny opening about half a length in front of his. As Conrad's chestnut went through, just behind Susan's grey, there was a loud crack as his knee collected the top of the flimsy, gum-fence pole. Loud howling joined the bleating and both sounds slowly receded as the horses disappeared into the distance.

We watched in silence as the dust settled.

Thulani clicked his teeth. 'Bludd fools,' he hissed under his breath.

There was another ten seconds of silence before the rest of us started howling.

We didn't see Conrad and Susan again on the outing. Thulani assured us that the horses would head straight back to their stables with such incompetents on their backs.

For the remainder of the ride, Thulani's only warning that we were going to have a 'little canter' was to hold his Stetson with his left hand. It was an incredible morning as we galloped over open fields and along paths lined with thatching grass that sometimes reached over my head. After two hours, the path crossed a stream and we cut sharply up towards a cave. A little while later we dismounted and unsaddled. Leaving the horses grazing beneath some trees, we walked into the shade of a rocky overhang. The walls were littered with bushman paintings to which Thulani alluded briefly.

As the horseman built a small fire for tea, I examined the paintings and told the guests the bits and pieces that I know about our Stone Age ancestors and their therianthropic art.

After that we sat around the little fire and absorbed the stunning view of the mountains across the valley to the north east. I spotted a small group of Cape vultures catching thermals in the distance and pointed them out to the guests. The water boiled presently and Thulani made some very strong tea which he served in ancient plastic mugs. The brew was accompanied by Hlolela Mountain Lodge's delicious homemade crunchies. I was utterly content with my back against a cool rock, sipping my tea and eating my crunchie.

The ride back was equally spectacular and I'd have happily sat in the saddle for the rest of the day.

We arrived back at the stables around 12h00. Conrad and Susan were nowhere to be seen although their horses, still fully tacked up, were greedily eating from a large wire and wood manger. This didn't perturb Thulani in the slightest. I had visions of the couple splattered on a rock somewhere but he assured me that they were already back at the lodge. Sure enough I found them drinking powerful brandy and Cokes on the terrace. They looked pretty sheepish and Conrad sported some heavy strapping on his left knee.

News from Sasekile is that the new fence doesn't seem to be performing its Mitchell-repelling job.

To: Angus
From: Hugh MacNaughton
Subject: Elephant

Hello Angus,

Thanks for agreeing to fetch those boxes.

Quick note from here is that the elephant is the Einstein of his species. It took him one week to figure the fence out. At tea yesterday, I watched him stand on the base of one of the fence poles, carefully avoiding the live strand, until the wood snapped. Then he stepped over the wire and into camp. I forgave him this time because the first place he went was Rhino Camp. Apparently Hanro was walking down towards her deck with a tray of welcome drinks when he stepped onto the path in front of her from behind one of the rooms.

Themba, her butler, says she screamed, dropped the tray and tried to push him into the elephant before waddling off at high(ish) speed.

See you next week,
Hugh

On my last afternoon at Hlolela Mountain Lodge, I took four guests on a teatime walk to some rock carvings in a forest. We returned to the lodge at dusk and I wandered through to the little admin office. The scent of wood smoke drifted in through the office window, mingling with the smell of dry thatching grass, end-of-winter dust and jasmine growing in a thick hedge on the stone wall outside. Allegra sat at an antique writing desk, concentrating but relaxed as she sorted the week's orders. She leant forward and turned on the lamp next to her. It cast a warm, yellow glow over the weathered, leather blotter and the one side of her face. A disobedient, dark strand moved over her cheek to hang over a wolf-grey eye.

From a cabinet, even older than the desk, an old LP spun on a turntable and the second movement of Beethoven's Fifth floated softly over the room, entwined with the smell of thatch.

I looked out of the window, down east over the valley to where the indigo horizon was climbing into the sky, revealing the faint glimmer of Venus. I stood there for a while, not wanting to break the moment. Eventually, I moved to put my hat down gently.

'Oh! How long have you been standing there?' Allegra turned her head.

'Not long. Would you like a drink?' I moved towards a butler's tray set underneath a large mirror on the western wall of the office.

'Yes, please,' she answered watching me as I took the stopper off the old crystal decanter and poured generous measures of whisky into two equally old crystal glasses. I added equal measures of water to each.

'You did not ask what I wanted,' she said.

'Look out of the window,' I replied, 'there's nothing else to drink on an evening like this.' I handed her the glass and sat on another ancient piece of furniture – this time a worn, cloth-covered sofa behind the desk, facing the valley.

'What am I looking for in this?' Allegra pushed her chair out, swivelled 180 degrees and leant back, swirling the scotch in her right hand. I sniffed the golden drink.

'I'm no expert but I'd say the scent of honeyed cherries,' I replied. 'It's from Speyside if I'm not mistaken.' She sniffed her glass.

'Cheers,' I said raising my drink.

'Cheers, Angus MacNaughton,' she replied and took a sip. 'I am not sure about the cherries but it is rather good.'

We sat for a while as the dark gathered outside.

'Did you have a good afternoon?' she asked and I told her about the walk.

There was more comfortable silence as we finished our drinks. The last sip gone, I stood, and Allegra looked up at me as I moved over to where she was sitting. She reached up and I took her hands, pulling her out of the chair quickly into my arms. We rocked gently to the last of the music. The sound of the needle scratching the label of the old record broke the moment.

It was a magic end to a magic two weeks.

Tomorrow we must make the long trek back to Sasekile.

Week 38

Boxes and bullets

On the morning of my departure from the mountains, I woke at first light and drank a coffee on my veranda while the birds stirred and the stars twinkled their last. Then I took my last breaths of crisp mountain air, packed my clobber into the Tazz, fetched Allegra from her aunt and uncle's cottage and off we set, the rear-view mirror reflecting the mountains bathing in the dawn light.

My mood dulled as I pulled into the Johannesburg driveway. String Bean's three or four boxes actually turned out to be fifteen so we had barely enough space to breathe on the way back to the lowveld. The Tazz is not designed to carry such loads, especially at its advanced age, and the trip was interminably slow. It started badly with my grandfather accusing Allegra of theft as I packed.

'Where are you going with my bloody wine you thieving harlot?' he bellowed staggering towards the garage brandishing his walking stick as she helped me. 'I may be old but I was a soldier and I'll be damned if I'll sit by and watch you thieve my drink!'

'It's not your wine, Granddad, its Hugh's,' I replied, emerging from the back seat.

'Rubbish! Hugh would never take my wine – he's my favourite you know!'

Mum came out of the house as my assailant (her father) moved towards me with the speed of an agitated glacier. 'Mother, please tell Granddad I'm not stealing his wine before he falls over and damages himself.'

'I'm sorry dear,' she said turning him round.

At this point he forgot about the wine and said to her: 'You know I do like the springtime!' He stuck his nose into a huge yesterday-today-and-tomorrow bush.

The stuffing of the car complete, we had some tea with Mum and Trubshaw in the garden. The dog lay on his back, mouth wide open, while Allegra tickled his belly. Then we made for the lowveld. The drive, apart from being sardined in the car, was fun and Allegra and I chatted most of the way about everything from the Big Bang to her pasty Brit (although she was evasive about the latter).

There has still been no rain so the bush remains parched but the knobthorn trees are in full bloom and there are new leaves on most of the trees. The mopane leaves are only now starting to drop off and they will provide a welcome food source to various browsers as we wait for the rains to bring the land to life again.

Petrus was sitting on a crate outside his door when I arrived at my room. His weight is increasing and he's in much better spirits so he's obviously adhering to his ARV regime. The number of empty beer bottles around our patch has also decreased substantially in the last few months. Petrus's self-discipline has not extended to my welcome drink however – the empty bottle rested on my doorstep.

'Hello Petrus,' I said in Shangane as I beheld the empty bottle.

'Yes, hello Angus,' he replied.

'How are you?'

'Very fine – no problems.' There was a pause.

'Well, I am also fine on the off-chance that you're interested – spent my leave in the mountains. Any idea what happened to my welcome drink?' He observed me for a moment, as though I'd asked a profoundly stupid question, which I suppose I had.

'The baboons were in camp. I have to drink it before they can steal it.'

'Ah, I see. Well, that is very kind of you. Here I was thinking that you're just a common thief and all the time you were actually looking out for me.

I feel suitably chastised and will flagellate myself accordingly this evening.'

Petrus scowled.

Bertie came to see me as I was unpacking and we debriefed. He says that between Mitchell and Hanro, the camp has been in a bit of turmoil. The elephant has now not only worked out how to stand on the fence poles but also sometimes picks up a big stick and beats the lines until they snap. PJ is becoming desperate and the camp gardens are looking pretty ropey.

Hanro is apparently rubbing everyone up the wrong way but has taken a shine to The Legend. She has told Carrie that she only wants him driving out of her camp because he's the only one good enough. That amused me no end. I have yet to lay eyes on the woman as she eschews feeding at the Avuxeni Eatery.

Kerry seemed relatively happy and relaxed having avoided the Cape. I went to say hello to her in the kitchen on my way to meeting my new guests on the Main Camp deck. She was mixing something for the evening's pudding.

'Hello Ginger,' I said to her sticking a finger into the mixture.

'Hey!' she shouted, slapping my hand with the wooden spoon.

'Ow!' I pulled my hand away and licked my finger. 'How was your holiday?' She smiled.

'It was good, thanks, spent most of it in Durban and then went to a food show in Jo'burg for the last few days with Richard and O'Reilly.' I nodded and then grabbed the wooden spoon from her hand and stuck it in my mouth. She retrieved another one and smacked my shoulder with it.

'No awkwardness with you and your boss in Johannesburg?' I mumbled, sucking the sweet, vanilla-flavoured spoon.

'No, we actually had a very cool time.'

I had cause to write to my sister this week – it was her birthday after all. I sent her some news about my time in the mountains and wished her all the best for the year. I even ordered some flowers online and had them delivered to her office. She sent the following when they arrived.

To: Angus
From: Julia MacNaughton
Subject: Thank you!!

Hey Angus,

Thanks so much for the flowers, they really made my day. You are very kind. There hasn't been much time for anything but work today so it's been fabulous having not one but two(!) enormous bunches of flowers on my desk in amongst the endless piles of paper (the other is from Alistair of course, very sweet). Otherwise, birthday celebrations will take the form of some quiet drinks tonight at the Foundry and then the usual family Sunday lunch on the weekend.

Thanks again for thinking of me and I hope you have a great day out there.

Lots of love,
Jules

No doubt The Legend's bunch was twice the size of mine.

Towards the end of the week, Elvis came to my house. We were free of guests and I had just returned from a run to the airstrip. He found me lying on the grass outside my room stretching and watching a woodland kingfisher that had just arrived from his winter north of the equator.

'Angus, *ta na* [come],' he said without preamble. When Elvis beckons, it is unwise to refuse and, from the look on his face, I could see that he was concerned about something. He led me back to Jacob's house. The conservation headman was examining an impala skin. This wasn't unusual in itself – impala are sometimes shot for rations and the skins are handed out to the staff according to seniority and length of service. The same goes for the impala that the new rangers shoot. But this impala skin was to prove rather interesting.

The pelt was hanging from a wire strung between two trees.

'What can you see?' asked Jacob in Shangane. I was a bit confused so I walked over to the skin and looked at it for some time. Slowly, realisation dawned. There were three distinct bullet entry wounds. There was an obvious one through the middle of the neck. Then, there were two others – one through the belly and the other through the top of the front leg that would have smashed the shoulder and crippled the antelope.

'Whose impala is this?' I asked. Ration hunting is done with a small-calibre rifle – from close range in a vehicle so that the animals experience minimal stress. These were large-calibre bullet holes – like the .375 or .458 rounds that the rangers carry.

'That new guy,' said Jacob.

'Matto?' I asked to be sure we were on the same page.

'Yes.'

'He only had one bullet left when he went out to shoot this one,' said Elvis.

'And he used at least three to kill this animal,' Jacob concluded.

'Where did you find it – I mean, why have you only discovered it now?'

'Timot wants to take it home. Anyone who wants to take a skin out of the property has to come and check with me,' Jacob continued. 'I have to check where he got it to make sure there is no poaching. It was his turn when that guy shot this impala, so Timot skinned it – he doesn't know the rules for the trainees but Elvis saw these holes when I hung the skin up.'

I stood there looking at the pelt wondering why Jacob and Elvis had chosen me to reveal this to and then what I should do about it. Carrie is on leave which means The Legend is in charge of the ranging team. Jacob isn't too fond of him – The Legend's childhood on a timber farm in Natal means that he addresses the Shangane staff with a supercilious tone like the one I imagine his father uses to address the farm hands back home.

While I'm fonder of *E. coli* than I am of Matto, I wasn't sure entirely what to do with the information. I couldn't go to The Legend because he is a chop and Matto's cousin and I'd hate for this to be swept under the carpet. Going to PJ seemed a bit formal – I felt like the field team should be able to deal with the issue on our own. Jacob, Elvis and I agreed to think about it for a while and reconvene a bit later to discuss the plan of action.

While I did my exercises, I considered the situation. How serious was it? To me, it smacked of a complete absence of integrity – Matto, as I suspected, was simply not someone prepared to admit his failings and accept consequences. He'd also obviously managed to steal more rounds and I suspect he probably lifted them off his dopey neighbour in the Bat Cave – in fact I remember Jeff being harangued for losing his rounds just after Matto shot his impala. The more I thought about it, the angrier I became. While I'm one of the last people in the world who buys into tradition for the sake of it, I've come to respect the rites of passage that the Sasekile rangers endure. They are, for the most part, well thought out and designed to unearth and test the characters of the trainee rangers. Matto had not entered into the spirit of a very valuable task and, instead, had clearly demonstrated some very serious shortcomings in his character. I reckoned he had to go.

Just after dinner, Jacob, Elvis and I met at the staff shop and plotted a way forward. They agreed that telling PJ was an option but that the rangers, trackers and conservation crew should deal with the situation. So it was that Jacob called a meeting for this morning at 11h00. No one else knew what it was about but when Jacob calls a meeting with the field staff, all arrive without question.

We convened in the rangers' room at the designated time and Jacob arrived carrying the skin. He asked me to translate what he had to say because he barely speaks a word of English. When everyone was sitting, he unfurled the impala pelt. There were a few confused murmurings. I glanced over at Matto and a flicker of recognition tinged with fear touched his face.

'This skin,' began Jacob, 'is the reason we are all here today.' I translated and Matto started shifting uneasily. The Legend peered at the coat. Jacob then explained that he had discovered something when Timot had tried to take it out of the reserve. Everyone looked across to the bespectacled Timot, perhaps wondering if he'd been caught poaching. Then Jacob moved to the nub of the matter. He pointed at Matto who instantly realised what was about to be revealed. The blood drained from his face.

'You,' Jacob's voice rose, 'this is the impala that you shot. You only had one round left when you went out to shoot this impala – there are three holes in this skin.' The trackers and the few rangers with a smattering of

Shangane began murmuring to each other while I quickly translated. By the time I'd finished, Matto was looking alternately at his feet and at his cousin. The Legend stood, arms folded and unsmiling. Then Matto, in a last-ditch attempt to save himself, went on the offensive.

'This is a fucken lie! I shot my impala once. How do you even know it's mine? How do you even know someone didn't make holes in it?' The murmuring in the room died down and everyone looked to Jacob to see if he had any more evidence. I translated. Jacob then looked Matto in the eye.

'*Mfana* [boy], every skin that comes in has a number written on it. There is no question that this is the one you shot. As for the holes, these are bullet holes and nothing else.'

He held the skin up and attention was once again turned on Matto. He looked over to his cousin who remained still. An awkward silence descended on the group as Matto realised the game was up. It was broken by Brandon in typically tactful fashion.

'What a *doos*,' he said. Matto then stood up and made to leave.

'I don't have to listen to this shit!' he shouted.

Elvis moved to the door and blocked his exit and then Jacob said, 'Either we can go and talk to PJ about this and you can try to fight to stay here or you can go to your room and pack your bags and be gone by tonight.' I translated and Matto glared at me.

'Al, man, jeez, say something to these okes. We all make mistakes, shit. It's no real biggie – I mean, fuck it, I was under a lot of pressure.'

The Legend looked at him, shook his head and said, 'You've really screwed up this time man – you need to leave – there's no room for that kind of shit here. You'll never be accepted.' Elvis stepped aside and Matto, with tears welling in his blue eyes, walked out of the door. He and his BMW X3 pulled out about two hours later.

That afternoon I was driving from Kingfisher. As per usual I headed down a bit early for some coffee. Simone was there arranging some fruit kebabs when I arrived.

'Shit, that was quite harsh on Matto. He's not such a bad dude!' she said after we'd exchanged greetings.

'Simone, it is my opinion that Matto has less to recommend him than the HI virus.'

'Well, I mean, isn't it a bit harsh to just fire him – does killing an impala really make a ranger?' I took the coffee and a biscuit over to my favourite burgundy armchair overlooking the river.

'It's not really about the death of the impala. Come over here and I'll explain it to you,' I said.

She sat in the chair opposite.

'That hunt is probably the most difficult thing a ranger will ever have to do – short of shooting an animal bent on killing his guests. It's a rite of passage that tests him physically, sure, but it's the emotional strain after months of training without a break that it really explores.' I sipped my coffee and a Cape glossy starling landed on the deck railing, looking for something to eat. I tossed my choc-chip biscuit crumbs onto the deck in front on him.

'Going out there with just three rounds means you have to be careful, show great bush skill but mostly, you have to be enormously patient. If Matto had shot all three rounds off and missed, then come home and confessed, I suspect Carrie would have re-done his shooting training and maybe made him spend some time on foot with the trackers. Then he would have been given another chance. Instead, he shot off three rounds, then stole more, shot the impala – wounding it first – and then he lied about it. His hunt showed him to be an emotionally immature liar and a thief – and that's not the sort of person you want in charge of people's lives.'

Simone nodded as I spoke and then said, 'Ok, well I see what you're saying but it's still harsh.'

'Yes, it is and it was meant to be. It shows the rangers who've completed it properly that they've achieved something really special and it also shows that we don't just take anyone in the field team.'

We watched the starling's precise beak picking up the crumbs for a minute and then I said, 'I assume you know that String Bean was thrown on the heap by Amber.' A smile crept over her face.

'Yes, I heard. I don't really like to gloat but I reckon I deserve to this time.'

Week 39

Anna and Arthur

This week saw the anniversary of Anna's death – the 26th of September. Arthur and Mavis arrived the day before. The old boy was in much better spirits than when I first met him at Anna's funeral. I have no doubt that the spritely and hilarious character that is Mavis is keeping him in good nick. They were both quite overwhelmed that PJ wouldn't allow them to pay for anything.

On the afternoon of the 26th, Carrie made sure that Arthur and Mavis were my only guests.

At 16h00, we set off west along the river bank. Ten minutes out of camp we came to the rhino path that leads to the spot where Anna and I often used to come to contemplate the world together; the same spot where we had her memorial. Elvis and I helped Mavis and Arthur off the vehicle, I pulled my backpack with our drinks off, and we walked slowly down the dusty path, through the riverine trees with their fresh new foliage. It was a hot afternoon and Elvis and I moved slowly to accommodate our aged guests and also to hear anything that might be lurking in the shade.

We saw a bushbuck ram, two nyala ewes and, down in the river, an old buffalo dozing next to a muddy pool.

After ten minutes of slow walking, we arrived at our destination – a glade of mahogany and large-leafed false thorn trees on the top of the bank. Anna told me it was her favourite place in the whole world. We sat down under the largest Mahogany and looked over the river. I then took a new bottle of Talisker, a packet of ice and five crystal glasses (carefully wrapped in cloth) from my pack. I poured a generous measure and a couple of ice cubes into each glass and handed them out, leaving one for Anna untouched. A grey-headed bush shrike called his high plaintive whistle in the branches above.

Arthur then pulled a photo album from his little canvas haversack. He opened it and leant back on the tree trunk, Mavis right next to him.

'I thought we might look at these photographs,' he began, opening the cover. 'Anna sent me pictures from her travels and I put them all in this album.' Elvis and I gathered around and looked as the old man flipped the pages wordlessly. There were shots of Anna from around the world – on all continents (except Antarctica). Towards the end, her time at Sasekile was chronicled. With the staff at rhino camp, at the Christmas party the year before I arrived, on game drive with some guests, playing touch rugby. The last photo was a self-portrait she took of the two of us lying on a blanket under the very tree we were leaning on. The dappled sun shone on our faces – we looked blissfully happy.

The bush shrike whistled again as my eyes filled.

When we'd all recovered (even Elvis looked a bit glassy), I raised my glass. 'To Anna,' I said.

'To Anna,' replied all the others and then Arthur added, 'To beautiful Anna.'

I savoured the peaty single malt and felt awfully sad but I forced myself to remember the fun that Anna was and the foil she provided to my volatile and possibly sometimes unpleasant character. When we'd finished our drinks, Arthur and I took Anna's down to the river – to the place where we'd scattered her ashes. I poured the whisky into the trickle of water that remains.

As we sat there, wiping our eyes, there was a rustle in the middle of the reeds halfway across the almost-dry river. I looked up and saw the back of an elephant feeding quietly, his trunk peeping over the top of the reeds towards us. Speedy retreat with Arthur wasn't going to be possible but the elephant, although obviously aware of us, seemed unconcerned. I led Arthur back to where Elvis and Mavis were waiting in the shade of a tamboti tree. From there I could see the elephant was Mitchell with his broken tusk. After a while he stopped and raised his head to look at us and then, as he moved off, he exhaled loudly and rumbled his infrasonic call.

We arrived home much later, having been on a long slow game drive. Arthur and Mavis were exhausted so I organised them dinner in their room.

Because of my lateness, there was nothing to eat at the Avuxeni Eatery so I wandered down to the kitchen, hoping for a repeat of the last time I went begging. Inside there was the normal hive of delicious-smelling activity. O'Reilly was leaning over the stove with a wooden spoon in his hand talking to Rufina – he persists with trying to teach her the chef's art despite the complete absence of a mutually-intelligible vernacular.

He was pointing at the spoon and yelling, 'Roofeena, dis chuculate sauce tests loik a bat vummitted in it!' Rufina then started yelling at her boss in machine-gun Shangane.

Kerry spotted me chuckling and came over.

'Hungry?'

'Ravenous. Nothing left at the eatery.'

'Go and sit under the tree and I'll bring us something. I've finished up for the night.' She turned and disappeared into the coldroom.

Ten minutes later we were sitting under the blue sweet-berry bush outside the kitchen. Our supper consisted of a delicious venison pie, some roasted butternut scattered with mixed seeds and some fresh asparagus from O'Reilly's garden. This we washed down with liberal quantities of Châteauneuf-du-Pape that the head chef had handed to Kerry when she told him we were having supper outside.

It was a calm, warm evening and the wine, spring air and privacy made for a comfortable atmosphere. I told her about my afternoon and then about Anna. I told her about the snake that bit her as she reached for a T-shirt in her cupboard; the sound of her scream; the rush to the hospital; my unshakable faith that she'd recover; then the terrible last minutes at her bedside when she told me she loved me and then made me promise to soften my outlook and allow myself to be a bit vulnerable.

By the time I'd finished the story both Kerry and I had tears flowing down our faces. It was cathartic because I haven't spoken about it for a long time.

The next morning, Arthur and Mavis flew out. Just before he climbed gingerly onto the plane, Arthur took my hand in his and smiled at me.

'This has been the most special few days. I cannot thank you enough. Please extend my profound thanks to all the staff for putting up with us,' he said.

'It has been an absolute pleasure and there was nothing to put up with,' I replied, a tear threatening.

'Please come and see us in England,' added Mavis warmly, 'it would be so wonderful to see you again.'

'And you had better not leave it too long; the flowers of our youth are withering somewhat.' Arthur smiled and I promised to pay them a visit early next year.

I suppose my openness inspired Kerry because last night I finally coaxed her into telling me her story.

It had reached the point where every time I arrived home from dinner, she was sitting on her veranda staring out into the sky, normally with tears streaming down her face. Last night I wasn't driving and I wanted to enjoy the new warmth with a good drink on my favourite koppie just north of the river. I wandered into the rangers' room around 17h00 to see if anyone wanted to come out with me. Carrie was in there with Jane and I suggested a little jaunt and they looked awkward and then confessed they wanted some alone time and were going for a walk.

I made my way to the staff shop to see if there was anyone tolerable there and all I found was Melissa and Candice who were arguing about the purple colour the latter has chosen to paint her long false nails.

I returned to my room to fetch my binoculars and on the way out bumped into Kerry walking back to her room.

'What ho, Ginger, Come into the bush for a drink,' I said.

'Cool,' she replied. I returned to the staff shop, added three milk stouts and three Heinekens to The Legend's account and went to the workshop where Kerry was waiting, dressed in some loose khaki cargo pants and a

T-shirt. She carried a moth-eaten, grey knitted jersey over her arm. Her hair was tied up carelessly and she was smoking again. It always kind of ruins her looks a bit to see her with a cigarillo between her fingers – still, they're better than cigarettes.

'I know, I know,' she said as I approached, 'it ruins the smell of the bush. Last one till we get back I promise.'

'Good,' I replied and we climbed onto my Land Rover and set off for the koppie which is only about ten minutes' drive from the lodge. 'What do you want to see?' I asked as we drove out over the dam next to camp.

'I like rhino,' she replied, 'but I don't really mind.'

'I'll see what I can do.' I had no intention of spending time looking for much – I just wanted some peace in the wild. We drove a circular route away from the river then back onto the southern bank in order to make for a crossing to the north just near the koppie. The riverine bush where we were driving was thick and I wasn't really concentrating as we bumbled along in silence. Some oxpeckers called to the south and I spotted a grey shape in the thick bush. I stopped the vehicle and peered at the animal – unusual habitat for a white rhino; bit early for a hippo to be out of the water; too small to be an elephant; too grey to be a buffalo. I pointed the shape out to Kerry and we peered into the greenery. I felt my heart beat faster as realisation dawned.

'Black rhino!' I hissed at Kerry.

'Oh,' she replied, 'that's nice.'

'*Nice?* Black rhino are highly endangered and they've only been seen here once every three or so years for the last century!' She was a bit more appreciative after that but not for very long because she dropped the binoculars she was holding. They bounced off the door frame and then clattered onto the floor of the Land Rover. The black rhino bull, as is their wont generally, was not amused at the disturbance and came rushing out of the bush snorting. We both froze instinctually as the stocky animal stopped about twenty metres off, his head held high. He was a magnificent creature and waited there for a few minutes, sniffing the air and affording us an excellent view of his stout front horn and hooked lip. Then he spun and charged off into the bush. Kerry turned to look at me.

'*Nice* indeed,' I said.

'Well I guess I saw my rhino,' she smiled.

We drove to the koppie feeling exhilarated and climbed up to the top, me carrying the little cooler box and Kerry the binoculars and a packet of Mexican chilli chips. We found a comfortable spot facing east, cracked open our drinks and watched the night begin to grow from the horizon.

We alternated between silence and some general chit chat and then, when the temperature had dropped a little, Kerry pulled on her stretched, grey jersey.

'I bet that garment has a few stories to tell,' I said, making light conversation. She didn't reply immediately and then sniffed, trying to wipe a tear away before I noticed it.

'Ginger, I think it's about time you unloaded,' I said. 'It's simply appalling for you to be so sad all the time.'

She was silent for a little while and then said, 'Well, I'm not very good at talking about myself and besides, who am I supposed to speak to?' The door was open.

'Me obviously,' I said gently.

'Alright Angus, I'll tell you my story but you have to promise not to tell anyone because it's *kak* and you have to promise not to bring it up with me after tonight. Okay?'

'Fair enough,' I shrugged. I handed her a Heineken and then opened my last milk stout. 'Fire away.' What followed was not pleasant to listen to but I think it made her feel a little better.

She began, 'I was born in Beaufort West and I never knew my father. My mom was only seventeen when she had me. She refused to ever speak about the bastard and she wouldn't even tell me his name. She never said as much but I'm pretty sure she was raped and I'm the result. So that was a pretty shit way to start life.' She took a sip of her drink. 'My grandparents were crazy dogmatic church people and they thought both my mother and I were going to hell – they refused to see either of us and when I was six, they were killed in a car accident. It didn't make much difference to us because we never saw them and they didn't help support us – all the while my mother was doing odd jobs for people, I never knew what exactly and when I was thirteen, she hooked up with Clive.'

She paused for breath and drank deeply. A spotted eagle-owl called down towards the river and she continued, 'Clive was a mechanic or a panelbeater or something. He was huge, like that rhino huge. He had siff tattoos all down his hairy forearms and I never heard him say a gentle thing. But it wasn't what he said that was the problem – he was an alcoholic and he was violent – fucking angry like I'd never seen. At the beginning, my mother said she hung around with him because he gave her protection but that was just bullshit – she was abused and had a massive case of denial as well as being not very bright. He'd come home late at night and the screaming would start – normally with her apologising for something hoping that he wouldn't punch her. Sometimes it worked, sometimes it didn't. I would lie in bed waiting for the thump as his fist hit her – normally in the body but sometimes it was the face and she'd wake up all black and swollen.

'Clive hardly ever said anything to me and I spent as much time away from the house as possible – at school, with friends and anyone who'd have me but always I'd have to go home because I was worried about my mom and I didn't have the courage to tell anyone. I'm sure people must have known about it all because it was hardly a secret but no one ever did anything about it back then. Then one night he came home. I was in bed and Mom was out doing a night shift cleaning job somewhere. I heard my door open and I could smell him straight away. I froze, shitting myself for what he was going to do – and I'm not going to tell it all to you, but it involved his fists – but thank God, he didn't rape me. I think he may have wanted to but my mother came home and he turned his anger to her.' She paused and took a long drag on her bottle.

'Shit Kerry,' I'm so sorry, this is unbelievable.' She didn't acknowledge me but carried on talking fast.

'I skipped school the next day but that night Clive came back to my room, he was naked and told me he was going to make me a proper woman. He jumped onto my bed and got on top of me – stinking of booze and sweat and engine grease. I was struggling but he was so big. He hit me but he had to let go of my arm to do it and as his fist hit my face, I grabbed the lamp next to my bed and smashed it into his face. It was made of china or something and it shattered on his face. He screamed and let go and I ran out of the house into the night – it was pissing down rain and I had nowhere to go.

'Anyway I need to back up a bit to tell you that at school we had this awesome maths teacher – Monty we called him. He was in his twenties with fresh ideas and even the worst students in my class – and it was a rough school – enjoyed him. Anyway, because he was a cool oke, people used to go to him with problems – he really cared. I didn't even think about going to him but that night, he was the only place to go. I ran the few blocks to his place and banged on the door. After what felt like a long time, the door opened and he came out. He didn't even ask a question, he just took me in his arms and looked after me. I woke up the next morning with my cuts all plastered up wearing only this grey jersey.'

The silence hung for a little while. 'Do you want to smoke?' I asked.

'Yes please.' I waited for her to light up. She blew the smoke out into the evening. It was completely dark by that stage and the ledge we were sitting on faced directly into the rising moon – two days waned from full.

'Anyway, the next day was a Saturday. Monty woke me up with a cup of tea and a rusk – I'd never had that before! He'd dried my clothes so I dressed and then put this old jersey over me and walked through to the kitchen where Monty had made us bacon and eggs. We sat and ate and he eventually managed to make me tell him what I've just told you. He said he was going to make sure no one ever did that to me again and then told me to sit tight for the day. I lounged around watching TV while he spent most of the day in his little study on the phone.

'That night, he asked me if I wanted to go live with his folks – they lived in Cape Town and he'd obviously spent the day talking to them and a school in Cape Town. I really didn't want to leave Mom but I knew Clive would come at me again. I didn't know how I was going to pass my exams – I was about to write my matric finals. Anyway after a lot of talking, Monty convinced me and I moved to Cape Town that weekend. I didn't even go home to tell Mom, I phoned her later but she was so pissed I hardly think she noticed.'

She took another long drag on her cigarillo. The night was broken by a leopard making his sawing territorial call below us and crickets chirruped gently all around the koppie. Kerry stubbed out the cigarillo and put the stompie in her pocket.

273

'Monty's folks were a bit like yours and they made me feel so welcome. Their only rule was that I wasn't allowed to drink in the house and that if I was going to be late home for any reason, I had to tell them. I struggled a bit at first but Monty coached me through it. I plugged my exams badly at the end of the year and I didn't know what I was going to do. Monty's mom, Betty, convinced me to repeat the year and stay with them, so I did. They weren't wealthy people but they were comfortable and during the year we all discovered that I really enjoy food and cooking and so when I passed my exams a year later, they helped me get a bursary for the chef's kitchen I went to.'

'That doesn't explain the tears,' I said, knowing there was more to come.

'No, the tears came later. Betty and Gavin became my parents and I spent four years with them until I came here. Monty was like my big brother but over the course of the next few years, I think I fell in love with him, although he pretended not to know. The first year at the kitchen went by so fast – it was probably the best year of my life. Monty was still teaching out in Beaufort West but he came home more and more often and I think it was mainly to see me. Then, at the beginning of winter during my second year at the kitchen, Monty got sick – very sick – he had a brain tumour but the cancer was everywhere. I didn't want to know all the details. All that mattered was that he only had a few months.' She sniffed and wiped her eyes and then continued, 'In the end, he only lasted nine shitty weeks.'

A breeze rustled the sparsely-leafed tree above us. The owl called again and I heard a lion roaring so far away it sounded like he was directly under the moon, which was just clear of the horizon.

'So, that's the story this moth-eaten old jersey has to tell.'

It's difficult to know what to say in situations like that and it's infinitely preferable to be silent than spew clichés or twee advice. After ten minutes or so I said, 'Well I have a little experience in these matters but I don't know what will make it easier for you.' I moved over to sit next to her, reached out and pulled her close. I leant back on a tree, she nestled into my chest and, for a long time, she sobbed as I stroked her hair.

Once again, the trials of my life are put into perspective.

Hanro and harlot

This week saw my first altercation with Hanro.

This woman's ten years working for a large but dubious safari company have imbued her with a sense of enormous self-importance matched only by her mass. Word on the game path has it that the Sasekile business is leaking cash because of poor controls. In addition, apparently our competitors have upped the levels of general hospitality and we are falling behind. SB was supposed to take care of all this when he was elevated to the position of LHCU.

SB was right about Hanro's size. She is over six feet tall and roughly the same again wide. She is big-boned and blessed with a covering of blubber that would make a Norwegian whale hunter salivate. This unfortunate combination of attributes is made even more unattractive by two things. Firstly her insistence on wearing shorts that end halfway down her thighs and secondly, an aggressively short haircut of dark spikey hair atop a head too small for its body. In short, she looks a bit like an engorged tick with a military haircut. Hanro's personality makes Joseph Stalin seem positively lamb-like. It is not immediately apparent if she has a gender at all.

Carrie dispatched me to drive out of Rhino Camp early this week. (The Legend has refused to drive exclusively out of her camp because apparently she keeps making sexual innuendos which are making him nervous. He is about six-foot-two and built like the proverbial outhouse. The fact that he is afraid of Hanro gives an indication of the 'impressive' physical specimen she is.)

So it was that I made my way down there before tea on the designated afternoon to pick up three couples – all unrelated but on safari for the first time. I arrived ten minutes early in order to have my usual cup of coffee and a choc-chip biscuit. Themba was in a corner cleaning a vase. He was showing signs of post-traumatic stress syndrome. I greeted him, wandered over to the tea table, poured a cup of coffee, helped myself to a biscuit and was about to go and consume these on the edge of the deck when the kitchen door swung open and the monstrous form of Hanro emerged, red-faced and pointing a finger.

'What are you fink you are doing?' she shouted. I looked behind me to see if there was a criminal making off with the silverware because I couldn't fathom another reason for her aggression. There wasn't anyone there.

'I'm sorry?' I replied, my choc-chip cookie already between my lips. She stormed over to me, the puckered flesh of her exposed legs wobbling, grabbed the saucer from my hand and then pulled the biscuit out of my mouth.

'Vis is not a ranger's camp! Vis tea and coffee and stuffs is for guests, not for you guys who drive in ve bush all day and call it work!' She glared at me, her eyes about four inches above mine. The smell of her breath, somewhere between dried apricots and turpentine, singed my eyebrows. I took a step back. 'I am Hanro du Toit, hospitality manager of Sasekile and also camp manager of Rhino Camp.' This, I assume, she thought would impress me to the point of genuflection.

'Good afternoon,' I said. 'I am Angus MacNaughton, hero of the bushveld and devourer of choc-chip cookies. How do you do?' This she ignored and closed the distance between us again.

'Fings have changed around here. If rangers want coffee vey come to ve kitchen and have Ricoffee in vere. Vis stuff is for ve guests!' I took another step back as her breath threatened to bring my lunch back up my oesophagus. She made to take a step forward again but I extended my arm in front of me.

'You may address me from there,' I said, placing my other hand over my nose. The guests wandered onto the deck at this stage and Hanro's demeanour went from truculent buffalo to smiling hostess.

She looked at Themba who ran over, took my coffee and biscuit and disappeared into the kitchen.

She then greeted the guests and introduced me as follows, 'Vis is your driver, Angus. You can tell him all vat you want to see.' My ego was stung by being referred to as a driver. She clearly expected me to wave from the background but I moved forward and stuck my hand out.

'Please excuse her, she's from Potgietersrus.' I heard/smelled her gasp. 'I'm Angus and I'll be your ranger while you're here.' The guests looked a bit confused but they shook my hand. Two American couples and a British pair – all in their late 50s to early 60s. Hanro then made to take charge again.

'What can you like to have to drink and eat?' she asked. Lucy Bonello of Cornwell asked for some tea and a piece of chocolate cake. The angry tick, who now wore the most cheesy grin I've ever seen said, 'Okay, vat is fine, not a problem.' This is, word for word, how she then greeted all the other requests while Themba, recently returned from the kitchen at a gallop, served. She just stood there saying, 'Okay, vat is fine, not a problem,' six times with her appalling gorgonzola grin while the butler and I worked up a storm.

'Please feel free to sit on one of the ve coaches [yes coaches, not couches],' she invited. I followed the guests and sat down on the table opposite them to try and garner some information about why they were in Africa – very important if you intend planning a game drive. Unfortunately, I didn't get a chance. As I was about to open my mouth, Hanro, clearly threatened by my talking to the guests, said, 'Angus, please go to prepare your veeecle,' as though addressing an obstinate school child. I was pretty irritated by this point and what I said next probably shouldn't have been uttered in front of the guests.

'Hanro, despite the fact that we've known each other for less than fifteen minutes, there are a few things you need to understand. Firstly, in order to make the sound th as in *there* or *theatre* or *threaten*, one simply places the tongue under the incisors – which in your case are long – and blow. Then you don't need to say *vere* and *featre* or *freaten* – none of which are, in fact, recognised English words.' The two Brits smiled and the yanks looked on with interest. Hanro looked like she might reply but I continued.

'Secondly, my vehicle – never *veeecle* – does not need further preparation. Thirdly, I am a ranger or guide, not a driver, rather like you are a host or a camp manager and not an Olympic steeplechase champion. Lastly, I'd like to speak to these good people alone so that I can ascertain their every wish before taking them on drive.' Hanro was a shade of red – somewhere between tomato and beetroot by the time I'd finished. Unlike me, she thinks staff conflict should not be conducted in front of guests and therefore turned and disappeared into the kitchen without another word.

Somewhat unsurprisingly, I was called in for a meeting with Carrie and Hanro the next day. PJ is on a short holiday and left a potentially explosive power struggle. The General Manager was obviously not quite clear enough with Hanro as to who is in charge while he's away. Carrie, however, is under no illusions and she is also not to be trifled with. I walked into the rangers' room at about 11h30 and Carrie was waiting for me.

She sighed. 'Angus, why does this always happen with you?' she began.

'I hardly think I'm to blame here,' I replied.

'You never do. I know she takes a bit of getting used to but nobody else has made her cry!'

'Wow. I made her cry!' I was impressed with myself.

'It's really not funny,' she smacked the desk in front of her as Hanro walked in carrying a Coke in one hand and a folder in the other. She was sweating like a Kentucky Derby winner – October in the lowveld is not good for someone with that amount of insulation. She slumped onto the chair Carrie had provided. Then she pulled a piece of paper from her folder and handed it to me – a written warning.

'Vis is a written warning,' she began, 'if you want to not be fired, ven you must sign it and write a apology letter to me and to my camp staff for bringing my camp into a bad name.' Even Carrie was taken aback. I started to giggle.

'Angus!' Carrie snapped, 'go and drink some water.' I rose and went to the water cooler in the corner. While I was pouring myself a glass, Carrie said, 'Hanro, with all due respect, I am in charge here and I will decide on the appropriate action.' Hanro tried to interrupt but was cut short. 'You do not have the authority to fire anyone and nor are you able to hand out warnings to anyone but the butlers in your camp.' I walked back to my chair feeling quite smug. Not for long. 'That said, Angus was out of line to take up his issues with you in front of the guests. Angus, you need to apologise for that.'

'I will not!' I said. Carrie became very angry at that point.

'Angus! You bloody will or I'll take you off the road until you do!'

I knew she meant it and so, like a petulant child, I said, 'Sorry.'

'Properly!' yelled Carrie.

'Okay, I'm sorry.' I repeated louder.

'Vat is not good enough!' screamed Hanro. Carrie silenced her.

'It will have to do. If you have further issue, please take it up with PJ when he returns. That is all.' I stood up and left. The sound of Hanro blethering on about God-knows-what faded as I walked out into the sun.

The next evening, I drove a family from Chicago out of Kingfisher Camp. These geniuses complained incessantly about the heat. The idiocy of whining to your ranger about the temperature when you come to the Lowveld in October didn't occur to them. When I explained my inability to affect weather patterns and suggested that they take the matter up with God, Mrs Chicago instructed me not to take the Lord's name in vain and rather consider 'portable aircon units' for game drives.

On the last night of their stay, a slightly sensitive incident occurred. Kingfisher is an old camp built on three levels, the bottom-most being a small, comfortable sitting area on stilts nestled in the riverine vegetation. It has a thatch roof, large, extremely comfortable leather sofas and an excellent library of old books.

That night, all the camp's guests had dinner together in this little open-air library. There were two rangers, ten guests and Melissa. My guests were Mr and Mrs Chicago and their two daughters (both in their early teens).

The most notable of Brandon's lot was a voluptuous Southern Belle. She was hourglass-shaped (think Scarlett Johansson) and had the largest set of nature-given bosoms I've ever had the pleasure of casting my eyes upon. The other obvious thing about her was the adoration she'd developed for her ranger over the few days he'd been guiding her.

Brandon Cunningham and I have become quite good friends this year. That is to say that he is a pleasant fellow with a good sense of humour – but he's no oil painting. Born of Irish parentage, Brandon has hair almost as red as Melissa's and skin so pale that his Shangane nickname is Spoko (ghost). He has a slightly overshot bottom jaw and more freckles than the Serengeti has wildebeest. Despite a design that many would consider seriously flawed, his uniform, rifle and Land Rover were sufficient to give the Belle a virulent case of khaki fever.

The dinner was interminable. Melissa slobbered endless drivel at the guests and somehow managed to include the phrase 'Chicago summer sunshine' (Thicago thummer thunthine) and, in so doing, covered Mr Chicago's prime juicy rump in spittle. Just after the main course, the Belle explained that she was considering vegetarianism because she didn't agree with the mass production of animal products.

Melissa, in case anyone at the table wasn't convinced of her idiocy, waded in with, 'I with wild dogth would be vegetarianth. They are tho cruel.' Conversation stopped. 'And altho the other predatorth – it'th jutht not fair that they kill other thingth – I mean thothe other animalth have rightth too!'

Crickets and frogs filled the silence left by this profundity. I placed my knife and fork down.

'They thould eat fruit and nutth and theedth!' she continued, mistaking the silence for interest rather than incredulity.

'I would support that wholeheartedly, Melissa,' I paused and she turned to look at me, surprised, then I continued, 'but for the fact that it would significantly reduce the number of potentially fatal animals you might encounter.'

Dinner, mercifully, finished soon afterwards. While the security guard was walking the other guests back to their rooms, I accompanied the

Chicagos back to their luxurious digs. When I had bid them a not-so-fond goodnight and turned their air conditioner to the 'Liquid Nitrogen' setting, I made for my quarters. Halfway back I remembered that I'd left my hat behind. I considered leaving it for the morning but decided that Basil, the security guard with fewer scruples than Robert Mugabe, would probably deny ever having seen it. I turned around and walked back down the path.

Halfway back, I saw a light coming up the other way. I couldn't see who the owner was because the beam burnt with the power of a thousand suns.

'Hello, Angus MacNaughton,' said Allegra.

'Hello, Sirius,' I replied shielding my eyes. She laughed and pointed the light at the ground.

'Oh sorry.' She was carrying a basket, dressed in a white shirt and some black shorts.

'Where've you been at this hour?' I asked.

'There is an old woman in Main Camp with a nasty back spasm. And you, where are you going at this hour?'

'To fetch my hat – I left it at dinner.' We stood in silence for a little while, listening to the crickets singing all around and the hippo calling from the river.

'Would you like some company?' she asked finally.

'Sure,' I replied and we turned back down the path.

The Kingfisher upper deck was deserted. The frogs called in the river below, a nightjar said 'good Lord deliver us' somewhere in the night, and a scops owl called from the big Albizia tree shading the deck. We made our way towards the library deck from which there was a faint, flickering glow emanating.

As we stepped through the curtains that separate the library from the stairs, an astounding sight met our eyes. There, more luminous than the moon, was Brandon's bare bottom on one of the sofas.

'Ahem!' I coughed. My colleague shot up and fell onto the floor leaving Belle and her giant bosoms, almost as luminous as her ranger's backside, exposed. She quickly covered herself as Brandon clambered back onto the sofa next to her. They looked at us speechless. I walked silently around to the table and retrieved my hat. At the exit, I turned briefly and said, 'As you were ... Good evening.'

Back on the upper deck, Allegra was chuckling with her hand over her mouth.

'Well, that's not something you see every night,' I said.

'That is the whitest piece flesh I have ever seen!' she giggled as we made our way back onto the path leading to the staff village.

'Whiter than your pasty Brit?' I asked. I'm not sure why I asked it but it dulled the humour between us immediately. Allegra wasn't exactly offended but she didn't answer immediately and then quickly took the path back to her room.

'Goodnight, Angus,' she said formally.

I have taken to referring to Brandon as 'Moon' on the radio. He does not think this is funny – especially since Carrie demanded to know why he had suddenly received this nickname.

The following came from Julia this week.

To: Angus
From: Julia MacNaughton
Subject: Visit and other bits and pieces

Hello Angus,

I had lunch with Hugh yesterday and he finally came clean about what happened with Simone. I have to say that I can't believe it. Well, unfortunately, I can but it's just such a cliché. And yet he still feels sorry for himself?! He said that he misses Simone a lot but maintains that he feels it was indeed she that pushed him into the arms of Amber. I told him I thought that was nonsense, and that even if Simone hadn't provided the support that he needed, I would have hoped that he'd have had more integrity than he showed.

Anyway, as you probably also know, PJ is in town and Alistair and I had lunch with him and Amy the other day. Apparently Sasekile needs some legal work done – contracts and labour stuff so your lodge is now the firm's newest client and I'm the attorney who has been put in charge of looking after them. While it's only a small client in the bigger scheme of things, it means a massive amount to me as it is the first one that I've been given charge of. Very exciting (for me at least). The upshot is that I'll be doing quite a lot of work down in the Lowveld during the next little while, which will be fun!

So I will be seeing you next week.

Love,
Jules

Well I'm pleased that she's excited about the work but I'm equally displeased with the fact that she's going to be spending even more time in The Legend's company – still, maybe that'll put her off.

Week 41

Dogs and discord

Julia came through this week for about three days to do some work on the Sasekile staff contracts. None of us has ever really had a proper employment contract and PJ is worried that the WANCRs will cause untold trouble if they ever find out how disorganised that side of the business is. Julia, as a labour–relations specialist, has been tasked with sorting it out.

PJ freed up a room in Main Camp but she spurned that in order to take up residence with The Legend. As can be imagined, I was less than cheerful about this. I said nothing, but an incident on the last afternoon of her stay severed the fraying threads between us.

On the afternoon in question, I was driving out of Kingfisher Camp and, unfortunately, so was The Legend. Julia finished work in time for game drive but I already had six guests so she went on drive with her boyfriend who only had four. All the Kingfisher guests wanted to see a pack of wild dogs that had crossed onto the reserve in the morning so that meant The Legend and I would have the same goal for afternoon drive. There is often some competition between rangers to see who can find animals first. Normally, it's pretty good-natured stuff.

With The Legend and I, 'good-natured' was never going to part of the deal and I was desperate to show him up. I couldn't bear the thought of driving into a sighting he had established.

I was confident because one would be hard-pressed to find a better tracker than Elvis anywhere – here or in the rest of the lowveld. The Legend, on the other hand, has to make do with Solomon Gumede who is almost as uninspired as he is lazy.

I was driving a family of four Dutch (Joss and Irina – mid-40s, Sabine and Jeroen – nine and ten) and a couple of New Zealanders (Justin and Nicola – 50ish). The Dutch, unusually, were as tardy as the Kiwis were laidback and loading them onto the Land Rover was like trying to herd termites.

'Hullo Engus,' said Justin in an accent from somewhere deep on the South Island. 'Heow's ut going?' He and his wife wandered onto the deck at a leisurely pace. The Legend's guests and Julia were already halfway through tea and the Dutch were nowhere to be seen. I was becoming agitated and hurriedly poured them some iced tea and then sliced two wedges of carrot cake.

'U thunk U'll have some iced coffee, thenks Engus,' said Nicola.

'Right!' I snapped, flinging the tea from the glass into the river below and refilling it with coffee. The Legend's guests were ambling towards his Land Rover by this stage and there was still no sign of the Dutch. When his engine started and they still hadn't arrived, my agitation grew to the extent that 'Guest Delight' flew out of the window. I rushed into the kitchen and retrieved a flask and a length of foil. Simone was standing in front of the tea table when I emerged.

'Please cut me four slices of cake,' I said, grabbing the iced coffee jug and emptying the contents into the flask.

'Angus what are you doing?' she glared at me.

'In a rush,' I said and then, as she was dallying, I grabbed the knife and attacked the cake. Four uneven slices were soon trussed up in the foil. I put the flask under my arm and went to the table where the Kiwis were consuming their tea.

'We need to leave now,' I said hoping they wouldn't ask any questions.

'U'd like some more coffee please,' said Nicola.

'Well you see, if we want to see those wild dogs, we need to get out there as soon as possible.'

'Oh don't wurry about thet,' said Justin leaning back, 'we've seen so much, ut's no problem.'

'Well, I'm afraid the coffee's finished,' I said.

'No, there's more in the kitchen Angus,' said Simone, mystified.

'Um, yes...but don't forget about the fumigators – they're coming through any minute, we need to be out of camp for that.'

'What fumigators?' she asked, failing dismally to see me winking or discern my anxiety.

'You know the ones that come and fumigate for mosquitoes,' I said through gritted teeth. She looked at me.

'Um...'

Before she could continue, I said, 'Right, good well, better get a move on then. Also don't want those dogs to get away!'

Nicola and Justin stood reluctantly and as we were heading off the deck, the Dutch family, moving with the urgency of frozen treacle, appeared. I took Joss by the elbow and spun him round.

'Quickly, fumigators are about to arrive, must get out into the bush. At the same time I thrust the flask and foil into Irina's arms.

'Takeaways! Let's be quick!'

They were a bit nonplussed but eventually everyone was bundled onto the Land Rover. I fired up the engine and pulled off. I probably dropped the clutch a bit fast because there was a squeal and I turned around to see little Sabine with a face full of carrot cake icing. I ignored her plight because the radio crackled to life and The Legend announced that he was nearing the area where the dogs had last been seen.

I drove like a man possessed and by the time we reached the spot where Elvis suggested we begin looking, his normally black knuckles where white. Luckily Elvis also likes to find animals before anyone else so he wasn't too put out. As we were hurtling down the road at a speed that would probably have resulted in my dismissal, Elvis held up his hand, meaning 'stop, there are tracks in the road'. The Land Rover came to a skidding, dusty halt and I leapt out to examine the spoor with Elvis. While Elvis examined the road, I chanced a look up at our guests. Their faces weren't exactly smiling – in fact all the adults were scowling and the kids looked like they'd been attacked by a carrot cake, so much icing was spread about their faces.

'Found the tracks,' I said, 'back in a few minutes. You chaps just relax here for a while.' I didn't wait for an answer and hurried to catch up with

Elvis who was standing about twenty metres behind the car, squatting on his haunches. He looked up as I approached and then headed east off the road. I followed.

A few minutes later we were cautiously walking through the bushwillow woodland. The tension brought on by my competition with The Legend dissipated and I was suddenly immersed in the peace of the wild – walking behind Elvis and searching for wild dogs in the gilded afternoon light. The bushwillows are in full leaf now but the grass is still bone dry and gentle puffs of dust rose off the ground with each step. There were birds calling in the trees all around and the smell of new leaves, dry grass and dust assailed me.

About fifteen minutes after the tracking began, the soft evening scent changed – wild dogs smell like wet domestic dogs and the air was unmistakably tinged with their odour. Elvis turned to face me – he smelt it too and a grin spread across his face. Then we heard a grey go-away bird alarm calling off towards a thick saffron tree.

The view to the tree was obscured by low bushes so we doubled back a bit and approached from an angle that offered a less impeded view of the tree. We crept slowly towards a mopane tree about twenty metres from the saffron and then sunk to our haunches. Elvis went left around the mopane, I went right and we peered into the shade of saffron. There, reclining and snapping at the occasional fly, was the pack of four dogs. They were just starting to look a bit restless – about to head out on the evening hunt. We inched slowly back, putting the mopane tree between us and the saffron and taking enormous care not to crunch the dry vegetation underfoot.

We'd been away from the vehicle a good twenty minutes by that stage, which meant ten minutes' walk back to it and another five driving to the restless pack. There was a real risk that they'd be gone by the time we could return with the vehicle. The upshot was that I had to call the dogs in on the radio in the hopes that someone else could reach them before they went off hunting. This wasn't ideal because it meant that our guests wouldn't be the first ones to see the dogs – to them it would look like we were just responding to someone else's sighting. At the same time, I couldn't risk them going off hunting because finding them again would be difficult in the fading light.

'Stations, located pack of four wild dogs, northeast of Hyena Road. Animals are lying in the shade but look like they will move soon. We're on foot and will try to relocate in the vehicle.' Almost before I let go of the radio button, The Legend arrived on air.

'Angus, I'm in the area. Please give directions, I'll go and relocate.' Of course this was reasonable but the fact that he would see them before my guests, drove my ego into an irrational frenzy. Reluctantly I gave him directions to the saffron tree. By this stage, Elvis and I were jogging towards where we'd left the guests and our Land Rover. As we arrived, panting, I realised I'd left the car parked in the sun – it was well over 30 degrees in the shade.

'Hello, everyone!' I said, 'We've found the dogs.'

I was about to leap into the driver's seat when Joss said, 'My son would like to take a toilet break.'

'What ... now?' I was exasperated and pictured The Legend driving to the dogs and claiming credit for finding them.

'Yes, now!' he snapped.

Justin then added, 'End we'd like some water. Wa've been puuhked here un the boiling sun for ages!'

'Can't it all wait till sunset?' I asked starting the engine.

'No ut cannot!' snapped Nicola. 'Wa're not on holiday to be rushed around. Now please guve us some water!'

I sighed. 'And my daughter needs some water to clean the cake you've put all over her face,' added Irina as the hostility towards me grew.

'Fine!' I ran round to the back of the Land Rover to fetch some water bottles from the cooler box. It wasn't there – not just the water, the entire cooler box. There was nothing in the rack. 'Elvis!' I hissed and the tracker removed himself from his seat and came round. 'Where's the cooler box?' I was becoming mildly desperate.

'I think maybe it fell off while you were driving here. You drove like a baboon,' he replied, unconcerned.

'Shit!' I kicked the back of the Land Rover.

The guests were even less impressed when I explained that there was no refreshment to be had. I tried to cheer them up by telling them we were about to watch wild dogs on the hunt. It did little to warm the collective disposition to me but I was still consumed by trying to reach the dogs before The Legend. I started the engine and sped offroad.

The Legend's voice arrived on the radio, 'Angus, come in.'

'Go,' I replied as we careened through the bush, guests ducking as vegetation threatened to maim or knock them from their seats.

'Relocated the pack but they're on the move – you need to hurry, it's getting really thick in here and I'm not sure I can keep up with them.'

'On my way. Stay with them!' I yelled into the radio and dropped a gear. The speed at which I was going was now causing the odd scream to emanate from the guests as they tried to avoid being bounced out of the vehicle.

'Why are you driving so fast!' yelled Joss.

'Angus, come in,' said The Legend on the radio. I grabbed the mouthpiece.

'Because the dogs are on the move!' I shouted at Joss and then into the radio, 'Go ahead!'

'They're heading into the mopane section in the north of this block and I can't follow them if they go in there,' said The Legend.

'Jones, do not lose them, I'm on my way!' I bellowed. At that point, the back right wheel slammed into a hole and then bounced out. I turned around in time to see Sabine about three feet in the air and her mother pulling off a spectacular slip catch to save her daughter falling out of the vehicle. 'Nearly there!' I shouted to the white knuckles and faces behind me. I could see The Legend's vehicle in front of me – stationary. We hared up next to him.

'Where are they?' I yelled. He scowled at me and pointed into an almost impenetrable mopane thicket. 'You go round and I'll try to go through the middle!' I said.

'Angus, they've gone bru. You not going to see them – we're off to the lions on the river.'

'I found these things on foot and my guests haven't seen them so you can help me re-find them!' I hissed at him through gritted teeth.

'Bru, we're going to see the lions, you'll never find the dogs again.' I looked at Julia who was sitting in the passenger seat. She, in turn looked between the two of us and then at the guests on the back of my Land Rover. With that, The Legend started his engine, reversed and disappeared.

Elvis said in Shangane, 'Angus, it's time to leave the dogs, the guests are not happy.' They were covered in a wide variety of new-season foliage; there were no smiles. They regarded me with a mixture of hostility and some fear. I couldn't even give them a drink to soften things so we went to see a herd of buffalo nearby and then made our way home in stony silence.

By the time we returned to the lodge I was seriously pissed off. I still don't believe The Legend made any effort to stay with the dogs before I arrived. It's an unwritten rule that you make damn sure you stay with an animal that another ranger is coming to see – especially if you've responded to a sighting he's established on foot. The way I figured it, The Legend had ruined any chance I'd had to save my appalling game drive – the hunting dogs may have saved me but without them, I knew there was going to be a complaint.

Julia and The Legend were having a pre-dinner drink, leaning on the Kingfisher bar, when I arrived. I walked straight over to him, ignored my sister and stuck my finger in his face.

'Fuck you, Jones. You only saw those dogs because I found them and then you couldn't be bothered to stay with them till I arrived.' Julia, wisely, backed off.

'Angus, calm down man, I didn't have a chance to stay with them.'

'Bullshit!' I snapped. 'I arrived a minute after you said they were disappearing – you couldn't have stayed with them for another minute?!' The Legend pushed himself off the bar and drew himself to his full height, his eyes a good six inches above mine. Simone emerged from the kitchen at that point.

'Don't talk to me like that, I did what I could. Get over it.' His ultimately cool disposition was starting to heat up. Perhaps he thought I would back down but neither of us was going to retreat in front of Julia. She realised this and stepped in.

'Guys, please, this can't be the right way to deal with this,' she said as calmly as possible.

Without taking my eyes off her boyfriend, I said, 'Julia, in your lawyer's wisdom, I have to say you've picked yourself a steaming, rancid, world-class turd here. He's not worth the foul air that he breathes.' With the last syllable I poked The Legend in the chest with my finger. This, predictably, pushed him over the edge and he took hold of my uniform and shoved me up against the bar. I was horribly outmatched physically and thankfully Simone averted any damage.

'Hey!' she shouted. 'Alistair, you let him go. NOW!' The Legend released me. As I smoothed my uniform out, she continued, 'Guys, this sort of animal behaviour is not going to happen in this camp!' Julia and The Legend then walked off onto the deck.

Simone pulled me into the kitchen. 'Angus, come on dude, what did you do on drive? The guests were like the most easy-going guests I've ever had. I left them with you for a few hours and they're ready to check out. It took me half an hour to convince them not to demand a new ranger.' She was angry and I had no answer – I'd lost control of my ego. I realised this and apologised to her.

Dinner was a silent affair. My guests were no longer talking to me; nor were my sister or her boyfriend. Julia left this morning and didn't say goodbye.

Advice and armistice

Things reached a bit of head with Mitchell this week. The fence, the electrified cattle grids and the egg tossing no longer deter him. There's still been no rain at all so the elephant continues to seek sustenance in camp – to the point that he has now changed the look of the gardens almost irreparably. The russet bushwillow that used to shade the Main Camp lawn is now a stump, the mopane trees that dot the paths between the camps are fractions of their former selves, and there isn't a knobthorn between the four camps that hasn't been pushed over or stripped of most of its bark. The conservation crew spend hours each day helping the gardeners to clear the paths and make the place look as neat as possible.

The worst of it, however, is that Mitchell is now seriously affecting guests and PJ won't stand for that. The elephant, as always, hasn't been overtly aggressive but if he's startled he tends to turn round and trumpet at whoever has disturbed him and if that happens to be Carl and Annabelle, aged close to their mid-130s, and one of them has a coronary, it's less than ideal.

These two aged but pleasant Scandinavians were staying in Kingfisher Camp and, freshly woken from their post-lunch slumber, were doddering towards the deck from Room 3 for tea and a game drive with me. The walk isn't a long one and follows a path lined with thick riverine bush, out onto the pool paving and then onto the Kingfisher Camp deck. They didn't make it to the deck however because Mitchell had snuck into camp for a drink at the pool and some fresh raisin bush leaves. The old couple are nearly stone deaf and therefore didn't hear the elephant slurping water or tearing up vegetation. As they were about to emerge into the pool area, Mitchell heard them coming and, perhaps suspecting egg-tossers, wheeled round and trumpeted.

Sipho and I were chatting on the deck when we heard the trumpet. Conversation stopped and then there was a blood-curdling scream from Annabelle. We dropped everything and ran for the pool area where I fully expected to find Carl or his wife skewered on the end of Mitchell's good tusk. All I saw of the elephant, however, was his backside and horizontal tail as he ran off towards the river, clearly perturbed by the screaming. On the path between the pool and the room we found Annabelle bawling and Carl flat on his back, eyes wide open, gasping for air and clutching his chest. Sipho ran to Annabelle while the rest of us went to the aid of Carl. None of us is medically trained, but for the most basic of first aid, so we had no real idea what was wrong or what to do about it. Melissa specifically.

'Thit, thit, thit, thit ...' was all she managed.

I grabbed the radio tucked into her belt.

'Candice, reception, do you copy?' I called. There was a pause and then I tried again – this time I shouted.

A few moments later she said, 'Go ... a ... head,' in her nasal Benoni. I explained the situation and that we needed advice from a doctor. Of course, she should then have followed the pre-determined medical plan (which I later discovered is pinned to the wall in front of her telephone). However, Candice is not one for an emergency and when she heard the words 'heart attack' she became hysterical.

'Oh my God, is he dead? Oh God, he's died, we've got a dead one!' was all I heard before the radio went quiet. In her panic, however, she had failed to release the radio button with the result that no one could communicate at all on the airwaves. All the while Carl was writhing on the floor and his wife had since passed out on the ground. Eventually, Carrie came on air. She had heard the interaction and rushed to the reception office to take control. Not too long after that, a helicopter arrived from Hoedspruit and the two Danes were taken off to hospital where they remain. Carl's heart attack was apparently minor but I don't think they'll be returning any time soon.

PJ called a meeting about Mitchell with Carrie, Jacob, Elvis, The Legend and some senior trackers. To my utter chagrin, Hanro was also invited – apparently as part of the senior management team. The outcome of the meeting was not divulged to the rest of us.

In the wake of last week's incident with The Legend and the continued, shall we say, strained nature of my sibling relationships, I received some communication from my father this week – on my birthday. When he takes to the computer, it is normally because he feels very strongly about something.

To: Angus MacNaughton
From: Dad MacNaughton
Subject: Happy birthday and the family

Dear Angus,

Our very best wishes for your birthday today. Your Mum and I hope you have a very special day and that everyone is very kind to you. We've put a little something in the post but who knows when it might arrive.

I have a few concerns which I wish to raise with you. I trust that you will take my comments in the spirit in which they are intended.

Firstly on the subject of you sister. You and she have had a wonderful relationship just about all your lives and to see it in the state it languishes currently makes your mother and me very sad indeed. I feel that you are being unreasonable and that you need to think beyond your own prejudices. I suspect your dislike of Alistair (whom I have met) comes from the fact that he reminds you of your peers at school with whom you struggled to get on – the 'jocks' for want of a better word. For some reason, despite all your achievements, some sporting but mostly in the cultural arena, you always felt inferior to the (often larger) sportsmen. I strongly suspect your dislike of Alistair has quite a lot to do with that.

Secondly, regarding your brother. Hugh had none of the problems you did at school but he is just as volatile in different ways. He is very emotional and, as you know, can tend towards arrogance, but just as quickly tends to depression when things aren't going his way.

The reason I am sending this to you is to ask you to do something for us, your parents. We would like for you to start playing more of a big-brother role in your siblings' lives. Julia, despite what you think, longs for your approval. Hugh needs some support and mentorship and while this may sound harsh, you have done a poor job of playing this role in his life.

I hope you will not be offended by any of this because it is all said with love but I ask you to please give it some consideration.

Love,
Dad

If anyone else had written that to me, I suspect I'd have tossed my computer through my recently replaced window. While I found the contents of this email difficult to stomach, my father is clearly writing with the best interests of the family at heart. Perhaps I do need to make more of an effort to heal the wounds with my siblings but my God, it won't be easy.

His words about my prejudice towards The Legend really stung. I hadn't looked at it from this point of view. I'll give it some thought although it's going to be really difficult not to puke when asking myself if I'm being unreasonable about him. As for SB, well he doesn't bloody listen so what the hell am I supposed to say to him? With my siblings alienated, I don't want to estrange my parents as well, so I replied to my father, thanking him for his concern and promising to consider what he'd said (made especially hard by the fact that SB gave me a very half-hearted birthday greeting and my sister failed to contact me at all).

A day or so later I happened to be driving out of Tamboti Camp. With my father's sentiments fresh in my mind, I went down to the camp half an hour early with a vague plan to talk to SB or, at the very least, just be around him for a while. I wandered into the main area and found him at his desk, writing.

'Hello String Bean,' I said mustering what I thought to be a fairly warm voice. He looked up.

'Hello Angus,' he replied evenly.

'How are you?'

'Fine. How are you?'

'Pretty good thanks.' SB returned his attention to the greeting cards he was writing. 'How's work going?'

'But for Hanro, not too bad.'

'She's not my favourite either,' I replied. He stacked the cards, put them to one side and smiled.

'Yes, I heard about your little boxing match and it was difficult not to laugh as she went on and on about you in our hospitality meeting the other day. Allegra, for the first time since I've known her, started giggling.'

'Well, I'll leave you to get on,' I said.

'I'm done here,' he replied and stood. We wandered down to the tea table and I poured myself a coffee.

'Did you hear about the group coming over Christmas?' he asked. I shook my head. 'Some sort of Arab prince. He's booked out the whole place and the entourage he's bringing sounds unbelievable. Chefs, hairdressers, security, entertainers, wives – you name it. It's incredible.'

'You'll have your hands full organising that lot,' I replied.

SB sighed heavily. 'Not my job. Hanro's in charge.'

'Ouch, that must have hurt a bit.' We watched a carpenter bee excavating a hole in the deck railing.

'Yup. Well, at least the pressure's off me.'

The guests arrived at that point and the business of looking after them began.

Week 43

Rain and ruin

The drought broke this week in spectacular fashion but my short life nearly came to an end with it.

A few days before the storm that restarted the flow of the Tsesebe River, turned the parched dust into soft, fertile earth and coaxed the new shoots of fresh green grass from their husks, the Mitchell plan was publicised. Sasekile's brains trust decided that the elephant had to go for good. The gardens are destroyed and life for staff and guests is becoming a hazard. The idea was to have him darted and transported to another reserve near Phalaborwa. Great White African Safaris, owned by a cousin of Hanro's, had offered to pay handsomely for him. While it all seemed a rather reasonable way to deal with the situation, I was suspicious of Hanro and whatever backwater cousins she had dwelling around the not-too-enlightened reaches of Phalaborwa.

'So pray, what kind of operation is Great White African Safaris?' I asked Carrie after the meeting announcement.

'It's a safari operation. They offered to pay the costs of having him darted and carted away so I don't think PJ asked too much about it. I'm just happy he'll be gone soon – I'm really worried about people in camp when he's around.'

'And you're not a tiny little bit suspicious as to why these people would offer to take a troublesome elephant? It's not exactly like accepting an over-friendly Yorkshire terrier.'

'Angus, don't read things into everything – it's not all a great conspiracy. They're coming to take him in two days so until then, please make sure you're extra vigilant around camp. We need to know where he is at all times.'

Over the course of the next two days, Mitchell was consistently in camp and keeping tabs on him was very easy. There were extra security measures in place and we instructed all guests how to behave if they saw him.

I wasn't driving on the day Danie Grobelaar and Ian MacDonald, proprietors of Great White African Safaris, arrived with about ten helpers to remove Mitchell. Danie was built much like his cousin Hanro – except that his stomach extended further and his moustache was bushier (only just). His cohort was a giant with forearms like my thighs. They pitched up in a huge truck with an oversized container and a crane on the back of it. The truck itself looked like it predated the Model T and the container was rustier than a shipwreck. It was solid steel, with double doors at the back and windowless walls. Thick steel bars, spaced about a metre apart, crossed the otherwise-open top.

I was in the rangers' room when they pulled up outside. It was already almost dark. PJ walked out of the office to meet them and Carrie soon joined him. She then returned to the rangers' room.

'Angus, they need a bit of help finding the elephant, please would you come and help?' she asked.

'They're a little late aren't they?' I asked.

'Yes, they're a good two hours late! So please come quickly, there are already guests about to come back from drive.' I acquiesced and a little while later Bertie and I wandered onto the Kingfisher Camp deck where Simone and Kerry were putting some finishing touches to the tables. I greeted Simone, tapped Kerry on the backside, received a half-hearted slap for my troubles and then asked if they'd seen Mitchell. There was a splash from the direction of Room 3.

'He's having a drink,' said Simone, 'there's no one in Room 3.'

I radioed Carrie with the news and ten minutes later Danie, Carrie and PJ arrived at Room 3. Danie assessed the situation and decided they could squeeze the truck in between Rooms 3 and 4 – there were no guests in either rooms that evening. We moved through Room 3 and out onto the deck. Danie stepped forward, cocked the dart gun and took aim at Mitchell's backside, which was facing us about twenty metres away. The elephant froze – sensing something amiss.

Danie fired and the dart hit home. Mitchell reacted with predictable irritation. He swung round and bellowed at us. Then he ran a few steps towards the deck and stood with his ears fanned out and head up. Slowly however, the anaesthetic started to take effect and he wobbled a bit and then his back end slumped underneath him and he toppled over onto his side.

Danie pulled a two-way radio from his pocket.

'Bring the truck,' he said. Soon the enormous machine was grinding backwards down next to the low Room 3 deck. With the aid of a spotlight and some torches, the workers trussed up the elephant and twenty minutes later, he was hoisted into the air by the crane. The arm swung around and the mighty beast was lowered onto a ramp fitted with rollers that led into the cage. A winch then manoeuvred Mitchell's slumbering form into the back of the container. It was all rather efficient up to that point and I was about to decide that Danie and his crew were not quite as cretinous as they first appeared, when things began to go wrong.

As the truck started, there was a horrible grating noise from one of the rear axles and then, as the driver pushed the accelerator and the truck moved slowly forward, the axle came away from its mounting. The driver failed to hear Danie yelling at him to stop so he continued forwards and the remaining axle, with all the weight now on it, snapped with a deafening crack. The elephant inside was comatose so he didn't mind but the truck was going nowhere. Ian turned the engine off and a standoff containing a lot of 'foks' ensued between him and Danie.

I sat on one of the pool loungers and watched as they nearly came to blows. Their shouting ended when PJ walked between them and asked them to try to behave with a modicum of professionalism. Then a meeting between the GM, Carrie and the visitors took place. The upshot of this was that they couldn't retrieve another truck before the morning and that

Mitchell was, therefore, to spend the night in his cage because, explained Danie, releasing and then drugging him again would be dangerous to his health. On the other hand, he couldn't be left lying down because an elephant's organs are so large that they can't function if the animal is on its side for an extended period. Mitchell had to be woken and kept sedated for the night before the entire container housing him could be relocated to another truck.

Danie climbed atop the container, and with his reloaded dart gun, administered the antidote. In a minute, Mitchell was stirring and a little while after that, we heard him stumble to his feet. Then there was peace – the only sound mixed with the night was the elephant's heavy breathing and the distant rumble of thunder.

'Right, there we go, let's go get some beers!' said Danie cheerfully.

'When are you going to sedate him?' I asked. 'As far as I can tell, you've just woken him up. Presumably, you'll need to give him something to keep him calm through the night.' Danie glared at me.

'Ja, no, he's fine, he's not going anywhere.'

'I can see he's not going anywhere, but if you don't sedate him, he'll go ballistic when he comes round fully.'

'Ja, ja, the M99 will keep him groggy till morning.' He sounded about as convincing as an ANC promise. I was worried about Mitchell and his future – although he'd nearly murdered me once, I'd become quite fond of him and enjoyed the thrill of having him around the camp.

As we walked away from Kingfisher I asked Bertie to go and speak to the labourers who'd arrived with Danie and find out about their employer's operation and exactly what they intended to do with Mitchell. They were all now staying for the night so Bertie said he'd ply them with a few quarts and extract the lowdown. In the meantime, I went off to the Avuxeni Eatery for supper. I helped myself to a plate of ham, cream and mushroom pasta and sat down next to Allegra. She was freshly showered, wearing a loose white linen shirt. Her hair has grown since our first meeting and was, unusually, not tied up.

'You do not look pleased with life, Angus MacNaughton,' she said as I twisted some spaghetti onto my fork.

'I'm not entirely,' I replied. 'Mitchell is currently residing in a crate outside Kingfisher Camp.'

'You mean the elephant that tried to drown me? So I hear,' she said, placing her knife and fork together. 'Is that a problem?'

'There's something about the guys who've come to take him that makes my toes curl.' I ate a mouthful. 'I'll go and check on him after supper and see how he is.' We chatted while I finished my meal and then I stood to leave.

'Do you think I might come with you?' asked Allegra. 'Nasty as he was to me, I would not like to think of him being harmed.'

We set off for Kingfisher Camp a minute later while lightning arced over the mountains in the west. As we approached Room 3, the sound of Mitchell trying to break his bonds touched our ears. We rushed out onto the deck to see the container rocking from side to side, the elephant screaming inside. It was gut-wrenching.

'Oh my God!' said Allegra with her hand over her mouth. 'That is dreadful!'

A few moments later we were rushing towards Main Camp where Danie and Ian were staying. I walked straight into the boma where dessert was being cleared – Danie and Ian were nowhere to be seen. We turned round and made for Room 6. I flung the door open without bothering to knock. There, inevitably, I found Danie and his companion lying on the bed with the entire contents of the mini-bar (empty) strewn around them. They were both unconscious. Allegra walked to the bathroom and returned with a glass of water. She flung it on Danie's face. He half woke up.

'Wat . . . die . . . fok?' he sat up groggily. I stood over him and pointed a finger in his face.

'You haven't tranquilised that elephant, you prick!' He just stared blankly at me and then shook his head. Allegra returned with the glass re-filled and emptied it on him. He spluttered and looked up but he was so drunk his eyes couldn't focus. I slapped his fat face.

'Where are the tranquilisers, you turd?' I yelled in his face.

'None . . . here . . .' he managed before passing out again.

'We are clearly wasting our time here,' said Allegra taking my hand and heading for the door.

Back outside, we made for Carrie's place. The head ranger's palace is situated on the banks of the Tsesebe just west of the camp. It's a slightly hairy walk at night but I was too irritated to worry about the hippo or buffalo that might be lurking in the thick bush lining the path. Besides which, Allegra's five gazillion candle-power torch was bright enough to be seen from space and any animal bent on harming us would have been instantly blinded for life.

I banged on the door and walked in. Carrie was lying on a sofa reading a magazine, her head on Jane's lap. The chef was sipping a glass of wine and watching the travel channel. My boss sat up immediately.

'Angus, what's the matter?'

'That dickhead hasn't sedated Mitchell. Danie's pissed as a lord and from what I could glean, there aren't any tranquilisers at all. The elephant's bashing the hell out of the container and screaming his head off.' Carrie sat up immediately.

She looked at her watch. It was 21h30. 'Let's phone PJ.' A few moments later she put the receiver down. 'Angus, I'm afraid there's really nothing we can do. We can't release him — he's just going to have to ride out the night. We can't afford to have him come back into the camp — he's going to kill someone soon and the sooner he leaves the better.'

'That's bullshit Carrie,' I said.

'Angus, it's not bullshit, and you know it's not. Hell, he nearly killed you! I know it's horrible but it's only a night. Please try and forget about it.' I turned and left without another word. Carrie called Allegra back but I didn't wait.

I went straight to Bertie's room.

'Those guys tell me that they are only doing hunting on that farm,' he blurted out as I knocked on the door.

I went cold. Any thoughts of trying to calm Mitchell went out of my head. I understand that selling trophies keeps a lot of land under wildlife and I also understand that hunting a few animals on some of our neighbours' farms pays for fencing, roads and various other conservation-related things. I do not, however, feel a lust for blood and hard as I've tried, I struggle to see trophy hunting as a humane, 21st century form of entertainment. (Hunting for the pot is another matter.)

I thanked Bertie and returned to my room to think about the situation. I'm told there are moments in life when you have to do things that just seem right, despite their lunacy. I decided that such a moment had arrived for me. I had to release Mitchell and somehow chase him out of the camp. At the very least it would give him a night's reprieve.

I waited half an hour and then walked out of my room. There were still a few revellers at the staff shop but I skirted them without being seen and made my way to Kingfisher Room 3. The noise from the container was muted now but every so often, Mitchell trumpeted and let out a long low rumble. I looked up at the sky considering my next move. The stars were dotted between some fast-moving clouds and a strong gust blew sand into the air around the container.

I was about to jump down from the low deck when there was some movement from behind me. I spun round to see Bertie and Allegra.

'Bertie saw you leaving your room,' said Allegra. 'I asked him to call me if you moved – I had a feeling you might try and do something, shall we say, ill-considered.' The wind thrashed the trees above the deck.

'Well, I'm buggered if I'm going to let this animal be butchered by Danie and his redneck clients.'

'Do you have a plan?' asked Allegra.

'Not really. The problem is that the stupid bastard won't stay out of camp. But I suppose releasing him now will at least give him another night – maybe he'll leave because of the trauma he's experienced today.'

The first drops of summer rain touched my face and the thunder rolled not far west of us. 'Whatever the case, the two of you don't need to be involved.'

'We are here because we want to be involved,' said Allegra, her face set hard.

'Storm's coming. Let's get a move on then.' I turned to the container.

With the human voices and the noise of the coming storm, Mitchell was again raising hell. I walked around to the doors of the container and examined the locking mechanism. It was pretty simple but we couldn't just open the back because whoever released the angry pachyderm would be flattened in seconds. The rain that broke the drought started in earnest as I considered the problem.

There was a ladder built into the rear side of the container so I climbed up onto the top and peered through the bars of the roof. A flash of lightning illuminated the cage and its terrified resident below me. Mitchell sensed me above him immediately and his frenzy increased. He head-butted the door which shook the container so that, with the increasing deluge, I slipped and nearly fell in with the enraged animal. Scrambling back onto the greasy roof bars, I turned my attention to the door but there was no way of opening it from the top – it could only be opened from the bottom.

I climbed back down and hatched a plan, which I explained to the others. The idea was for Bertie to distract the elephant from the far side of the container while I opened the door. It was fraught with unpredictable variables but I didn't really see any other option. While I went round on the ground to the door, Bertie climbed up the front of the container and started shouting at Mitchell. Allegra remained on the deck relaying information from Bertie to me – above the din of the screaming elephant and the raging storm overhead.

There wasn't space for the elephant to turn around inside the container but at the sound of Bertie bashing on the roof and shouting behind him, he reversed towards the front of the container and swung from side to side trying to see his tormentor.

Allegra shouted, 'Okay, open now!'

I started hauling on the opening mechanism but the levers stuck firm. I pulled with all my strength but they hardly shifted. Allegra saw me struggling and leapt the three feet from the deck to the muddy ground and took hold of the lever next to me.

'Get back on the deck!' I shouted.

She put her face close to mine so that I could hear her – I don't think Allegra ever shouts – and said, 'Not until this crate is open. I am in the habit of finishing the jobs I start.'

I should have insisted Allegra move back onto the deck. It was my decision to let him out and I hadn't fully considered the awful possible scenarios of being in such close proximity to an angry, abused, six-tonne wild animal.

Slowly the levers gave way but they made a horrible wrenching sound as they moved and this attracted Mitchell's attention where it wasn't wanted.

As the levers came free, the doors opened halfway. For a frozen moment, lightning flashed across the sky and the great bull's head was illuminated as he bore down on his freedom, his ears splayed out.

Allegra was still hanging onto the right-hand door, trying to pull it free when Mitchell's head crashed into the gap. The solid steel doors burst open. I saw him coming but I wasn't quick enough to duck the door. It caught me on the left temple and I fell back out of the way. Then the night went briefly pitch black as six tonnes of elephant flew out of the container.

Allegra wasn't so lucky.

As Mitchell clattered into the door, I watched in horror as she was flung out and away from the container and the deck. She hit the ground about three metres clear of the door with a sickening thud. As she looked up groggily, Mitchell was standing just above her. I don't think he saw her at first but when she started scrambling backwards, he spotted her and moved in, his huge feet stamping the mud beneath them. I shouted at him for all I was worth but he took no notice as he trumpeted at Allegra who was lying in the mud, pinned against a mopane tree. The elephant dropped on to one knee, ready to push his good tusk through the only human being he'd so far managed to corner. What happened next is a bit of a blur.

I found the last reserves of my courage and managed to raise my bleeding head from the mud and crawl out from under the deck where I'd landed. What I did next, I did for purely selfish reasons – I simply knew that life with Allegra's death on my hands would be utterly intolerable.

I found a heavy piece of wood and, staggering to my feet, I yelled, 'Mitchell!' and flung the log. It collected his right ear hole. He stood up and swung to face me – I was in no man's land between him and the deck – five metres from each. Mitchell came forward and I shut my eyes – fully expecting the world to go blank. I felt the spray of mud hitting my legs in slow motion as the elephant arrived to mete out his revenge.

Then there was just the sound of the rain and a dim peel of thunder off to the east. I opened my eyes and the elephant was gone. Allegra was leaning against a mopane tree, covered in mud, soaking wet, her arms wrapped around her knees. I looked to my right and saw to my horror that Carrie was standing on the deck watching in shock. On the ground, between the deck and the container was Bertie, he'd clearly been thrown off during the commotion. He too was sitting up, a cut above his eye bleeding down his face.

'Angus, go and see if Allegra is alright,' Carrie shouted at me.

I snapped out of slow motion, walked over to Allegra, sat down in a puddle next to her and pulled her to me. She fell against my chest and we sat there for about five minutes while the drought ended around us. Carrie broke the moment – she was helping Bertie up.

'Angus, this time you've bloody done it. Get that girl back to her room and make sure you are down here first thing tomorrow morning.'

Just after Carrie and Bertie left and when we'd calmed down sufficiently to walk, I lifted Allegra gently to her feet, and walked her home. While she sat silently on her bed, still dripping wet, I drew a hot bath and emptied a bottle of some sort of bath product into it. I probably overdid it because by the time I turned the taps off, the bath looked like someone had stuffed a cloud into it. I told her it was ready and she came through to the bathroom.

I was about to leave when she said, 'There is a bottle of brandy in my bedside table. I would like to have some. Would you mind?' I fetched the bottle of Martell and the two crystal glasses sitting next to it.

'Where do you want it?' I asked.

'In here please.' I walked back into the bathroom, expecting her to still be clothed but her wet and muddy rags were lying in a pile and she had all but disappeared into the cloud – only her head was visible. I held out the glass and a bubble-covered hand retrieved it.

'Thank you,' she said and drained the glass. I refilled it for her, sat down on the loo lid and took a deep drink myself. We sat in silence for a while, the brandy warming my insides while a puddle of the summer's first rain gathered on the floor around me.

'I'm sorry,' I said finally. 'I nearly got you killed.'

'I did not do anything I did not want to,' she replied.

I drained my glass.

'You nearly paid that price too,' she said. 'I am glad your friend Mitchell has a reprieve. I hope it lasts.' I stood up to leave and her hand emerged from the bubbles again, reached for mine and squeezed it. She smiled. 'All's well, etcetera.' I reached down and touched her cheek with my other hand and then left quickly.

I walked back to the village. Bertie was sitting on his veranda with Kerry. She was dressing the wound above his eye, the rain still clattering down on the tin roof. His eyes were wide open, his hands shaking. Bertie doesn't drink but he needed a little help. I crossed the patch of mud between our rooms – that was dust until this evening – and retrieved a bottle of scotch. I handed Bertie the bottle and, without a pause, he unscrewed the lid and took a long sip. He coughed, spluttered and then choked but took another long drink almost immediately. The whisky worked its magic on him.

While Kerry finished her first-aid job on Bertie and then attended to the cut on my temple, I related the evening's events.

I woke the next morning – supposedly the first morning of my leave – feeling anxious. I showered, shaved and made my way down to Kingfisher. There, I found Danie, Ian, PJ and Carrie all staring at the open door of the crate.

'I'm fokken telling you, vis fokken door was opened from ve outside! No fokken elephant could have opened it. FOK!' said Danie, his finger pointed at PJ and Carrie. The General Manager, realising the sort of people he was dealing with, lost his patience.

'I suggest you calm down and start using a few less "foks" or I'll have you thrown off the reserve. I don't know how this elephant escaped but he did and he's nowhere to be seen. Frankly, given your level of professionalism yesterday and the state of your room this morning, I don't think you're fit to be transporting animals. You can consider the deal off. You'd also better get this truck out of here before I have it removed by the police.'

After a few more 'foks' Danie and Ian left.

PJ turned to me when they'd gone. He walked over to the mopane tree where Allegra and I finished up and, from the mud, he pulled a cap and a black slip-slop. 'Any idea whose these are and how they got here?'

I said nothing.

The GM continued through gritted teeth. 'Let me see if I can help you,' he said turning the hat over. 'It says Angus MacNaughton in bright red marker pen, just on the brow line. And this looks quite a lot like Allegra's.'

He held up the slop. I still didn't say anything. PJ and Carrie stepped up onto the deck.

'You've done some bloody stupid things in your time here,' said PJ stepping close to me, 'but until yesterday, they hadn't endangered the lives of anyone else.' He was working himself into a bit of a frothy. 'From what I understand, you very nearly got Allegra and Bertie killed. I've had enough. You've gone too far this time. Your irresponsibility, unwillingness to see the big picture and total disregard for the way we do things around here have nearly resulted in the deaths of two Sasekile staff. If you like, we can go through the motions of yet another disciplinary hearing but I'm bloody sick and tired of them and let's face it, you wouldn't have a hope. I'd like you to pack your bags and get off the property before the day is out.'

I just stared at him as what he said sunk in and I suppose I must have looked a bit confused.

'Do you understand what I'm saying to you? You're fired! Pack your bags and fuck off.' With that, he stormed off the deck leaving me standing there. A green pigeon called in the jackalberry tree shading the deck and the sound of the newly-flowing river touched my ears. I smelled the fresh, wet earth all around me. Then I slumped down onto one of the pool loungers and became aware of Carrie standing there. She pulled a wrought-iron chair closer, and sat down backwards – her arms resting on the back.

'I'm sorry about this,' she began, 'but I have to agree with him. That elephant nearly killed Allegra and Bertie could easily have been badly hurt too. You know PJ hasn't even mentioned the fact that you let the elephant out – in fact I reckon he's probably secretly glad about it. But at the end of the day, he's responsible for the safety of the staff and the guests. You've really made it difficult for him to do anything else.'

I didn't say anything as a pair of lesser-striped swallows landed in a fresh puddle to collect mud for their new nest. A sense of unreality descended. Carrie eventually stood up and left me to ponder my fate. The swallows flew off and returned a few minutes later to collect their next load of building cement. I lay back on the pool lounger and shut my eyes, hearing and smelling the early summer. Twenty minutes later I made my way back to my room. I felt nauseous, embarrassed and, worst of all, I didn't have any will to fight my situation. PJ was right: I had endangered my two friends' lives because I hadn't bothered to think the situation through.

With a sense of sick numbness, I packed my few belongings into a hold-all. It didn't take long. Then I went to the workshop and retrieved a box to put my books in. I really wanted to leave without being seen – it was simply too embarrassing experiencing the same disgrace that Matto had a few weeks earlier. Unfortunately word spread – probably via Carrie. SB was the first to arrive. He burst through the open door as my *Smithers' Mammals of Southern Africa* went into the box.

'Shit, Angus – what the hell's going on!?' He sat on the bed, genuinely upset. I went through the events of the last night with him. 'Jeez ... that's ... it's just so shit. I'm really sorry!'

'Well ... thanks. I'm not exactly leaping for joy either.' I closed the box. 'Listen, would you mind fetching the car for me, I can't face seeing anyone right now.'

'Ja, sure, shit. I'll get it for you.' I thanked him and went into the bathroom to pack my wash bag. There was a knock on the door.

'Angus,' said Kerry.

'In the bathroom.'

She popped her head in. 'What's happening?' she asked, 'someone said you've been fired! The box on your floor says that's true!'

'Well I ain't going on a holiday,' I replied zipping up my beaten-up Old Spice sponge bag. It was given to me one Christmas by Mum and Dad and the memory made me feel ashamed about letting them down.

Back in the bedroom Kerry threw her arms around me and started crying.

'That's so *kak*, I'm so sorry.' I let her go before a tear could escape my eyes. 'What are you going to do?'

'Don't know, haven't given it a moment's thought yet.' I tossed the sponge bag onto the book box. 'I better go and tell Bertie.' We walked across to their block and I knocked on Bertie's door. He was lying on his bed, recovering from the bash he'd taken to the cranium as he came off the top of Mitchell's container. Kerry leant in the door frame and I sat down on a wicker chair to explain the situation. Bertie nodded and said he was very sorry. He was in a bad way, pretty groggy, and about to be driven to the doctor. Seeing him lying there, concussed, made me feel even worse. A few minutes later I stood up, patted him on the shoulder, apologised for my role in his injury and walked out.

SB pulled up in the Tazz soon thereafter. He and Kerry helped me pack. We shook hands and then Kerry, tears streaming from her eyes, hugged me again.

'Hey, it's going to be fine,' I lied, fighting back the urge to vomit and cry.

I started the engine and wound through the village towards the vehicle entrance. A few heads turned to see the unusual sight of the car but I was supposed to be going on leave anyway so no one paid too much heed. Then I was out onto the reserve and leaving the wild that had absorbed me into its rhythms over the last 22 months. There were animals all over the place enjoying the new, fresh earth. They didn't seem much concerned with my departure. I still felt numb six hours later when I drove into Johannesburg.

A Highveld storm was brewing to the south of the city as I turned into the driveway. The scent of Mum's summer garden filled the air and I was glad to be home. Mum emerged from the house looking concerned – obviously SB had phoned ahead. I appreciated this because it saved my having to confess to my dismissal.

Despite the feeling of dread that enveloped me, I wanted to deal with the saga as fast as possible so I told the whole story at dinner that night – without embellishment or emotion –while my parents listened, the Major sucked the marrow out of his lamb stew bones and Trubshaw tried to steal my paper napkin. Mum was notably distressed, particularly when I reached the bit about Allegra nearly being skewered. Dad didn't say anything until about five minutes after I'd finished.

'Well,' he began, 'there are a few lessons for you to learn here I suppose. It's not the first time you've heard people telling you to think things through and consider the effects your actions might have on other people. God knows, your mother and I have been doing it for ages.' He paused and sipped his wine. He was very disappointed which makes me sad.

Week 44

Unemployed and unemployable

I spent most of the week feeling sorry for myself and cursing the universe for defecating on me, despite my providing some of the laxative this time.

A few days after returning home, I dragged my limp carcass from its bed to check my emails. Well, more precisely, Dad came into my room at 06h00 and told me to 'get the hell out of bed, accept some responsibility and get on with [my] life'. I didn't really have a choice because Trubshaw landed next to me like a slobbering bomb.

There were eight mails in my inbox. Four of these came from sources offering to enhance my manhood, one from PJ, one from SB, one from Julia and one from an address I didn't know. The kind offers to make my whatnot larger for bargain prices I deleted without reading. The one from PJ contained no text – it simply had an attachment with my termination letter and last payslip. I suppose I harboured some hope that it might be a retraction of my dismissal but it was not to be. He was kinder than he could have been in the five emotionless lines.

Sasekile
Private Game Reserve

Angus MacNaughton
60 Sutherland Ave.
Parktown North
Johannesburg
2913

01/11

Dear Angus MacNaughton,

Re: Termination of Employment at Sasekile Private Game Reserve

Period of employment: One year and ten months.

Position and responsibilities: Game Ranger, responsibilities included taking guided game drives and walks for Sasekile guests.

Reason for termination of employment: Personal values divergent from those of Sasekile Private Game Reserve management.

We wish Angus well in his future endeavours.

Sincerely,

Paul John Woodstock
General Manager
Sasekile Private Game Reserve

Not a letter I'll show to a future employer but at least it didn't use the words 'dismissal' or mention any of my three disciplinary hearings. The thought that my sister would have vetted it before it was sent (in her capacity as Sasekile's attorney) wasn't entirely comforting. I scratched the week's worth of beard on my face.

Mum came in while I was reading so I shared the letter, which drove her into a frenzy of worry about the fact that her baby finds himself in the predicament he does.

'Oh Angus, what are you going to do?'

'Mother,' I replied rubbing a hand through my greasy, unkempt hair, 'I plan to look for inspiration in the vast array of liquor available at the Jolly Roger.' She didn't seem to think I was serious and went off to make some tea for me. I clicked on the next unopened item.

String Bean's letter was kind but lacking in any form of practical worth.

To: Angus
From: Hugh MacNaughton
Subject: Hope you're okay

Hi Angus,

I hope you are feeling okay there at home. Mum says you haven't really come out of your room much since you got there. Everyone here is a bit shocked that you have gone and they were all very confused. Carrie had to hold a special meeting to explain everything to the rangers and the information sort of filtered to the rest after that. Surprisingly, no one seems too happy about it.

Allegra has kept almost totally to herself since last week – apparently she only eats when everyone else has left the eatery.

Bertie is fine, you will be glad to know. He just had a mild concussion so he's okay but he doesn't look happy so I think he is quite sad you are gone. Maybe you could send him a message sometime.

Anyway, I hope things are fine with you and despite our differences over the last little while, I'm really sorry that things have ended up like they have.

Your brother,
Hugh

I realised suddenly that it was his birthday so I replied quickly, thanking him for his concern and wishing him a happy day.

The next one was from Julia.

To: Angus
From: Julia MacNaughton
Subject: What's going on?

Hello Angus,

I've been trying to phone you all week but it would seem that you've turned your phone off. I've obviously seen your termination letter but I wanted to find out what happened. I've only heard from Mum and Dad. Call me sometime and let's talk.

Love,
Jules

P.S. Despite your behaviour last time I saw you, I'm really worried about you.

One of the last things I felt like doing was talking to Julia. I didn't want to rehash the whole thing, listen to someone else telling me I need to consider my actions more carefully and, mostly, I didn't want her then talking to The Legend about it. I'm sure he's thoroughly pleased with my axing.

I closed Julia's mail and wasn't up to reading anything else so I left the remaining one unopened. Then I went into the morning sun with Trubshaw to drink my tea. The dog managed to spill scalding-hot beverage down my front as he grabbed my arm and pulled it when I had the temerity to stop tickling him. I swore at the hound and went to make some more but gave up halfway and went back to bed.

The rest of this week was unproductive. I watched TV, lay on my bed and walked down to the Jolly Roger to drink large volumes of beer from mid-afternoon until I could barely stand. I spent a number of nights at Donald Gilbert's house in Parkhurst because I was pissed and didn't feel like facing my parents. His wife Lauren was tolerant of my lazing in their small livingroom although I began to feel like Dupree come Saturday (yesterday) morning when they came through to go cycling and I was lying on the sofa, still drunk from the night before and smelling like stale brandy and Coke. I don't imagine it was pretty and as Lauren went out to pump her tires, Donald told me it was time to pull myself together and go home. I promised to be out by the time they returned.

I wove the Tazz home and collapsed on my bed. Mum and Dad were out shopping and the Major was having his porridge in the kitchen. At about 12h00, I woke up, the beginnings of a massive hangover setting in. Dad walked into my room – unimpressed.

'Right, that's it. Get out of bed right now. You are now 28 years old, unemployed, and being bloody pathetic. I'm not going to put up with it. Either get up and get on with your life or get out.' He slammed the door and I heard Mum remonstrating with him to be gentle on me. As I lay there staring at the ceiling, nauseous, my head pounding, I realised some time alone to think was what I needed.

Kenton seemed like the best option. When I'd showered and eaten 46 Disprin, I went through to the veranda where Mum and Dad were having lunch. Trubshaw enraged my father further by chasing flies and in the process, knocking over his Peroni. My parents agreed that some time away was a good first step forward.

The Tazz is now all packed and tomorrow morning I'll depart for the coast to be alone and consider my options.

Week 45

Solitude and sorrow

The drive to Kenton was as beautiful as ever. Once out of Johannesburg, the flat green farmlands of the Free State stretched out in all directions sprouting the new crops that will feed the country come the harvest. Then it was into the Karoo, past the Gariep Dam and through the tiny towns of Steynsburg and then Hofmeyr. These intriguing little settlements somehow eke out a living on the farm trade of the arid lands in which they exist. They always seem to be on the brink of becoming ghost towns but somehow survive. I stopped at the renowned Hofmeyr butcher and bought some Karoo lamb and boerewors.

Then the road winds its way on to Cradock where I always stop under the pine trees at the cemetery to have lunch and weed my great grandparents' grave. After Cradock, comes Bedford – the small town nestled in the moutains with its spectacular gardens that go on display once a year in late spring. From Bedford, the bleached and potholed road traverses a number of scenic and precipitous passes and then drops down to Grahamstown, home to more churches per soul than any other place in the country. Halfway along the last 60 kilometres of winding road, lies the tiny settlement of Salem (which sports one of South Africa's most picturesque cricket grounds). The home stretch passes farms and land turned back to wildlife after centuries of agriculture.

With fifteen kilometres to go, the sea appeared on the horizon and I opened the windows. The Eastern Cape air filled the car – salt, sea and early summer coastal bush.

I pulled into the short driveway at about 16h00, collected the key from the resident neighbours, politely refused tea with them, unpacked the car and then headed through the garden, over the heavily-wooded dune and onto the river.

On the bank of the river, the sight, smells and sounds filled me with an enormous sense of peace and nostalgia from the many holidays we have spent here as a family. A pair of southern boubous called to each other upstream and a bar-throated apalis shouted 'prrp prrp prrp prrp' from an exposed twig just behind. The tide was going out so I walked to a jetty a few hundred metres upstream and tested the water with my big toe. It was warm with the last of the outgoing tide. The water, the dune greenery, the estuary birds and the salt in the air seeped into me.

I leapt into the water and swam for the other side. It was a short swim of just over 50 metres before my feet touched the sand on the eastern bank. As I stood, a puff of air alerted me to a Cape fur seal fishing in the water behind.

I waded the rest of the way out onto the soft, warm, wet sand. A flock of whimbrels fluttered off, one or two of them calling irritably. In the middle of the sand bank, I dropped to my knees and then lay down. The late afternoon sun warmed my back and I sucked in the smell of the sand. After ten minutes or so, I rolled onto my back and watched the gulls and terns swooping about overhead. I've always loved the feeling of sand and salt on my skin so I remained there until the sun set. By the time my body touched the water for the return swim, inspiration to do something about my situation was growing – there were no plans yet, just the will to move forward.

I went up to the house, changed into some dry clothes and then ferreted about in the drinks cabinet for some whisky. There was a bottle of Black Grouse so I poured a healthy measure and returned to the boathouse roof to drink the smoky scotch and watch the last of the day. Across the river, yellow lights illuminated the old farmhouse on the eastern bank, a tree hyrax made its somewhat terrifying call in the dune behind, and upriver a fruit bat began its metallic 'tink tink tink'.

As the whisky level dropped, I forced myself to think things through and it was surprising how clear and how fast ideas arrived. Firstly, I realised that no matter what happened, I wanted to work in a place of natural beauty – the thought of moving back to Johannesburg made my throat close. Secondly, I've developed some skill as a ranger and I enjoy lodge life for the most part and while I don't wish to be a guide for the rest of my days, perhaps some sort of training role in the future would be enjoyable. Thirdly, I acknowledged the extreme sense of loss I felt at being ejected from Sasekile. With those thoughts I made Plan A and Plan B. The former (and most preferable) was to somehow convince PJ and the brains trust at Sasekile to take me back. Plan B would be to seek employment at a game lodge somewhere else – a road I hoped to avoid entirely but one I accepted may have to be travelled.

So, early the next morning, I fired up my computer and set about mailing the relevant people. My inbox contained a few more offers for penile enhancement and bedroom performance drugs. There was still the unopened one from the unidentified address. I didn't open any of them, so intent was I on winning back my job.

The execution of Plan A was somewhat more complex than its conception. Turning PJ 180 degrees remains a seemingly impossible task so I needed some allies on the inside. Carrie was the most obvious one.

To: Carrie Barlett
From: Angus MacNaughton
Subject: Apologies and a possible way forward

Dear Carrie,

I am sorry that it has taken me this long to write to you but I have been thinking (drinking) things through in the wake of my eviction from Sasekile. From the outset I would like to tell you that I accept full responsibility for putting the lives of Allegra and Bertie at risk. I am quite sure that my actions put you, as my former manager, in an invidious position and this was never my intention (not that my objective makes an enormous difference). In short, I apologise without reservation for endangering my two friends and threatening the good name of Sasekile.

The second purpose of this letter is to ask a favour and please read to the end. Over the last two weeks or so, I have come to realise the special place that Sasekile holds in my heart. I am bereft at the thought of no longer living and working there. To that end, I would like to ask you to consider taking me back (I have written that sentence 150 times trying to make it sound less pathetic and less like I am begging but there is really only one way to say what I need to). I realise this is more than you owe me (which at this point is about nothing) and that it is an enormous cheek even asking but if I do not explore all avenues of reprieve, I shall regret it. I also realise the decision will lie ultimately with PJ so if you do decide you would like to give me my umpteenth chance, I know it would require seeking his approval.

Once again, I am sorry for putting you in the position I did. Regardless of how this eventually turns out, it has been something of an honour to work for you.

Sincerely,
Angus

Winning her over may just be able to provide the push PJ needs. The two of them are close confidants. I also wanted the victims of my ill-thought-out plan to rescue Mitchell to approach the GM and convince him they bear me no ill-will. That said, I didn't want Bertie and Allegra doing that without really meaning it. I wrote to Bertie next but realised I didn't have Allegra's address so I moved onto PJ's letter. I left the subject line blank because filling it with 'I want my job back' would just make him delete it on sight.

To: PJ Woodstock
From: Angus MacNaughton
Subject:

Dear PJ,

This letter serves to say a few things. Firstly, I would like to apologise wholeheartedly for putting the lives of Allegra and Bertie in danger. I accept responsibility for the incident completely. I understand why you fired me and I bear you and Sasekile no ill-will because of it.

Secondly, I would like to ask you to reconsider my termination. I know the audacity of this request will probably take your breath away but please read to the end of the mail before dismissing it totally. I realise I have a less-than-sterling record on the disciplinary front, mostly as a result of my inability and/or unwillingness to control my temper and my tongue. While it may sound twee, after two weeks of soul-searching, I believe that I have finally seen the error of my ways. I shan't lie to you and try to pretend that I shall never be offensive again but I believe I shall learn to be much more measured in the future.

Like I said, I know this letter is filled with temerity bordering on psychopathic but Sasekile has gone from being a prison to a treasured home and I believe that while I have been a difficult employee, I have demonstrated some commitment to Sasekile. I ask that you reconsider my termination and take this letter in the humility with which it is intended.

Sincerely,
Angus

P.S. I am happy to accept just about any conditions of re-employment that you might care to impose.

I thought it remarkably controlled of me to not mention his poorly-researched Mitchell plan.

PJ's letter complete, I needed a bit of a break so I went off to the beach. It was wonderfully hot and deserted. It's always a little nerve-wracking swimming in the sea completely alone but the tide was far out, there was a gentle southwester blowing and the waves were breaking in even, untroubled lines. I plunged in and spent about half an hour in the water. After that, I lay on the hot sand and after a swim in the lagoon, I went home.

A gin and tonic in my hand, I clicked on the unopened item from the unknown address still sitting in my inbox. The letter, written five days after I was fired, negated the need for me to seek Allegra's address.

To: Angus MacNaughton
From: Allegra Gordon
Subject: Various vacillations of the mind

Hello Angus MacNaughton,

I hope you are in relatively good health although I imagine you might be mentally fatigued and at something of a loose end.

I am sad that you did not come and say goodbye before you left. However, I understand that you were probably ashamed and just wanted to escape as fast as possible. I thought the emotions I was feeling would disappear but they have not yet. I am not sure what they mean but I do need to tell you that I remain sombre that you are not to return.

I feel it would also be remiss of me not to tell you that I am not the only one who is saddened by your departure. I know that Jacob, O'Reilly and Incredible have all been to see PJ about you. Although I am not party to what was discussed, I saw O'Reilly leaving red-faced and saying 'fek' a lot as he returned to the kitchen. I believe Jeff also barged into the office while PJ was meeting with all the department heads. He threatened to chain himself to a desk unless you were re-hired. Apparently Jacob and Carrie removed him physically.

In conclusion, I hope to see you again at some point in the future and I wish you good fortune in whatever endeavours you choose to pursue.

With love,
Allegra

An encouraging letter which made me feel surprisingly elated. I responded immediately, explaining that I hadn't responded earlier because I'd been wallowing in too much self-pity to actually read my emails. I also outlined my plan for re-employment and told her that I hoped to see her soon.

After that, I shut down my computer and phoned Mum and Dad to explain what I had done. Dad was pleased and even said he was proud because it was the first time he's ever seen me eat more than a teaspoon of humble pie. Mum fussed about my future again but said she felt better about it now. I also mailed Julia and SB, thanking them for their concern and telling them I planned to be re-employed. The talk of pie made me hungry so I went up to the home industries and bought a chicken pie for lunch (and supper).

Three days after I sent off the mails, I'd had no reply and it took some will power not to check my inbox every five minutes. In the end I limited myself to one look three times a day. In the meantime, I made some half-hearted attempts to look for other employment opportunities around the country – I don't want to work in the Lowveld if I can't be at Sasekile so I investigated places around the Eastern Cape and in KwaZulu-Natal mainly. The rest of the time I spent reading, going for long walks along the beach with my rugby ball and swimming in the river and the sea. I managed to cut down substantially on the drinking although I imagine that will ramp up again if my attempts to be re-employed are unsuccessful.

On the morning of the fourth day, there was one mail in the inbox. It was from SB.

To: Angus
From: Hugh MacNaughton
Subject: Sasekile news and your plans

Hey Angus,

I believe you're in Kenton, which is nice. I hope you're not too sad.

I think it's a good thing that you're trying to get back here and I saw PJ and Carrie having a heated argument the other day so hopefully it was about you. I also know that Bertie and Allegra went to see him. Julia must have told Jonesy your plan because he asked me about it the other day at lunch. At the end of the discussion he said, 'Well Angus can be a real prick but at least he had the guts to take action for something he believed in.'

Other news is that the elephant (I think you called him Mitchell) hasn't been seen since you released him. The bush is bright green all over and there is water everywhere so either he was so traumatised by the incident or there is enough to keep him going out in the bush for now.

Let me know if you hear anything from PJ and I will keep you posted from this end.

Good luck!
Hugh

P.S. Hanro is still a nightmare and is ordering us all around like a sergeant-major with the planning of the Arab visit at the end of the year.

I haven't had another mail this week. I figure this isn't necessarily a bad thing because it might indicate some sort of discussion on the subject of Angus MacNaughton and his connection with Sasekile Private Game Reserve.

Reprieve and relief

Three more agonising days followed with no word. On the fourth day this week I had a reply from Bertie. He apologised for not writing earlier and confirmed that he is not angry with me in the slightest. In fact, he and Allegra went off to see PJ the day I sent my mails to them. PJ thanked them for going to see him but then gave them hell for being part of the hare-brained scheme in the first place. He did, however, admit that he was glad Mitchell was free.

Then, the next day, I finally received a reply from Carrie. It wasn't entirely encouraging. She accepted my apology but said that although there was some support for my re-employment from the field team, PJ was still angry and proving very difficult to sway.

Two days later, I headed back to Johannesburg to begin my new job hunt in earnest. I suppose I could have done it from Kenton but I was running out of cash so a few family meals were always going to be appreciated as was any advice my parents could give.

The next day, I had all but given up hope. It was a Saturday morning and Dad and I were putting the finishing touches to my CV (trying to state delicately the reasons for my departure from Sasekile) when my phone rang. It wasn't a number my phone recognised so I wasn't going to answer it but Dad said he wanted some tea. As he left the table, I answered.

It was PJ.

He didn't greet; he just said, 'Angus, I'm in town for the weekend and I have half an hour to spare. I would like to meet you to discuss a few things. I'm at Vovo Telo in Parkhurst.'

'I'll be there in five,' I replied trying to hide my excitement and ran through to the kitchen where Dad was pouring water into a pot and Mum was arranging flowers on one of the counters. I blurted out the news and was about to run out when Dad stopped me.

'You'll probably want to wear something other than your sleep shorts and that T-shirt – you'll also need to put some shoes on.' All valid points. I threw on a pair of jeans and a decent shirt and a minute later was hurtling down the road at break-neck speed in the Tazz. A minute and three near collisions with pedestrians after that, I parallel parked outside the café. It was only then that nervousness welled up inside me. I was sweating and my mouth went dry.

PJ was concentrating on his phone as I walked in so he didn't see me. Without thinking, I lifted a napkin off a table, dried my sweating palms and then replaced it absently.

'Hey!' said a surprised woman eating scrambled eggs with her pre-teen daughter.

I smiled at her. 'Yes, good morning Madam,' I replied and carried on.

PJ lifted his head as I approached. He indicated for me to sit down while he continued his phone call. I ordered and drained an enormous glass of water. When PJ eventually disconnected, my heart rate was dangerously high.

'Hi Angus,' he said without smiling. 'How are you?'

'Fine, hi, thanks and you?' I replied.

'I'll come straight to the point. I'm still very angry about what happened to Bertie and Allegra and while you didn't force them to come along with you, you were the only ranger there and the senior staff member. I expected more from you and actually, until then, harboured some hopes that you might fulfil a leadership position at Sasekile in the future.' He sipped his coffee and then ordered another without offering me one.

'You will notice that I have not once mentioned the actual release of the elephant. I don't condone your methods but you stood up for what you believed and I respect that. Besides which, I made a mistake with those idiots.' The BlackBerry next to PJ rang again and I was left on tenterhooks, sweat dripping down my back.

'No, three rooms need the cream curtains, four the blue...' his voice tapered off as I spotted Jenny walking past the café's wide concertina doors on the pavement. I turned away, hoping to avoid being seen. Unfortunately, in my haste, I knocked the empty water glass off the table. It was one of those large, heavy ones so it made a spectacular noise as it shattered into a million pieces. This made everyone in the restaurant and a few passers-by stop and stare. PJ scowled, 'Sorry about that,' he said into the phone, 'yes the Egyptian cotton ones...'

Staff descended to clear my mess and as I looked up, Jenny was standing next to the table. I felt a numbing sense of embarrassment.

'Hey!' she said cheerfully. 'How are you?'

'Good,' I lied, 'very good. You?'

'Ja, really great. I just got back from three months in London doing odd jobs. I'm here for a month, then making a more permanent move over there for the next year.'

PJ remained in deep conversation with whatever supplier he was talking to so Jenny pulled a chair over.

'What's been happening at the lodge? Are you on leave?'

'Both pertinent questions and unfortunately entwined with each other,' I said. PJ, who misses very little, smiled at Jenny and frowned at me before continuing his conversation.

'So?' said Jenny.

PJ covered the mouthpiece on his phone. 'Tell her, I'd like to hear your version.' I sighed and gave Jenny a basic and emotionless rendition of Mitchell's story – his capture, escape and the near death of three of us. Jenny's brown eyes became larger and larger and she said 'oh my God' a lot. When I arrived at the bit about being fired the next day, things became uncomfortable.

'Oh...I see...so you're not really on leave.'

'Not really no.' I could see that she felt sympathetic and probably wanted to find out what on Earth I was doing having breakfast with PJ. Thankfully the GM finished his phone call.

He gave Jenny a hug and then said, 'We're here discussing Angus's future in case you were wondering.' He then, obviously revelling in my discomfort, asked Jenny if she'd like a coffee. She accepted and there followed a further fifteen excruciating minutes as PJ and Jenny caught up on life.

Eventually Jenny looked at her watch and said, 'Oh, I'm going to be late!' She stood and we exchanged hasty farewells.

'Right,' said PJ as Jenny departed, 'here's the deal Angus.'

'Mango has just resigned – he's moving to Cape Town to be with his girlfriend. We're extremely busy till the end of the year and so we're going to be short of rangers.' I began to feel much better. 'I am prepared to offer you a month's fixed-term contract. There are no promises after that – it's up to you to prove you are worth having around.' He drained his cappuccino. 'I'll say this for you, your popularity has increased quite a lot since you started. I remain unconvinced, however – I think the job might not present the right sort of challenges for you.' The silence hung briefly.

'Thank you,' I said.

'Thank Carrie and the others who stuck their necks out for you.' He checked his watch, called for the bill and said, 'You're driving out of Tamboti tomorrow afternoon. Don't be late.' We shook hands and my commander-in-chief-again left.

I walked out feeling like a million bucks tempered by the hope that one month would be sufficient to prove myself.

Back at home, my parents were going about their Saturday tasks. My father was sorting through some stuff in the garage – he's already readying himself for the Kenton holiday such is his excitement at the thought of leaving Johannesburg. Mum was deadheading the roses and Trubshaw was lying in the middle of the lawn on his back absorbing some rays, tongue lolling to one side. We gathered on the veranda where the Major was reading a newspaper and muttering about the government. AIDS Cat was curled up on his lap. I explained what had transpired. The relief on both my parents' faces was palpable.

'Oh thank God,' said Mum enveloping me.

'Well done, boy, that's great news,' said Dad smiling, 'now don't bugger it up.' The Major looked up for the first time.

'What's happening?' he snapped. 'Who's been buggered? Pah, today's men, need more time in the army I say. That'll cure them of the tendencies.' He returned to his paper without waiting for a response.

There was one thing I had to do before my return to the wild – see my sister. Mum said she was at home so I went straight round to her place, making a mental note not to make any comments about its design. She was surprised and reticent in equal measure when I arrived.

'Hello Julia,' I said as she opened the door.

'Hello Angus,' she said turning away and walking back into her apartment. I followed her in. Files and a laptop covered the entire surface of her small diningroom table. I thought it best to just go with the humble approach – I had no desire to go down the road of discussing her detestable boyfriend.

'Julia, I'm sorry I haven't contacted you. I guess I was just ashamed and didn't feel like rehashing it all. I appreciate your concern though.' She sighed and shook her head.

'Why are you such a difficult fucker?' She hardly ever swears so she was obviously quite worked up. She sank heavily onto her sofa.

'I don't know,' I said, pulling a chair out from the diningroom table and sitting down. 'I don't mean to be.'

'So much of your life has been about "I didn't mean to". All the stuff you broke as a kid when Mum, Dad, Hugh and I told you what would happen. The hurtful things you've said – especially to me and Hugh.' She looked up at me. 'You've hurt me so much this time you know.' A tear escaped her left eye. I hate it when she cries; it really chokes me up. I swallowed hard as my eyes began welling.

'I'm sorry,' I croaked and then wiped my eye. We sat in silence for a little while.

'It's time for a drink,' she said walking to the fridge and extracting two Peronis. As we drank the beer, conversation returned to relative normality. I told her about the whole incident leading to my axing. She knew about my being re-hired for the month because she drew up the contract. I stayed for lunch and then made my way home to pack.

This afternoon I wrote to Arthur to tell him about the last month and then Julia came over for supper and we had the first relaxed family dinner in about six months. The Major even made a few amusing contributions. I felt much better about things, especially as I'm heading back to the lodge tomorrow.

Week 47

Return and reunion

The drive into the lowveld has never been as pleasant as it was on my return to employment at Sasekile – albeit under a cloud of disgrace. I arrived around 13h00 and drove to the office because I wasn't even sure where my home was to be. PJ was still away so Carrie was in the hot seat again. The first person I encountered was the delightful Hanro as she emerged from the office with a file under her stained armpit.

She clicked her teeth, her rather impressive moustache mingling with the sweat on her top lip. 'I can't fokken believe vey let you back here.' I bit my tongue hard. 'You a fokken lie...um...liab...liebel...fok it...you a fokken problem!'

'You mean a liability?' I asked. She glared at me. 'Hanro, that's the most accurate thing you've said since I met you.'

'*Ag fok jou*,' she spat and waddled off. There was no one in the office so I went to the rangers' room. Carrie was tapping away at her computer.

'Ma'am,' I said. Her chair swung round.

'Ah, Angus. Welcome back.' She smiled finally. 'Can I help you with something?'

'Well, I don't really know where I'm to live...you know...as an independent contractor.'

'Same place,' she said. 'You'll need to sign this though.' She pulled my one-month contract from a folder.

I walked over, signed it and then said, 'Thank you for doing this for me. I probably don't deserve it.'

'You definitely don't deserve it!' she said but there was some humour in her voice. 'You can thank me by not causing any more shit.' I made for the door and then turned back.

'Why did you do it?' I asked, 'Why stick your neck out? There are any number of part-time guides knocking about who'd only too gladly have come to work here and probably have been infinitely less risky.'

She considered me for a while.

'Because I think you have a role to play here in the future if you can learn some self-control.' She turned back to her desk.

Back at my room there was even a welcome drink (empty of course) but a nice gesture all the same. The accompanying card, pinned to the door, was fuller than any I've received before with a number of 'so glad you're back' sentiments. I was quite overwhelmed.

SB arrived as I was unpacking. He was dressed in a pair of board shorts and a T-shirt – the Mozam Dream Team had been reconstituted and was about to depart for the sunny east coast (minus The Legend who is returning to Johannesburg to see his girlfriend). We shook hands warmly.

'I'm really glad you're back,' he said.

'You mean that, String Bean?' I asked.

'Ja, I really do,' he replied defensively.

'Well thank you very much. I'm really happy to be back.'

'I'm not the only one who thinks that, by the way. There are quite a lot of pleased people.'

'Makes a change.'

'It sure does. Anyway I wanted to tell you a few things quickly before we go off to Mozam.' He sat on my bed and took his hat off. I could see he was serious so I sat on the desk chair and gave him my full attention. 'First, dealing with Hanro has made me realise what a knob I was as the hospitality manager; so much of what drives people mad about her I know that I did. It's painful for me to admit it but I know that PJ made the right decision in demoting me.'

'That's very big of you,' I said.

'The second thing is that I finally swallowed my pride and went to apologise to Simone. I know it's taken me much too long but I guess I was just too proud and then embarrassed. She shouted at me for a long time and I didn't even say anything back to her. I'm not sure she'll ever forgive me for what I did but at least we're on speaking terms again.'

In my head I heard myself say, 'I imagine the Lord himself would have trouble forgiving you,' but instead I said, 'Well done, that must've been tough.' I tapped him on the shoulder in what seemed like a fraternal way. 'Have a great time in Mozambique.'

As I unpacked my wash bag, Bertie and Kerry burst into the room and enveloped me in a cheerful hug and by the time I'd sorted out my room and showered, it was time to head down to Tamboti Camp to meet my guests and talk to the other person involved in the Mitchell saga.

On the walk down to the camp, a cocoon of serenity enveloped me. It was like being plugged into a primal source of energy. The cicadas were out of the ground and their song filled the hot afternoon – that most quintessential summer sound.

As I approached the entrance to Tamboti, apprehension gathered in my stomach. It was difficult to pinpoint where it was coming from until I heard Allegra's voice. There is a small flight of stairs leading down to the deck where the tea table stands. I paused at the top and looked down. Allegra was arranging some lilies in a large vase while Redman sliced the cake and added vanilla bark to the iced coffee.

'...And honey badger, I still struggle to remember the word for it?' asked Allegra.

'*Xindzhele* is honey badger,' replied Redman. He then spelt it out for her.

'So the "sh" sound in Shangane is spelt with an x?'

'Yes but not always,' replied the butler-cum-Shangane teacher.

Allegra finished her arrangement, scooped up the offcuts, turned round and saw me watching her. She froze and after a slightly uncomfortable period, she said. 'Hello Angus MacNaughton.'

'Hello Allegra,' I replied moving down the stairs.

'How are you?'

'I'm fine now,' I replied. 'More to the point, how are you?'

'I believe I have just about processed the events of what is now being referred to as "Angus's Elephant night". Ambiguous I know.'

As she spoke, I realised that Allegra's subtle expressions say a lot more than is first apparent. The corners of her eyes turned up slightly – an expression of humour. 'Frankly I think it is a bit unfair that only your name is associated with the evening.' Then the corners of her mouth turned down a little and she blinked a few times. 'I thought it tremendously unfair that you were dismissed on my account.' She paused and then added awkwardly, 'Anyway, I am glad that you have returned.'

'I was fired because I should have led the situation far better than I did. It was in no way your fault.' Another slightly uncomfortable moment ensued, and then, acting on impulse I stepped forward and put my arms round her slim waist. 'I'm sorry I didn't come and say goodbye,' I said.

For a moment she just stood there like a post, which made things even more awkward, then she dropped the flower cuttings she was holding, stood on her toes and returned my hug. We remained unmoving until the swing door from the kitchen opened. We let go quickly and while I pretended to be engrossed by the leopard canvas hanging on the wall, she picked up the fallen cuttings.

I collected a cup of tea and a biscuit and then asked, 'What are my guests like? I was rather hoping the first lot of my second term of employment would ease me back into the swing of things.' Allegra smiled properly at that point and before she could answer, the sound of Ronald 'Tex' Meadows's nasal Texan twang reached my ears. It wasn't the accent that made me realise life was going to be tough for the next few days but the fact that I could hear him emerging from his room – at least 80 metres away.

The Meadows family (twelve in all) were mostly from Texas and their money, an apparently inexhaustible supply, comes from oil. If ever there was a group of stereotypical guests, this was it.

Tex is the patriarch of the family and is still president of the oil company at age 78. He thinks everything in Africa is too small. His suite was too small, his bath was too small, the helpings on his plate were too small, my rifle was too small and the lions were too small.

'Ayngus,' Tex told me before dinner over a Garrison Brothers bourbon (which was specially imported), 'y'oughta come to the US one day. The grizzlies up in Yella Stone make these laahns look like house cats.'

Marilyn Meadows, who married into the family, was tasked with planning the annual clan vacation. She was educated in upstate New York and has therefore heard of places outside of the United States. I don't believe the rest had the foggiest idea where in the world they were.

At dinner one evening, Ronald Meadows III (about thirteen I think) asked me if there was a possibility of doing some surfing in the morning. I fetched an atlas from the Tamboti library and asked young Ronald to point at where he comes from on the world map. He managed to point at the correct continent. I then asked him to indicate where he thought he was now. He pointed to a remote part of the Florida coastline. I considered young Ronald and his wrap-around Justin Bieber haircut briefly.

'Ronald, my boy, your current position is further removed from the Gulf of Mexico than your grandfather is from Archbishop Tutu.'

Because he has no idea who Desmond Tutu is, he looked mildly confused and said, 'So can we surf or not?'

'Ronald, I'm afraid surfing is not an activity we are able to offer here on account of the fact that we're about 200 miles from the sea.' His expression soured.

'Oh she-it,' he said.

The Meadows group was unable to ruin my enjoyment of being in the bush again, however. The first game drive will linger in my memory as one of the most memorable of my time out here. Elvis chuckled heartily when I arrived at the Land Rover. He slapped me on my back (which knocked the wind out of me) and told me he was very pleased about my return.

My six guests, excluding Tex, were very quiet on the drive. This was either because they were jet-lagged or because their brains were unable to process the unfamiliarity of their surroundings.

A tremendous sense of well-being developed again as we headed parallel with the river into the setting sun. Elvis suggested that we cross north to find a leopard which had been seen earlier that morning. There's been a lot of rain in my absence so the river was flowing strongly over the rocky drift. As I eased the nose of the vehicle into the water, there were some gasps from the Texans but the tires gripped the rock and we moved slowly through the two-foot deep water. Halfway across, I switched off the engine.

'Wattarrwee doin?' asked Nancy Meadows, 40ish.

'Listening to the sound of the water,' I replied feeling marvellous. The afternoon sun danced across the ripples and a fish jumped in a pool in a lee of the northern bank. A little egret watched us, momentarily distracted from his fishing while a pair of pied kingfishers called to each other as they scudded past the front of the vehicle just three feet above the surface. A hippo grunted in the distance downstream. Then, about 100 metres to the west, a herd of elephants arrived at the water's edge. They emerged from the greening reeds, young ones in the centre, and it wasn't long before they were all splashing about in a wide, shallow sandy section of the Tsesebe River.

I didn't utter a word of explanation – it seemed to me that the lowveld was speaking for itself during the twenty minutes or so that we sat there watching the elephants drinking and horsing about – spraying water and sand onto their bodies.

Then it was out onto the northern bank and up towards a dry tributary where the leopard had last been seen. At the designated spot, I switched off again and while Elvis scanned the surrounds for black rosettes on gold, I reiterated our leopard plan to the Meadowses. When satisfied that there was no cat watching us from the shadows, Elvis climbed down from the tracker seat. He beckoned me to follow so I took the rifle from its rack and explained that we were going to track the leopard on foot.

'Who's gonna diffaynd us if it curms this way? You're tayeken the gurn!' said Billy, mid twenties. It took a little while for me to process this utterance.

'Well, if she happens to wander back this way, you'll be perfectly safe. Just sit still and don't stand up – we shan't be gone longer than twenty minutes.'

Elvis and I descended the low bank into the tributary and the tracker found the leopard's pugmarks almost immediately. They were heading upstream so we began to follow slowly. It was blissful walking in the dappled shade of the tamboti, jackalberry and false thorn trees overhead. A cardinal woodpecker pecked around for food in the bark of a knobthorn and a European golden oriole flew over while its black-headed cousin called somewhere further upstream. The banks were lined with shorter, thicker vegetation all in full leaf; blue sweet berry, guarri, fever tea and sweet-scented num num bushes in flower.

Then, we heard a drongo calling up ahead and Elvis stopped. He turned to me and whispered in Shangane, 'That drongo is alarm calling at a leopard.' To me it sounded like a fairly normal drongo call but I've learnt to trust Elvis in these matters. We edged slowly forward, my skin tingling and my heart beating much quicker. Then, about twenty metres further, Elvis froze. He turned his head.

'Can you see?' he whispered. I stared at the dappled sand up ahead, expecting to see a cat coiled and ready to spring. 'Up,' he added. So I began scanning the branches and then I saw it. About 50 metres in front of us, there was an enormous nyala tree, its gnarled old branches stretching out over the narrow drainage line. Hanging down just below the line of the foliage, there was a tail – gold and spotted. I smiled up at Elvis. We stood for a bit longer scanning the area.

'She's killed something,' he added and then pointed to a secondary fork of the tree where the fresh carcass of a small duiker was hanging. Then Elvis did a very kind thing. Normally we would both walk back to fetch the Land Rover or I would go and he would wait with the animal. Perhaps he could see how much the afternoon meant to me.

'You wait here,' said the tracker, 'I'll fetch the guests.' He turned and walked silently back down the drainage line. I sat down to wait on a flat rock, the earthy bank providing the perfect backrest. The lower angle offered a view of the leopard's head and I was surprised to see that she was staring straight at me, clearly unconcerned.

I can count on one hand the number of times I've felt as satisfied as I did sitting there in the golden light, chewing a piece of new grass, watching a leopard with every sub-atomic particle of my body sucking in the bushveld summer.

For the rest of the week, I drove flat out from all camps including a three-day stint in Kingfisher Camp where Melissa lavished well-meaning idiocy on me.

'Oh Anguth, I can't tell you how upthet Jeff wath when you left – he wath totally incontholable!'

Every time she saw me, her flaming red hair seemed to glow a bit brighter, she'd sigh loudly and then hug me. 'Jutht tho happy that you back!' It is an eternal mystery why the two people who've been at the sharpest end of my sarcasm for the last two years should continue to harbour such fondness for me.

Arthur sent me another very balanced view of things this week.

To: Angus MacNaughton
From: Arthur C. Grimble
Subject: Life's little lessons

Crocus Cottage
West Road
Wragby
Lincolnshire

Dear Angus,

I am so glad that this will find you back in the employ of Sasekile. What a testing few weeks you have had. I am even more glad that your two friends remained uninjured in the wake of the elephant rescue. From what you say it could well have ended differently but the two of them now have an amazing story to tell!

It has become very cold here and we even had a bit of snow last week. Since Mavis moved in, I have had to pay more attention to the heating and I am beginning to regret being so frugal about it for so many years. It makes the winter infinitely more bearable when you live in a warm house with someone who is kind.

Please keep sending your news, I still so enjoy it, and try to stay out of trouble.

All the best,
Arthur

Week 48

Storm and suspense

There was some disturbing news for Sasekile this week. Carrie and Jane have resigned on the back of an offer to set up and then run a camp up in Tanzania. Carrie is going to build a field team of guides and ecologists from scratch while Jane oversees the refurbishment of the old hunting camp and the training of the hospitality staff. It's a wonderful opportunity for them but very unsettling for the rangers and trackers here. Carrie has been a genuine inspiration and whoever takes over from her will have enormous boots to fill. They leave at the end of the month. Apparently PJ has known about it for a little while but the lodge has only just been told. The worst part of course is that The Legend is now frontrunner for the head ranger position again. Still, my contract runs out at the end of the month, so I may not be here to put up with him.

Julia sent the following little missive at the beginning of the week.

To: Angus; Hugh
From: Julia MacNaughton
Subject: Visit

Hi Guys,

As you know Mum and Dad are heading down to Kenton soon. I'm going to join them for Christmas but I'm coming down to the lodge to see Alistair (and you guys obviously!) for a few days beforehand. I hear there will be some sort of Arab royalty staying in camp so I expect things should be quite festive about the lodge?!

Anyways, just thought I'd give you ample forewarning so that my older brother can prepare himself to be polite (and if necessary stock up on some Valium) and my younger one can become over-excited about my imminent arrival.

See you next week!

Love,
Jules

Pushing succession battles from my mind, I continued my enjoyment of the summer. Given that the head ranger has now resigned, Sasekile is going to be short-staffed come the end of the month so if I keep my head down, perhaps the arrangement will become more permanent.

The most notable part of my week was hosting some Norwegians in Tamboti Camp. The muggy heat played havoc with their Scandinavian physiologies' normal experience of December. There were three couples and while I made a valiant effort to remember their names, it was impossible because they sounded so unfamiliar. I think there was a Bjorn and an Inger in there somewhere but I may be wrong. They were very formal; all dressed in freshly-pressed khaki safari gear – long-sleeved and breathable.

While the temperature has been molten, there's also been a lot of rain. Puddles dot the roads and clearings, the waterholes are full and two of the three river crossings are impassable. The grass is long and always wet so tracking in the mornings means squelching shoes, legs wet to the thighs (knees in Elvis's case) and a good covering of sticky white sap from the guinea grass flowers. The rain normally arrives in violent afternoon thundershowers which results in rangers charging for home at dangerous speeds, guests hanging on for grim life, their ponchos streaming like green capes behind them.

Some guests like to brave the rain, doggedly determined to make the most of the bush despite the inclemency of the weather. There are a number of solutions to this problem, the most effective being to aim the Land Rover into the wind and drive fast. Within ten minutes or so, guests are cold, wet and miserable which makes convincing them to return to camp easy.

The Norwegians were as impervious to my homing methods as they were impermeable to the sheets of water streaming from the afternoon banks of cumulonimbi. When the thunder started rolling in, they unsheathed expensive and sophisticated Scandinavian wet-weather apparel. They remained bone dry as the rain belted down while Elvis and I made do with the lodge-issue ponchos which rival chicken mesh in their ability to resist water. Coupled with this laughable gear, Land Rovers are designed so that water running off the steering wheel is channelled directly into the crotch of the driver. Of the infinite number of design flaws that the Land Rover Defender 110 possesses (sharp stabbing edges on every corner, a dashboard made of cheap plastic, knobs that fall off after a week's use, fans that break after a day's use) the funnelling action of the steering wheel is the most irritating.

One afternoon, the deluge began fairly late. We spent the afternoon at a hyena den where there were two litters of cubs – one about a month old and then another about three months. The clan had picked a termite mound on a west-facing slope, so there was a superb view of the storm gathering over the mountains as we watched the hyenas play.

The cubs amused themselves charging up and down the termite mound, the little ones running in and out of the burrows dug into the side of the mound. The older ones came right up to the Land Rover and then proceeded to remove all four oil caps from the wheels. These they chewed to pieces in seconds. A particularly brave one approached the driver's door (where there isn't a door). I was sitting sideways with my feet on the running board and the cheeky cub sniffed once at my shoe and then tried to take a nip.

'Oy!' I shouted. This made him scamper back. The two adult females looking after the den hardly lifted their reclining heads when I shouted, so habituated are they to our presence.

The youngsters chewed on bits of old bone, the shell of a long-dead leopard tortoise and two of them chased a Swainson's francolin which chanced upon their game. The bird squawked loudly and flew off just in time.

A few minutes before sunset Elvis tapped me on the shoulder and pointed. The gathering storm had broken, sending isolated sheets of grey to the earth interspersed with streams of gold and yellow afternoon sun. It had cleared the Drakensberg in the west, so as the shafts of water streamed towards us, the western horizon above the mountains turned peach and then crimson. Ordinarily, I'd have told the guests we needed to head for home but the quite stunning sight of the coming deluge twisting towards us had the Norwegians, Elvis and me wrapped.

Then, thunder roared across the sky and a cloud on the next ridge shot a blinding bolt into the earth and, quite suddenly, we were no longer viewing the storm's awesome beauty rolling by but living in the middle of it. The wind hit first and the temperature plummeted. Then the first big drops of rain fell as the Norwegians waterproofed themselves and Elvis and I donned our useless ponchos. The small hyenas made for the cover of their burrows at the first peal and the adults lazily moved across to shelter under a big guarri bush.

The rain proper started then while lightning and thunder exploded all around. The normally stoic Norwegians agreed that we should make for home as soon as possible given the amount of electricity stabbing into the ground. It took almost an hour to reach camp and it was dark by the time we arrived and the power was out. Elvis returned the Land Rover to the workshop while I walked the guests to their rooms – the security guard absent in the torrent. All the time the rain was becoming more ferocious, so I decided to take shelter in the Tamboti main area before returning to my room to change.

The ramp and three steps leading onto the deck are polished concrete – dangerously slippery when wet. This, of course, I failed to remember as I ran for the shelter. As soon as my feet touched the ramp, they lost purchase and I flew straight over the lip of the steps and into Allegra. A large ottoman slowed our momentum and, reflexively holding onto each other, we tripped over the soft furniture and onto the deck behind it. Allegra landed on top of me, her knee slamming into my solar plexus. I looked up, unable to breathe, to see Allegra's grey eyes boring into mine. The moment hung as the rain clattered down outside and I gasped for air. She rolled off me and I turned onto my side, the air slowly returning to my lungs.

'Are you alright?' she asked.

'Will be just now,' I gasped. When my diaphragm had recovered sufficiently, I sat up next to her and spluttered, 'Allegra, are you trying to flirt with me again?' We were leaning against the back of a sofa, looking out beyond the deck as the lightning lit the ridge opposite.

'I have told you that I do not know how to flirt,' she said quietly, turning her face to mine and smiling.

We were sitting very close, our legs touching. The smell of her clean hair and subtle perfume mixed with that of the rain.

'What are you wearing?' I asked, our faces now just millimetres apart.

'Other than this burgundy dress?' she whispered.

'Yes – your scent.' I moved my nose to her neck and inhaled softly. She tilted her head to the side.

'Coco Chanel,' she whispered. Lightning struck the river bank opposite and thunder split the sky above the camp. We both started and laughed. 'For a second I thought you were referring to my lingerie,' she said.

'You can tell me about that too,' I replied turning my head back to her and lifting my hand to her olive cheek.

'I would but you would accuse me of flirting with you again.' She put her hand to my face.

'Which you would be, of course.' Her crimson lipstick glinted as her mouth opened slightly.

Then, suddenly, the power came on and the sound of Redman, Nora and Incredible arriving discharged the air between us. Allegra stood quickly.

The next day the whole staff was forced to sit through a meeting with Hanro about the arrival of the Sheik Abdul bin Ismail al Maktoum. (I had to write it down to remember.) We're not allowed to know from which part of the oil-rich Middle East His Excellency hails, but the demands and requirements of him and his entourage are as many as they are bizarre.

Hanro delivered her address to us in the sweltering midday heat around the table at the Avuxeni Eatery. PJ and Carrie were away meeting the managers of the neighbouring reserves about something or other. Their absence left Hanro as the most senior member of staff for a few hours and she wasn't about to miss out on her command opportunity.

It was the same day the Norwegians left. Their plane was late so I wasn't on time for the meeting. Everyone was seated and Hanro was about to hold forth when I walked in. From her reaction to my late arrival (almost seven minutes late), you'd be forgiven for thinking I had just singlehandedly had her family deported.

'*Ag nee fokkit man!*' she shouted. 'Always a problem wiff you. Fok!' This made Brandon snigger. I didn't want to react with my employment on such a knife edge.

'I'm sorry I'm late,' I said sitting in the only empty chair – right next to Brandon.

'Is not acceptable! I'm trying to prepare for vis important group and you fink you too important!'

Brandon whispered in an excellent take-off of Hanro's accent, 'Fokken funny vis sort of fing.' Hanro didn't hear him but this utterance ignited a case of giggles deep in my belly and I started shaking. This made Brandon and Sipho (who had also heard him) also start sniggering. I stared at the tablecloth in front of me, hoping that concentrating on the intricacies of the floral design would calm me. Tears began dripping onto the surface. The incandescence radiating from Hanro was palpable.

'It's not fokken funny!' she screamed. This, of course, made it twice as funny and when the first 'pfff' escaped from Sipho's lips, the three of us collapsed in hysterics. A second later everyone else at the table was rolling about. I think even the repugnant Abbot had a smile on his face. Hanro stormed out.

Ten minutes later, everyone had calmed down and Hanro returned. She simply pretended nothing had happened and continued with her presentation.

In short, the sheik is bringing his own hairdresser, team of chefs, food, enormous security entourage, massage therapists, personal trainer, wives (fifteen!) and various other hangers-on. They have booked out the entire camp. He, unlike many of his brethren in that part of the world, has an extensive list of exclusive liquor requirements including malt whiskies and various ancient brandies.

Apparently he wanted to fly his plane straight in but our humble runway isn't big enough to take the sheik's Gulfstream so they have had to charter a few smaller aircraft, at enormous cost no doubt.

I received a message from SB at the beginning of the week, sent from an Internet café in Inhambane.

To: Angus
From: Hugh MacNaughton
Subject: Marvellous Mozam

Hey Angus,

A quick one to let you know that we're having an awesome time here. Came to town to get some supplies so I thought I'd drop you a mail. We've drunk more rum than last time (didn't think that was possible) and I've spent the rest of my money on diving – it's my new favourite thing. The dudes here are a bit lax on the safety front so diving with a hangover doesn't seem to be a problem.

Anyway, hope you having fun and haven't been fired again! Ha ha!

Cheers and see you soon,
Hugh

Ha ha indeed.

Week 49

Festivities and foolishness

Iwrite this week's update in the wake of the Staff Christmas Party – my left leg up on the desk. This is because my ankle is throbbing, strapped and much larger than it was a few days ago. The reasons for its unusual proportions will become clear.

There is a holiday atmosphere about the Sasekile staff village at the moment because a lot of the staff have their children visiting with the end of the school year. Often while I'm sitting at my desk or lying on my bed reading, the sensation of being observed develops. Turning my attention to the open door normally reveals a small grinning face or two.

'Hullo,' I say sternly. Much giggling follows. If there is a brave one he (or normally she) returns my greeting and then there is more giggling and the game continues elsewhere.

There were a number of other meetings about the sheik's imminent visit. Carrie, as the head ranger, will be driving him. The Legend and Brandon will be driving the wives that don't accompany their husband. The rest of us will drive the entourage or track animals for the others. Hanro is in a complete state about the whole thing and it's been a steep learning curve for String Bean as he's seen himself revealed in her methods.

I was driving out of Tamboti at the beginning of the week and just before the guests came through for dinner I poured my brother and I a large measure of excellent malt whisky each (thanks, Legend) and sat down on the sofa next to where he was lighting some tea-light candles. A scops owl called from the sausage tree below the deck. I handed him his glass.

'Thanks,' he said sitting down. 'You know the more I watch Hanro, the more I cringe at my performance earlier this year.'

'Well, String Bean, as our dear father has always tried to impress upon us, mistakes are only bad if you don't learn from them.' I sipped the Ardbeg ten-year-old, savouring the feeling as it slipped down my oesophagus. 'I reckon we've both had our fair share of hard knocks in the last while.'

'With no one to blame but ourselves.'

'Depressingly, that is the case.'

The Christmas Party was as amusing as last year's. Because the pantomime that SB and I performed twelve months ago was such a success, PJ asked us to produce another. I penned a piece called *Little Red Hooding Ride*. I played the hyena, which replaced the wolf. This I had to do with a severe limp and tremendous pain in my lower back. My discomfort was caused by the three-legged race – the final event of the traditional children's sports day. String Bean played Hooding Ride, an obnoxious teenager with a hoody and a tiny bicycle; Carrie played the Huntsman, with an enormous fake moustache; and the grandmother was performed by Bertie. The tale isn't very well known by the Shangane staff and their kids so the setting was a lodge in the lowveld, the Huntsman was a ranger and Hooding Ride a guest. The grandmother, much to the delight of the staff, was a parody of Gladys Khoza (poacher of fish and cleaner of the village). Bertie did a hilarious job of taking her off and everyone roared with laughter at him. Even Gladys cracked a single-toothed smile in between threatening to behead him.

The ridiculous piece was half in Shangane and half in English with a huge amount of improvisation. The apogee for me was a scene where Hooding Ride was accosted by the hyena for the first time as she rides through the bush on her bike. When I stepped out from behind a pillar, he was genuinely taken aback by my ridiculous costume (a mask hastily cut from a box, the teeth drawn on in black marker pen) and the rest of me covered in a smelly hessian sack. He started laughing and wasn't able to continue with his lines for about five minutes. The audience found SB's hysteria just as funny as he found my get-up.

The traditional children's sports day took place just prior to the play. Elvis's daughter Zodwa cleaned up in the sprints and the egg-and-spoon race. The sack race saw a fist fight between two six-year-olds. The reason for their displeasure was never gleaned and Simone (in charge of proceedings at the athletics for the day) disqualified them from the apple-bobbing for unsporting behaviour. As is traditional, the sporting spectacular culminated in the three-legged race.

This year, I was paired with Rufina from the kitchen. Despite our near victory, the race didn't end well for me. The stars of the event were O'Reilly and Gladys Khoza. These are among the most hot-blooded people at Sasekile. The latter is also the most competitive and the show the two of them put on in their quest for glory was nothing short of epic.

Everyone lined up along the southern end of the soccer field, partners firmly attached by lengths of twine. The bindings were all checked by PJ – he chose his partner (Zodwa) and checked his own bindings which were loose to say the least. He then explained that this year, the race would be two lengths of the field.

As per last year, the General Manager began the race by false starting. The mayhem that ensued was predictable, dangerous and, for the most part, painful. Most of the 80 or so pairs fell over themselves and each other before they could make it twenty metres down the track. Rufina and I skilfully negotiated the turmoil by starting on the far west of the field – almost in the fringing bush.

O'Reilly and Gladys, wearing expressions of grim determination, made sure they started in the middle of the field, jostling their way to the front of the pack before the start. The only rule for this race is that leg bindings must remain in place for the duration. Some people are quite inventive in the way they cheat but none more so than Gladys. In her right hand she carried a hooked stick and by the time she crossed the start line, she'd used it to trip four other pairs. String Bean and Rhandzu (aged thirteen) were her first victims and they failed to make it across the start.

By the halfway mark, the leading group consisted of about twenty pairs with the cheating GM and the lowveld's junior athletics champion in the lead. Rufina and I were somewhere in this group. As soon as we turned for the second length, there was another major scrum as we ran into the rest of the field coming the other way. It was pandemonium. The air was filled with mud, flailing limbs, punches and curses small children shouldn't have heard. It was in this chaos that most of the injuries took place. I copped a horrible blow to the shin from someone's shoe but the adrenaline was such that I didn't notice and Rufina had spotted a chance for victory and the 500-rand prize.

By halfway through the second length there were four pairs left in contention. The GM had long since become too exhausted to continue – he was sitting on a stump on the eastern side of the field. Out front Allegra and Elvis were steaming to victory. They were followed closely by O'Reilly and Gladys who were competing for second with The Legend and Gift (unbelievably agile for someone so rotund) in third place. Just behind them Rufina and I were making excellent progress.

Gladys was swinging at The Legend's heels wildly with her stick. O'Reilly by this stage must have been dangerously close to having a heart attack, so excited had he become by proceedings.

'Get out da way ya fekkers! Hit de fekkers Gladys, hit em so dey never fekken walk again!' he shouted. In his effort to avoid being smacked by Gladys's flailing bushwillow branch, The Legend swerved left – into his partner. Gift, being of the same proportions as a giant beach ball, bounced him straight back and he tripped on the hooked stick. As he fell forward, his shoulder collected Allegra's ankle just in front of him – she and Elvis went down about five metres short of victory leaving just Gladys and O'Reilly competing with me and Rufina still way off to the west.

We gave it a final effort, but the head chef and the village cleaner pipped us to the line. Coming second was the least of my worries, however. The southern edge of the soccer field is not straight and falls away suddenly to the west – into a ditch full of rocks. Rufina and I were concentrating so hard on Gladys and O'Reilly that we careened straight over the edge and into the ditch. My ankle caught between two rocks and there was a nasty tearing sound. My body pitched forward, turned and I landed on my back. Our bindings snapped and Rufina was catapulted into the sandy bottom of the ditch. Jagged rocks pressed up into my flesh but my head mercifully landed in some sand.

I lay there for a moment before the searing agony in my ankle registered. The pain was astonishing and I struggled not to scream as a great crowd arrived to see what was going on. Carrie was first on the scene and she took command. She quickly released my twisted foot. It sprung painfully back into place so at least it wasn't broken but it would bear no weight. String Bean and Carrie then helped me to my one good foot and guided me out of the ditch and back to the staff shop.

I sat down and the ankle swelled up almost immediately. As Carrie tied an ice pack to it, String Bean examined my back which was covered in grazes. Jeff brought me a quart of milk stout. We chinked bottles and raised them towards The Legend who was observing proceedings.

'A toast to our benefactor!' I said.

'Ja cheers, benefit guy!' Jeff chorused.

By the time I'd finished that quart, half another one and three Myprodols, the pain in my ankle was a mere dull ache. We performed the play immediately after a dinner of spit-roasted impala, veggies, potatoes, pap and ice-cream in cones for pudding. After that, the dancing began. The tunes were provided by a DJ from Acornhoek who brought speakers that distorted the music to such an extent that it was difficult to make out what was coming out of them. It made no difference because we could hear the beat and that was all that was required.

Julia arrived just after the sun went down and it was great having her there despite the fact that she spent most of the evening dancing with The Legend – I made sure to buy a lot of drinks for people on his account. I believe Hanro has a greater dislike for Julia than she does for me. This is because she wants The Legend for herself – a pursuit in which I support her wholeheartedly. The most amusing part of the evening was therefore watching Hanro not-so-subtly bumping Julia out of the way and then gyrating her folds in front of The Legend and sweating like an unfit carthorse.

Melissa and Jeff, despite the fact that they've been seeing each other for just over a year, were still publically affectionate to the point of offence – this time on the pool table. Candice, who has been celibate since her leave which ended three days ago, homed in on Brandon. Josta (who runs the staff shop) was highly indignant when she found them enjoying each other on her stock of orange corn chips and crushing them in the process. Simone and SB spent some time chatting to each other under a marula tree but the former went to bed quite early.

I had a good dance with Kerry and the group formed a circle as we twirled around the floor. She really is a great dancer. There was rapturous applause when we'd finished. I then found Allegra and after much cajoling convinced her to take to the floor with me. She began enjoying it after a little while and, because it was the first time anyone had seen her dancing, she was quickly swept into the cheering crowd.

After that it became clear that my ankle was in no state to be receiving the abuse it was and I removed to a bench a little away from the crowd and watched the party progressing – it was already 02h00. Allegra extricated herself from the sweating mass and plonked herself next to me.

'How is your ankle, Angus MacNaughton?' she asked.

'It's actually difficult to tell the difference between that and my back,' I replied.

We looked at each other and then she said, 'Would you like a massage?' I turned to look at her. 'And no, I am not flirting with you.'

'That would be utterly spectacular,' I said. She helped me to stand and we wandered off. It was too far to go to the spa so we just went to my room and while I showered, Allegra fetched some oils. A few minutes later I was face down, on my bed in nothing but my shorts. Allegra found some classical guitar music on my iPod and this mingled with the sound of the night outside. I heard her rubbing oil into her hands, kicking her shoes off and then she shuffled round to my head. Her hands came down on my neck just below the hairline and then slid down either side of my spine. The sensation that shot through my body was so pleasant that I groaned.

'Are you alright?' she asked.

'I will be if you keep doing that.'

The only thing I could see was her feet – neat and high-arched with bright turquoise nail polish – rocking up onto the toes as she stretched forward and then down onto the heels as her fingers rubbed the knots from my neck and spine.

'Cute toes,' I said as her fingers probed the intercostal muscles down either side. 'What would your "I-suppose-it-is-serious friend" in Scotland have to say about your 02h00 massage?'

'No talking,' she replied gently prodding my ribs with a finger. I shuddered and she giggled. That was the last thing I uttered as a feeling of bliss enveloped me. I must have passed out a little while later.

At 05h00 this morning, I woke up, the painkillers and booze all worn off. The fire in my ankle was indescribable to the point of making me see stars. I eventually managed to haul myself onto my one good foot and move to the bathroom. Four glasses of water and three extra-strength Disprin later I fell back into bed, foot raised on a pillow. The pain hardly subsided and I drifted in and out of consciousness. By about 07h00, I was pretty desperate. The ankle was the size of a small soccer ball and my back was also in a bad way– to say nothing of the hangover.

Thankfully, Bertie stuck his head into my room on his way to work. I explained my predicament to him and a little while later there was a knock on the door and it opened.

'Angus MacNaughton,' said Allegra.

'Allegra Gordon,' I replied.

'I believe you are not quite ready for work?' She came in and pulled the covers off my foot. 'No, this will not do. You need an X-ray. Can you move?'

'No, I just want to die,' I moaned. She came round to the front of the bed and put her hand on my forehead.

'I don't think your mortality is in question at this stage,' she said and smiled. Taking a deep breath, I gritted my teeth and she helped me upright and then into the bathroom where I showered and cleaned my teeth. A little while later, Bertie was driving me to the military hospital in Hoedspruit for X-rays and an ultrasound. We returned to the lodge around lunch time with a bag full of pain killers and the news that I have a grade-one ligament tear – nothing too serious. The doctor reckoned most of the damage was done on the dance floor.

I hobbled into the Avuxeni Eatery for my first meal of the day. Just about everyone had left already but Allegra was just finishing her meal. She quizzed me on my visit to the hospital while I consumed a hamburger.

'What time did you leave last night?' I asked.

'I think about a quarter to three,' she replied. 'You ceased being very entertaining company after a little while.'

'That was your fault, you put me to sleep – for which I am grateful.' We looked at each other across the table. Then, suddenly, she looked at her watch.

'Oh shoot, I am late for a massage,' she jumped up and ran out of the eatery.

Week 50

Arabs and accident

One would have thought the arrival of one of the Middle East's richest sons would have provided the bulk of the entertainment for this week but alas this was not the case – I would far rather it had – more on that later.

Sheik Abdul bin Ismail al Maktoum, aged roughly the same as the Great Pyramid, was dreadful and I could not have wished him on a more appropriate person than Hanro. He had every able-bodied person running about after him and his fifteen wives – the youngest of whom should still have been in school.

He was, however, accompanied by one of his 25 (yes 25) sons. Meslar (aged 40) turned out to be a deeply intellectual man with a vast general knowledge and some fascinating opinions on the world. He read engineering at Cambridge, was fascinated by sub-Saharan Africa, and wanted to experience as much as possible during his stay. For the most part, he was mortified by his father's behaviour.

The entourage (60 in all) arrived in various aircraft. My ankle, although still large and unpleasantly coloured, was sufficiently recovered for me to drive a Land Rover so I was at the airstrip with the rest of the staff as the squadron landed. Hanro, sweating with the profusion of the Tsesebe River in full flood, was striding past the front of the neatly-parked Land Rovers holding a clipboard and bellowing orders.

I was sitting somewhere in the middle, my injured foot up on the dashboard.

'Get your fokken foot down!' she yelled at me.

'Hanro, you may notice that my ankle is rather larger than the good Lord intended. It needs to be raised – thus spake the doctor.'

'I don't give a shit who spaked what, it looks fokken unprofessional!'

Before I could answer, Brandon called out, 'Incoming!' as the first plane was sighted. Hanro quickly forgot about my foot and flew into a panic. She charged over to the refreshment table where September, SB, Simone, Melissa and Amber (moping) were waiting with various concoctions and some ice-cold facecloths.

'Fok, quickly, hurry, vis fokken oke's about to arrive!' The camp managers didn't move – they were all quite ready.

The main source of Hanro's concern was the fact that she had no idea which of the four aircraft about to land contained the sheik – she was determined that only she could meet a guest so important. The first plane touched down – a twenty-seater turbo prop. As it came to a halt on the apron the hospitality manager (by this stage, dripping from every pore) waddled over as the door opened. The rangers and trackers (except me and my gammy ankle) moved quickly to the luggage bay and began to unload. Carrie joined Hanro at the bottom of the stairs as the guests emerged. As they descended slowly, another plane of the same size landed. Hanro was frantic about seeing all the guests in the first plane before she moved to the second in case old Abdul should emerge.

The first aircraft disgorged mainly the sheik's staff. Some of them unloaded their hand luggage onto Hanro without greeting her and then made their way to the refreshment table. She was still trying to hand this stuff over when the guests from the second plane began wandering down onto the tarmac. I saw this happening and hobbled over to greet them, which freaked Hanro out even more and she almost redid my ankle in her effort to have at the guests before me. This plane was also staff, most of whom unloaded onto the hospitality manager when they saw me limping.

The next plane of similar size contained the fifteen wives and some security. Hanro repeated her frenzied performance. By this stage her normally spikey hair was plastered to her head with sweat, her white shirt sticking to the dripping folds on her stomach. Old Abdul and Meslar arrived in a small Citation shortly after that. By the time the little jet landed, Hanro had passed out from dehydration. Jamie and Sipho had to drag her behind a termite mound so no one would notice. September put cold towels on her head.

Carrie met His Excellency who barely greeted her before climbing onto his (and only his) Land Rover. With that, the fleet of vehicles departed for the lodge. I was fortunate enough to have Meslar and his security attachment on my vehicle. He was unfazed by the midday heat and it took nearly an hour to drive the short distance back to the lodge because he was so fascinated by everything he saw.

(Hanro was left at the airstrip by mistake and it wasn't until PJ asked after her once all the guests were settled in their rooms that we drew straws for going to fetch her. The Legend pulled the shortest one which made me laugh a lot.)

The group demanded that their food be prepared by their imported chefs. O'Reilly met them all on the Main Camp deck and took them into the kitchen to make lunch. The meals, until the last night, went off without a hitch although a number of the security detail took O'Reilly aside and asked him to make them bacon for breakfast.

After our jaunt down from the airstrip, Meslar insisted on driving with me for the duration of his stay. This suited me as we got on like a house on fire. For the first three days, Meslar, Elvis and I went out into the bush alone where the prince sucked up information like a sponge – trees, invertebrates, mammals, birds, geology – he was fascinated by the lot.

The highlight of our time in the wilderness came on the third evening. Meslar had enjoyed a massage with Allegra at lunch time and he insisted that she join on us on game drive. I was surprised to see her on the Rhino Camp deck at tea time, a pair of binoculars round her neck and a bird book in her hand.

'Good afternoon Angus,' she said.

'Good afternoon Allegra,' I replied, 'what are you doing down here?'

'After his massage today, Meslar asked me if I would like to accompany him on game drive.'

'He did, did he?' I raised my eyebrows.

'No, not like that,' she said evenly.

'Oh, why not?'

'Because he told me not like that.'

'Ah, I see.' A black-headed oriole called its liquid song. Allegra's eyes smiled.

'You aren't jealous are you?'

'Of him and the pasty one?' I replied dryly. 'You had your hands all over my body the other day – now I find you've been doing the same with Meslar. I thought I was special.'

'I have to confess,' she took a step forward and then whispered, 'Meslar was one of many.'

'No!'

Before this exchange could continue, Meslar and his father swooped down onto the deck. The sheik ignored us all and demanded some sort of delicacy from one of his chefs. Meslar didn't have anything and in a few minutes, we were out in the bush.

It was a hot afternoon, with a deep-blue sky, dotted with tall puffy clouds. A storm gathered far over the mountains as we drove west through a grove of mopane trees where the new leaves of the season diffused into dapples of tannin-red and, closer to the ground, summer-green. A myriad cicadas sang in the foliage above, drowning the sound of the engine. We were silent, each of us wrapped in a sense of peace and wonder as the Land Rover eased through the spicy sweet scent of the mopane. Out of the grove, we made for a little-visited waterhole on the far western boundary of the reserve. Elvis and I didn't really have a specific plan for the afternoon but I knew we'd see bits and pieces that interested Meslar.

On the way there, Meslar asked if we might spend a bit of time on foot. My ankle was sufficiently recovered to acquiesce and we stopped about twenty minutes' walk from the waterhole. The essence of wild aniseed and saffron crushed underfoot drifted up and mingled with clean air and the vague hint of Allegra's Coco Chanel.

Halfway there, Elvis held his hand up and pointed at the ground. We were crossing a well-worn animal path and there were very fresh rhino tracks heading towards the water. I explained the need for quiet to Meslar and Allegra and then we proceeded in silence. As soon as we were in sight of the pan, Elvis once again held up his hand in the freeze position – he pointed to a muddy section shaded by a low-hanging red ivory tree. A huge rhino bull lay snoring in the mud, totally oblivious to us. Every time he exhaled, bits of mud sprayed out from below his nostrils.

We were standing in the shade of a false marula thicket. In the middle of it, an old trunk lay perpendicular to the other stems about two feet off the ground – a perfect bench. I indicated for everyone to be very quiet and we threaded our way through stems to the bench, being very careful not to snap any twigs or crunch the leaves underfoot. There we sat in a line, Elvis on the far left, then Meslar, Allegra and me. We faced east, the late afternoon behind us. It was the perfect cover.

After a few minutes Elvis made a clicking sound with his teeth and pointed across the waterhole into the clearing beyond. At the far side, another three rhino were approaching for their evening drink. The three of them (a cow, her year-old calf and a sub-adult bull) approached with caution. It took the slumbering bull until they reached the edge to react to their presence although their caution indicated that they were fully aware of him. As he woke, the big bull stood quickly, which frightened the others, but after he and the cow puffed at each other, ears pricked forward, the tension dissipated and they all drank.

We watched them for almost an hour – wallowing, drinking and scratching themselves on the surrounding stumps. Eventually, as the sun was about to set, all four rhino grazed off east into the clearing. A white-browed scrub-robin called its evening rattle from the middle of the thicket. I was happy. A single tear made its way down Meslar's cheek and into his beard and Elvis looked even more chilled out than normal.

Allegra turned to look at me. The olive skin of her face glowed in the last of the sun's light, her grey eyes shone and her dark red lips smiled. The overpowering desire to lean towards her and kiss her was broken by Elvis sliding off his perch to the left of us.

'Sun is setting now,' he said, 'time to go.' We made our way back to the vehicle in silence. Allegra sat next to me on the way home.

Back at the lodge, things weren't progressing with the same peaceful ease of my game drive. I dropped Meslar off at Rhino Camp and then headed to the kitchen to drop off the cooler box. O'Reilly's domain was twice as full as normal because of the number of chefs the sheik had brought with him. The head chef, as has been the case for much of his life, was dangerously close to apoplexy.

He was wagging his finger in one of the guest chef's faces, 'You moost be fekken out of ya desert-cooked fekkin moind. We don't surrve gorts here!'

The short chef, clearly not used to being verbally assaulted by anyone other than his employer, slapped O'Reilly's hand away and then began yelling in Arabic. Halfway through his diatribe, O'Reilly said, 'Oi don't understand one fekkin wurrd you just said ya stchoopid fekker but it better not have had anyting te do wit gorts if you tink yu're gonna murrrder dat ting in here!' The Arab then took a swing, which the Irishman ducked, grabbing his diminutive attacker by the throat and pushing him up against the wall. PJ arrived in the kitchen.

'What the hell is going on in here?' the GM asked O'Reilly.

The head chef turned to his employer, his grip still firmly around the Arab's windpipe. 'Dis stchoopid fekker tinks he's going te be cooking gort meat fur dat crazy fekkin Bedouin!'

'A goat?'

'Dat's what I said, a fekking gort!'

'O'Reilly, he's not breathing. Let him go,' PJ observed. O'Reilly released his by-now red-faced and choking counterpart. 'We don't have goat meat lying about do we?'

'NO, I don't keep fekking gort meat around! It's fekkin inedible!'

'Well, where does he plan to get it?' At that point, the unmistakable sound of bleating touched our ears. Everyone looked towards the coldroom.

'What the hell is that?'

'It's de fekkin queen modder returned from de dead! Whut de fek da ye tink it is?!' PJ became irritated with his chef.

'O'Reilly calm down and do not talk to me like that,' he said firmly. 'I can hear it's a goat — how did it arrive in the coldroom?'

'Dis, fe…fella put it in dere,' he snarled at the Arab. 'How de fek he got it, Oi've no idea!'

There was silence as the bizarreness of the situation permeated the kitchen. Gift stepped forward.

'I saw Incredible with a goat a little bit earlier.' At this utterance, Richard, Jane, Rufina and Kerry started giggling. PJ rolled his eyes heavenward.

'Go and get him,' said PJ through gritted teeth to no one in particular. Seeing a chance to ingratiate myself, I made for the door of the kitchen and PJ added, 'And bring someone who can translate.'

I found the moronic butler fishing for candles in the storeroom, grabbed him by the elbow and marched for the kitchen. On the way, we passed one of the security detail I'd heard speaking English. He said he would gladly translate.

From the Arab chef, via the translator, we managed to glean that boiled goat and yoghurt sauce is the sheik's most favourite thing in the world. His Excellency demanded it on his last night. The chef, rightfully fearing for his job, sought help and found it with Incredible. He parted with a few hundred dollars and Incredible (who was pale by this stage of the story) phoned a friend and smuggled it onto the reserve through a hole in the fence.

There was silence before O'Reilly added, 'Well Oi'm not havin dat fekkin ting killed in here!'

'I'm afraid the ultimate decision for that lies with me,' said PJ. He turned to Incredible. 'Open the door and get that thing out of there before it destroys our entire coldroom stock.' Incredible looked like he might protest but PJ was having none of it. 'Now!' he snapped. The kitchen went silent as Incredible approached the reverberating door. The butler pulled the latch and the door burst open as the animal flew out into the kitchen.

It wasn't a small goat. In fact, as African billy-goats go, it was huge and it was very angry at being locked up in the coldroom. The first people it saw were O'Reilly and the Arab chef (what with Incredible dazed and peeling himself off the wall behind the fridge door). It ducked its head and charged.

'Feeehk!' yelled O'Reilly vaulting onto a small piece of counter. His counterpart made for the same narrow surface. They both narrowly avoided having their shins smashed to pieces by the irate little bovid. As they moved, the door to the lowveld presented itself and into the night the goat ran, blissfully free and equally blissfully unaware that his domestic instincts were unlikely to see him through the night.

As the goat escaped, the two chefs fell onto the floor and resumed wrestling. PJ instructed Richard and I to tear them apart, which we managed to do before any further damage could be done. I left to change just after that.

Dinner was some fairly rank mutton which apparently passed as bad goat — not that goat can be anything but.

Allegra and I were the only Sasekile staff sitting for dinner — this because Meslar asked if we would join him. The sheik felt it beneath him to eat with the 'servants' as he grouped all the Sasekile staff. Hanro was on point to host and it peeved her no end to be part of the crew serving me dinner — especially when Meslar asked why she hadn't offered me a drink. Other than the 'goat', the dinner was edible. Conversation between Meslar, Allegra and I flowed easily and we drank a good deal of the excellent wine which Meslar selected from the list. SB was on hand as the sommelier because it was found that, contrary to her claims, Hanro knows nothing about wine and in fact the only thing I've ever seen her drink is Coke — often with lashings of brandy.

My brother did a great job. With new-found humility, he explained the estates that the eight bottles came from and then gave an excellent description of the wines. The sheik managed the first 'thank you' of his stay after SB delivered his address on the Viognier we drank with the starter.

Just after the main course, I excused myself to go to the loo. SB joined me and instead of going to the ablutions we wandered a little way out of the camp and into the car park. We were relieving ourselves and chuckling at Hanro's antics when there was a terrible scream. The high-pitched voice made my blood run cold ... it belonged to my sister.

SB had his torch with him so we ran in the direction of the noise. A scream like that, although indicating distress, also means life. When it stopped, I was gripped with nauseating fear. The sound had come from somewhere near The Legend's house. From the open space of the car park, we turned onto the path that leads to his residence. It's not clever to run along that path at night because the bush is thick on either side and it winds around so you can never really see much. Neither of us thought about this, however, as we charged to our sister. The one thing I did notice was the very obvious dairy smell – the unmistakable odour of buffalo. My fear for the fate of Julia ramped up.

In a minute or two we'd reached the open area in front of The Legend's room. The sight that greeted us was harrowing. Julia was lying in a heap in the moonlight. She was clearly not conscious, face-down in a puddle, her shattered right femur protruding from the skin. Even in the dim light, it was obvious there was a tremendous amount of bleeding. I ran over to where she was lying, forcing down the rising panic.

The first priority was to take her head out of the puddle. I was loathe to move her because of the risk of spinal injury but she had to breathe. I needed help. SB, however, was in a state of shock. He just stared.

'String Bean,' I called softly at first. Then I shouted, 'String Bean get over here now.' He moved over dumbly. 'Get to her hips and when I say now you turn her over to the left, understand?' Still gasping, he nodded. 'Right, one, two, three.' I held her shoulders and head as still as possible and we turned her over onto her back. The broken limb dragged behind and moving her made the bleeding much worse. SB vomited.

'String Bean, get into the house and fetch a pillow.' He nodded, stopped retching and ran for the house. The door was locked but without flinching he kicked it in. With the hand not cradling my sister's bloodied head, I felt for a pulse.

There wasn't one. Again panic threatened to overwhelm me.

SB returned with a pillow. I laid Julia's head down.

'There's no pulse and she's not breathing,' I said. String Bean stared at me. 'We have to give her CPR.' He nodded.

My brother and I then set about trying to save our sister.

I compressed her chest and he filled her lungs with air. Every time he gave her two breaths, I checked for a pulse. I don't know how long we were at it. Time blurred and memories flooded my consciousness – Julia, aged about five, pushing her pram full of soft toys. Julia having a tea party with her dolls in the Wendy house. Julia, SB and I building sand castles on the beach. Julia dressed for her first social. Julia comforting SB when he grazed his knee on the driveway falling off his skateboard. Julia in her first school uniform. Julia learning to ride her bike on the lawn. Mum, Dad, Julia, SB and I on the boat in Kenton.

I looked at my brother. Tears were streaming down his face as he stared into our sister's lifeless face. Still we carried on, without speaking, without wanting to acknowledge what was happening.

When I thought about fighting with her earlier in the year, tears began to stream out of my eyes as well. Still my brother and I, crying freely, persisted with the CPR.

It was only then that I noticed The Legend lying about five metres away. He was just coming round. He sat up, staggered and shook his head.

'Jones!' I shouted through the tears. He looked up. 'Jones, where is your radio?!' He didn't react immediately. 'Jones, get your radio now!' His head cleared sufficiently and he realised what we were doing. He made to speak. 'Get your fucking radio right now!' I shouted again. The Legend staggered into his room and retrieved his radio. He was so groggy he could hardly speak. I grabbed the radio from him as SB breathed into Julia again.

'Jones, you have to help Julia breathe.' He looked at her. 'Do you understand?' He nodded. 'String Bean, take over from me.' SB came to her chest while The Legend took over the breathing.

I turned the radio on and prayed like mad that Carrie would be on air. The head ranger answered immediately. I swallowed back the bile and forced myself not to look at The Legend and SB.

'There is an emergency at Jones's house. Julia has been hit by a buffalo, her femur is broken and she is not breathing.'

'Copy. Stand by,' she said calmly and I knew she'd be running around like a mad thing. I knelt back down and checked Julia's pulse. Still nothing. String Bean was tiring so I took over from him. At that moment, there was a commotion on the path behind us and a small crowd of people burst onto the scene – Allegra, Johnson the Rhino Camp security guard, Themba and Meslar. Johnson had clearly heard my call to Carrie. He told Allegra, Meslar overheard and they all ran to assist. Carrie arrived almost simultaneously from the other side with Jacob, Bertie, a backboard and a first-aid kit. For the first time since I'd know her, she froze, staring at the protruding femur.

'Stop the bleeding in the leg,' I snapped at her and she went to it.

'They won't send a plane at night,' she said, 'we're going to have to drive her.' Meslar stepped forward.

'If I may,' he said kneeling down, 'our aircraft are still here. I can pilot the jet – with a moon like this, I am confident I can do it.'

'Thank you,' I said. The prince stood and disappeared with Johnson.

I checked her pulse again – and there it was, faint, but her heart was beating.

Meanwhile, Carrie had dispatched Bertie to round up the rangers so that they could light the runway with Land Rover headlights. We moved Julia onto the backboard carefully and then Jacob and I carried her to a waiting vehicle in the Rhino Camp car park. Meslar arrived at the same time carrying a bag of whatever he needed to fly us out.

A few minutes later we were on the airstrip, the rangers positioned at intervals all the way up. We gently eased Julia into the Citation. When the door closed, Meslar was in the cockpit firing up the little jet's engines. The Legend, who was bleeding from a deep gash above his right eye, was sitting groggily, being attended to by Carrie. SB made up the remainder of the crew and in very little time we were airborne. Julia was spread across two seats and I sat at her head, checking her pulse which was still very faint and erratic. The bleeding from her mangled leg had stopped.

We were advised to fly straight through to Nelspruit given the extent of the injuries and specialists required. About twenty minutes later, Meslar landed and we handed Julia and her concussed and bleeding Legend over to the paramedics. We then watched the flashing lights and sirens disappear towards the hospital. There was silence as we stood there on the airstrip and I remember hearing frogs calling – bubbling cassinas and painted reed frogs – as we made our way to the small terminal building. PJ had phoned ahead to a Sasekile supplier who met us and then drove us to the hospital. Our little crew certainly drew a lot of attention as we walked into the hospital – SB and I muddied with quite a lot of Julia's blood on our clothes, Meslar dressed in his white thobe and keffiyeh and Carrie in a pair of rugby shorts and a T-shirt (her standard sleepwear).

The worst part of an incident like this is the waiting. We sat in the waiting area for about an hour. All we knew was that Julia was having her head and leg scanned. A nurse came through to tell us that they couldn't operate on the femur because she wasn't in a state to cope with an anaesthetic. While we waited, Carrie went through to the general ward to check on The Legend. He had a concussion but nothing too serious although they wanted to keep him under observation for the night.

Meslar went off to buy us all coffee and it was only then that I realised I had better speak to Mum and Dad. Before that, however, SB needed some help. He was sitting in a corner, eyes glazed. Meslar arrived presently and we added four sugars to SB's coffee and took it over to him.

'String Bean, you need to drink this,' I held out the cup.

He didn't look at it and tears started flowing from his eyes again. His lips turned down and quivered as he spoke, 'What's going to happen to Julia?' he sniffed. I bit my lip, forcing my own tears back. I placed the coffee next to him on the floor and squatted down.

'I don't know, String Bean but she's with the doctors now and we need to be as positive as we can. You are in shock so you must try to drink this.' I handed him the coffee and he took it. 'We just have to focus on one thing at a time, okay? You finish this and soon they'll come and tell us what's going on.' He sniffed and nodded.

I then went over to the desk and asked to use a phone. Being a privately-run business far more than a place of care, the hospital has a strict no-phone calls policy. The highly-efficient and personality-bereft administrator gave me directions to the pay phone in the corridor. I didn't have any money with me so I had to borrow some from Meslar who was only too happy to oblige.

It was almost midnight when the Kenton phone rang. After about ten rings, my father's sleepy voice answered.

'Dad, it's Angus,' I began. 'Julia's been in an accident. She's alive but badly injured. We're not sure of the extent just yet but she's in hospital in Nelspruit.' I said all that slowly and as calmly as I could and then added, 'I think you and Mum need to get up here as soon as possible.' There was a short silence.

'What happened to her?' My father asked.

'She and Alistair were hit by a buffalo but he is not really in a state to talk about it just yet. He's okay but concussed.'

'Right. We'll get on a flight tomorrow morning.' Before he rang off he said 'Are you and Hugh okay?'

I bit back the tears again.

'A bit shocked but we'll be fine. Just come quick.' I gave him the hospital phone number and then hung up.

Not too long after that, a nurse came through to call us to Julia's bedside. SB and I went into the ICU and there was our precious sister, unconscious, with machines beeping in the background. The trauma specialist was standing at her bedside. He explained that she was breathing on her own and her heartbeat was much stronger and more regular. The scans of her head revealed no major bruising – it seemed she'd hit the side of her head on the ground rather than being crowned by the buffalo, so her skull was fully intact. She said they needed to operate on the leg as soon as possible to prevent infection but that they couldn't do this until Julia was more stable.

There was nothing left but to find a place to sleep for the night. Carrie had organised us some rooms in a budget road lodge around the corner but Meslar refused to allow that and insisted on putting us all up at a five-star boutique hotel. It was something of a comfort to walk into the softly-lit and beautifully-appointed room. I told SB to have a shower – we were both still covered in grime. He went into the bathroom and shut the door.

As I sat down on the bed, the phone next to the bed rang.

'Hello,' I said.

'Hello Angus,' said Allegra and then there was a pause. 'Are you alright?'

Hearing her voice made my emotions explode and I bit my lip hard as a tear escaped.

'I'm okay thanks,' I said.

'How is Julia?' I took a deep breath and gave her a brief summary of things.

It was tremendously comforting to hear her voice. She asked about SB and The Legend. I explained their situation and then asked her about things at the lodge, wanting her to remain on the line for as long as possible. Eventually SB came out of the bathroom and I felt awkward.

'I have to go now,' I said.

'Well, sleep well and ... I am thinking of you ...' She hung up.

I had a long shower and while I dried myself I heard SB crying on the phone. I was initially irritated thinking that he shouldn't be freaking our parents out further but it soon became apparent he was talking to Simone.

'I know, I know,' he sniffed, 'it's just really shit.' There was a pause as she comforted him on the other end. 'Thanks for calling,' he snuffled, 'it means so much to me.' His tears began again. I went about my ablutions methodically which helped take my mind off things and when I emerged from the bathroom he was asleep.

I woke with the dawn. SB, I suspect from the shock, was still in a deep slumber. After a glass of water I phoned Dad's cellphone. They were on their way to Port Elizabeth and said they'd be in Nelspruit by the afternoon. I told them to keep safe and then made some coffee. As I depressed the plunger, there was a gentle knock at the door. Meslar walked in bearing a bag of toiletries for us. His kindness was quite overwhelming.

We shared the coffee on the east-facing balcony, the sun just rising. It was only just after 05h00 and still a good two hours before we'd be able to visit Julia. Meslar took my mind off the medical scenarios by telling me stories about his prized stable of Arabs — bred for desert endurance racing. He kept me occupied until it was time for a shower, some breakfast and the return to the hospital.

When we arrived, the ICU sister told us that Julia was in theatre having her leg operated on. Apparently they decided they couldn't wait any longer and still be able to save the leg.

More interminable waiting.

Two hours later, the doctor called SB and I. The leg was set and she was stable but heavily sedated. He let us see her and there seemed to be more colour in her unconscious face. We left her after half an hour or so.

Before returning to the hotel, I needed to do something. I walked through to the general ward, fully intending to tell The Legend that I blamed him for what had happened — I wanted to know how on Earth he'd failed to see a 600 kg buffalo. I wanted to shit on him for being a prick whose arrogance and complacency had nearly killed (and might still kill) my sister. As I wandered down the sanitised corridors, the anger built and by the time I turned into the ward, my whole body was seething. The five-bed ward was empty but for The Legend, lying as he was in the foetal position, facing the window. As I drew up to deliver my scalding greeting, I noticed his whole body shaking. I thought maybe he was having a fit of some sort but it quickly became apparent that he was wracked with sobs. He turned his head as he heard my footsteps and then returned his gaze to the window.

'I've killed her, haven't I?' he said. 'God I don't know how I didn't see it.' I stood there and stared at him and slowly the anger drew back and, to my eternal surprise, it was replaced by something approaching sympathy. I swallowed hard and then, gritting my teeth, I put my hand on his shoulder.

'It's not your fault, Jones, I saw your torch lying in the mud . . . it could have happened to anyone.' I swallowed again. 'No one can blame you. She's out of theatre and looks much better now. She's not out of the woods yet but they say the worst is over.' He cheered up a bit and then turned over and looked at me.

'Thank you, that means a lot.' I nodded, lips pursed.

'You just get better,' I said turning around.

Mum and Dad arrived around 15h00 this afternoon. About twenty minutes before that, Julia regained consciousness. She remained heavily sedated but managed a smile at the concerned faces of her family. Our mother was very calm although I know she was dying inside. Dad was controlled but obviously shocked by the state of his daughter. Meslar left around lunch time – he had to return to fetch his father and the rest of the entourage. He paid the hotel for the next four nights.

By the time we left Julia this evening, she was talking and the doctors said there was nothing to worry about. The relief was profound. String Bean was much better by the evening too and we managed to have a scotch at the bar together before bed. We shared our impressions of what had happened and were thoroughly drunk by the time we fell into bed.

Tomorrow is Christmas Eve.

Week 51

Allegra and ascension

Julia spent almost a week in the Nelspruit hospital before Mum and Dad could take her home. Jones was discharged soon after I saw him. He returned to the lodge to recuperate and, from what I could glean, spent most of his time on the phone to my sister.

The MacNaughtons experienced Christmas Eve in the hospital. Julia was moved to a general ward and we celebrated with a foul takeaway meal which Dad supplemented with the hospital-issue jelly and custard that Julia had rejected. SB and I had to return to the lodge on Boxing Day but Julia was recovering well. Mum and Dad took her home three days later and they're all returning to Kenton soon for some well-earned rest. (Trubshaw is still at the coast and the neighbours who naively offered to look after him are on the verge of feeding him to a shark.)

Two other noteworthy things occurred this week – the one fairly predictable and the other unexpected in the extreme.

SB and I arrived back just after dark. Rain was heaving out of the sky and the power was out again. I returned to my room and then just as quickly realised I didn't want to be there. I walked back out into the deluge, already drenched and made my way down through the front of the village. My feet sloshed past the back of the kitchen and on to the little building between Tamboti and Main Camps. Soft candle light flickered in the windows and lightning split the sky overhead.

She was standing barefoot on her toes on the little balcony that hangs precariously out over the river, leaning on the balustrade. Her hand extended out beyond the leaking shelter offered by a thick mahogany tree, catching the rain. She turned and smiled as my feet touched the wooden decking behind her. Without a word, I walked over, took her face in my hands and kissed her. Her lips parted immediately and she slipped her arms round my waist. We remained in the embrace as the intensity of the rain increased. Eventually, she broke away and pulled me into the spa. The smell of the vanilla candles mixed with the rain outside while flames danced across the walls in the breeze.

Allegra handed me a robe and said, 'Angus MacNaughton, you are sopping wet.'

While I replaced my soaking clothes with the robe I asked, 'So, what of the pasty one?'

'He and I had a conversation about a week ago. Probably our last.' She returned with a bottle of Aberlour fifteen-year-old. 'I bought this for you for Christmas. I hope it is a good one.' I took the bottle with one hand, put the other one round her waist and pulled her close.

'It's magnificent and very kind,' I said.

There's a wide white sofa in the spa waiting room and on this we lay entwined until we'd drunk our fill and the candles had eventually flickered out.

The next day, PJ called a meeting about the new head ranger. Carrie was to leave in a few days' time and there was still no replacement. The General Manager arrived a little late and the room was abuzz with expectation. Jones was sitting on one of the sofas, sporting a black eye, crutches and a limp, but otherwise he was fine.

'Right, let's get straight to it,' said PJ. 'Normally, as you know, we hold an interview process for the head ranger position. Carrie, however, felt that the rangers, trackers and conservation crew should vote this time around. I'm not convinced this is the best route to take but I am going to allow it – on the understanding that it is still my prerogative to remove the new head ranger if he isn't performing.' Murmurs went around the room. 'It will work as follows: I will ask for nominations. These will then be written on the board and we will vote by a show of hands.' He went over to the whiteboard and took up a marker. 'Right, nominations are open.' Duncan raised his hand.

'I'd like to nominate Jonesy.' PJ nodded and wrote Jones's name on the board.

'I'd like to nominate Sipho,' said Jamie.

'Well, I'd like to nominate Jamie,' said Sipho. Everyone giggled. PJ allowed ten minutes for any further nominations.

'Right, voting will now commence,' he announced. 'All those in favour of Alistair, please raise your hands.' As he finished the sentence, Jones struggled to his feet using his crutches.

'Hang on a second,' he began, 'there's someone missing from that list.' The room stared at him. We were all convinced he wanted the job more than anything.

PJ sighed. 'Well?' he asked, 'don't keep us all in suspense.'

'I'm nominating Angus MacNaughton.'

'What?' exclaimed PJ and I together.

'I know this may come as a bit of a surprise but you all need to hear me out on this. Angus can be,' he paused, 'well a prick, basically, we all know that.' There was a murmur of assent from the room.

'I assume there's a "but" coming somewhere,' said PJ, becoming slightly exasperated.

'There is,' said Jones. 'He's also consistent and he has the balls to stand up for what he believes. He released that elephant. Quite apart from the fact that he nearly got Bertie and Allegra killed, he knew he could lose his job but he made a choice based on his convictions. Kerry confessed something to me the other day which I think I can share in the present company. It was Angus who got rid of that shit that Abbot was using to rip off the staff.' He then swallowed hard. 'And he showed unbelievable calmness and leadership under pressure during...' his voice cracked a little, '...during the accident last week.' He took a few breaths.

'And in case anyone should forget, he took on the task that everyone else thought was totally hopeless – training Jeff.' He turned to Jeff. 'No offence, bru, but shit, you were bad.' Everyone laughed and he continued. 'Angus not only took it on but thanks to him, Jeff actually takes game drives today.

We're going to have a lot of new guys next year and Angus is just the guy to do their training.' PJ, wide-eyed, turned to the board and my name was added to the list.

There was great murmuring in the room when Jones sat down. My face flushed, I didn't know what to think.

'I'm going to leave the room for you lot to think about this and discuss it for a while,' said PJ. I didn't want to discuss anything so I just went to the loo. When I returned, Jones was standing under the buffalo thorn tree that shades the area between the rangers' room and the office, leaning on his crutches.

'Why did you do that?' I asked.

'For the reasons I gave,' he said. He picked a leaf absently and then looked at me. 'And because I know you wanted to blame me for Julia and you didn't. Instead, somehow you managed to comfort me ... Situations reversed, I don't think I could ever have done that.' His voice cracked again.

A little while later we were all back in the rangers' room. As PJ was about to begin the voting process, Jacob stood up and with Sipho as his translator he said, 'Wait. There is no need for voting. We have decided. Angus is the one we have chosen.' My face flushed afresh. I had never won any kind of popularity contest – not ever. PJ looked around the room.

'Is there anyone here, other than me, who thinks this might not be the best idea in the world?'

Jamie stood up. 'No, it's unanimous.'

PJ went quite pale as he stared at the assembled field team.

'Right, well I guess I'd better re-employ him then.' He walked over to me and shook my hand. 'Don't make a mess of this.' There was a hint of a smile on his face as he walked out of the door. Then everyone started clapping, cheering and patting me on the back. Carrie embraced me bodily and squeezed the wind out of me.

'I'm so glad about this,' she said. 'It's just what you and this place need.'

Everyone eventually filed out and I was left alone with Jones who had returned to his place on the sofa. I walked over and sat opposite him.

'I'm still mildly confused,' I said.

'About what?' He hauled himself to his feet again and leant on his crutches. 'I would have liked the job a year ago but I'm not sure how long I'm going to be around. The last few weeks have made me think about things, and besides, I'll probably want to spend a bit more time in Johannesburg now.' I nodded. 'I hope that's not going to be an issue anymore.'

'Oh, I think I'll manage.' I stood up and held out my hand. 'Thank you,' I said. Jones transferred his crutch and took my hand firmly.

'I didn't do you a favour. I meant what I said.' Just before he limped out into the sun, he turned. 'I have to tell you I'm bloody glad this year is nearly finished – your and Jeff's bar bills have put a serious dent in my pocket. That said, every time I've had to pay the damn thing, I've felt bad about being so rough about him.'

Week 52

Well and wilderness

It's New Year's Eve and I am without guests this evening. Instead of eating in the boma, I will be attending the staff party in the Twin Palms. I write this from the desk in my room, looking out onto the mopane tree, full of rich green leaves, and the knobthorn tree — both of them bathed in soft blue moonlight mixed with the yellow glow from my room. Allegra is lying on my bed, leafing through a book on evolutionary psychology. She's in her navy-blue party dress — the one that she thinks hugs her figure a bit closely but that I think is just right. She has on some burgundy lipstick and dark eye make up. I look over at her and the grey eyes twinkle back at me.

Allegra makes me happy.

The only slight damper to my mood is that Carrie and Jane depart tomorrow and I shall miss them both, especially my old boss. During the last week, I've had moments when I fear that I'll bugger up all the good work that Carrie's done. A few days ago, when my self-doubt was threatening to become a panic attack, I received this message from my father.

To: Angus Mac Naughton
From: Dad Mac Naughton
Subject: Coming of age

Dear Angus,

I hope this finds you basking in the afterglow of your election.

I wanted to say how very proud your mother and I are of you. All reports suggest that you handled the night of Julia's accident with phenomenal skill. Your brother says your sister would be dead had it not been for your clear thinking and ability to stay calm.

Secondly, I do not recall your ever having been elected by your peers for anything. That you have been chosen to lead the field team at Sasekile fills me with pride because it shows that you have matured enormously. I have no doubt it will be a huge challenge for you but I have faith that you have become sufficiently self-examining to be able to modify your methods as required.

We look forward to seeing you soon.

Love from us both,
Dad

This encouraging missive was sent from Kenton where the family, but for SB and I, is now well ensconced. Julia is pretty much immobile but recovering well. I imagine it will be some time before she is fit for work. I received this from her earlier today.

To: Angus
From: Julia MacNaughton
Subject: Thank you

Hello Angus,

I am writing this from the veranda in Kenton. Mum has been fussing over me as you can imagine. My leg, in full cast, has been carefully balanced on the low table in front of me and there is a medicinal G&T on a stool next to me. My leg still aches a lot but it's bearable now and I'm getting pretty nimble on my crutches.

The sun is shining, there is hardly any wind, and the sky is that glorious late-afternoon blue. Trubshaw is asleep next to me, snoring gently, the edge of one of Mum's hand-embroidered throw cushions between his lips. AIDS Cat is watching some tiny birds eating from the seed dispenser. (I think they are called manakins). Mum and Dad have retreated for the afternoon siesta and the Major is in a gin-induced coma.

I just wanted to say how amazing I think you and Hugh were on that truly dreadful night. I hardly remember anything about it but I know that I have the two of you to thank for the fact that I'm even able to write this (tears dripping on to the keyboard as I write). Alistair says that you were completely calm and showed the kind of mettle and leadership that he says he wishes he had (told you he's not so bad). Anyway, I am incredibly grateful and so very proud to have a brother like you (more tears).

I also want to congratulate you on your election as the new head ranger – it makes me so happy for you. Fantastic news!

Anyway, tonight is New Year's Eve and I will be staying at home but some friends of mine are in town and have kindly agreed to come round and drink the New Year in with a cripple.

Thank you again and I trust there will be something fun going on there tonight.

Lots and lots of love,
Jules

P.S. Word on the bush telegraph is that you have a female friendie
to share the New Year with!

Arthur also sent me a congratulatory mail – from a resort in the Caribbean
where Mavis's family have taken them to escape the winter for a few weeks.

This afternoon, in lieu of a farewell, Carrie organised a group of us to go
into the bush – SB, Elvis, Kerry, Bertie, Jane, O'Reilly, Sipho, Jacob, Allegra,
Jones and even PJ. I drove us to the far northern boundary where there's
a dolerite outcrop. From the rocks, the view extends out west towards the
mountains and we spread out on the rocks, facing the sunset. PJ brought
three bottles of Veuve Clicquot and when we all had a glass, Carrie stood
up and made a short speech. She thanked everyone for making her time
at Sasekile so meaningful and said how much she and Jane were looking
forward to their new challenge. Then she took up her spotless rifle and
turned to me.

'This rifle was handcrafted for Dennis Hogan's father in 1925 and since
his family bought this land just after that, it has been assigned by the person
in charge of the field team. Its enormous value symbolises the importance
of your job as the custodian of this wilderness.'

She unlocked the bolt, slid it back, checked the chamber and handed it
to me. I took it, rechecked the chamber and closed the bolt.

'Thank you,' I replied, 'I hope I will do the job half as much justice as
you did.'

PJ then raised his glass. 'Congratulations Angus. Despite your very
chequered history, I look forward to working with you next year. I'm
hoping the extra responsibility will keep you on the straight and narrow.
May the future be full of adventures and devoid of disciplinaries.' Everyone
chuckled and a chorus of congratulations went up.

O'Reilly added, 'Ah well, fekken muurvelues dis. Congratulations
Ungus. Ull de best te ya and Currie and ull de rest of oos!' There was more
clapping and everyone had another drink. He and Kerry were sitting next

to each other, comfortably close. I doubt whether anything romantic will transpire between them but it's not beyond the realm of possibility. I'll have to quiz her soon.

After two glasses, I climbed to the top of the rocks and over to the other side of the outcrop. I leant against an old star chestnut tree and looked east into the great expanse of the Kruger National Park. A movement in the dry drainage line below arrested my attention – I couldn't see what it was for the thick riverine vegetation. Then there was a rustle from the behind me. It was Allegra. She put her arms round my waist and her head on my shoulder.

'Are you alright?' she asked. At that moment, a bull elephant broke cover in the drainage line. He was about 40 metres away, his right side facing us. Then he stopped and turned to look up. His left tusk was broken halfway down. A deep rumble emanated from Mitchell. Then he snorted once and ambled off.

'Perfect,' I replied putting my arm round her and kissing the top of her head, 'just perfect.'

Acknowledgements

The Gatesian wealth and bodyguard-demanding fame that comes with publishing a book does not come without a lot of help from many people. While it is my name that appears on the front of this pile of pages, the creation before you has been a collective effort by many humans.

I am eternally grateful to Pan Macmillan for agreeing to publish me a second time. To Terry Morris and Andrea Nattrass for taking the risk on this and the latter for her brilliant guidance and encouragement through the whole process; Laura Hammond for her sterling, original and tireless publicity efforts; Wesley Thompson for his scary proofreading skills; and Sharon Dell for editing.

I should also like to thank my parents for funding most of my education. I hated writing and was terrible at it when I left school but despite this, they have been a constant source of encouragement. Indeed, my father has tirelessly read and critiqued just about every word I have ever written. Likewise, my sister Kathryn made very valuable suggestions during the process of this book's creation and added her touch to Julia's letters. From the lofty altitudes of high finance, my brother Douglas continues to encourage his volatile brother unflinchingly.

Then to the friends, family and colleagues who have shared their lives, stories, suggestions, titbits and given pieces of themselves to some of the characters (often unwittingly) in these pages – specifically Graeme, Mike, Scott, Derek Jax, Hobb James, Duncan, Elvis, Alex, Michelle, Jilly

(GAJ) – thank you all. And let me not forget Trubshaw and Phoebe who agreed to have their real names and characters used.

Lastly, thank you dear reader for taking the time to peruse these pages – I truly appreciate it more that you know.

CPSIA information can be obtained
at www.ICGtesting.com
Printed in the USA
BVHW032122171119
564070BV00030B/332/P